Charlotte
SEENING

****

CW00557224

SEEING WHITE

An erotic novel
The first part of The White Trilogy
Copyright ©2015 by Charlotte E Hart
Cover Design by MAD
Formatting by MAD

License Notes

Table of Contents

To See

English definition of "See".
-To be conscious of what is around you by using your eyes.

To Look

English definition of "Look".
-When we look at something, we direct our eyes in its direction and pay attention to it.

To Watch

English definition of "Watch".
-Similar to look at, but usually means that we look at something for a period of time, especially something that's ever changing or moving.

Belligerent

English definition of Belligerent
Line breaks: bel/li/ger/ent

Adjective:
1, Hostile and aggressive
2, Engaged in War or Conflict

Origin
Late 16th century: from Latin *belligerent-*"waging war", from the verb *belligerare*, from *bellum* "war".

SEEING WHITE

By
Charlotte E Hart

2015

"A belligerent state permits itself every such misdeed, every such act of violence, as would disgrace the individual."
Sigmund Freud

Charlotte E Hart
SEENING WHITE

Chapter 1

Alexander

Sitting on the bed, he took a few calming breaths and absorbed the dull ache that continued to enrich his battered body. He hurt, every fucking inch of him. Not as much as it did an hour ago but nonetheless, the impression marks on his skin still enhanced the same integral feeling: pain.

Interestingly, it was a sensation that he couldn't honestly remember experiencing for a very long time. Of course, the occasional bruise here and there was reasonably normal, but this feeling radiating through his whole body was almost excruciating in its grip of each tendon and ligament, each muscle still in a spasm of sorts.

He chuckled to himself, clicking his neck and staring at the wall. It felt comparable to pure ecstasy in reverse. Heaven being poured into hell with abandon. And while he'd very nearly forgotten just how therapeutic pain could be when received in the correct mind frame, he certainly hadn't lost his ability to relish in it when it happened.

Reaching down to untie his trainers, he winced as his right shoulder reminded him that he wasn't getting any younger. Maybe this form of entertainment was coming to an end. Perhaps it was time to find a new interest to unleash his irritation on.

He rolled his eyes at his own apathy on the subject and hung his head between his knees, recalling the visions of this evening. He'd never stop and he knew it. It was just a part of who he was, or what he was created to be. He was more careful now, but fundamentally, he adored every fucking minute of it simply because his somewhat aggressive tendencies seemed to define him. Whether people knew the extent of them or not wasn't relevant. He hid it most of the time these days anyway, mostly because he had to. But even he had to admit that there were other ways to determine the future now, or at least varying ways to manipulate it to his advantage. Unfortunately, it

7

was still there, though, scratching away just beneath the skin and clawing to get out, aching to release itself and forget.

Pushing his head back and stretching his arms above his head, he lowered them to rub his sore neck. Another stab of pain. He smiled and reminded himself that regardless of the tension, he also felt good, cleansed, washed free of the never ending aggravation and torment if only for a few hours. Essentially, he knew his infuriating memories would return to haunt him again but for now they had subsided a little, and his release had given him a small sense of peace. Although, it wouldn't last long. It never fucking did.

These were his evenings of pure freedom, of unadulterated pleasure - freedom to do pretty much whatever he chose, to whoever he chose and at a level that he chose. Tonight he'd chosen to fight; he'd needed to relieve his tension a little more vehemently than most women would allow. He'd wanted a man or two. In fact, he'd taken three. After all, that's what the male of the species was built for, wasn't it? To receive pain? So that's what he'd delivered with a smile and a wink, friends be damned.

Thankfully, Westfield had given him everything he needed tonight, hotly pursued by Deville. After he'd let them have their fun and wind him up to the point of no return, he'd given more back, revelling in the sadistic thoughts that crossed his mind and fuelled his body forward - always forward. Now his wrists and knuckles were bloody to say the least, but they'd be better tomorrow.

They always were.

Standing, he moved towards the bathroom mirror, noticing all the clothes that were neatly arranged in the dressing room and the soft glow of the lamps illuminating the hall below - that slight red hue that seemed to bring calmness to his world. Calmness - the word in itself was ludicrous. It was a state of being that Alexander White very rarely seemed to have in his world. His world mostly consisted of a multitude of things to do at any one time. So these were his evenings to appreciate the quietness he envied other people of having in their everyday lives. Did they even know what peace they had? Did they appreciate it? Or did they just see it as boring and mundane?

Mind you, they probably didn't have the accumulated wealth that he had, either - the niceties and added extras. Whether he deserved them or not was still debatable but, regardless, he had them.

Work hard; play harder. With input comes growth in all facets of life. Eternal peace was not on that list of achievements and he doubted it ever would be. It probably wasn't deserved anyway, given his history.

Looking at himself in the mirror, he looked at the bags under his eyes and the bruises already forming around his ribcage and stomach. He looked dirty and tired. His shorts still clung to him from the sweat and filth he'd been rolling around in, and his hair was sticking to his face with the blood that shouldn't have been there. He'd definitely be having a conversation with Conner about that tomorrow, the sneaky bastard.

This man he was staring at was not the Alexander White that everybody saw each day. He was nothing like the person people knew and admired for his genuine acumen or uncompromising business brain. No, that man was accepted or acknowledged every day for his wealth and status. He was loved by all the sycophants and money grabbers. He sneered at the thought of their nasty little games and then sneered again at himself and the way he played those damned games so well. If only they knew who he really was or what he really felt deep down in the pit of his stomach.

His portrayed image was completely in control of every single moment of his life. Order and discipline were the mainstays of that man's environment and the people that worked for him, or anywhere near him, fucking knew it. There were three evaluations of Alexander White from his associates or workforce: they liked him, were terrified of him or respected him. He was happy with all of the above, but he doubted any of the above would be the correct description if they really knew him. Terrified was almost acceptable. Horrified was probably a more fitting word.

In disgust, he stepped into the shower and let the water wash away the day and rejuvenate him to some degree. The icy spray made his chest muscles constrict and the pain that shot across his ribs again made him grimace in shock. So, heaving in a breath, he ramped up the lever to turn the heat on and let the warmth cascade. He chuckled to himself. At least he felt something. Good or bad, at least it was something other than the nothing that was becoming increasingly normal.

Dropping his head down, he dipped it under the water and let the torrent wash the grime from his head. He hissed instantly when the heat hit the cut that his supposed friend had caused this evening. He pushed his hand over the damaged area and watched the blood falling from his fingers. He was so mesmerised by the swirling liquid as it hit the white tiled floor and disappeared that he couldn't help but remember all the blood that seemed to do that over the years - dry up or simply be made to disappear. The shame of it was that no matter how hard he tried, it never seemed to do the same from his own mind. Small nagging reminders tore into him occasionally. A family name here or a particular street there. It was enough to pull him back to his old self - the version of himself who'd done his job with some sort of pride, swiftly, efficiently and with no remorse whatsoever. There was also that constant corruption of money and backhanders to deal with.

The little shits in his past just loved that form of torture.

He shook his head and growled at himself. He didn't care about any of it. His own head would heal. His body had been through far worse than this when he was weaker, and yet here he was, still standing. He might be fucking lost and far from happy, but at least he *was* still standing, regardless of all that had happened in the past to torment him.

He was rinsing the last of the day from his body when he heard the phone ringing. Who was calling him at this time of night? It was close to ten. Whoever it was, it wasn't going to be fucking good. He mumbled and cursed to himself, walking towards the phone and grabbing a towel on the way.

Rubbing his wet hair with the towel, he stood in the middle of the bedroom and looked at the caller ID. His frown deepened. Why would Louisa be calling him? And did he really want to know? These were his evenings. She knew that. Emergencies only. Fuck it. He'd get a glass of wine and call her back. He had at least two hour's worth of emails to look at anyway, and much to his annoyance, he simply couldn't avoid them any longer. Pulling on some jeans, he grabbed his phone and made his way down the stairs to the kitchen. Feeling the tell-tale vibration of the voicemail in his hand, he sneered. Obviously it was an emergency.

Leisurely, he strolled along the hall, taking note of the cleanliness and neat order that had appeared since he left this morning at five thirty. Mrs Jenkins had been busy today because everything was as spotless and impeccable as usual. There was a reason he paid her so well. No doubt he would find all his favourite food and wine neatly stacked in the cupboards and racks, too. The woman was a rock of unwavering fortitude, almost mothering him but not quite that close. Whatever it was, he quite liked it, not that he showed her that too often.

He stopped abruptly, as he felt something like anguish roll over him at the thought of her never having the chance at motherhood, and tilted his head. It being taken from her at such a young age was presumably unjust to some degree. He tried to process the emotion for a few moments, knowing that she would have made a wonderful mother but as usual, the sensation left as quickly as it arrived. He sighed at his inability to empathise and kept walking. Maybe one day something would make him care enough to actually feel something for longer than a second or two.

As expected, there were ten bottles of wine, so he chose a Merlot and made his way back towards the study. Pausing in the doorway, he looked at the library shelves stacked with books that he loved so much and exhaled. He never really got a chance to read much anymore and missed the space that a good book created for him. There was a certain pleasure in living someone else's life for a while just to forget the realities of his own. He really should make more time for it but the concept of more time was just another personal fantasy that was yet to be realised.

"Louisa," he barked. She'd picked up on the first ring as usual.

"Sir, I'm sorry to be calling so late. However, there has been a substantial problem with the New York deal that I'm afraid requires your immediate attention. I've already contacted Mr. Westfield and emailed you all the details. Mr. Westfield is booked on the 3am from Heathrow and I've ordered the jet for refuelling and take-off at five tomorrow morning for yourself. Mr. Westfield is meeting with the client at one and I have you scheduled for a meeting at three."

Alex sighed as he scanned the emailed document and realised the depth of the issue. Damn, the woman was good. Yet another person he paid incredibly well. She deserved every penny. Not that he let her know that he gave a shit about her flawless service. It never pays to give any one person too much praise, especially not a woman.

"No, Louisa, have the jet booked for four. I want to talk with Westfield before the meeting."

"Yes, sir. Is there anything else I can do for you?"

"Yes. Get my meetings at the office changed for a more appropriate time and advise the staff in New York to expect me for two weeks."

He sighed again as he read the next document in front of him and ran his fingers through his hair, immediately wincing at the cut to his head.

"Yes, sir."

"Also, arrange some flowers for Mrs Jenkins to be delivered on Tuesday. Lilies. Make sure she knows they're for her."

"What would you like the card to say, sir?"

"Something... happy," he said after a shrug. He hadn't a clue why he even wanted her to have the flowers, let alone what he wanted to say to the woman. Flowers were normally just a thing he did to chase the rare type of woman who needed it. They liked them - always the best, boring and dull. "Also, cancel Rebecca Stanners. I won't be able to see her tomorrow evening." Or ever again if he could help it. Mind you, she had been an acceptable distraction for a while, and she was at least from the right type of family - not the usual for him at all. His type of women were rarely from the right sort of family. It seemed that most women from the right social circles were not that interesting, in the bedroom or out of it.

"Yes, sir."

"Thank you, Louisa. As always, you have been useful," he clipped as a sort of praise.

She'd get the point.

"Enjoy your flight, sir," she responded as he ended the call.

Finishing the call, he let out another long breath. He was beginning to feel a little agitated again. He'd planned on at least a few more hours of calm.

Obviously this was not the night for his pleasure or relaxation.

As he looked at the screen, he rubbed his forehead, a headache already beginning to form across his brow. *"Enjoy your flight, sir."* It was almost hilarious. He hadn't enjoyed a flight for a very, very long time. Others may have seen it as exciting and interesting, but after your fourth year at the top, nothing was ever a challenge anymore. Nothing appeared to deserve his respect or admiration, and quite frankly, that was becoming dreary.

12

At thirty-one, he'd conquered most of his ambitions and there wasn't a place he couldn't get into at the drop of a hat. The accounts were fantastic. He would never want for anything money could buy, and of course he appreciated the beautiful women that threw themselves at him daily to some degree, but something was missing, something else, something more…

He sucked in a breath and downed his wine, then poured another one. Maybe he should have Andrews drive him. He downed the next glass. He'd definitely have Andrews drive. After all, that's what he was paid for, wasn't it? There was no need to get anything together. His things would all be waiting for him in the New York apartment. All he needed to do was grab his briefcase, phone and keys. He'd sleep on the plane.

Engrossed in documents, financial statistics and reports, he was surprised to notice that time had flown by so quickly. Time flies when you're having fun. No matter what he thought of his life, he did enjoy the fundamentals of it. Business was easy for him, natural. He'd never seemed to struggle with its concepts and complications like some did. The main structure of a healthy business was quite simple: brains, charm and strict discipline. Don't let people walk over or under you, and have enough power that everybody is wary. Trust no one. Be ruthless, and never let anyone know the real you. Weaknesses showed a route in.

There was only one person that knew him with anything close to actual reality. Well, maybe two, but Conner was the more appropriate of them. They had been friends from their first meeting and had always been close. Even their three years apart hadn't diminished their grasp of each other. Conner was like the big brother Alex never had. Having often been guided and driven by deep-seated anger and frustration, it was Conner who moulded the fury into something more sustainable and stabalised it. He'd found a path for Alex to channel himself and a hobby to rid himself of the anger - several actually, some more pleasurable than others.

Conner had given him a focus he'd never known before, a way to try to achieve something more worthwhile. Without Conner, he would probably be in the East End somewhere, barely keeping himself out of jail and not giving a fuck about it. More than likely drinking himself to death, fuelling himself with coke and probably killing anything that interfered - quite happily at that. There was no doubt that he owed Conner a lot, and he reminded himself that he'd never really thanked him for that. No, he'd just fucked him over a few times like the bastard he was - thoughtless and deviant to the last. That was just his natural disposition unfortunately, and the actual words - *thank you* - well, they were a little harder. And frankly, how could he say what needed to be said anyway without confessing everything, without revealing it all? It was for another time, or maybe never at all.

Who fucking knew?

Standing at the desk, he moved his head from side to side and headed up the stairs to find some clothes. Andrews would be ready in half an hour and he needed to get organised. He dragged his fingers along a line of neatly pressed shirts in the walk-in-wardrobe and selected one along with a jacket. Then put on the shirt and shoes, grabbed his watch, switched out the lights, and headed back downstairs. Such was the order of his life. How women made the process of getting dressed so difficult was beyond him. They were strange creatures really, beautiful and stimulating in a few ways, yes, but strange nonetheless. To be honest, he'd yet to meet one that interested him for more than a few months, so they deserved little of his respect or thoughts at all for that matter. They all seemed to lack depth or substance, no real quality that intrigued or surprised him, tiresome really. All he needed to do was flash an Alexander White smile and lift an eyebrow and he had them, any of them, anywhere. It was yet another dull element of his life.

His phone beeped, informing him that the car was outside waiting, so he picked up his briefcase, phone and coat and walked out the door.

"Andrews," he said as he climbed in.

"Good evening, sir."

"Is it? I think it's actually morning." Alex almost chuckled in response.

"So it is, sir. However, we are both alive and well so that has to be a good start," he replied, his bark of laughter surprising even him. As an ex-military man, Andrews was apparently happy simply to be alive. He supposed in that line of business it was crucial.

He only fucking wished it was enough for him.

"Ready, sir?" Andrews said, closing his door.

"Yes."

~

Standing outside the sleek, grey jet, he nodded at Andrews, signalling his dismissal, and then stared at the jet. He loved the look of it and gazed for a minute. It always brought a smile to his face, continuing to be one of the only things that genuinely made him beam with pride. He had achieved this, his first real goal. Since he was a boy, he'd dreamed of it. That little red plane had been the only toy of any consequence he'd been allowed at the time, so regardless of the fact that the bastard had continued to remind him what a worthless little shit he was, who wouldn't achieve anything of any value, he'd kept dreaming just a little in the hope of another existence. This was supposedly it, his better existence. Why the hell it suddenly seemed so unfulfilling was a complete fucking enigma.

At the top of the jet's steps stood the pilots. John and Phillip had been regulars for him since he got the plane and had always proved good at their jobs. He regarded them and made his way up the stairs.

"Good evening, sir," said Phillip. John had already made his way to the forward cabin.

"Phillip."

"Everything is ready to go, Unfortunately Tara couldn't make it on such short notice, but Jo Meyers comes highly recommended," he said, directing a hand toward a woman. She was about five foot four, a bit slim for Alex's liking, but everything was in the right place. Her long blonde hair was piled into a neat bun, but her make-up was far too heavy so he immediately presumed that she was yet another vapid and undeserving whore like all the others. One bat of her false eyelashes proved him exactly right.

"Thank you, Phillip," he said as he pulled his eyes from the reasonably cute blonde's short but well-formed legs. He would have preferred them longer, but unfortunately not all women were blessed with such good genes, and it made little difference while they were on their backs anyway.

"Mr. White, it's a pleasure to meet you and I hope I can serve you well for the flight," she said primly, glancing at his chest. It was pathetic.

15

"I'm sure you will," he replied with a slight sneer, passing her by and walking towards the black leather chair. He sat heavily and proceeded to buckle himself in, dropping the briefcase on the floor.

"I'll just stow your bag, sir," she said, all flushing cheeks and nervous fingers as she bent to pick it up. Those legs might have been a little short but the familiar stirring in his groin as he watched her arse reminded him that maybe a little amusement could be in order. Perhaps she should work a little harder for her probably overpaid salary.

"Is there anything I can get you before take-off, sir?" she asked, reaching above him.

"Yes, take off your skirt, buckle into that chair facing me, put your legs on each of the arm rests and make yourself come," he said, flashing a very weak smile and lifting his eyebrow suggestively.

She gasped and recoiled a bit. "Sir, I'm not sure that's…" Struggling to find the words, she wobbled in her shoes. "I wasn't told it was that sort of contract."

"It isn't in the contract, Jo. I don't need you to sign a contract to make you feel good. We've got a long flight ahead of us. I don't want to work and you're a diversion for me. If you want to thoroughly enjoy working for me then you'll drop the pretence that you don't find me attractive and just accept my request," he said, staring long and hard at her with no emotion whatsoever. She really wasn't worth his effort in the slightest and he couldn't be bothered with another smile. "Of course, you don't have to do anything you don't want to."

"I'm still not sure it's appropriate, sir," she stuttered again, nervously shifting from side to side. He sighed and pinched his brow. Was she really going to try this *I couldn't possibly* shit?

"Trust me, Jo, it's more than appropriate, and when you've finished having your first orgasm and we're high enough, you'll be on your knees giving me the best blowjob you can manage. Ten minutes after that, I'll be fucking seven shades of shit out of you across that bar." He directed his hand towards the black granite bar. "You'll have the time of your life, feel things you've never felt before and be screaming my name out for at least two hours. By the time you leave my plane, you'll be sore and fully sated," he stated nonchalantly, continuing to stare with narrowing eyes. He could see her rather pitiful defences breaking down and shook his head. "Now, be a good girl, get in the chair and do as you're told before I strap you there myself. You know you want to so don't disappoint yourself. Embarrassment and guilt have no place on my plane."

Again he raised an brow.

She looked at him for ten seconds, made her decision, gave him her best impression of a seductive smile and began to lower her skirt, so he relaxed into his chair to enjoy the show. Maybe one day someone would surprise him with a no, or maybe an argument. Even a fucking slap would go somewhere towards relieving the constant monotony. He frowned as he watched her lift her legs and wished he hadn't started this. Those legs really weren't doing a thing for him; they barely reached over the bloody armrests.

"Well done, Jo. Now tell me about how much you want me inside you," he said as the wheels left the tarmac beneath them. Her mouth parted with apparent shock. Given that she didn't know him ten minutes ago and she was already spreading her legs for him, he thought her surprise was unwarranted to say the least.

He continued to stare at her until the words began tumbling from her mouth and then lowered his eyes to something a little more appealing as her hand reached downwards. Her fingers were too short as well but at least the talons she sported reminded him of his baser instincts, so he continued to watch with a bland expression in the hope that it might pass the time somehow.

It really didn't, but with a little thought, maybe he could increase the entertainment factor. He eyed the cords on the curtains with a smile and ran his fingers across his lips as his imagination grabbed at various images.

He needed his lighter and a calculator.

Chapter 2

Elizabeth

*"*You're such a bloody cow. Unbelievable! I can't believe you told him he was tepid in the bedroom." I can hear Belle laughing about their story with Teresa as they load the last of the client order onto the catering van for the Torrington wedding.

"What was more amusing was the look on his face. You wouldn't believe it, named and shamed as being shit in the sex department," says Teresa, still chortling to herself about the whole event.

"But honestly, Teresa, did you have to do it in front of the whole bar? He was actually a reasonably lucrative client for us."

"Who was?" I ask, as I walk through from the kitchen with a tray of chocolate éclairs that have been left behind.

"John Dixon. Can you believe that Teresa screwed him stupid after the Linton party then he had the audacity to parade his girlfriend around in INK the other night? Apparently he's been dating her for a few months. The bastard actually laughed when he saw her and tried to pretend to the girlfriend they were just friends. So, she called him out on it and told most of the bar he was, and I quote, '*Tepid* in the bedroom at best,'" Belle replies, screaming with laughter as she finishes the explanation. My fit of giggles bubble to the surface at my sister and best friend jumping up and down in fits of hysterics, Teresa very nearly falling over a crate of champagne as she walks around the counter towards the door.

We've owned Scott's Catering Company for four years, starting as a small firm run out of our mum and dad's bakery in Surrey. We took the huge leap of starting the shop in London two years ago, running it alongside the existing business, and it has thankfully taken off with startling results. We only managed to do it by using the country pub our family bought for a steal as collateral, but we managed it. Belle, having done her degree in business and marketing, is the brains with the balls to back it up. Teresa works the shop front, has done since the day we employed her to help, and I'm the creative cook. I've always loved the kitchen. I pestered my mum my entire childhood, spending most of my evenings making some new cake or pudding for the family to taste. It's rubbed off well on me. Lord knows how we all keep our weight down. Frankly, we should all be the size of houses.

Scott's has become well known for special event catering, and the shop has become a firm favourite on the high street for all the well-heeled people of London to purchase their pastries and cakes. More often than not I'm in the shop until the early hours of the morning creating another order of delicious treats for the rich and famous. As long as I never have to meet them, I'm very happy. Wealth has always had a funny impact on me. The people make me feel inadequate and unkempt somehow, which I know is ridiculous, but I just don't feel able to converse easily with them. They just seem to make me feel very uncomfortable without really doing anything at all. Belle has told me on many occasions to "sort my shit out," as she so eloquently puts it, but I just can't make that nervous feeling go away. Of course, it helps that Belle went to a private school full of money. She finds it easier to converse with the landed gentry. I went to state school. Mum and Dad's bakery was struggling when I hit eleven so I ended up in the local comprehensive, not that I minded at the time. It would have been unfair to pull Belle out of St. Peter's so they somehow managed to keep paying for her to remain there.

However, life is good. The business is doing incredibly well and all I have to do is keep doing what I love - cooking. Belle manages to find new clients weekly and the orders keep coming in. We're on the brink of expanding and just need a few more wealthy individuals who appreciate our worth and then we can go to the bank and plead for more money. The kitchen space at the back of the shop has started to become limiting in its size and we are becoming confined in how much we can produce. Bigger events are not an option unless I can share the cooking with Mum in Surrey, which unfortunately is definitely starting to become too much for her. I know there's only so much Mum can do for us without making herself ill again, and as she's already battled cancer once, I'm not harassing her too much anymore. Besides, the constant two locations thing is ridiculously tricky to manage and fuel costs are beyond unreasonable.

Having finally managed to get the last of the racks of food inside the van, we tap the roof to let the driver know he's set to go. We'll meet him there in the morning. The catering manager at Torrington Hall will unload it all into the kitchens and then I'll have free rein over the luxurious, state of the art workspace from nine in the morning until midnight. I can't wait.

"Right, it's four o'clock. I suggest we all go out and get shitfaced," Belle says, smiling brightly.

"I'm up for that. I just need to get a change of clothes at the flat and I'll meet you there at, say, six, Beth?" Teresa replies at lightning speed, not unlike her at all.

"Umm, I don't know. I've got to be up pretty early and it'll be a very long day. I was thinking about a lazy night in by the television if I'm honest," is my pathetic reply as I turn my back to them and grimace, waiting for the tornado that is about to hit me.

"I can't believe you're going to do this fucking shit again. You're a twenty-five year-old independent woman of means who is beautiful and funny. You cannot continue to hide yourself away in that apartment and watch the sodding television or read your romantic drivel. I simply won't fucking allow it a minute longer," Belle screams. She does this a lot.

"And think of those men who are being denied that fabulous body and those incredible legs because you continue to cover it all up in that slobby, comfy shit you keep wearing," Teresa barks, joining in on the tirade.

"It's Friday night and you are coming home with me now so that I can strap you into something more appropriate, and then we're going to INK to get drunk and enjoy the merits of our success," my sister states, with a finality that I know means the end of the conversation. I fold, not unusually, and twitch my nose in irritation at myself. I have got to learn to say no to that woman.

"Fine, but if the Torrington meal goes arse about tit, it will be your fault. I warn you now." I know it won't. I would never mess up the day, no matter how awful I feel, but I do need to make my point.

"Sister dearest, you would never let the bride down on her big day. You know it as well as I do," she quickly responds with a grin.

"Bitch," I reply with a frown.

"Snotbag," Belle states with gusto and a smile. I smirk at the term of endearment my sister always uses. I can't help it, bitch as she is.

"Right then, I'll meet you there," Teresa says as she races out of the door so fast I literally see the dust flying off her shoes.

"You're such a smartarse," I mutter, starting to set the alarm as Belle collects our things from the back.

"I know. However, I do radiate charm and I always get my way in the end." She chortles behind me, pushing me toward the door.

As we pull the shutters down and lock the main doors up, Belle turns to me and pulls me in for the biggest hug she can manage.

"You know it's because I love you and I just want you to be happy, right?" she says, looking directly into my eyes. Oh god, she's so good at that.

"Yeah, I know, and I love you, too. Just don't push too hard, please," I reply, turning away and giggling at her effort of love. She doesn't do it often.

We link arms, smiling warmly at each other and head off to the tube. In twenty minutes we'll be home and then the makeover will begin. It's pretty unlikely we'll make it to INK by six; it will definitely be nearer to seven, not that it will matter to Teresa. She'll have found at least two men by then and probably have bumped into at least ten other girlfriends. She's undoubtedly one of the most well liked people I know. Who wouldn't like her? She's gorgeous, funny, wild and always up for a party. Men love her, women don't seem overly disarmed by her and she has enough charm to bring Satan to his knees. I narrow my eyes at my own pang of jealousy. I've envied her ease of nature for as long as I've known her, much as I love her. Nothing fazes or unnerves her. She just seems to be happy with exactly who she is. If only I had that ability. Tonight will probably be awkward, difficult and tiring. INK is the only place to be seen at the moment and that's why Belle's so intent on being there as much as possible. I would much prefer a quiet drink in the pub down the road, but that will never be good enough for my sister, or my friend, I might add.

We managed to break through the door security at INK about six months ago when a few well-known clients gave the doorman the nod and let them know we were allowed into the elite crowd. Funny how a few well-baked cakes can get you accepted into a world of power and snobbery. I've avoided going as much as possible because of the rather unnerving people in there. However, since then the business has gone through the roof and I've been persuaded, against my better judgement, that it's detrimental to Scott's for me not to be seen out and about. No matter how much I find it uncomfortable, I can't deny that my sister can work a room like a pro and her brilliance at schmoozing the clients has been exactly what we needed. Unfortunately, it appears that people actually want to know who cooks their food as well as who organises it.

It's only a matter of time before she finds those elusive new clients we need to upscale, and unfortunately she does need to be in INK to do it. Anyone who's anyone is constantly there. The place is owned by one of the hottest young entrepreneurs London has to offer and most of his friends and associates are frequently there in their private booths and VIP areas, drinking the best that money can buy and eating the finest food the top French chef has to offer. Yes, INK is definitely the cool place to be and it makes me feel dreadful. Not that I have any problem with wealth in itself. In fact, I've quite enjoyed spending my money since we've started to make a good living, but I'm just not a natural at it as so many others are. They've grown up with it or are married to it or just have it, but with it seems to come a confidence that I just don't possess, and try as I might, I just can't seem to find it.

I look at Belle as we make our way through the entrance foyer of our building, heading towards the lift.

"Do you think that Mr. Avery will be there tonight?" I ask casually as I step in.

"Don't know, don't care." She's short with me. I know why.

"When will you accept that you like him?" I reply with a grin.

"I do not date or like spiky haired, tattooed Neanderthals."

"Even when they're incredibly charming?"

"Especially when they're charming, not that he is. He's an arrogant pig that believes he's special because he invented some software and made some money," Belle scoffs as she stabs at the lift buttons.

"It wasn't just some software, as you well know." I chuckle.

"Okay, some really very fucking cool software, but he's still a pig and I dislike him immensely."

"Right, any reason you're getting so wound up then?"

"Shut up, little sister. You know nothing. Now get in that apartment so we can sort your shit out and go get drunk."

I smile to myself as I push the door to our apartment open. This is going to be a long night and an even longer day tomorrow. *Dig deep, Beth. Dig deep.* Belle immediately launches herself at one of the three bottles of white wine that have been chilling in the fridge, and I begin to wonder if this evening has been planned a little longer than the last minute decision to go out for a drink would suggest. Neither of us are huge drinkers and we only ever have a few glasses in the house before going out. Normal procedure is to then get roaring drunk as soon as possible. This is a usually a delicate affair for Belle as she makes her way through many drinks and becomes steadily more inebriated with an elegance I can only dream of. For me, it tends to be a different time scale of events entirely, going from stone cold sober to really, earth spinningly drunk within a few hours. The last big night out resulted in me being lifted into the cab from the floor by midnight and stopping twice on the trip back to the apartment to relieve my stomach of its entire contents. A horrendous hangover occurred the next day, resulting in a promise to never touch the damn stuff again, while Belle seemed to wake up the next morning with a beautiful smile and a craving for the largest cooked breakfast I've ever seen.

That is not going to happen again this evening. It's a very important wedding tomorrow that I will get perfectly right. Unfortunately, as I watch Belle down the first glass of wine before she heads for the shower, it occurs to me that maybe my sister doesn't have the same commitment to tomorrow's job as I do.

"Get your arse into my room and dig out something clingy and short," Belle shouts on the way to the bathroom. "And don't choose the backless black one 'cause that's mine tonight."

I gingerly pick up the overly full wine glass that has been poured and mumble various expletives to myself while walking up the hall.

Belle's wardrobe is something to behold - a long, sleek, sliding door affair that runs the entire length of her bedroom, neatly stacked with everything a girl could need. Unlike my own that mostly comprises of jeans and shirts. Anything elegant is arranged in the one wardrobe I hardly ever open. If I ever want to learn how to dress, I only need to look at my sister. From her flamboyant, thrown together look to a business suit, Belle always looks fabulous and radiates a sense of style that I don't have a clue about.

Sliding the doors open, the first things I see are the shoes - rows and rows of them. Belle picks her clothes depending on which shoes she likes that morning. I'm pretty sure that's as good a place to start as any so I start to peruse the selection. I'm lucky enough to be about the same shoe and dress size as my sister, albeit about three inches shorter at only five foot seven.

A striking pair of red, very high-heeled, patent shoes gleam at me from the corner. The last evening out I had with that type of heel went drastically wrong, with me flying down the stairs at an awards ceremony and looking like a complete idiot. I also managed to throw my entire glass of champagne over the chairman's wife with horrific results to the lady's hair.

"So are you going to continue to stare at them or do you think you might have a go at picking them up?" Belle asks, throwing her towel on the bed behind me.

"Oh, I didn't see you there," I say with a shrug as I glance at the shoes again.

"Obviously not, otherwise you would have been looking at the very sad, black, flat pumps on the other side of the wardrobe," Belle affirms casually.

"I don't think I'll manage to walk, drink and dance in them. You do remember the last time I wore heels that high?"

"Yes, dear sister, I do. But with practice comes perfection. You just need a few more drinks and you'll forget all about them."

"But..." I notice my sister's glare. "Okay then." There really is no messing with Belle this evening, it seems.

"So what we need now is a fantastic little something, maybe with some tassles." Tassles? Christ. Belle runs her fingers through the dress selection until she pulls out a short red dress with a fringed hem that's longer at the back than the front. It has a modest neckline and is

24

cut off the shoulder. I shudder at the thought. She looks pleased as punch at her choice.

"Umm, I think that might be a bit too much," I protest on completely wasted ears.

"Don't be ridiculous. It's Friday night and we're going to the hottest club in London. You wouldn't want to look out of place, would you?" she retorts. "God knows... You might even find an attractive man to entertain you." I sigh in response, wishing she would just give up on this obsession she has.

"I always feel out of place, Belle. You know that, and dressing me up like that is not going to help me blend in."

"I don't want you to blend in, Beth. I want you to stand out. It really is time you started to believe in yourself a little more. You are utterly gorgeous with a body to die for and a beautiful mind. You know how hard I have to work at my figure. You don't even have to try." She's right.

I've been lucky enough to inherit my grandmother's genes, which results in very long legs, a petite but curvy figure and perky breasts that happily just stay just where they should. My long reddy, orangey, browny, whatever you want to call it, hair is also a result of our grandmother's family. As are the brown heart shaped eyes. I know I'm not unattractive, but for some reason I've never felt comfortable in my own skin. My sister, whose hair and eye colour are about the same, has inherited our paternal family's height and weight, which results in her having to work hard to keep her weight down. Three nights a week she will be found at the gym and she eats very healthily, unlike me. I eat nothing but utter rubbish and yet the weight stays off. Thank God.

"Okay, let's do this then," I reply, basically to placate my sister and avoid the ensuing argument that's surely coming if I deny her wishes. She stares in amazement and drinks some more wine.

"Well, fuck me," she says, her eyebrows shooting upwards at the thought of a complicit sister. "Green light for everything then?"

"Whatever, just get on with it." I'm seriously going to regret this, and oh shit, she's reaching for the curling tongs. I back away slightly at her advance.

"Just drink the damn wine, Beth." Right.

By the time we have gotten ourselves together and filled our handbags, it is indeed a quarter to seven. Belle calls a taxi and we head down to the foyer to wait. Even I have to admit that my sister has done an amazing job on me. My hair is piled high in a messy up do and the outfit looks fantastic. Even the make-up, which has been over applied as far as I'm concerned, looks wonderful - smoky eyes and a sultry red brown gloss lipstick. I feel beautiful, and as long as I don't have to walk too fast or talk to anyone who unnerves me, I feel like tonight might be a good night.

Belle's joy at going out is infectious and when she's like this, I always feel her confidence rubbing off on me. She's right, a few drinks and a killer outfit later and I do feel like I'm ready to paint the town a vivid shade of her shoes, which are already killing me, regardless of how fantastic they look.

We saunter arm in arm to the revolving door and then to the taxi. I immediately trip over the lip of the carpet and almost fall to my knees. Thankfully Belle grabs my arm and hauls me back up.

"For God's sake Beth, watch what you're doing," she scolds.

"What? It's your fault for putting me in these things. Jesus, I told you they were too high," I giggle in reply, both of us bursting into laughter to the point where the tears begin to leak.

"Nooo... I did not spend thirty minutes on that look to get it all messed up again," Belle says, wiping the tears from my eyes.

"Sorry."

"Don't ever say sorry for making me laugh, you idiot. Just remember to stay upright tonight. If you can't, sit your fabulous arse down. Hopefully nothing can go wrong then. I'm not sure I can be there all the time to catch you, although you know I'll try my hardest," she responds with another infectious cackle of laughter.

"You've never let me down yet. Well, apart from that time at-"

"Yep, you're right."

"And that time at-"

"Yep there too."

"Also there was that incident at-"

"Okay, okay, so I'm a bit shit sometimes, but I do try," she says, smiling and pushing me at the taxi.

"I know. I promise I'll try not to be so clumsy tonight."

We lift our heads, take a deep breath and open the taxi door. Teresa is waiting and so is the exclusive INK.

Charlotte E Hart
SEENING WHITE

~

As the taxi rounds the corner that will take us to the club, I feel my anxiety levels starting to rise again. The alcohol has started to wear off on the thirty minute drive because the London traffic has been especially heavy this evening. Belle has found out, via her mobile, that some major celebrity is apparently at a film opening and this has caused most of London to descend on the middle of town to try and get a glimpse of the elusive film star. I couldn't care less. I just need another drink and fast. Hopefully it will make this feeling of deflation disappear.

The taxi pulls to a stop outside the understated white building and I glance nervously at it, anxiety shooting through every pore at the very thought of the people inside. The only colour is the elaborately written INK in black over the door and three lights over that. The red carpet and ropes barricading the entrance are surrounded by three normal looking men in black tuxedos - the doormen. Their size isn't to be confused with their strength. I saw them handle some unwelcome members of the public just a few weeks ago. The ambulance arrived to pick up the nine men in under ten minutes. I've never seen people fight with such precision and viciousness. It was both arousing and stimulating, and I completely surprised myself with the effect it had on me as I breathily watched the whole thing unfold in front of me.

Is stare at the roped off entrances and think about what that sensation was. Something about the brutality made me feel, well, remarkably horny for some unknown reason. I spent several long moments trying to process the feeling at the time, but there wasn't an answer so I just accepted I might well be a little perverted or something equally odd. I mean, nobody else gets horny at physical violence, do they? Okay, some probably do, but none that I've ever met. Actually, I'm disgusted by violence most of the time, so confused wasn't enough of a word for my feelings regarding the situation.

Belle pays the driver and pushes open the door.

"You ready?" she asks.

"As I'll ever be. Get me in there quick so I can get a drink, and don't leave me until we've found Teresa." Belle chuckles and sorts out her dress, although why she's bothering I have no idea. She looks fantastic as usual.

"You'll be fine, darling. You look amazing. Just have some fun and loosen up. Failing that, get pissed and dance your sexy little arse off."

The entrance foyer lighting is dimmed low and screams indulgence. The black, opulent granite floor and plush lounge areas for meeting guests feel warm and relaxing, immediately letting you know you've arrived in first class. People are milling around, talking to each other while they check in their coats, and there's an overwhelming feeling of quality in the clothes and surroundings. The soulful, sensual music playing in the background gives a feeling of desire and comfort as the tell-tale swishing of dresses lulls you into a slightly hedonistic tranquillity. Three sets of double doors lead off from the foyer, one to the lounge, one to the very upmarket restaurant and the last to the bar and club. If you hadn't been here before, you wouldn't know where to go next. None of the doors are labelled - yet another sign of the exclusivity of the place. You can tell who the longstanding members are by the way they don't even check where they're going. They just seem to know the feel of the place as they wander around and open doors without looking.

"Straight through?" Belle asks.

"Definitely," is my reply, anxiously scanning around. There is nothing I worry about more than having to make polite conversation with people I don't know. The quicker I can get lost in the music the better.

The moment we enter the dark tunnel that leads to the bar, the music kicks in. While we continue to walk it grows louder. Bassy dance music ripples along, not the heavy beats of later in the evening but enough to get you in the mood for a great night. The walls are all white and heavily decorated. The owner got the three best tattoo artists in Europe to design the entire wall space of the building. The intricate designs climb up the wall and over the ceiling, intermingling with each other and creating a warm sexy feeling, revealing the inner woman within, letting you become what you might want to be for the night and also somehow calming your mind to free itself of the day behind you. It really is very clever.

As Belle sashays toward the glass door in front of her, it glides open, disappearing into the wall and reveals the main bar and dance area. The heat and sound hit us first. Warm air rushes against my skin and music fills my ears. The screams of laughter and clinking glasses assault my senses and

I can't help but smile. The ambiance is exactly what it should be, relaxed and inviting with a sensuous, raw appeal. If it wasn't bloody full of so many daunting people, it would be perfect.

"Don't let yourself be intimidated by anyone, little sister. You deserve to be here. You've made it on your own. Stand tall," Belle says. I smile warmly at her. She always knows the right thing to say, always seems to understand how I'm feeling.

"Come on, honey. Let's get some mojitos and start having some fun."

We both cackle like two old women as we wander across to the bar area. I just can't help but move my feet to the beat of the bass line as the music starts to have its resonating effect. Closing my eyes and letting the rhythm take me for a few seconds, I almost forget where I am for a moment. The bar is crammed full of all the beautiful people, watching me, waiting for me to make a mistake and fall flat on my face. I snap my eyes back open to notice all the trendy London social elite not bothering to take a second glance and wonder why I ever thought they would. I really don't fit in at all. *Stupid Beth.*

"Just, wow," a divine looking Teresa says as she approaches from the high stools. Her short, dark, cropped hair looks every bit on trend and she's wearing a green dress that barely covers anything.

"I know. Doesn't she look fabulous?" replies Belle with a grin.

"Beth, good god where did you get those eyes from and that dress? My lord, the men are dribbling. We'll have to scoop up the saliva with a spade," Teresa says with a giggle as she ruffles the bottom of my too short dress and blows a kiss.

"Don't be so ridiculous. I know I look okay but I think you're pushing it a bit far," I reply, lowering my head and feeling fully embarrassed.

"Beth, darling, you have no idea, do you? You are by far the sexiest bit of red stuff that has entered the building this evening. Those legs simply go on forever," Teresa replies with a smile.

"Well if you're going to continue your flattery debacle then I think a big drink is in order."

"Fantastic idea. Gin slings all round," she exclaims, flouncing off through the bar, men actually drooling after her.

We find a high table and stools by the dance floor and start talking about the trials and tribulations of the social network - who's sleeping with who and what's happening to each person in the room. Teresa grabs a passing barman - yes, I do mean grabs - and orders three drinks, apparently making them large. Within what seems like minutes, the drinks arrive swiftly on our table and Belle smiles sweetly enough to ensure the next round will arrive just as speedily. I pick up my drink and close my eyes to listen to the euphoric melody that's singing out.

We talk, laugh and giggle for ages until I notice that Belle has gone a little rigid, her demeanour a little more closed off than usual. Scanning the room, I soon notice why. Mr. Conner Avery is making his presence felt as he ambles around the room. Women are falling over themselves to put their eyes in front of his. He's a tall man, about 6ft 4inches with blue hair and tattoos, very solid and good looking in a dangerous kind of way. He knows it and uses it to full effect. He should have been a rock god really. Unbelievably, that isn't the case at all because it seems the man's far too clever for that.

He made an absolute fortune when he developed one of the best pieces of software in the last ten years, and the two big rivalling software companies battled for a year to licence it. Blutech Inc is now a very wealthy company and Avery continues to design more and more. He seems to work hard, but he's constantly papped for doing something that he shouldn't be doing. It's usually something naughty. However, he is one of the most charismatic men I have ever met and I really like him in a big brotherly kind of way. Scott's has been delivering pastries to him for a year or so, and he continues to pop into the shop every now and then, always asking if Belle's about. More often than not, I tell him that she isn't even though she's hiding in the kitchen, which kills me laughing. I've never really seen a man have that kind of impact on her before and I still wonder why she just can't talk to him. But regardless of my slight concern on the matter, it is hilarious to watch her suffer.

Suddenly he's approaching our table and I watch Teresa stand and start to leave with a conspiratorial wink. I take this as my cue to leave also. Belle lunges at my hand.

"Don't you dare leave me," she whispers.

"Darling, you'll be fine. Stand tall," I reply with a smirk. She gasps at my retaliation from the earlier comment as Conner gets to the table, looking effortlessly casual in black jeans and a tucked in blue shirt.

"Belle, lovely to see you tonight. You look incredible as usual," he states, lifting the corner of his mouth.

"Conner, you do not, and what are you doing here anyway? The papers said you were in LA," Belle says stiffly, trying not to look at his face. I smirk at her unease and put my drink on the table.

"Ha! I'm here to meet a good friend if you must know. Are you keeping tabs on me, Belle?" he chortles. "Beth, is that you in there? Fucking hell, girl, you look like a goddess. If I wasn't so interested in your sister, I'd be hunting your arse all night."

"Why thank you, kind sir. I'll take that as a compliment, I think." I blush a little, feeling slightly uncomfortable because that's not entirely big brother like and the quite intriguing sneer that Belle is trying to mask does not go unnoticed by me.

"You should. I never knew your legs were such a sight to behold," he says, scanning my shoes – well, Belle's shoes.

"I think I'll leave on that note before it gets uncomfortable," I say, turning from him and frowning.

"Beth, I think I could get really fucking uncomfortable with you whenever you like," he says with a wink. Okay, really not comfortable at all now. His chuckle at my need to look anywhere but at him has me smiling again, thankfully.

"Mr. Avery, you are not quite as charming tonight as you normally are," I reply harshly, swatting him with my clutch and turning on my heels. Thankfully, he doesn't mean anything by it, and I know this because his eyes have only ever been for Belle.

"My apologies, Madame," he says, bowing in an attempt at chivalry. It looks quite ridiculous.

"Forgiven, just once. Now get on with wooing my sister."

With that, I turn to leave as he takes up a stool next to Belle, smiling a megawatt grin and proceeding to exude every inch of his raw

31

sexual spirit he can muster in an attempt to convince her he is the man for her. Unfortunately, I can't help but think that he'll probably have a very hard time and a very long wait. Bless him. Poor man.

Chapter 3

Alexander

He stood watching over his club from the office above the bar and leaned his head on the glass to feel the throbbing of the music. He couldn't hear the sound but he could feel the beat thundering through the fibre of the building, sense it pounding through his body, reminding him of years before. He'd put his heart and soul into this place, let his creative flair open up on it. His company normally broke things up and made as much money as it could from selling off pieces to the highest bidder. Big fucking pieces that were worth a lot, but nevertheless, he still basically traded on failing businesses. He'd retained a few and pumped some capital in and they were doing well now, but most of his wealth had been made from someone else's misery.

Actually, he'd made a habit of ensuring businesses failed to make sure he got the right deal. He'd also been an utter bastard to the nicest of people just so that they were too scared to argue with him. But INK had been his dream, a place to make people happy, and more importantly, to make him a lot of money making people happy. The security was very tight and the members list very limited. He'd seen plenty of clubs fail miserably by letting the wrong people through the door, collapsing the perfectly balanced atmosphere.

He hadn't been here for about three months. Tom Bradley, the club manager, was very experienced and had earned Alex's respect within the first few months of opening. He knew that the club was in very safe hands, and was only called in on the odd occasions when something was seriously wrong or when Tom needed to talk with him about something relevant.

Tonight had been the latter. They'd had an interesting chat about increasing profit via various mediums and the potential for a new club in Rome. They'd already begun work on the venue in New York, but both his ideas were promising and required a little thought.

He kept out of the day-to-day business and tried not to put in too many appearances. There were only a few people that knew he owned the place. A few more thought he was simply an investor. He was fine with everybody guessing so he never really discussed the place with anybody at all. It was his little piece of a dream. Prying eyes were not welcome in the slightest.

However, his main objective tonight was to meet with Conner. They hadn't seen each other for about month or so. Conner had just spent some time in LA with Tyler Rathbone, CEO of Rathbone Industries, going through the latest of his software designs and probably making himself several more million in the process. In the meantime, Alex had been in New York for three weeks, dealing with the complete incompetence of his fucking useless employees, firing most of his senior level team and poaching an entirely new team from the closest rivalling company. He had most definitely announced himself in Manhattan as a person not to be taken lightly. That may or may not have been a mistake. For once he may just have been a little too ballsy in the wrong place. He'd just have to wait and see. He'd damn well enjoyed every minute of it though. There was nothing better than pissing people off.

From the corner of the door he noticed a flash of red entering the bar area with legs that went on for a damn mile and long, slender arms. He admired a woman who would allow herself to stand out in a crowd. The world was full of little black dresses. He followed the long legs as they moved gracefully toward a shorter, dark haired woman, pretty enough but not a patch on the redhead. Her luscious locks were piled high on her head with tendrils tumbling down her neck onto her bare shoulders, and her skin was so creamy white that his mouth was salivating at the very idea of taking a bite out of her. His dick jumped at the prospect. So, chuckling at himself, he went toward the phone. No woman had ever refused an invite to the office when asked and as he was determined to have her within half an hour, his cock would get what was coming to it regardless of its impatience. However, he was so mesmerised by the way she moved that he couldn't help just watching for a while longer. He stood with his hands in his pockets, just staring at her. Her eyes had a heavenly glow and those lips... Christ, they were made for kissing or fucking - preferably both, maybe even at the same time. He really didn't care as long as they were wrapped around something of his. Fuck, she looked perfect. She had a quality he hadn't seen for a long time. She didn't have any hardened edges. She looked soft and warm. Her smile lit up the room and her animated way of chatting made him grin to himself with an affection he hadn't felt before. When was the last time he did that? Just smiled with affection? Fuck knows if he ever had - probably not because it was one of those ridiculous emotions that happened to brainless people.

There was a sudden, sharp knock at the door, and before he could turn, the door had opened. He smirked at his friend's entrance as he heard Conner walk in, loudly, as always.

"Sorry, man. Should have waited, shouldn't I? I keep forgetting that bit." Without turning from the redhead, Alex responded.

"You're still hoping to catch me at it with a couple of girls so you can join in, aren't you?"

"Well, now that you mention it."

"No." It wasn't happening with Conner - not that.

"Oh all right then. Come here and give me a man hug then. I've missed you, Mr. White."

"Too busy looking at a piece of rather extraordinary skirt down here."

"Right behind you. I love this one-way glass shit you've got here. I keep meaning to get it installed in the office - great for perving. Which one?"

"She's wearing red," he said. Conner peered over his shoulder and then head butted the window randomly with a sigh.

"Oh dear. That is not the cup of tea for you, my friend," Conner replied with a shake of his head, rubbing his hand across his forehead. "You have no right whatsoever picking her."

"What? Why? Do you know her? And what are you trying to say about me?" he said, swinging his head to meet Conner's face for the first time.

"Nothing, man. Only that she is by far the sweetest woman in the club and is absolutely not going to be up for the sort of stuff you want to do to her. But I agree, she does look incredible tonight. Never really seen her like that before," Conner replied, taking a sip of his drink.

"Really? I think that needs more defining." Conner sighed again and scanned the crowd.

"Honestly, Alex, she's just not into it. What about the girl in blue over there?"

"Fuck the girl in blue. I probably already have anyway. Tell me about the redhead," he ground out, looking back down at her long legs and tilting his head to the side. She glided her way towards a taller woman who looked similar somehow - harder though, not as ethereal or beautiful by a long shot, but still a worthy viewing.

"Okay, okay, calm down. Fuck. Her name's Elizabeth Scott. That's her sister over there in the scorching, backless black dress. Frankly, I wish it was frontless. I've been trying to get into her for about a year. So beautiful. Her name's Belle. They own a catering company that serves high-end parties. They've also got a shop in town. God, she's just too fucking sexy for her own good. Look at the way she sways. I love a woman that sways," Conner replied.

Alex watched them meet up with each other and laugh at something. Christ, her mouth was simply fucking divine. She suddenly swung her head round and looked up towards them as if she sensed she was being watched. Her eyes narrowed a little and bore straight through to his soul for a second, seemingly accusing him of past sins or something equally disturbing, before she turned back to the others.

"The red dress, Conner?" he pressed again, slight irritation lacing his voice now and some strange sense of fucking guilt addling him for no reason. She couldn't have seen him, but he somehow felt that she saw straight through him to places even he hadn't visited for a while.

"Oh, yeah, well there's not really much else to say. That's all I know, man," Conner replied with a shrug.

"What's the shop called?" Alex asked.

"Scott's." He continued to stare for a few moments longer as she drank a cocktail of some description and then bowed his head, turning to Conner.

"Not the girl for me you say? Are you sure you know what I need?" he said with a raised brow.

"Well, there's what you need, man, and what you want. Which one are you asking me about?" Alex smiled and shook his head in resignation

"Okay, let's go find us what we *want* for the night then, shall we? The suite is waiting for us," he said, making his way to the door, glancing back at the redhead again.

"Now you're talking. Lead the way."

Conner closed the door behind them as they made their way toward the private elevator at the end of the corridor. The moment they entered the bar area, Alex immediately scanned for the redhead again. Gone. Fuck. That irritated him.

"Any more ink, man?" Conner asked.

"Two more added in while I was in New York."

"Lisa do them?"

"Who else? I think she'd have my balls if I went elsewhere," he replied with a chuckle.

"Fuck, I'd let her near my balls anytime. Mind you not with a sharp object - that girl is some crazy shit."

"Agreed, but she does know her art."

"Damn right. So who are you having tonight?" Conner asked as they entered the bar, scanning it for prey in his usual relaxed manner. Alex shook his head at the man and continued onwards.

"I thought we'd just catch up. It's been a while since we just talked and drank like the old days."

"What the fuck was that? You're not going soft on me, are you?"

"It's not all about your dick, Conner. I'm actually quite interested in how you are and what's been happening in your life."

"Yeah well, sweet as that is, I'm fucking ravenous. That Scott woman is infuriating and I need to get laid," Conner replied, running his fingers through his blue hair and sidling up to a blonde who was leering at him. That Conner smile was firmly plastered across his lips as she nudged him back and did that fucking giggling thing that stupid women do. Why the man found it interesting was a complete mystery. Mind you, she'd probably open her legs within ten minutes so if Conner was desperate, why not?

Alex chuckled to himself and signalled to the barman on the way past the bar. He was a new chap, which was a ball ache, as he wouldn't know what they drank. The guy completely ignored him and carried on talking with some girls, so he calmly walked to the divider, opened the hatch and strolled into the serving area, walking towards his favourite malt whisky.

"Hey, what the fuck do you think you're doing?" the barman shouted, rushing towards him as he lifted two bottles off the shelf, suddenly aware of his presence.

"Having a drink or two," he responded, deadpan.

"Who the hell do you think you are? You can't just walk in here and take the booze. I'm calling security."

"Please do, and while you're at it, call Tom as well," Alex said as he picked up two tumblers and started pouring. The guy hastily picked the phone up and dialled while looking at him in complete amazement.

"Get out of the bar area, you dick, before you get yourself beaten out of it," the little, now infuriating, shit shouted. So, he waited calmly while chatting over the bar with Conner and handed him a drink.

"You're going to fire him, aren't you." Conner said. It wasn't a question.

"Probably."

"Give him a chance, man. He clearly doesn't know who you are."

"Well he should."

"Fuck, you're an arrogant bastard," Conner responded, mouth twitching in amusement. Alex smiled and drank some scotch. Christ, that burn was good.

He smiled as his security team began throwing people out of the way as they pushed through the crowd. The two guys stopped abruptly when they saw the barman facing off with him, practically knocking the blonde to the ground. She giggled again so he rolled his eyes at her and waited for the dick to speak.

"What the fuck are you idiots doing? Get him out from behind my bar," the barman whined as he threw his hands around. It was fucking pathetic and overly dramatic to say the least. The boys looked over to Alex for instruction.

"It's all right, guys. Go back to the door. Tom will be here in a minute. Good response time, by the way," he said smoothly, watching them frown in puzzlement at the situation.

With that, they nodded then turned and left without a word to the barman who was now looking very confused. Alex watched as Tom Bradley made his way toward the bar and scowled at him. He always liked a chance to remind him of his job. It really didn't happen very

38

often, but it was still good to have a reason to pull him down a peg or two every now and then.

"Alex," Tom said across the bar.

"Tom, we seem to have a useless barman," Alex said, nodding toward the guy.

"Really? That is quite a novelty in here."

"Quite."

"Right, can someone explain what the fuck is going on? Am I being filmed or something?" the barman ordered. Conner chuckled and tipped the bottle of scotch up to have another drink.

"Constantly. Didn't you know that?" Alex retorted.

"Mike, this is Alexander White. He owns the club and you just broke some major rules in here," Tom explained politely. "What would you like to do, Alex?"

"I'd like an apology for a start. Then you can fire him," Alex explained calmly to Tom as he downed another Scotch and smirked at Conner. It appeared he needed to keep up with his friend who had clearly begun the game of *let's get trashed*.

"Please, Mr. White. I need this job. I didn't know who you were. I'm very sorry for my mistake," Mike said, almost pleading. He fucking despised that. Why did they all beg like dogs? From women it was acceptable, beautiful even, but from normal men? No.

"The problem is, Mike, you were thinking with your dick. The women are attractive; a lot of them are, but you let them distract you from your focus, which should have been my bar and my money. Due to that issue I have no choice but to let you go," he said with a smile while still looking at Conner who was refilling again.

"I was doing my job serving the ladies." Alex turned to face Mike with a sigh.

"No, you were trying to serve your sex life, badly, I might add. What you do in your own time is not my business, but on my time, it very much is. There is no more to talk about. Tom, please sort the rest of this out. I am going to drink. I'll be in the White if you need me. Also, give the ladies a bottle of the sixty-four on the house. After all, they're the reason I've been so entertained for the last ten minutes." He threw his dazzling smile at the women. They all instantly melted and gave doe eyes straight back at him with varying giggles. He wasn't in the slightest bit interested and quickly scanned for that red hair again. Where the hell was she? Then he saw her.

He was just moving to the divider when the stupid barman did the unthinkable and launched toward him with a fist raised. It all felt like slow motion and as his arm raised to block the swing, he placed the other hand around the idiot's head and shoved him to the floor. The dick crumpled, cracking his head off the shelving below the bar.

Lowering himself down to a crouch, he lifted the guy's head by his hair.

"Are you still breathing, Mike?" The spluttering of blood indicated that he was.

"Fuck you, arsehole!" the shit seethed from the floor. He had to admit the guy had balls - stupid, but ballsy nonetheless.

"Do you want some more?" he asked quietly. "I'd be happy to oblige. Or would you rather I asked the guys to take you out the back? Talking of arseholes, I think Jerry's on tonight and we both know how he enjoys his fun with little ones like you." Mike instantly stopped struggling and stilled. "I think maybe we'll leave it at that then, shall we?" he continued, letting go of the guy's head and pulling himself upright again.

Nodding at the two bouncers who had arrived to see the commotion, one of whom was indeed Jerry, he turned his head to Conner with a smirk of amusement then instantly frowned again as the word "shithead" drifted up from beneath his feet. He sighed again - begging and now being a complete moron - the guy had some serious issues to deal with.

"Jerry, go have some fun," he said, wiping his hand on a napkin and lifting his scotch. Jerry smiled and walked around the bar to haul Mike from the floor.

"No! Mr. White, please. I'm sorry. I shouldn't have..." the idiot shouted as he was pulled around the corner by the very large man.

"No, you shouldn't. Fucking stupid," he said quietly as he exhaled and made his way through the divider toward Conner.

"Christ, man, you really are a fucking arsehole," Conner stated with a smile as they walked away from the bar and he waved off the blonde who pouted like a child at her dismissal.

"Yeah, I know."

"The kid was only doing what you would have done."

"Well then, he'll have learnt a good lesson today. Never let anything distract you from the task at hand, especially a woman," he replied with a smirk. "And I would never fail as badly as that. The runt had no chance with any of them."

"But Jerry? Really?" Conner asked.

"He'll be gentle with him, I'm sure," he replied, not really thinking about the situation. He was still too busy searching the room for the elusive redhead out there who had disappeared again..

"No, he won't. That monster doesn't know the meaning of the word gentle." Possibly true, to be fair, but still of no fucking interest whatsoever.

They chuckled as they made their way across the floor to the private bays at the back of the dance floor. His friend still scanned the room for more, probably inadequate, prey, and continued with his downing scotch. He swiped his card against the door to the White Suite and raised a brow at Conner as they entered, who was clearly on some sort of mission to destroy some brain cells this evening.

"What?"

"Are you planning on slowing down at some point?"

"Why the fuck would I do that?"

It was a good point, and the man could drink most people under the table. He barked out a snort of amusement and nodded to the door as his friend damn near glared at him in frustration. It appeared he really did need a drink or two so he extended a hand and watched Conner head straight for the seating at the bar. Breathing in the smell of the room as the door closed behind them, Alex smiled at the sight of blue hair mingling with the design of the space. The burgundy leather and grey smoked glass still reeked of the timeless elegance he'd been after when he built the place and Conner just clashed. He always fucking did to be honest, but that was just part of his character - different, unusual.

"These booths are such a cool idea man. I still love this one-way glass shit," Conner said as they poured two tumblers full of the amber liquid. "Good to see you again, man. You never fail to make an evening interesting. I can't believe you fired the guy for fun and then sent him to a fate worse than death."

"I didn't fire him for fun. He was abusing my trust and then he thought about hitting me," he replied, gazing out of the window hoping to spot the red dress again.

"Don't pull your crap with me. I see right through it. You picked a fight with him when you could have let him off."

"He won't be so stupid again though, will he?" Conner simply stared and shook his head. Why was a mystery. The man knew him well enough.

Knocking back his drink and refilling his glass, Alex returned the stare and waited for a comeback. The shaking head situation carried on until a smirk appeared.

"So what are we eating tonight? I'm still starving."

"The entertainment will arrive in about an hour. Christ, you're insatiable," Alex groaned as he removed his jacket. It was always the same with the man. He was surprised his cock was actually still attached.

"That comment coming from you seems a little ridiculous if you don't mind me saying so," Conner chortled in response. Alex raised a brow, but couldn't deny it. The man was probably right.

The next hour passed swiftly. They had a lot to catch up on, and there was always a bit of business to discuss. However, the first bottle of scotch had disappeared far too quickly and they were half way through the second by the time ten o'clock approached. He felt his stomach beginning to ache at the hysterics his friend was causing about some ridiculous situation he'd gotten himself into while surfing in Bermuda when there was a knock at the door. He looked at his watch and laughed again at Conner's eyes lighting up at the prospect.

He buzzed the door open and four women walked into the room, taking off their long coats as they moved. The flesh that followed was varied in colour and appeal.

"Miss Trembell said we should come by at ten," said a cute brunette as she did that false head flick that seemed to be a requirement of the job.

"She did," he replied as he followed the blonde's legs wandering around. They looked... flexible. He tilted his head and then remembered another pair. What was it about that damned red dress and the woman in it?

"What would you like from us this evening, sir?" She directed her question at him and smiled seductively. He looked into her eyes. They were vacant, weak. He wanted nothing from them. That fucking red dress was what he wanted, right now. Christ, this was pathetic. He waved a hand toward the front of the booth and turned toward his other entertainment.

"Just do what you do, ladies, in front of the glass."

"Fuck me, man, where do you find them?" Conner said, gawping and cracking his knuckles as he zoned straight in on the blonde. Blondes were always his go-to fuck of choice. Any other colour was apparently too complicated. Alex still hadn't got a clue what that meant other than there might have been a brunette in the man's past that he wasn't aware of.

"Do we need more scotch?"

"Well, looks like I'm going to need something. Those girls could actually be scaring me," Conner exclaimed as the girls moved to the glass panels and started their performance.. They were quite good - dull, but good nonetheless.

The champagne and scotch arrived quickly and the women continued to grind into anything that was available, but he just couldn't keep the image of the redhead out of his mind, no matter how much the girls waved their reasonably impressive tits in his face. Elizabeth... That name rolled around his mouth quite nicely. Where was she now? And was she with another man yet?

The thought fucking disturbed him immensely, to the point where he almost got up to leave at one point. He hadn't seen her pass the window at all. He'd been scanning the entire time they'd been in here, hoping for a glimpse. Maybe she'd left. That thought damn well annoyed him too.

"Are you still thinking about Beth, man?" Conner asked, sharp as a fucking razor.

"Who?"

"Miss Elizabeth Scott, pastry maker extraordinaire, hands all doughy and wet. You know, red hair and mile long legs. I wonder what she could do with those fingers. I bet they're quite dexterous." Alex barely contained a fucking growl that came out of nowhere.

"No."

"You're a shit liar. Well, to me anyway," the dick said, laughing out loud. "You've been scanning that fucking window all night. I'm surprised you haven't left yet."

"I am not and I have not," he replied, pushing the short-haired one away who was reaching for his cock and directing her back to the glass. She was becoming irritating in her desperate advances. She'd be better off in a fucking whorehouse.

"Yes, you are. You know I love you, man, but you've got to be ready for it," Conner proclaimed rather quietly as he gazed at the brunette. "I won't let you through to her unless you're ready. She's just too, well, nice for the likes of you."

He stared at him, trying to work out what the hell the man was talking about.

"What are you talking about, you drunken fool?" he asked, watching Conner refill their glasses and collapse on the sofa with a sigh.

"Reality, Alex." Conner sighed again as he looked down at the woman positioned between his legs and sneered slightly. "Love, commitment and all the things that you don't have a fucking clue about or any sort of want for."

Alex slumped down beside him and watched the other girls parade about again. Unfortunately, they were becoming boring and more perplexingly, Conner was right. Feelings of any sort were normally the last thing on his mind, but Christ, those long legs had been nice and that mouth was captivating him beyond belief for some unknown reason. And those eyes that seemed to burn into him were so fucking mesmerising that he could still almost feel them on him now, ripping into something that he hadn't even remembered was still alive.

He picked up his drink, while gazing at his nearly passed out friend, and pondered if perhaps she might be worth some effort on his part for once. She clearly meant something to Conner and that could be a problem he'd need to think carefully about. Pissing Conner off was not to be recommended at any point.

"Ask me again tomorrow when we're not fucked up," Conner slurred without opening his eyes as the woman unzipped his trousers. Alex chuckled as he finished his drink and tapped the girl on the shoulder.

"Enough. You can get up and go." She pouted. What the fuck was that pouting shit? She should have snarled if she was that into Conner, fought for him. Instead, she scrambled to her feet and took the money he was holding out to her with a smile. Whore.

"I think it's time to get you home, my friend." He waved the rest of the girls over, gave them some money and called for Andrews. "Come on. Up you go," he said, almost to himself really as he grabbed onto Conner and hauled him upright. It wasn't easy. The man weighed a bloody tonne and, regardless of his own size, he was struggling a little to say the least.

"You'd destroy a woman like her, you know? You're a fucking cock like that," his friend said as he half carried him to the private entrance next to the booths. Hopefully, Andrews would be there to take some of the weight off him. He frowned then sneered at himself. Conner was right; there really wasn't anything else to say on the matter because he absolutely didn't deserve a woman like that. Why the hell would he? He'd corrupt, degrade and humiliate her then throw her to the wolves so he could watch them devour her. One green-eyed wolf in particular sprang to mind and he smiled at the visual as he watched Andrews heading towards them.

Andrews dragged Conner into the car and basically threw him onto the floor in the back as Alex fell in beside him and leant his head back. Unfortunately, the moment he closed his eyes, all he could see was a pair of hypnotising brown eyes staring back at him and pink lips being licked. Fuck. He shook his head to try and dislodge the image but it wouldn't leave so he let it swirl around with a smile. Then that strange guilt-like feeling emerged again and knocked him for six in the gut like a damned freight train. He opened his eyes and let the emotion channel through him, felt it build into something unknown and uncomfortable. Disgust or self-loathing poured across him in waves as it took hold and then slowly began to warp into something warmer inside him - something close to contentment or maybe even that elusive fucking peace he'd been searching for.

The car moved off and he gazed down at a now definitely passed out Conner who was filling up the entire floor space beneath him. He swung his feet up onto the seat and reached for the Cognac.

"Love sucks," came mumbling from the floor by his feet, presumably originally from Conner's mouth.

Did it? And why the fuck was Conner even saying that it did?

"Care to expand?" Nothing. Silence.

He tipped his head back again and sighed as those visions instantly took hold again. It appeared the woman stirred a feeling of some sort - an emotion of consequence that he thought had long since departed, one he definitely had no fucking clue about and one he could probably do without.

But Christ, they were incredible legs.

Chapter 4

Elizabeth

I can feel the pounding in my head before I even move, so I gingerly lean over and slam my hand against the alarm clock I rather cleverly set before I even left the apartment last night. Today is going to be hell and I only have myself to blame. Yes, I may have been cajoled into going out, but the drunken stupor that ensued from the night's entertainment was entirely my fault. I should have stopped and come home early, but the inevitable happened and I got so drunk so fast that I forgot to be sensible and just went with the flow of the evening. We all danced our arses off in the back of the bar area for several hours as the dance floor was so densely populated, and we supplied ourselves only with tequila shots as hydration. *Stupid and more bloody stupid, Beth.*

I can't deny it, though; we all had a fabulous night. I laughed until I cried on several occasions and had some pretty nice attention from several men, which helped loosen me up.

However, now it's time to work and I have a little under an hour and a half to get up, shower, dress and get to Torrington Hall. *Belle, I hate you.* I squint one eye open and look at the clock. 7.30 am. God, it was 3.30am before I fell into bed. How on earth am I going to make it through the day? Gently, I edge my way to the side of the bed and swing my legs to the floor, hoping for salvation of some sort. I force myself upright and head for the bathroom. Salvation isn't forthcoming in any way.

Grabbing my coat and bag, I head for the kitchen, thankfully feeling somewhat refreshed from my shower, and having applied makeup to make myself look more human, I realise that I don't actually feel too bad anymore. That will undoubtedly catch up with me later when I'm needed most.

"Belle," I shout as I push the door open to her bedroom.

"Yep, wrong room, you dork," Belle responds from the kitchen.

"Oh, you're up!" I exclaim, completely mystified as to why she isn't still snoozing her way until eleven. She doesn't have to get there till one.

"Of course I am. We've got to be at Torrington in 45 minutes," she says as she pinches her forehead and hangs her head.

"Oh, I didn't know you were coming first thing?"

"Do you think I'd let you go on your own feeling like death when I pushed you to go out?" she replies as she raises her head again and looks into the mirror to apply her lipstick.

"You are by far the best sister ever." I giggle as I pat her shoulder and walk across the lounge for my boots.

"I know, honey, but honestly, I'm so hung-over I'll probably be no use whatsoever," she says as she gets up and shrugs on her coat.

"Just being there will be enough. Thank you." I smile.

"You're welcome, honey. I can't say Teresa will be quite so pleasant or care free about it though," she huffs as she picks up the keys and switches off the lights in the kitchen.

"She's coming, too? How did you manage that?"

"I gave her the phone number of John Dixon's girlfriend. It made her more pliable. So she arranged some cover in the shop. God knows how she did that, though. I think she phoned Julia Stevens at two in the morning."

"Wow, I bet that went down like a shit-storm, huh? I suppose we better get going then," I reply in shock as I pick up my bag and open the door.

"Yep, but, honey, we must get coffee on the way. My head is in far too much pain because of the stupid amount of alcohol you made me drink, and without coffee, you know I will be completely useless." She chuckles.

"Oh, yes, because it was definitely me pouring that stuff down your neck all night. Next time, though, I think we'll go with the no tequila shots technique, or at least not so many of the bloody things in a row," I reply with a snicker and a nudge as we head for the elevator.

~

The day seems to fly by, and actually, the team with the three assistants that have been hired pull the day off to perfection. This was totally expected by Belle. I was far less optimistic about the day's events. However, with a great deal of will and determination we've manage to stave off the incredible hangovers we are all suffering from and also deliver the bride's faultless day.

The newly appointed Lady Torrington sashays into the kitchen around eight-thirty in the evening to congratulate us all on a fabulous day and gives us all a bunch of flowers. So sweet really, to think of your caterers on your big day. I'm very surprised, but Belle simply smiles sweetly and nods as if there was never any question of excellence. We leave shortly after that, grinning from ear to ear and feeling happy but extremely tired.

As we walk into the apartment, Teresa heads straight over to the fridge and grabs a fresh bottle of white wine and three glasses. Belle slumps straight onto the sofa as I move toward the chair and Teresa starts to pour the wine

"You ladies mind if I crash here tonight? I cannot be arsed to get the tube home now," she asks.

"God no, the spare room's ready to go. Besides, we have to catch up on last night," Belle responds.

"I can't believe today went so well," I say, ripping off my boots and launching them behind the chair.

"There is nothing we can't achieve together," Belle replies, smiling with her eyes firmly shut. "I think that's a quote," she continues to muse as she stretches out her legs.

"Well, I say we give ourselves a huge pat on the back. We pulled it off with style and no one was any the wiser that we were all still shitfaced from last night," Teresa states, glugging back her wine.

"Cheers," we all chime in together.

"Talking about last night, did anyone notice the utter sexpot that was standing behind the bar with Conner Avery?" Teresa asks.

"Oh, God, do we have to talk about him again?" Belle groans, reaching for the wine bottle.

"No, I'm not talking about him, although I can't believe you don't want him. He can have me any day. The man's utterly gorgeous, even with blue hair. No, I mean the guy he was talking with across the bar for a while," she continues, leaning forward across the breakfast bar and giggling.

"He was probably a new barman," I chirp in.

"No, definitely not. He was far too well dressed. Dark brown Armani suit, and his shoes were worth more than the barman makes in a month I should think. His eyes were the most stunning pools of icy blue liquid I've ever seen. I was salivating. Honestly, it was all I could do to stop myself from launching over the bar at him and screaming take me now," she says, sighing and staring wistfully up at the ceiling.

"Well that would have been interesting. So not you at all," I laugh as I pop my feet up onto the coffee table and get comfortable.

"Yes, Teresa, I don't recall ever watching you throw yourself over a bar on purpose before. Obviously we all remember you doing it accidently though," Belle joins in, chuckling.

"Sod off, ladies. You know that wasn't my fault," she responds with a frown.

"No, of course not. You most definitely just fell off the bar while grinding onto Mr Blonde's knee. I still can't believe you did that." Tears begin to run down my face at the thought.

"In my defence, I was very drunk. I haven't done it since and won't be doing it again anytime soon."

"Oh, feel free to do it again as soon as you want. It was the most entertaining moment of my life," I remark, trying desperately to contain my hysterics.

"Well, anyway, I have to find out who he was. Black hair, blue eyes and an arse so yummy I would eat breakfast off it. The suit was cut to perfection and there was just something about his demeanour. So arrogant and yet so smooth. I just wanted to be whipped away and never rescued. Mike went to hit him for some reason and he just threw him to the floor as if he were an insect or something. Very appealing. If you'd have seen him you would have felt it, too," she says, returning to her far away state.

"Wow, I don't think I've ever seen you so dreamy before. Maybe he was a new bouncer?" I question with a smirk, having just about contained my giggles.

"Ooh, I forgot to tell you. I had a call today from Louisa Trembell. She's something to do with the White Buildings in town and we've got a meeting set up for Monday to bid for their catering. If it comes off, it'll be a gold mine. Just what we need," Belle interjects, raising her glass.

"Wow, that's a bit of good luck," I exclaim.

"Isn't it? She said she'd been given my number by a good friend who had recommended us very highly," Belle responds.

"Any ideas who?" Teresa asks.

"No. As far as I'm aware, I don't have any connections to Miss Trembell. Mind you, it's a small world so I'm sure I'll find out soon enough." Belle laughs.

"Well, we're not looking a gift horse in the mouth. We just have to win the contract now. Belle, I'm sure you'll do a fantastic job. But, honestly, I can't see how we can do much more cooking in that kitchen. It's far too small. That sort of regular contract will push us past our limits at the current location," I say with a small frown, thinking of my sweet but completely not acceptable any more kitchen.

"You're right, and maybe after this meeting we'll be able to go to the bank."

"Ooh how exciting. Do I get to come with you to the new shop?" Teresa chimes in.

"Do you think we'd leave without you?" I reply with a genuine smile. As if my life could be happy without her in it every day.

We all smile warmly at each other and proceed to chat into the early hours. Tomorrow is Sunday and that means a lie in, a happy breakfast, a gossip and coffee all day. Life couldn't get any better really. I smile at my sister and best friend while they chat about everything and anything and I feel completely comfortable in my skin. I've had a great night and day with the people I love, and as I watch them, I know we will never change. Life will move forward and alter its course, but the three of us will always remain strong together. We are all rocks of stability for each other, constantly helping out with varying issues or dilemmas, our own varying strengths and weaknesses complementing each other in a way that only the closest of friends can ever achieve. That has always been and will remain the most important thing to me - friendship. Relationships will come and go but no man will ever know me as they do. I'll never be able to open up to a man with such complete abandon. My girls simply know me inside out, and I them. They don't even need to speak and I can tell how they feel. I can see it in their movements and appearance. I adore the relaxed mood that we can create around each other through times of stress and turmoil, or the sense of excitement that we can produce if we are all inclined to.

Yes, life is good and we all know it.

"Well I, for one, am pooped," I say, yawning and stretching my arms above my head.

"Looks like you're ready for bed, young lady," Belle says as she heads to the sink. "I think we all are. It's been a fucking long day and I am exhausted."

"Yep, I can't keep my eyes open anymore," Teresa replies as she waves her hand and wanders off to the spare room. "Night, all."

Belle and I nod at each other and go our separate ways, to our beds and our duvets and our dreams.

~

Sunday morning comes round in a slow and easy manner and soon we're all laughing around the kitchen table about another indiscretion Teresa involved herself in a few weeks earlier. She is undeniably a girl who can get herself into a tight spot without any degree of difficulty. Fortunately, she usually seems to be able to wrangle her way out of it with the same ease. Belle continues to talk about the possible White Contract with a grit and determination I haven't seen for a while, but bizarrely she appears to be a little nervous, unsure of herself even.

"Belle, are you okay? You seem anxious about this meeting," I ask.

"Of course I'm fucking anxious, Beth. Do you know anything about the White Building? It's... It's... The fucking White Building," she snaps at me. I recoil instantly.

"Okay, calm down, honey," Teresa soothes.

"I'm sorry. It's just... I've never done anything this big. Christ, do you know how much these types of people make in an hour? Even I'm a little intimidated by their wealth, and frankly, we've never catered to this level. I don't know if I can pull it off," she stammers. I stare at her in shock. If she's worried then perhaps we all should be.

"Of course you can, Belle. You've never let yourself down, and I couldn't think of a more appropriate person to put in a room full of those *types* as you so aptly put it," I say with a rub to her shoulder.

"Alexander White is not someone I can just wing my way through, Beth. I need to be completely prepared for him."

"You didn't say you were meeting him. You said Miss Trembell."

"But what if he's there?"

"I doubt someone like Alexander White will be hosting a meeting regarding company lunches, Belle. I'm sure he'll leave that to other people," Teresa states, quite rightly.

"Tell you what, let's Google him, see what we can find out," I interject. "We'll grab our stuff, head down to the coffee shop and go from there. I'm sure we can find a way to make you feel more comfortable about it."

"Good plan, Beth. Always the planner," Teresa agrees enthusiastically.

"Okay, sorry girls. I'm just wound a bit tight about it, that's all. Its major league stuff and I'm really concerned. It's such a big thing for us."

"Well let's go and get you some fire power then, shall we?" I reply with a smile as I head to my room to find my boots. He's only a man for God's sake. I'm sure we'll be fine.

~

For October it's a surprisingly nice day, crisp and cold, and at least it isn't raining again as we stroll arm in arm along the street to the coffee shop that we so often frequent. The traffic is quiet because it's Sunday and it gives that slightly odd feeling to the otherwise loud and hectic London streets. I love Sundays - my one day of the week to relax a little and do something other than cook, and thankfully, it's an absolute necessity that everything is take out on Sunday.

I usher the girls into the coffee shop and go to the counter to order the drinks and pastries. It's the same standing order as it always has been for the three of us. A double macchiato for Belle with a chocolate twist, cappuccino with nutmeg sprinkles and a chocolate brownie for Teresa and a vanilla latte with a cinnamon swirl for me. I pay Tristan with a smile and take the tray over to the girls.

"Oh my fucking god, that's him," Teresa shouts at the screen. I almost drop the tray at her outburst.

"What the hell are you talking about?" Belle questions.

"That's him, Mr. Sexpot from INK," she says, pointing at the screen.

"No, honey, that's Alexander White. He would not be behind the bar at INK," Belle retorts, laughing.

"I would never forget that face, Belle. I'm telling you. Holy shit, you're going to meet him," she screams, clapping her hands together like a child.

"Could someone show me what's going on?" I ask, giggling with them, completely oblivious.

"Just look at this. Actually, I'm not sure if you should look. You might faint or something."

"Just turn the screen round, you idiot." I glare at her as she turns it towards me.

Oh. My. God.

I just gape at the vision of sexiness smiling at me from the screen. Open-mouth stare.

He is the most striking man I've ever seen in my life. Jet black hair that very nearly tickles his collar with that messed up look about it. Light-blue eyes that seem to draw me towards them somehow with their mesmerising and icy cold gaze, like you know you would be playing with the unattainable and probably bloody dangerous but you'd be willing to give him anything anyway. A smile that very nearly brings me to my knees and has me drooling like a hungry puppy, and a stance that exudes a confidence that definitely needs no explanation. I skim my eyes over the length of him, barely containing the drool as I digest his broad shoulders and long legs looking lean under a tailored black suit. His hands are in the pockets, and the open white collar shows off his incredibly sexy neck and jaw line to perfection. I'm seriously struggling to know where to look next.

Unfortunately, my eyes hover over his crotch area so I lift them again to meet his and almost feel my insides melt under his gaze. Even from the screen it seems like he's entering my deepest thoughts. My thighs have begun trembling or something. I have no idea what the hell that's about and I can't help but lick my lips as I look back towards his mouth again where there's a long, wide, enigmatic smile that lifts slightly more at one side, giving a slight hint of amusement. He's looking sideways at the camera with a woman draped over him who's equally as stunning. They make quite the dashing couple. He looks like a runway model, the Greek God of casual style and he knows it.

"Oh my..." I say, still open-mouthed.

"Exactly," Teresa agrees fanning herself. "I did try to tell you."

"That is quite unfair, ladies, and you are not helping at all," Belle remarks.

"I know, Belle, but good god, why didn't you say something? How the hell does a woman present a decent pitch with those eyes looking at her? I wouldn't be able to speak, let alone sell," Teresa states, quite rightly.

"Well I'm not going to back out of a meeting because the guy happens to be reasonably handsome. It's his profile I'm more worried about. Have you seen the write up on his businesses? He appears to own half the bloody world and is both loved and loathed because of it. He's been known to bring companies to their knees by challenging them through the courts. Some chap called Tate Westfield runs his law department and he's apparently the devil incarnate. He dabbles in the casino and entertainment sector but doesn't like to gamble too much. Most of his capital has been made through acquisition or asset stripping. He also owns a ridiculous amount of property, private and commercial. He does most of his dealings in either the States or the Far East, got in there about eight years ago. He must have seen that boom coming, or he created it; I'm not sure which. He's been at the top of his game for the last four years with several million between him and his next viable competitor, and if all that's not scary enough, it seems he donates ridiculous amounts of money to various charities and institutions each year," Belle explains, occasionally sipping her coffee.

"So what you're saying is that he's a cutthroat bastard who likes to appear the hero? How very charming of him." I smirk.

"I still can't get past *reasonably handsome*. At what point do you call that *reasonably handsome*?" Teresa almost shouts, knocking over her coffee. "Oh, shit. Even my bloody hands are shaking."

"Teresa, have you not heard a word I've been saying? The guy is a fucking machine. He gets whatever he wants by going through whatever he needs to and doesn't take any prisoners. That's not attractive; that is a pure business brain on a killing spree. There is no sweet and well-mannered in those eyes or fingers I dare say. They're meant for pure butchery," Belle says.

"I know, but look at that backside, and why did you mention those fingers?" Teresa replies dreamily, making my eyes swing to his hands, which I have to say look incredibly inviting - strong, and given my sister's explanation, probably very precise. My inner slut leaps at the thought, so I chastise my own ridiculousness and look across at Belle.

"Well, I think he's probably a complete arsehole, granted a very cute one, but no one who operates at that level can be a very nice person. He's probably a complete control freak who has to spank his employees and I'm sure he donates to charities simply to give out a decent appearance. He probably doesn't even know who he gives money to. In fact, I'm sure that is how you need to approach the meeting. Think of him as an unworthy opponent, someone who simply needs a bit of sucking up to and flirtation and he'll be putty in your hands," I declare, while secretly continuing with my absurd panting for the man on the screen, who appears to become even more attractive as we speak. There's a damn hotline to my groin or something, and he's still looking at me as if I'm not allowed to remove myself from his gaze.

"I'm not sure a bit of flirtation is going to work, honey," Belle says with a frown.

"Well why not? Just go in and picture him naked," Teresa chimes in. "That'll definitely get the flirtation level up."

"Really, ladies, I don't think I can go with either option but at least you've made me laugh about him. Maybe if I just keep it light and breezy, I won't let myself get drawn into a death stare." Belle laughs.

"Oh, I think I'd quite like a good death stare from him. Actually, I think I'd give him anything he asked for." Teresa smiles as she plays with her hair. I can't stop my eyes from rolling - such a princess.

"Belle, honey, you're going to be great. Hopefully he won't even be there and none of this will matter. You said that Miss Trembell sounded very efficient and I'm sure she just wants to know the facts and figures, which you know like the back of your hand, so please stop worrying about it," I reply with complete sincerity, flicking my eyes to the screen again. I'm pathetic, I know, but honestly, I can't think of anything other than his bloody hands all of a sudden.

"Well we'll find out tomorrow, won't we? It's a one o'clock meeting so I just need to take a few sample platters in so they can have a taste."

"That's fine, honey. We can knock up something fabulous in the morning. You'll get a taxi there and before you know it, you'll be back, contract in hand," I say as I sit back, Mr. *Reasonably Handsome* having now timed out on the screen, thank the lord.

I have no doubt in my mind of my sister's ability to pull this off. While this is by far the biggest challenge she has faced, Belle is a master of her art. She's never lost a new deal and it's unlikely this will go any differently.

~

The next day comes and goes in a flurry of excitement, nerves, anxiety, tension and finally relief.

Mr. Alexander White is not at the meeting, and therefore Belle is, as usual, exemplary. She only has to convince Miss Trembell that we are the catering company for the White Buildings' business functions and it works. She calls me immediately from the taxi on the way back to Scott's to inform us that we've been given the green light, and we are, of course, completely jubilant. We've been given a date of the twenty-sixth of October to cater for their first luncheon. It'll be twenty-five businessmen from several different countries attending an all-day conference at Mr. White's request. Something to do with rising oil prices and the index linking of such things. I really don't have a clue what my sister is talking about and frankly, I don't care. However, that date is only a couple of weeks away and I need to get planning. This is not something to get wrong, it would be devastating to our business if we get bad feedback and would probably wreck any hope of us ever expanding. Never mind the major arse kicking I would receive from my sister.

Lists. That's what I need, lots and lots of lists. This most definitely requires a new notebook, and a big one at that. Maybe even a new pen.

Chapter 5

Elizabeth/ Alexander

The weeks leading up to the White Lunch fly by in a whirlwind of varying clients and orders. We cater for a particularly fantastic Bond themed evening at the Chesterfield Mayfair, which is a resounding success, picking up several new names and numbers along the way.

The White lunch has, if truth be told, been causing a great deal of tension between us all because we all know it needs to be perfect. We've been squabbling over the course choices and bitching at each other for no apparent reason. We all know what the cause is and yet no one seems able to broach the subject rationally. Eventually we go with a safe Mediterranean type affair that I will spice up a little with some flashy new ingredients, along with a kickass dessert. The wine is being provided by the venue, or actually by Richi's, but White has gone direct. It's the only decent high-end wine distributor in town. We've used them before for several events, so I'd called Anthony to discuss the dishes with him and worked together to bring the perfect balance to the meal.

The day eventually arrives and here I sit, nervously chewing my nails at the kitchen bench. Everything is prepared. I've looked over the crates god knows how many times to ensure that everything is in perfect order, so now all that's left is for the catering van to come and pick it up. Belle will be meeting the driver at the other end with the waiting on staff to help her unload and serve. It's eleven o'clock. It'll take a good forty-five minutes to get across town at this time of day, so we've ordered the driver for eleven-fifteen, giving ourselves plenty of time. I stand, deciding to take one last look at everything. It's still perfect, so I let out a long breath, mumbling to myself. "If they don't like this then I'm really just not good enough for them."

Hearing the van pull up, I race to the back door to help the guy start loading and direct him to the correct crates while carrying the first one through. Just as I'm heading back through for the second one, my phone rings, scaring me half to death.

"This is just so crap!" Belle exclaims rather loudly in my ear.

"Why? What's the matter?" I ask, grabbing the next crate and beginning back towards the van.

"The fucking tube's broken down. I'm stuck under fucking ground and I've been delaying calling you hoping they'd get the fucking thing fixed, but I'm still sat here."

"But you're supposed to be at the White in twenty minutes, Belle. Where are you?"

"On the other side of fuckerty town. I've been sat down here for nearly a fucking hour. I gave myself plenty of time from the Croswell meet this morning but the sodding train's broken down and now I don't know what to do. No amount of me screaming at the fucking driver is making any difference and I'm going to fuck it all up because the London underground is completely fucking shit." She's almost crying with rage and frustration. I put the crate down and continue to point to the driver about the others.

"Right, calm down, Belle. What can we do to sort this out?" I ask, trying to think of a quick solution to our issue.

"Nothing, absolutely nothing, unless you can get a train engineer down here pronto," she huffs.

"Okay, well the waiting on staff will just have to do it on their own until you get there," I say, closing my eyes and praying that Belle isn't going to say what I think she's going to say.

"Beth, that's no fucking use and you know it. They'll mess it all up. Without someone there to direct them, they'll end up throwing it all over someone."

"Belle, I..."

"Beth, you're going to have to go," she states dramatically. I can imagine the arm waving and pointing.

"Belle, I can't. I've got too much to do and you know what-"

"You don't have a choice, honey. You're going to have to go there and head the lunch." *Fuck.*

"I can't. I don't have anything to wear for a start, and the thought of standing in front of twenty-five businessmen is making me want to be sick already. You know how I am around that sort of money. I just can't," I stammer, hoping desperately that there's a different way forward, but even I know there isn't if I'm honest. My shoulders slump.

"Beth, listen to me. There is no time to argue about this. You have to pull your shit together. I am not going to make it and this has to go perfectly. There is a work suit and shoes in my office and make-up in the top drawer. Go in there and get yourself sorted out. Put me on speakerphone so I can talk you through what you need to do. Make it snappy and tell the driver you're going to need a lift."

Resigning myself to the fact that this is happening, I proceed to listen to Belle as she gives me tips and tricks to get me through any variety of tricky situations. She explains each of the businessmen in detail and gives me a detailed layout of the room. She also gives me directions to the conference room and the names of all the people I will need to see upon arrival. God knows why she's bothering. I've almost tuned her out because of the nausea that's gracefully rising its way up my stomach toward my throat, but she's still chattering away while I get into the van. The drive seems to go by in minutes and before I know it, I'm at the White Building. I direct the driver around the back to the caterer's entrance and step out of the van, wobbling ever so slightly and taking in a long, deep breath. Apparently this is supposed to help me feel calm. It doesn't.

I'm now sweating and feel clammy all over. Sickness is raging up inside my stomach again and there isn't a thing I can do to stop it. I'm wracked with nerves and my head has that fuzzy and confused thing going on that always helps me make a complete arse of myself. Who am I meeting and where am I meeting them? *Christ, pull it together, Beth.*

I shake my head about and walk towards the first door, nodding at the girls who have gathered near me. My waiting on staff look immaculate. I only wish it was the same for me. Pushing the buzzer, I explain who we are and the lady on the intercom says she will meet us and show us through to the room. I almost curtsey at her high, clipped, English accent. It's yet another thing that increases my state of inner chaos.

The next forty minutes goes by in a flash of cutlery, waitresses, napkins, wine glasses and general nerves. I have to admit that the room is a stunning design of white and smoky blue glass. The tableware is the highest quality and I'm pretty sure that one glass was worth as much as the waitress's wages for the afternoon. The walls are decorated with modern art, all in differing tones of blue, giving a cool edge to the room. It's not a space to relax in. This is a place of work, probably one of ruthless business decisions, and it feels as if there is no room for emotion or geniality in here.

I sigh and try to gather my thoughts. Everything is laid out beautifully and all we have to do is serve. The girls are good, some of the best we've used, and hopefully they will all do their jobs perfectly so we can get the hell out of here as quickly as possible and leave without an accident occurring. I have to do this. It will be fine. I am strong. I am an independent woman of means. Who am I kidding? I'm screwed. *Fuckety fuckety fuck!*

I open the glass doors and hear the rumble of the guests arriving. *Keep it together.* One by one, they start to approach along the corridor. *Keep it together.* Old, young, grey suit, blue suit. *Keep it together and smile.* Tall, short, they're all a blur of business suits and ties. They are all talking vigorously and making so much noise, I hardly notice as they start to find their places at the table. I turn to the serving table and tell the girls to proceed, but as I reach for the first plate to hand over, I hear a lone voice coming from the corridor. *Shit. Wait.* I hold my hand up to the girls.

"Don't get me started on that fucking idiot. Has he any idea how much of my money he might have lost? I swear, I will have his balls on a platter if he comes within a mile of my building, and it's a bloody good job you're on the other end of a phone because if you weren't, you'd be getting an arse kicking as well. How could you let this happen? I gave you control for two weeks while I was in New York. Can I not trust anyone with anything? Fuck!"

I cringe and slowly turn to the door to await the arrival of the obviously very angry last guest, and oh God, there he is - Mr. Alexander White himself.

Oh. My. God.

There is a moment in time that seems to last for an eternity. Eyes so blue that they somehow sear into my soul, meet mine and my body immediately goes numb as he continues forward. I can't move. I'm frozen. My heart rate was already high, but now it begins to tear through my chest like it might explode or just give up at any point. I'm even struggling to breathe as I look up at him and gaze into those icy eyes that just continue with their assault of mine. The unyielding stare directed back at me has me quaking in my heels and whatever it is that he's thinking, for some reason has me questioning my very existence in his presence. His completely unreadable expression doesn't change in any way as he ends his call and pockets his phone. I watch as the corners of his mouth lift slightly, his probably permanently fixed frown dissipates, and the most glorious smile I have ever witnessed graces his delicious face. I instantly wobble a little on my heels and swallow down the gasp that is about to leave my mouth as that smile turns into something infinitely more wicked.

I'm so screwed here.

"Miss Scott," he says as he enters the room with that smile, and time comes racing back to normal speed. I can't help thinking that such a devilish smile probably endangers everyone in the room, possibly the world given a chance, and how the hell did he go from raging beast to calm and agreeable anyway? And how does he know who I am? *Breathe, Beth, breathe.*

"Mr. White, please be seated. We can start whenever you're ready." He stands for a moment longer, just staring at me, his face changing to one of puzzlement.

"Is there something wrong, sir?" I ask, hoping to god there isn't.

"No, not at all. It's just that I expected the other Miss Scott today. Please, carry on," he says as an amused smirk sets in and his eyes leave mine to address the rest of me.

"Thank you, sir. We hope everything will be to your liking."

Fortunately, his gaze returns to my eyes as he nods and walks towards the centre of the table, looking back over his shoulder at me briefly. Had I not been staring at his arse, I would never have noticed. My face flames and my heart rate escalates again. He narrows his eyes a little at me and continues on to the table. *Stupid Beth.*

I hear him launch into a humorous tirade at someone across the other side of the table and take that as my cue to begin service. Nodding towards the girls, I motion for them to start with the service and drag in a long, calming breath. This is going to be a very long ninety minutes.

Actually, the first hour flies by and I find I have even enjoyed myself at some points. I haven't needed to talk with anyone, which helped calm my nerves enormously. The conversation from the table has been both informative and strangely interesting. It appears that Mr. Alexander White can be quite the entertainer. He's been both comical and motivating. The group of businessmen sitting around him are completely enthralled with what he's discussing and most of them are constantly muttering sounds of approval or agreement. On a few occasions, the tension level has risen to an unacceptable level and he's quickly diffused the situation by complementing the inaccurate party or bringing harmony with an amusing anecdote. Even I have to admit he's utterly astounding, well, for a manipulative bastard that is. No wonder he's done so well for himself. He holds people in the palm of his hand without even trying. God knows what the man could achieve if he was really challenged, or what lengths he would go to get the correct result for himself.

We're down to the final course. We only have to put the desserts on the table and then we can pack up and go. We've done it. I've done it. I'm jumping up and down on the inside. Ecstatic isn't the word for it. Just for the formality of it, I choose to serve Mr. White myself. We need this contract to be perfect, and so far, it has been. Everyone has eaten heartily and I've heard several positive comments regarding the food, so I'm confident that all is well. I know that extra bit of effort to promote the business will only help to secure a good working future with them.

Taking the dessert in my hand, I walk across the room, making sure that everyone else has been served before I place the food in front of him as has been requested. I am three feet from the table. This is it, the last minutes of our perfect performance are almost finished and then I feel my toe catch the floor and it's slow motion all the bloody way.

I actually watch the plate leave my hand and fly scarily close to his head before the entire fresh strawberry and balsamic mousse tumbles from the dish, down his shirt and straight into his lap. Oh buggery shit and bollocks. I've stumbled and fallen, clearly looking like a complete imbecile, and somehow managed to end up kneeling at his side.

Silence. Utter silence. Shit. Which way is this going to go? And what the hell do I do now? Should I try to wipe it off? Probably not. I look up at the other gentlemen, not sure what to do with myself. A few are smiling, but most are frowning at my ineptitude. Shit. Realising that I am only a few inches from his crotch, which smells of strawberry mousse, I decide to make the grave mistake of looking up to his face. Beautiful, cold blue eyes stare down at me in complete shock, and then slowly, a smirk of amusement rolls over them. He's laughing at me. Great. Well at least that's better than anger. I stand quickly and begin to apologise profusely.

"I really am incredibly sorry, sir. I must have tripped on something and I couldn't hold onto the plate and it slipped from my fingers and... Oh, God, I am just so sorry," I blurt out. My face is more than likely the colour of beetroot and my body is shaking beyond belief. He simply continues with his assault of my eyes, his eyebrow raising at me.

"Elizabeth, please don't worry about it. Sometimes we all embarrass ourselves and really, there's no harm done. Unless you count the distress caused to my suit that is," he says as his smile softens to one of concern or something. I have no idea what it is, but it's bloody lovely; I know that much.

"Sir, please let me pay for the dry cleaning," I say, digging into my pocket to pull out one of Belle's business cards. "We could pick it up and return it to you or just send us the bill, whatever is convenient for yourself. I really would like to apologise for my blunder and I don't know any other way to..." I'm rambling again, my standard response to any awkward situation.

There is another pause long enough to eclipse the sodding sun while I look at my feet and wait uncomfortably for his response.

"Okay, thank you. I'll be in touch. I think perhaps it is time for you and your staff to leave now," he replies with a soft but dismissive tone, turning back to the table.

"Oh right, yes. Sorry again," I mumble.

I can't even begin to look at anyone again so hurry towards the door, ushering the girls out and being careful not to trip over my own feet again. No need to make myself look more of an incompetent fool than I already have. Looking at my girls is also not an option, so I wait until they're far enough away before I call over my shoulder to them.

"Girls, I have to rush so please pick up your wages on Friday. Thank you. You all did a great job today."

With that, I turn in the opposite direction, listening to them giggling and recounting the ridiculous situation. Embarrassment surges over me again as I try to remember how the hell to get to the main foyer, while berating myself over and over again. How could I be so stupid, so pathetic? Bloody hell, I can't even walk properly. No wonder I don't fit in with these people. Every eye in the building seems to follow me as I pelt in random directions, hoping that something will look familiar. Nothing does. Clearly not even escaping a bloody building is possible for the likes of me.

Eventually I find a corridor that happens to lead me in the right direction, and hitting the fresh air, I run down the steps towards the nearest taxi rank. I have just ruined my own business, and Belle is going to kill me.

~

Alexander

"Gentlemen, it appears I have some cleaning up to do and a suit to change." Alex looked at his colleagues and then at his lap, feeling a smirk crawl over his mouth again. He couldn't help it. The last hour or so had involved some of the most entertaining moments of his life.

"Yes, it appears so," one of them retorted.

"Please excuse me while I go and change. I won't be long so have another glass of wine." He left the room, which filled with laughter the moment he was through the door.

"It's a shame really. It appears you just can't find a pretty one that isn't completely inept at everything else," he heard Bill say and then snigger. The room erupted in laughter and agreement again, which was completely fucking unacceptable. He abruptly turned and stalked back into the room, rage welling up inside him for some unknown reason.

"Bill, did you not enjoy your meal?"

"Excuse me, Alexander?"

"I asked if you enjoyed your food."

"Yes, I did, very much. It was exquisite actually."

"Then perhaps you should have the decency to be thankful to the chef that created it for you. I am not sure why she was here, but Elizabeth Scott is the chef. Her food was exemplary and the service was perfect apart from the accident, which I'm pretty sure you didn't suffer from. So I suggest you keep your opinions to yourself and check your information before you jump the gun on someone's abilities." Alex fumed with a cold calculation. He had no fucking idea what the hell he was doing, but he couldn't stop it.

"I'm sorry. I didn't know," Bill stuttered, looking at Alex with a shocked expression.

"No, you often don't. That's probably why when I bought your last company, which you'd failed, and tripled its profits in the first year, I couldn't help but laugh at your fucking ineptitude. But then I had the right to do so. So please, if you want to remain in this room for future gatherings, keep your bloody assumptions to yourself."

At that, Alex left. Again.

What the hell had happened in there? What was he thinking talking to Bill Armstrong like that? Not only did he need Bill, he was also very closely aligned to a huge deal he'd been working on. He just couldn't stop the rage that forced its way through him. He normally had such control of it. He'd learned through various ways to keep a tight rein on his anger, but Christ, the fucking nerve of the man had completely thrown him. He walked swiftly toward the elevator that would take him to his apartment on the upper level, trying to calm himself down and analyse his own stupidity.

As he dropped his card on the entrance table, he smiled at the smell of strawberry mousse wafting up towards him. She'd been inches from his cock, and however absurd the situation had been, he couldn't help but be aroused. When he'd looked at her on her knees looking up at him, he'd instantly been hard and would have given the other guys anything they wanted just to get out of the room so he could have her on the boardroom table. Or the floor. Frankly any surface would have been acceptable in that moment. Her striking eyes had been almost tear filled and begging for forgiveness as her mouth searched for the right thing to say, and her lips trembled beautifully. He couldn't help but smile at her and interestingly, he'd wanted to -

not out of amusement but out of kindness or compassion or some other emotion he wasn't aware he owned. Maybe it was to try and ease her embarrassment, which was in itself enlightening because he'd normally enjoy the sight of humiliation with relish. But she'd had nothing to feel remorseful about. In fact she had been simply wonderful and the room had been filled with some sort of warmth that he hadn't ever been aware of before.

He wasn't sure why she'd been there. She certainly wasn't expected. He'd been told that her sister ran the show so he'd assumed she would be on point today. He'd been so shocked to see her, he'd almost tripped over his own words when he first noticed her, which was so confusing it had taken a moment to realise what was happening. Stunning was the only word that he could think of at the time as he'd gazed into her eyes. That's what he was - stunned. She'd looked less carefree and more businesslike, with her hair in a chignon and the dark blue knee length suit, but it was still sexy as hell. So he'd continued staring at her, not knowing what to say.

Realising that a lack of articulation had never happened to him before, he tried to formulate something to say. Nothing had come to mind as his heart raced and his fingers itched to reach out for her and pull her closer, or maybe just throw her over his shoulder and fuck the life out of her. Time simply seemed to stall for the few seconds they looked at each other. Her chocolate brown eyes bore into him for the first time and he felt his throat tighten, so much so that he'd had to move his eyes from hers for a second before she saw it all. But as his gaze had returned upward, her sublime lips had trembled in front of him, showing her apprehension. She'd simply held her head as high as her nerves would allow and then she'd called him sir. Christ, his balls had coiled so tight he thought he'd explode just looking at her.

As he changed into a clean suit, he found himself still smiling and thanking God for Conner's soft side. Yes he'd given him a good talking to, but he had eventually relented and given him Belle Scott's number. He'd received several stern words from Conner in his time but not many had come close to the severe berating he'd received about treating the Scott girls with the respect they deserved and keeping the hell away from Belle. The man was concerned that he would taint her as well. Unfortunately, he'd deserved every mouthful of venom that left his friend's mouth. Not that Conner was aware of it, but his past sins still haunted his life occasionally.

He buckled his belt and pondered what it was about her that was making him want to be just a bit better, or maybe even decent. Fuck knows what it was, but he hoped he could be because he sure as hell was going to have her, and soon. Where it went from there he didn't know, but for the first time in his life he felt something more than pain. He didn't know why or how she was able to do this to him but he did know she was making him smile and feel an sense of tension for some reason. Maybe it was the challenge of someone so innocent; maybe it was the thought of someone real and not another insipid whore; or maybe it was just her and those damned consuming eyes she possessed.

His phone vibrated on the table in front of him, pulling him from his fucking odd little daydream so he swiped it up and read the text.

• I have two new ones, dear boy. Do come and play. I am thoroughly bored without you.

Mmm, tempting. But given his last half hour, the thought was, quite bizarrely, a little dull. Having said that, his cock was definitely in need of some attention because that woman's very appealing body had thrown all sorts of fucking visions at him during the meeting. In fact, he might as well not have been in the damn room for all the work he'd actually completed.

He pulled on his jacket and walked back towards the hall. Stopping briefly in the kitchen, he ran his fingers over the portrait of the boy in the rain and gazed at the small child's huddled position, his knees pulled up to his chest in fear as the storm raged on around him. He drew his finger along the tiny shadowed figure in the background and sneered as his throat tightened again. It appeared that regardless of the reasons why, Miss Scott seemed to have the ability to make him uneasy, slightly uncomfortable even, and while it was exceptionally stimulating to some degree, both of those were emotions he had long since fucking buried. Deep down, where they could damn well stay.

He shook his head and carried on down the hall. He needed to get his control back around her and quickly at that. No woman would want to see the part of him he kept so well suppressed and he wasn't about to let Elizabeth Scott see his flaws or know the depth of his sins any time soon. A woman like her needed to see Alexander White, to experience the performance, and as he raised his head again and looked in the mirrors, he decided that Alexander White was exactly who she would get.

Chapter 6

Elizabeth

*"*Are you telling me that you threw strawberry fucking mousse over the most high profile client we've had to date?" Belle screams at me from the other side of the room, her eyes apparently having transformed into daggers.

"Yes," I reply as I sit with my head lowered at the kitchen table, trying to think up a decent enough excuse for my stupidity. There still isn't one.

"All you had to do was serve a fucking meal, Beth. Jesus. One fucking meal. I can't believe you screwed this up," she continues, walking around furiously, hands waving about as she mutters to herself.

I simply stare at the floor, wishing she'd calm down and give me a break but she has a right to be furious and all I can do is sit here and take it.

When I ran to the taxi the day before, I cried all the way to the apartment. I refused to go back to work and ignored the twenty missed calls I received from Belle because I just couldn't face it, or in reality, face her. When she returned later in the evening and asked how it had gone my reply was fine. It was the best I could come up with at the time, and then I lied that I had a terrible migraine and that I just needed to get to bed and rest. She was clearly not convinced and tried to obtain more information but I just blagged my way through it and went to bed anyway. I knew I wouldn't be able to avoid it the following morning, but at the time, I didn't care, so now here I sit.

"Belle, I'm so sorry. I just tripped. It could have happened to anyone," I try to protest. She cuts me off with such ferocity I actually shake a little.

"No, Beth, it wouldn't have happened to anyone. It would only happen to you. You're fucking ridiculous. I cannot believe this shit," she erupts at me as she paces some more, very nearly snorting with disgust at my obvious uselessness. She's right... I am a complete idiot.

"Belle, please, I am completely aware of my own incompetence. I don't need you feeding my subconscious any more than I do on my own." I can feel the tears pricking and unable to hold the flood back, I begin with more crying, as if I didn't do enough of that last night.

"Don't start that snivelling shit either. I've had enough of it. Why do you think tears are going to somehow make it better? Fucking hell," Belle says as she sighs and sits down across from me then bangs her head on the table repeatedly until she stops and leaves it there.

"I'm so sorry," I splutter through my sobs.

We sit in silence for several minutes as I continue to stare at the floor and try to contain my ridiculous crying fit. I can feel her wrath directed at me even though she's still face down on the table. Her muttering and occasional head bangs still warn me to keep my mouth closed, so I nibble at my nails and hope for the best.

"On his dick?" she eventually mumbles.

"What?" My head shoots up as she lifts her head slightly to look at me. Her chin is still connected to the surface and her eyes still dangerously narrowed at me.

"The mousse, was it on his dick, in his lap?" she asks again with no smile whatsoever.

"Yes," I reply, lifting my lips just slightly. She chuckles a little as she sits herself upright.

"Well, I suppose you at least fuck up in style."

"Oh, Belle, everything else was perfect. You would have been so proud. Honestly. There were positive comments and they were all very happy. I'm sure we won't lose the contract because of my mistake. I could always try to talk to him again and make it all right. I offered to do his dry cleaning and he seemed okay with that." I'm rambling again. Belle looks at me with a flurry of affection and strokes my hair soothingly, which just makes me feel worse.

"It's okay, honey. You tried your hardest. I know that, but I'm afraid with a man like Alexander White, there is only one chance and we just blew it," she states, shaking her head in resignation and getting up.

I watch Belle leave the room and then just stare at the closed door to her bedroom, knowing that I have just blown everything we've worked so hard for. Seriously, what is the bloody point? Of course the tears start again and I hold my head in my hands, mainly to stop it from exploding.

Twenty minutes later, Belle reappears in the kitchen.

"What are you just sitting there for? We need to get to work," she says in a strangely calm manner given the last half an hour, as she picks up her bag.

"Well, I thought I might just stay here. I've nothing pressing there and I can pick it up tomorrow. I'll just go in early," I reply blankly. I'm really in no mood for it whatsoever.

"Oh no you don't. You are not going to sit here moping around all bloody day. We've got work to do. It'll take some doing but we'll just have to find another client. If I can get one in the next few days, hopefully the grapevine won't have already spoken about our little faux pas," she says with her don't mess with me tone.

"Okay," I say as I get up. While her response is unexpected, I'm seriously not going to wind her up any further, but I really did think there would be more sisterly chats about this. She gives me a squeeze as I grab my coat.

"Seriously, honey, we'll just move on together," she says with a smile.

~

We've been in the shop for three hours. Belle's working hard on the phone and I'm trying to put the incident behind me and move on, as she suggested. So, I'm working on a set of new pastries that a colleague has suggested. Thankfully they're going well. The kitchen is soothing my spirits back to some sort of normality and seems to be helping relax my mood, but undoubtedly the strain is showing.

"Beth, get yourself out here," Teresa shouts from the front of the shop. She's mad at me as well. The fact that I pay her wages seems to have gone unnoticed for some reason.

Now what have I done?

As I round the corner, I'm confronted by a very tall man wearing a chauffeur's uniform. He doesn't have a hint of a smile to comfort me in any way. Slightly scary, frankly.

"Are you Miss Scott?" large man asks. I'm unsure whether to say yes or not as I narrow my eyes at him. Eventually I relent.

"Umm, yes," I respond quietly as Belle emerges from the office to stand behind me.

"I have been asked to deliver this to you personally," he says, and with that, he hands over a flat, rectangular, blue box.

"Are you sure you have the right address? I am not expecting anything," I reply, eyeing the box with confusion.

"You are Miss Elizabeth Scott?" he asks again, more sternly this time, with an accusing stare. He reminds me of some MI5 agent or something.

"Yes, but-"

"Then this is for you, Miss Scott. Please enjoy your afternoon. Goodbye." He turns and the doorbell chimes as he leaves the shop without another word.

"Thank you," I shout after him. I don't know why I bother because he's already gone, probably on another covert operation of some sort. We all look at each other with perplexed expressions, then at the box, then at each other again.

"You know where that's from, don't you?" Teresa whispers. "Tiffany's," she says as she jumps up and down with glee.

"Who do you know that would get you something from Tiffany's?" Belle asks, looking shocked.

"I... I don't know," I stutter. Clearly this is a mistake.

"Well open it then," Teresa screams at me.

I flinch at sound in my ear and look at the box, starting to open the beautifully tied bow and reach for the clasp. I openly gasp as I see the twinkle of diamonds beneath the card that has been placed inside. My left hand shoots to my heart and my fingers fumble with the card. It falls to the floor so I retrieve it and gaze down at the words.

Thank you for adding some sparkle to an otherwise very dull meeting. I thought you might like some sparkle of your own this morning.
AW

I slowly look back at the box to see the most stunning bracelet I have ever seen. It's vintage in style with a continuous treble row of diamonds separated by four vertical baguette-cut linking stones that gleam in the bright shop lights. The clasp in itself is a work of art and its deco appearance screams of an elegance and timelessness that has no business being in my presence at all. I stare at it some more, not really knowing what to say as Teresa snatches the card out of my hand.

"Does AW mean who I think it means?" she asks as she stares at me. She's clearly as confused as I am but I really can't think of anyone else I know with those initials, let alone someone who could afford something like this.

"What?" Belle grabs at the card and scans it herself.

"Beth, what the hell did you do to him? If I'd known throwing food all over a man would get me a bracelet from Tiffany's I'd have done it myself," she says, a small giggle escaping from her mouth.

I just continue to gape at it, as do they. What am I supposed to say to something like this?

"Try it on. Try it on," Teresa excitedly urges.

Slowly removing the bracelet from its box, I undo the clasp. Belle reaches forward and gently hooks it around my wrist. I'm not only shaking from the sublime beauty of the piece but also the fact that I have thousands of pounds worth of diamonds wrapped around me. Still, regardless of the cost, I can't help but continue gazing down at it as I twist and turn my wrist. It's simply too stunning to not look at and I take the card back from Belle to study it again. The beautifully hand-written note is on thick, white embossed card that has his name and a mobile phone number on the back. Why would Alexander White send a diamond bracelet and a personal phone number to me?

"Well, someone made a good impression yesterday. I thought you said you'd fucked it up?" Teresa says, grabbin my wrist for closer examination.

"Yes, we shall have to send you to all the new clients." Belle smiles as she stares at the bracelet.

"Well, beautiful as it is, it will have to be returned. I can't possibly accept it. I did nothing to deserve it and even if I had, it would still be too much," I say, removing the bracelet and placing it back in its box carefully.

"Don't be ridiculous. It's from Tiffany's, and he clearly wants you to have it for some reason," Teresa says in surprise.

"Well, he might have meant well but it's almost certainly worth more than I make in a year and it just doesn't feel right. I'm sorry, ladies. Take another look if you like but when you've finished, could you put it in the safe. I'll take it back tomorrow," I reply, leaving the box on the counter and wandering out of the room.

The moment I've turned my back on them I palm the card and tuck it into my pocket, grinning with delight. I won't keep it but that doesn't mean I don't like the sentiment attached to it, and whatever it is that Mr. White is trying to achieve, he's at least made me smile.

The rest of the day passes by more jovially and the earlier tension seems to have evaporated. Clearly the gift and note has lifted the anxiety that we had lost the contract and we are once again jubilant. With any luck he won't be there and I can just deliver it to someone significant and that will be the end of the matter, because I really don't want to see him again. It was embarrassing enough last time, and lovely as he may be to look at, I simply can't bear the thought of him looking at me again. He made me uneasy, and that was regardless of the strawberry mousse incident. Something about the way he looked at me just sent shivers of fear or waves of pleasure up and down my spine. I'm still not sure which it was so I'm not putting myself in front of him again anytime soon.

Unfortunately, my decision to not see him again doesn't seem to stop me from fingering the card repeatedly all afternoon while random sexual images float through my brain, and in spite of how much I chastise myself, there's just a small part of me that wishes I was more like either of the other girls in the shop.

That night I place the box on my bedside table and dreamily stare at it, still wondering why he would send me a gift. Or why someone like Alexander White would even give me a second thought.

But as sleep pulls at me and I close my eyes, I can't deny that those ocean blue eyes are still continuing with their penetrating gaze. They're still seemingly asking me for something that I'm unaware of, and quite unnervingly, they're the last thing I see as I drift off.

~

What does a girl wear to return a gift? Well, after much deliberating, I choose a green silk blouse and a pair of my most well-cut skinny jeans. I pull on my long, heeled boots and add another swipe of mascara. That will have to do. I'm not sure why I'm bothering so much about my appearance but for some reason, I have butterflies in my stomach and it matters to me. I want to feel at my best as I walk into that building again, and lord knows if he happens to be around I want to feel at my best in front of him. Running the brush through my loose hair once more, I add some lip-gloss and push in my diamond studs. There. Done. Spraying some Chloe on my neck and wrists, I walk through to the lounge with purpose. I can do this.

"Still taking it back then." Belle states rather than asks while painting her toenails.

"Yep," I reply breezily.

"Shame. It's such a beautiful thing." She sighs and looks somewhat wistfully out of the window, which is odd.

"Yep." I narrow my eyes at her. *What is she up to?*

"Beth-"

I interrupt her before she can finish. "Listen, Belle, before you try and talk me out of it, I really can't accept it, honey. It's just not something I do. This life you two live is not for me. I just want to keep it simple." I smile at my own ability to be assertive. It happens every now and then. She sighs again.

"I was just going to say please be careful. You're about to refuse Alexander White and I don't think you understand what that means," she says with some annoyance.

"What on earth are you talking about?" I ask. I really have no idea.

"The man doesn't understand the word *no,* Beth. He will not be amused by your rejection and we... Well, we need this contract." I suddenly see her point.

"Oh, I didn't think about it like that," I exclaim, my brain beginning to process the information and what it means to us.

"Well, on your journey please do, and think hard about how you handle it. We do not want to get it wrong again, do we now?" She raises an eyebrow. *Bitch.* Sometimes I hate how clever she is. I'm still not changing my mind about giving it back though.

"Right, I will. I'll see you later then."

I sigh as I head to the door, swiping my brown leather jacket on the way.

"Okay bye. Good luck."

Even though I take the tube this time, the journey still seems to last only minutes. It doesn't. It actually takes at least an hour, but unfortunately I'm so absorbed in thinking about how I'm going to *handle the situation* that I arrive before I know it. So I give myself a little time to appreciate Mr. White's building in all its magnificence. It's a tall and imposing Georgian structure that has been painted completely white, allowing it to stand out against the other grey facades on the road. It's covered in six strict rows of fourteen beautifully restored sash windows, which give it an air of elegance, but the underlying tone of the building shouts power. The very modern looking revolving door at the entrance entices me towards it steadily, somehow beckoning me with its draw, while at the same time scaring the hell out of me. And Christ does the whole thing suit him well. I can almost feel him emanating from the fibre of the structure - charismatic, elegant, impressive and clearly somewhat daunting.

As I approach the foyer, I notice things I missed before while exiting the building at speed last time. The black and white chequered floor reminds me of a chessboard, which makes me smile, and the huge arrangements of flowers that adorn the tall, pillared columns in the front are stunning. Each piece of artwork that hangs on the walls seems to have a softer feel than the art I saw in the conference room. They're somehow more welcoming and sociable, as if inviting you calmly into the hornet's nest with a smile and a wink. I can't help but giggle at the thought because regardless of his butchering hands, he's a sneaky bastard.

I step towards the unfairly stunning woman at the desk and tell her that I'd like to leave the package for Mr. White.

"Hold on please. I'll just buzz through to Miss Trembell. She will collect it for you," she says smiling. "What is your name please?"

There's a short conversation on the phone and then I'm directed to the sofa to *make myself comfortable* while I wait. That's just hilarious. I've never felt more on edge in my life as I try to disappear into the waiting area and somehow morph myself into the sofa. From where I sit I can see the elevator so I just wait for the efficient Louisa Trembell to materialise in the hope that it will be quick and painless. Flicking through a magazine and trying to relax, I find myself desperately hoping that the sinfully sexy Mr. White won't appear and ruin my seemingly natural disposition because at present, I'm managing to at least appear like I'm in control of myself for her.

I suddenly feel shivers run down my spine and stiffen. It's just like the feeling in movies when there's someone bad on the other side of the door that the heroine's about to open. My heart rate leaps bizarrely and before I calculate the possibility of an actual threat, I become aware that it's him. It's the same strange shivery thing that I had when he looked at me, and now for some reason, I can feel him, perhaps near me again, or in me, almost all over me. I have no idea what it is but the anxious experience from before has now returned with a vengeance. I sink down into the seat and try to hide behind my magazine, then peer over the top in the hope of spotting him in time so I can run, or maybe try my hand at evaporation or something similar. But as the hairs on the back of my neck stand on end, and I swiftly realise that he's probably behind me. *Shit.*

I should turn round with poise and flair to check out my theory. I could stand up and walk directly out of the building without even seeing him. Unfortunately, my curiosity at this random sixth sense that I seem to possess gets the better of me so I narrow my eyes and take a deep breath.

I slowly turn to look up at the most breath-taking vision I've ever seen, still peering over my magazine. Those light blue eyes gaze at me from the wall behind. He's standing there with his hands in his pockets, seemingly waiting for me to speak. I have nothing for this moment as I continue to gawp at his somehow announced presence and stupidly run my eyes over the exquisite grey pinstripe suit. Seriously, it's a really stupid move because now I'm imagining his body beneath it as I scan his broad shoulders and then those long legs, which obviously just increases my heart rate again. He cocks his head to the side at my perusal of him, so eventually I find the wherewithal to stand and turn myself fully towards him while closing my gaping mouth. Opening it again to say something, I realise I still haven't got control of functioning thought, apart from several inappropriate ones, so I close it again. He still looks at me as he smirks a little, probably at my discomfort. It only makes him look all the more glorious. Bastard. I need to get a grp.

"Elizabeth." And, oh, I love the way my name sounds from his lips, so much so that I mouth my own name to myself and gaze at his. This causes more unacceptable images to interfere with my other ridiculous thoughts, so I shake myself from my hedonistic visions.

"Mr. White, I-"

He cuts me off. "We can't talk here. Come with me for a moment and we'll go somewhere more private," he suggests. Private, yes. Good.

"Okay," I reply, while thinking this is probably the most stupid thing I have ever done, but it will absolutely be better to refuse him in a private room. I really don't want to make a scene and embarrass myself further.

With a swipe of a card, the wall seems to open up behind him and I realise there's a hidden elevator there. No wonder I didn't see him arrive. He gestures his hand towards it with a smile and I awkwardly manoeuvre my way around the sofa and step in. Elegant as always.

I feel him follow at a polite distance, being careful not to touch me, acting the gentleman. I can't help wondering if it's always so as more of those sodding images enter my brain. More than likely not. He never for a second takes his eyes off mine as he leans on the wall and crosses his arms. My insides clench at the vision that stands before me, and hard as I try, I don't appear to be able to stop the shaking thing that is beginning to occur within me. I exhale a breath and accept that this really is far too close for comfort. I haven't got a hope of appearing in control and I definitely won't be able to hold his gaze for much longer. His casually aggressive dominance is so completely overbearing and undeniably panty dropping that I feel the moment when I begin to fold. It's the second he nonchalantly licks his very beautiful lips and pushes away from the wall towards me. I immediately shudder with something odd and drop my eyes to the floor in defeat.

A small chuckle leaves his mouth. It's probably more a recognition of my surrender to his obvious superiority in staring contests, so I fidget with my hands as I feel him studying me. Quietly smiling to myself, I think of the effect he's having on me. It really is absurd. I'm even amusing myself with my ineptitude so I steel myself and look up again. He doesn't pretend he isn't looking at me, or rather my chest area. He just raises an eyebrow and tilts his head a little as if he has every right to be looking me over. He's possibly right. God knows every other woman in the world would probably be dropping to their knees at the thought, let alone the reality. He suddenly says the word "six" aloud, so firmly that I flinch at his tone and stumble backwards a little as the elevator starts to rise beneath us. He smirks again. Apparently I'm amusing him.

"Where are we going?" I ask, trying for casual and balanced, inwardly shaking like a bloody leaf.

"Somewhere more private," he reiterates, flashing a true megawatt smile at me. It's disturbing to say the least. Women would die for it, I'm sure.

Before I know it, the door slides back and I'm ushered into a large, white, granite-floored foyer. Imposing double oak doors lead off from the foyer on three sides and I notice the walls are also painted white. In fact, everything's white. He drops his card onto the table by the elevator and proceeds to walk through one set of doors into a large the kitchen area.

"Would you like some wine, Elizabeth?" he calls over his shoulder in a relaxed fashion as I study his rather impressive back view and follow him.

"Uh, yes please," I reply. Okay, so this isn't what I was expecting and now I'm in an apartment with him. Probably his apartment. How the hell did this turn into a drink in his home? "Is this your apartment? It's wonderful," I ask, feeling a bit flustered as I look around the vast, modern, open-plan space. Three huge, black leather sofas that dominate the lounge area are placed around a large glass coffee table, and behind that is a wall of glass overlooking the city. Other than that, there seems to be no colour at all, only white. Glass and white everywhere. The place is extremely sparse and for some reason seems very little like the man who stands in front of me. Not that I'd know, because I know nothing about him, but it all just feels wrong somehow.

"Yes, I spend most of the week here when I'm in London. I go home at the weekends or when I get the chance. I try to protect my free time but I'm afraid it's not always possible. Red or white?"

"Excuse me?" I stutter in surprise, turning my head back towards him and dragging my eyes from the stunning view of the London skyline.

"The wine, Elizabeth. Red or white?" he asks, poking his spell binding head above the kitchen counter. His near black hair twinkles amongst all the white, making me gaze at it in wonder, and god those lips are moving again. "Elizabeth?"

"Oh, yes. White please, if you have it, although I'm not staying, I-"

"I have everything you might need here," he cuts me off again. He seems to like doing that. He smirks at me, cocking that damn eyebrow again.

Is he flirting with me? No, I must have misread that last comment, surely. I need to get out of here and quick. I'm absolutely going to make an utter idiot of myself soon, and if he is flirting, there's only one thing on his mind and that is not going to happen, regardless of my still clenching insides.

"Mr. White, I just came by to return the bracelet. I can't possibly accept it and I really don't need to take up any of your time," I say, placing the blue box on the countertop and hoping my tone is pleasant enough. "So I'll just leave it here and go." *Stay positive, Beth.*

"Why on earth not?" he questions incredulously as he pours the wine and hands me a glass, completely ignoring my request to leave and not even glancing at the box.

"It's simply too much. I don't even know you and I've done nothing to warrant such a wonderful thing so I'd like to give it back," I reply. He looks at me quizzically for a moment then sighs and walks towards me, his eyes narrowing with each pace forward. I take a hasty step backwards.

"Louisa will be very annoyed if you don't take it, because I will have to send her across town every day until you do accept it, and that will be quite infuriating for her. It will also mean she can't be as efficient for me as she should be, and therefore I will not be as enamoured by her skills as I normally am," he states calmly while he walks behind me and removes my jacket from my shoulders, taking my bag with it. I let him for some reason and shrug my arms out awkwardly, trying to stop myself from spilling my drink as his fingers brush my back. "So unless you want to cause all sorts of trouble, I suggest you just accept it for what it is meant to be. A gift."

"Really, Mr. White I-"

"Alex," he cuts me off as he gazes at me with an arrogant *in control* pose. He's right. He is. In fact, I'm still trying to process the fact that he said a whole paragraph to me because his voice in full swing was like hearing the devil beckoning. A low, gravelly and somehow hypnotic tone came from his mouth, causing all kinds of reactions to erupt within me, mainly in my groin, and him actually touching me did nothing to stop the damn feeling at all.

"Right, Alex, yes. I just can't... Please?" Am I now begging him to take back the bracelet?

"Please what, Elizabeth?" He lifts that bloody eyebrow at me again as he puts my coat and bag on the counter softly.

"Please... Please, just accept that I'm returning it and that attractive as it is, I couldn't take it from you and feel at ease with myself. It's just..." I struggle to finish quite as effectively as I'd like to and his amused expression is doing nothing to help me find the right words.

"Look, Elizabeth, I am not in the habit of accepting no for an answer and I'm not about to start now. If the price tag worries you, please don't let it. It's not like I can't afford it." He gestures his wineglass around the room. "If it makes you feel more comfortable that small artwork cost more," he says, pointing towards a painting of a boy in the pouring rain behind me. I move toward it, feeling bizarrely drawn for some reason as he continues. "The point of sending you the gift was to get you to contact me. That part has worked. If you really don't want the bracelet then give it to someone else. I quite like it though. It reminded me of you. Besides, I very much hoped you would wear it for dinner." I swing my head back to him so quickly I could have whiplash and find that he's moved closer - only two feet away. I look up into his eyes in disbelief.

"Excuse me? What are you...?" I reply as I retreat a bit, feeling completely breathless at his proximity. Did he just ask me out?

"Dinner at my house next Saturday," he says, looking directly at me, motionless and smiling beautifully. I still can't breathe. Yes he did ask me out. That can't be right.

"Are you… Are you asking me out on a date, Mr. Whi- Uh, Alex?" It's not possible. I can't help smiling.

"I don't know about a date. I haven't had one of those for a quite a while but I would very much like to cook you dinner, surprisingly enough," he says, laughing at himself and ushering me into the lounge area. "Drink some wine. It's really very good."

"Right." Good idea. I slurp at it. A date, really? Well not a date, but still.

"Do you like it?" he asks after staring at me for some time. It's at least given me a small chance to get my head around the thought of a date with him.

"The wine, the bracelet, the painting or the view?" I reply with a smirk. Apparently I'm now feeling a little more confident in my demeanour because my sarcasm comes rushing back to me.

"All of the above, but mainly the gift," he asks again with a chuckle.

I pause for a long moment and look into his eyes, then realise I can't hold onto that amount of connection with him so stare out at the skyline again. He's far too intense. The man needs to relax, frankly, and regardless of his request for dinner, has he just played me to get me to come back to his office? For what exactly? A quickie? I think not. I need to get myself together. That incredibly well carved body and glorious face is distracting me from the fact that he is, of course, a complete arsehole who will eat me alive given half a chance. It's completely inappropriate where that thought leads me to as I imagine being *eaten alive.*

I turn back to him and raise my chin a little.

"Alex, you've just implied that you sent me the bracelet so you could see me again."

"Yes." Still he doesn't move, just stands there looking glorious. He's even undone the button on his jacket now and shoved his hand in his pocket, which is giving me a glimpse of his shirt against his skin. It's completely unfair of him.

"Did you think I would come back here to give you some sort of *gift* in return for your rather over the top gesture?" There's not a bloody chance as long as I can keep him away from me. If I'm honest, it really wouldn't take much at all - pathetic really.

"I'm not sure what I thought, Elizabeth. I just wanted to see you again. You intrigued me," he responds in a calculated manner, moving the glass to his beautiful mouth.

"Why didn't you just call me then and ask?" I narrow my eyes at him. He notices, smirks at me and then looks out of the window.

"Because if I had, you would have been too flustered to answer, given your mousse incident, and then you wouldn't have given me a chance to show you that I'm just a man who's really very interested in you," he says, bringing his eyes back to mine. "The gift was the quickest way to get you in front of me again." At least he's an honest arrogant shit.

"Well, I would prefer it if you would refrain from sending such things in the future. And besides, you never know, I might have said yes if you'd just asked. I'm not very keen on someone presuming what I will or will not do." I raise an eyebrow and take a sip of my very nice wine. I can't believe I'm even thinking about flirting with him. This is not going to end well.

"No, Elizabeth, you wouldn't and you know it. Please don't insult my intelligence. I'm far too good at reading people. I've made my career out of it," he replies with a slightly agitated tone. He's right again, but I still don't like the fact that he's played me so well.

"So you thought the best thing to do was spend thousands on a piece of jewellery and then potentially incite irritation in me by presuming my reaction? Really, Alex, I'm not sure that's the safest way to attract a potential date. Well, not a date, but you know what I mean." I will stay in control of this. God, those eyes are so enthralling.

"No, probably not, but you're here so I won the first move, and I never said I was looking for something safe, Elizabeth. I haven't played in a *safe* world for a very long time," he says, taking a step forward. Player, definitely. I should leave, immediately and at speed. I don't.

We once again stare at each other for quite a while until I can't hold it any longer and fold, looking to the floor nervously. He chuckles, and I wait for whatever's coming next still feeling him watching, assessing me. Then he breaks our little silent bonding session or whatever it is we're having. Confusion isn't the word for what I'm feeling at the moment.

"Did it feel good to stand up to me?" he asks.

I look up to find an amused expression staring back at me. It's too beautiful, confusing me even more, so hiding behind and looking across the top of my wine glass, I mumble a *yes* in response. His face lights up like a schoolboy who has been given a new challenge or toy of some sort. I'm not sure which. Probably both. Conceited bastard.

"Good, I'm glad you're enjoying yourself." Those lips twitch again into a smirk as he lifts his glass to drink. "I am."

Once again I have no clue how to move this conversation along so I just gaze at him with a confused face and fall hopelessly into his eyes. His sudden frown throws me. I quirk my lips up into a smile in the hope of ridding his beautiful face of it. It works, and I feel myself fall a bit more as he takes another step and reaches a hand towards my cheek. It's like a magnet drawing my face toward his fingers with no help from me at all. My feet move forward and his lips part to say something. I watch in anticipation as my body begins to hum with something like electricity, or maybe its random spasms. I don't know. It's a moment, though. A quite lovely moment.

His phone abruptly rings and makes me jump back a step in shock. He pulls his hand away from me just as quickly and looks down at his watch, his frown returning again.

"Louisa," he barks then listens for a short while, never removing his frown from me.

"Yes, apologise for me. I'd forgotten the time." Suddenly his amused expression is back. I can't keep up. He puts the phone back in his pocket and presses a button on the wall behind him.

"I'm sorry, Elizabeth but I have to go. I have an appointment that you have made me forget about. That is ... unusual for me." He chuckles to himself and leads us back over to the kitchen again.

"No, no, it's fine. I should get going anyway," I reply nervously.

"I've called Andrews. He'll take you wherever you need to go." Who's Andrews?

"That's fine really. I'll get the tube. It's no problem."

"No, you won't. Please take the car," he says, closing the distance between us.

"Alex, lovely as that offer is, I would rather take the tube. I have some things to do."

I go to the counter for my bag, placing my wine glass down, and as I turn to grab my coat our hands collide. I quickly try to remove mine but he clasps on and turns me to face him. I drift to his eyes and feel that pull again, that heat inside me building effortlessly. He moves his other hand to my face and runs a thumb down my cheek. God knows why, but I find myself nuzzling into his hand involuntarily and relishing in the feel of him on me, as he gently brushes his thumb over my lips. My mouth parts as I watch something warm flicker in his icy eyes, drawing me closer again and readying me lips on mine, but he removes his hands abruptly and backs away a step.

Shaking his head, he lifts my coat for me and helps me slip it on gently. It makes my confusion escalates so I grab my bag and turn for the hall, not knowing what I should be feeling as we head to the lift. It miraculously opens as I get closer so I step in and turn to wait for him, but he stands outside the doors and watches me.

"If you're still agreeable, I'll be in touch regarding Saturday. Andrews will meet you in the lobby."

I nod, affirming that I am and smile a little. I'm still not entirely sure that I actually am, and given the last ten minutes I'll probably be in deep shit if I do, so I'll make that decision later. The man is far too ravishing for me to actually be able to think at the moment.

"And by the way, you look incredible today. I've done nothing but smile since I saw you. You've been a breath of fresh air for me and I very much look forward to our *date*."

"Thank you," I reply quietly as I smirk at his *date* comment.

"Can I ask you a question?" he asks politely as he stands there looking absurdly attractive.

"Of course. Anything," I reply. I might not answer but he can ask, and frankly I'm still too busy with my wandering thoughts, which have once again lead me to his chest.

"Actually, two if you don't mind?" And now I'm mouth gazing. I lick my lips; I can't help it.

"Yes?" His lips curve into another wicked grin as he watches me watching him.

"Do you find me attractive?" he asks. My eyes whip to his, utterly flustered. I don't know where to look or what to say so I gaze firmly at the floor. It's safe there, and how does a girl answer that anyway? Of course I find him attractive. What bloody idiot wouldn't? "Do you, Elizabeth?" he repeats. Good God, where did that sexy growl come from? My legs buckle beneath me.

"Umm, yes," I squeak as I lift my eyes a little.

"Good," he replies, scanning my body for a moment, as if he hasn't done it enough in the last three quarters of an hour. Heat creeps up my cheeks at his blatant inspection of me. He quirks his head to the side, smiling devilishly. "And when I make you come, Elizabeth, will you tremble under my fingers? Will you beg for more?" I gasp audibly and take a step backwards, astounded at the comment.

Before I get the chance to express any emotion other than the ridiculous panting that has suddenly started, he steps in toward me aggressively and backs me up into the corner. I gasp again as he leans his weight into me, planting his hands either side of me on the wall. He's so close I can feel his skin against my cheek, his hips on mine, his breath against my ear. His spicy aftershave assaults me. Actually, his whole body assaults me as he pushes himself harder into me, now covering me completely and letting me feel exactly how solid his body is. He's going to kiss me, and quite randomly, I feel like pleading with him to kiss me as I tilt my head into him, but as his lips move against my cheek, I only hear whispered words leave his mouth.

"You don't need to answer that. I'm sure we'll find out soon enough, Miss Scott," he says, slowly releasing his weight from me inch by torturous inch. My body instantly screams from the loss as it watches him moving further away, buttoning his jacket and pulling at his cufflinks. I grab onto the handrail for support, still staring and trying to stand. "When the doors close, just say one."

I open my mouth to say something and then close it again, not sure what it is that I'm supposed to say to anything like that. I can't even breathe, let alone think. What the hell was that about? My traitorous body is firmly convinced of exactly what has just transpired as it continues with its apt trembling and reminds me that he is absolutely right about my orgasms. And given that I have now trembled by only his movements near or on me, I can't even begin to imagine what would happen if he actually tried to achieve something more than that. So of course my eyes move to his fingers without thinking as I try to keep my body from keeling over. He notices and raises a brow at me as I nervously flick my eyes away from him again, but the wicked smirk that forms over his delectable mouth pulls me back to his face again. I'm completely lost in him. Utterly immobile. Absolutely in lust and so wishing the bloody doors would close so I can escape the moment, or possibly revel in it on my own, but absolutely not with him watching.

The elevator doors swish to a close as he continues to retreat backwards, still grinning at me like a cocky bastard and chuckling to himself like the God of all things evil.

"One," falls from my lips, as I exhale a breath and he disappears from view.

I lean on the wall as the lift descends, trying to regain some composure and stop my legs from giving way beneath me. I've never felt so in shock in my life. I'm flustered. Probably bright red. And now I'm about to hit the lobby and meet whoever Andrews is. Clearly I don't want to frighten him with my ridiculously distressed state, although it appears half an hour or so with Alex White is enough to distress any girl. What on earth just happened in there? Well at least I've given the bracelet back, which was the purpose of the visit in the first place, and I've sort of held my own in some extravagant game that Mr. White is playing. Thank God.

The elevator stops and I reluctantly step out, instantly seeing Andrews. He's the MI5 agent, come chauffeur that bought the gift to the shop in the first place.

"Miss Scott, please follow me to the car," he says with no emotion at all, still looking very MI5. I sweep my hair from my ruffled face in an attempt to look calm.

"Mr. Andrews, I really don't need the car. I can get the tube. It's no trouble," I reply, smiling sweetly.

"Miss Scott, this is my job and Mr. White has requested that I do something for you. Please think nothing of it. Where can I take you?" he questions as he looks at me impassively.

"Yes, of course. I'm sorry. I wouldn't want to get you in any trouble. Back home would be great then, thank you, Mr. Andrews. The address is-"

"Just call me Andrews, Miss Scott, and I am familiar with the address," he cuts me off.

"Oh. Right, okay then," I reply, more puzzlement and confusion racking my nerves as I watch the back of his black suit and bald head walk off with military precision.

We approach the revolving door and I see the car immediately. The sleek, black thing sits imposingly at the kerb, twinkling at me as Andrews opens the door. I climb in the back and try to get comfortable. Regardless of the luxury interior, it feels weird to me somehow. Probably because I'm simply not used to sitting in the back of anything. In fact, if he wasn't quite so scary, I'd ask to sit up front with hm.

As the car pulls away, my thoughts still linger on the man upstairs and my groin. I have never been so confused before in my life. What on earth have I gotten myself into? The world of Alexander White it, appears. The man's a complete arsehole, a stupidly beautiful one, and actually quite a charming one in a roundabout way but still, he's obviously a player of the greatest proportions. I am absolutely not going for dinner at his house. I'll have no hope whatsoever of defending myself against him if alcohol is introduced, and my obvious idiotic behaviour around him is actually scary. My phone chirps at me, signalling a message, so I delve into my bag to find it and my lip-gloss. Staring at me is a very familiar blue box. How did that get in there? I put it on the counter, didn't I? Frowning, I lift the bracelet from the box and look at its sparkling diamonds for a time while I grab my phone and look for the message. It's from an unknown number so I swipe across it.

• Wear the bracelet for dinner. I want to see it wrapped around your wrist. AW

I narrow my eyes.

"Well, Mr. White, it appears you don't take no for an answer," I mumble to myself, wondering how he got my personal number. Funnily enough, it doesn't surprise me in the slightest. I have a feeling the man could probably get hold of anything he damn well pleased, and it seems that includes me at the moment. My body spasms at the thought, as more of those very inappropriate visions consume me, and I close my eyes to let them do their worst for a minute. They do, very suggestively, so I quickly open them back up again to stop the moment that he hovers above me while I try to level my breathing. Shit, no. Absolutely not.

I promptly roll my eyes at myself. It's a dismal attempt at no. Even I'll admit that.

What on earth am I thinking? I should have said no upstairs. A quick drop off was the plan. In fact, I should have simply given the bracelet to him before I even went upstairs, because I was so not prepared for him, or for any of these aftereffects that he's left me with. I quickly irritate myself with my own response to his delectable body and his ability to control everything around him, myself obviously included in that deduction. I then incite myself further by his amusement of the situation I found myself in while he dictated every move. I have an awful lot to learn, especially given the fact that I am now actually contemplating going to dinner with him simply because my groin is telling me to. And who would ask that sort of direct question of a girl? Mr. White would, it seems. The man is obviously very wicked and way out of my league. I have no business even thinking about flirting with him. He is definitely going to eat me alive. I burst out laughing at the thought and squeeze my legs together, enjoying both sensations. Although, how the hell does Andrews know where I bloody live?

I scowl at the man in the front as he winds his way expertly through London traffic in the direction of my apartment, his eyes coming back at me in the rear view mirror with a frown.

Blowing out a long breath, I gaze out of the window.

I really need to speak to the girls.

Chapter 7

Alexander

He watched as Tate rammed his fist into Conner's ribs repeatedly, causing him to cough. As he backed off, Conner rose to bring his head level again and was swiftly knocked to the floor by an uppercut to the chin. Alex smirked. The man might be smaller than the rest of them, but he was not to be underestimated. It was one of the main reasons he employed him, that and the fact that he was the best corporate lawyer he had ever witnessed in action.

"Fuck, man, watch the face," Conner sneered, rubbing at his jaw.

"Come on, Tate, you know there's no headshots," Alex shouted over at his friend - well, his version of one anyway.

"He'll be able to pull it off. He's normally brawling at some skanky dive anyway, fucking his way through yet another whore," Tate replied, springing around the floor. Alex actually felt himself cringe at what was about to happen.

"What the fuck? You little shit."

Conner ran at Tate and delivered a leg swing that landed him on his arse then threw a few brutal punches to the kidneys and lower back. Grunting in disgust, Conner pulled his huge frame upward and watched as Tate grabbed his side and rolled around the floor shouting in pain

"Okay, okay, I think you two are done for a while," Henry exclaimed as he slowly walked over and helped Tate from the floor. Alex clicked his neck as he gazed at the two of them.

"Shit, man, what did you make me do that for? You know how pissed I get when you say crap like that," Conner said, moving toward them.

"I don't know. Just a bit tense, I guess," Tate spat, still riled.

Alex watched as the pair sat down on the floor and patted each other on the back, both breathing hard. They'd been at it for a good twenty minutes.

They'd been doing this for about a year or so, meeting at Ripkins Fighting Ring after hours. Alex had known Tony Davies for a long time, since the days when he wasn't known just for being the owner of Ripkins. At that time, he'd been known for far more vicious pursuits than the legitimate boxing club owner he had now become. The man was a fucking monster in all reality, and although Alex found him amusing, he wasn't the sort of man he ever dared turn his back on. Even now, at the age of fifty-five, he continued to have that demeanour about him that made men cower in fear. Thankfully, he owed Alex his life and therefore there was a mutual respect of sorts. Not that he'd saved him out of decency. He'd done it to manipulate a situation at the time and keep the favours coming when needed. Tony Davies was still paying for his existence, and as far as Alex was concerned, he always would be.

The fact that he was also a mortal enemy of Aiden Phillips was also very fucking helpful.

There were only two rules when the four of them fought: taped hands and no headshots. None of them could afford bruising to the face or too much to the hands. Anything else could be hidden or explained away. Alex was known for kickboxing, Tate was a boxer for his fitness, Henry constantly rode horses, well- fell off them, and Conner was always fighting somewhere anyway. Tate was right, he was the only one who could actually get away with it and it was really only his vanity that was offended if someone hit him in the face.

Alex looked at Henry and nodded toward the floor, inviting some much needed fun.

Lord Henry Deville was one of his few good friends. They'd met while his company was heading up the wealth ranks, and as DeVille sat on the board of one of the largest investment banks in London, he held an lot of power in his hands. At first Alex had simply found him useful, but eventually they'd found they had a lot in common and quickly formed a strong alliance. It made each of them a great deal of money doing exactly what they both did very well. Alex manipulated, cajoled and bullied his way to profits; Henry backed him with wealth and provided room for manoeuvre with the banks. He'd been to university with Tate in the states and had also trained in law, but after his father died suddenly, he'd been titled and then called to do all the things a lord should do. Henry, it seemed, wasn't exactly comfortable with the status his father had left him though and often needed a place to expel his frustration as much as the others did. He was as brutal as the rest of them when it came to fighting and he seemed to relish the contact with abandoned pleasure. It was hilarious given his stature in polite society, but not surprising really, given his well renowned reputation in the boardroom, which Alex had witnessed on several occasions.

"You up?" Alex asked.

"Yes," Henry stated in his upper-class accent, strapping his hands.

Alex started to circle his opponent with a smile. This was the bit he loved - the weighing up of each other and waiting for the first move, the calm before the storm, so to speak. And storm it was. They fought almost for their lives, forgetting the friendship and just barely holding onto the fact that they shouldn't kill each other. The reason there were always four of them was so that two of them could pull the other two off if need be, and while they were all angry men with a past or a present that dictated their emotions, they also all knew that Alex was the only one truly capable of going too far. There had been several occasions where he'd been hauled off to the side by two of them and a bucket of water had been tossed over him to bring him back to their version of reality. He never thanked them for it. It was always the closest he'd been to his own reality in a long time.

Still circling, Henry's step started to speed up. Alex saw it coming a mile off. He always did, so he launched at him first, fists and legs spinning like a tornado, then rolling to the ground and away, he stood and started bouncing. He chuckled venomously, looking back at Henry as he watched him panting and holding his right thigh, exactly where two of his leg hits had attacked it. The dick had always been too slow. It was pitiful to watch really. He needed at least two of them most of the time. All three was a little more challenging but still doable.

"Painful, Henry?"

"Fuck off. I hate it when you're cocky. What's got you in such a good mood? You're bouncing around and smirking like a bloody idiot." Henry grimaced as he levelled himself and stretched his leg out.

Alex smirked in response. He couldn't help it. It hadn't stopped since he'd seen her again with that beautiful hair and those fucking lips that were made for… everything.

Henry stepped forward again and held up his fists as he resumed his lethargic bounce and stretched his head from side to side. Moving slowly, he stalked his way toward Alex and then let rip, old England style boxing. Alex feigned a duck and then let him attack, savouring in the contact, which helpfully increased every aggressive tendency he possessed inside. Henry held nothing back as he slammed his fists into his chest and ribs, hurling every bit of his large, six foot two inch Nordic frame. He wasn't as tall as Alex but he was much heavier and broader and Alex wheezed as the fifth strike hit his shoulder, feeling like he had just about dislocated it. He dragged up a breath and pushed back on Henry with all his might until he gained the bit of room needed between them to swipe his leg. Stretching it out wide, he brought it back down hard on Henry's already injured thigh and sneered as the idiot howled in pain. Pathetic. He'd never once in his life been known for mercy and it wouldn't be forthcoming anytime soon. If there was a weakness, he'd find it and then use it. They both backed off again for a time, giving them a chance to catch their breath.

"Is it dislocated? I heard it click," Henry chided, limping a little.

"One punch and you think you've knocked my shoulder out?"

"Well, you are getting old now."

"Dickhead." The cock was younger but that wasn't going to help him in the least.

"Language, Alex. There are ladies present." He laughed, pointing at Tate and Conner.

They barrelled toward each other again in a flurry of punches and kicks, rolling around on the floor and pouncing back to each other, sparring and jostling as they both found room to connect blow after blow on each other. Alex felt his muscles stretching as he continued to swing his frame around in a rhythm of unruffled and calculating malice, but suddenly he felt his jaw crack as Henry's head connected with it. It was unexpected and just what was needed to fuel the anger, so he used it. Grabbing for Henry's arm, he got him in a wristlock and pummelled fist after first into his stomach until Henry spat out some blood. He took a step backwards to assess the situation, but an unwelcome tremor of the familiar rose through his chest and shot to his spine. He narrowed his eyes. Something was wrong. Henry wiped his mouth with his sleeve and spat again.

"Fuck you, you bastard." Henry spat, scowling as he cracked his neck from side to side.

Alex stood confused for a second as the recognizable venom gripped his stomach and reared its ugly head, but before he could disengage the anger that was surfacing from beneath, his vision turned overly focused. It was too late. Conner and Tate disappeared from his mind and as expected, he was just facing off with a man he was struggling to see in reality - just doing his job. Clenching his hands and trying desperately to regain some composure and balance, he stood completely still and waited, not quite understanding where his emotions, or lack thereof, were coming from. Why the hell was this happening? This hadn't happened for a long time and it certainly shouldn't be happening with these guys. He clutched desperately at logic and reason, but as the well-used engine engaged and pushed itself to the surface, he felt what little sense of moral obligation he had disappear.

Henry leapt towards him with frightening speed and caught him by surprise around the head with a right hook, then made a grab for his neck and held him tight by the throat while he repeatedly kneed him to the chest. The last shred of control that Alex had tried to hold onto evaporated the moment he felt the hand tighten. He flipped Henry off, and forced the room needed to meet his enemy with an onslaught of hits and kicks. He didn't give the man a second to breathe, just kept the assault coming. He enjoyed this feeling too much - no thoughts, just being what he was or maybe what he was made to be. His movements became more of a fluid glide as he let his adrenalin finish the job for him, each swing flowing like the well-oiled threat mechanism it had originally been honed for. The enemy was retreating. He could see him losing his balance and becoming weaker, simply trying to defend himself from the pain.

Lining up for one last spin, Alex threw his leg around his hip to connect swiftly with the jaw in front of him. The body landed on the floor in a heap. He leant down over it, panting and heaving from the exertion, right fist still poised behind him for the next hit. Looking down into the faceless human, he noticed its pupils dilating and the fear shining in its eyes. He felt himself sneer at the weakness then smile at the potential underneath him. Just one more hit. Just one more fist.

"Alex," he heard in his mind, his cheek twitching at the sound. "Alex, you hearing me, man?" *Irritating fucking noise.* He frowned and shook his head. "Alex? Fuck, man, you in there?" He felt something touch his back and spun around, barely stopping his hand before it connected with the face below the blue hair. Conner rapidly held his hands up in submission and backed off. *Conner.*

"You back with us, man?" his friend asked.

He felt his surroundings come back into focus and locked onto Conner's face for a second as he tried to find an answer to his confusion. There still wasn't one, so exhaling a long breath, he lowered his fist and began shaking his hands out.

"Yeah," he replied, lowering his hands and his head.

"Fuck, man, where did you go? You just flipped the fuck out." Conner looked surprised, concerned even. Alex turned around to see Henry still sat on the floor with Tate helping him to stand.

"I need to go home," he said, unwrapping his hands slowly and moving to his bag. "Are you okay?" He directed his question at Henry through narrowed eyes.

"Yes, I think so, but Christ, could you get a rein on it next time?" Henry asked. Alex looked the man in the eye and searched for deceit. It's the only reason he would have lost it. The mist only came when something was off. There was nothing unusual there to speak of.

"Don't ever grab me around the throat if you want to continue breathing. Do you understand?" Henry nodded in response. He sneered at the man then immediately turned and walked to the door with Conner following. Something was not right at all.

"Hey, man, what's going on?" Conner asked, grabbing onto his shoulder to stop him. He bristled instantly and Conner let go. "Okay sorry, man. It's just... Fuck, I haven't seen that for years."

"Don't know. Something just doesn't feel right," he replied, sighing as he pulled open the doors.

"You will call me if you need anything, won't you?" Conner asked.

"Probably not. You know how I hate your sanctimonious bullshit." He chuckled.

"Oh good, we're back to big words again. At least I know you'll be able to ride now without killing yourself," Conner stated as he slapped him on the back and launched into a karate kid fighting stance, "Are you going to try and kill me now? Wax on, wax off..." Alex raised a brow and snorted in derision.

"You're not worth the effort. Besides, I'd hate to mess that pretty face up... again."

"Point taken, and why deprive the ladies of such perfection?" Conner said, fiddling with his chin. Alex shook his head at the absurdity of the man.

"I'm going."

"Cool, stay safe man. Call me," Conner replied as he blew him a kiss.

With that he nodded at Conner, inwardly smirking at the idiot, and strolled out the doors towards his Ducati. The moon was high in the sky and he felt the wind whip through his sweat-sodden hair. Pushing it off his face, he looked at his watch. Ten thirty. He thought for a minute. There was still time to call a convenient woman to release the rest of his tension on. He shrugged on his leathers and swung his leg over the bike, pulling his phone from his pocket, and then thumbed through the numbers looking for the right prospect. Allison Denver? No, not tonight. Sarah Pearson? No. And then he saw the name he wanted, so called it and waited for the answer.

"Alexander, darling, what can I do for you at this time of night?" the woman said. He breathed in the way her mouth surrounded his name with her Russian accent.

"I think that's quite obvious, Tara."

"Yes, sir." She chuckled throatily. "How long will you be?"

"About twenty minutes," he stated, pressing the end button.

Pulling down his helmet, he knocked down his visor and kicked off the stand, slowly pulling out onto the road. He needed to clear his head. What the fucking hell was wrong with him? That hadn't happened for years, losing it like that. Yes, Henry made a mistake grabbing his throat, but that was all it was, a mistake. Why had the cloud come over his brain so rapidly? That only ever happened when he was feeling threatened or felt he was being lied to. Henry was his friend. Why should he be feeling that way about him? Only last month Conner had done exactly the same thing and he had simply shrugged it off with a joke. He hadn't responded with the fury that had presented itself this evening.

He slowed for some lights and indicated for the right side of town. He just needed to get to Tara and let her give him what he needed to think more clearly. She was a long standing acquaintance and knew exactly what was necessary to make him let go of it all for a while, or at least try to define his parameters again.

Tonight he needed her experience. He needed to push harder than he had for a while and there was only a few he trusted enough to go that distance with. She would be bruised and raw for days and he needed to know that she would take it with a smile and enjoy every minute of it as much as he would, because that was what he intended to do - use the woman utterly and completely. He would feel much more solid afterwards and she would appreciate his anger and frustration for a while as he refocused himself. She always did. After all, that's what a masochist wanted and he was happy to give it. She wouldn't want anything more than he was offering and they would part as more balanced individuals, each for their own reasons. These submissive types were cute, but fundamentally he wanted a woman who liked her pain, who found a euphoric high in the combination of submission and sweet agony. Actually, he was reconsidering the submission part. Lately, submission in itself lacked bite, or maybe it was the substance he was after, the argument. Fucked if he knew. What he did know was that he needed to inflict that pain, to see it radiating across flesh and preferably to see a woman aroused by it, not that the latter mattered too much. He'd happily done it on occasion, regardless of their consent.

As he turned into the road where her apartment was situated, a girl with long red hair crossed the road in front of him. She turned her head towards him and smiled, thanking him for stopping and walked on. *Elizabeth*. The thought flashed across his mind and brought him back to the present.

What was he doing? He was supposed to be being better for her, trying to be a decent man. Fucking Tara to her limits was not part of the dating plan, he assumed. Well that couldn't be helped this evening. He'd be no use to Elizabeth in this state. He had to regain some semblance of order to this shit that was in his head. Besides, they hadn't even had dinner yet.

He parked the bike in the underground car park and kept his helmet on as he walked to the entrance. He did not want to be recognized here in the slightest. The door opened automatically, as he pressed the buzzer, letting him find his way to apartment seven quietly. Her front door was slightly ajar, soft music leaking out into the hall, so he walked in to find Tara knelt in the middle of the floor, naked with her eyes downcast.

"Good evening, sir. I am yours for as long as you need me." Of course she was, depraved psychopathic bitch.

He took off his helmet as he closed the door behind him with a chuckle. Walking towards her, he lightly brushed his fingers over her long black hair and strolled towards the bar where he poured himself a large scotch and took a deep breath. Turning, he looked at her for a moment. She was truly a marvel. Her ability to take whatever was given in enjoyment was indescribable and as he felt her tension increase, he sat down and slowly finished the rest of his drink just to push her further. Scanning the room, he noticed a candlestick on the sideboard. He fished in his pocket for his lighter and flicked it back and forth, then walked over to the candle and opened the cupboard beneath it. Pulling out his favourite type of rope, he walked to the centre of the room and began the hooking process above his head.

"Stand over here." She instantly stood and moved in front of him so he began wrapping her in the intricate knots he loved. Her first delicious squeal came as the rope bit into her thigh. "Up you go," he said, pulling on the pulley system he'd created and watching her lift from the ground.

Another thirty minutes passed as he manoeuvred her around until he was happy with his trap. She just lay there, suspended beside him as he ran his hands over her and watched her twitch under his fingers. Her calm smile remained firmly fixed in place and her eyes closed. She was a pretty thing really. He could see why she was so desired, but to him she was simply a tool, a very intelligent tool he had to admit, but a tool nonetheless.

"Tell me about your day in court, Tara. Did you jail anyone?"

"No, sir. He got away today," she replied quietly.

"Mmmm, shall we see how you feel about that then?" he replied, pulling hard on the rope in his fingers. She gasped as her body turned upright in front of him. He tied it off and lit the candle behind him. Her eyes widened in fear so he chuckled a little and took his shirt off. There was nothing the woman was really frightened of - well maybe a few things but even he wouldn't go that far.

"What was our last count, Tara?"

"Fifteen, sir," she said as her panting started and a sly grin crossed her mouth. He growled then quickly pulled the other rope to his left and her head whipped backwards. She shouted in pain.

"Tonight is not the night to piss me off," he snarled, continuing to pull and watching her squirm mouth-wateringly at the tension he was creating for her. She giggled. Well fuck it, maybe he would go that far. He pulled again and her moan of satisfaction was all he needed to confirm his thoughts. "I did warn you, Tara. Remember that tomorrow."

"Yes, sir. Thank you, sir," she said.

He chuckled at her response and held the candle out to her.

For a human rights lawyer the woman was really far too attached to torture.

Chapter 8

Molly Peters

Molly Peters sat at her desk going through the papers and documents she had been researching for the last three years. The only thing she had to go on was half a sheet of paper that had been found after the fire at Risebrook.

"Where are you, Nicholas?"

She'd been trying to piece together the limited information she had but she wasn't getting anywhere quickly. She hadn't even got a surname, only the letter W. When the paper had been burnt, the fragment that remained readable was his new first name and W, the case number 1283719 and the words *"abusive father, remains exceptionally aggressive and unreachable via normal mediums."*

The best course of action was to try and find the psychiatrist, Mr. Patrick Callen. That name had luckily been legible but she'd had no luck reaching him. He'd apparently moved out of the States for another job after Risebrook had gone up in flames.

She at least knew that Nicholas had gone by the time of the fire and so he was alive somewhere, hopefully. The lady that had helped her retrieve the fragment of paper from the archives had worked there for a while and was helpful enough to explain that from her memory, case numbers beginning with 128 would have been from the year 1996. Molly knew he'd been born on January 1st 1982, making him fourteen at the time. He would have been released from care at sixteen so he should have gone by 1998. Given that the Risebrook fire had been in 2000, he should have been long gone by then. But where to?

She understood, having spoken to a few people that had worked there, that the children from abusive or violent parents were renamed to provide anonymity from the abuser. There had been no other family known of and so no one had been contacted. Molly understood only too well why her dear brother-in-law hadn't told anyone else that there was more family available to help.

Richard Adlin was an extremely cruel and deceitful man. He was unbalanced and unpredictable. He was also highly intelligent and had been able to wrap anyone around his fingers including her sister, Julie. Oh, he was always seen as the perfect parent and husband, but she knew better.

He was undoubtedly responsible for the death of Julie but there was never any proof of that. He was far too clever to be caught. Her nephew had only been removed from his home because someone had informed social services that the boy had been left at home alone most evenings and he was starting to become troublesome in the neighbourhood. There had been talk of bruising and scars but Molly didn't know the facts. It was more than likely true though. By the time she had returned from Devon, there wasn't any sign of her nephew or his father - if that's what he could be called. Neighbours at the time seemed reluctant to talk about it and the little information she did find out was sketchy at best.

Now she just needed to find out who he was and where he was? He had family and he needed to know they were here for him.

She had never forgiven herself for not being stronger at the time, but she was simply too scared of Richard and had fled as far away as she could. Her sister had needed her and she'd run away. Her nephew had then also needed her and she didn't have the guts to return and help. Now in her fifties, she would find him and she would tell him everything. She would let him know he was loved and wanted. She would tell him everything he wanted to know about his mother and their family.

He would never remember his mother. He'd only been two when she died so there would be no memory of the love she had for him - no memory that Julie had begged Molly to take him with her to start a new life somewhere else where Richard would never find them.

When she'd finally agreed and they'd tried to make a plan, Richard had found out about it and showed Molly exactly what he was capable of. He'd grabbed her by the hair, tied Julie up and made her watch while he repeatedly raped Molly until she bled. They put on a show for weeks while he held them prisoner until Richard allowed

Molly to go to the shop one day. She ran as far as she could and she didn't look back.

She'd chastised herself repeatedly for being too scared to do anything, but when she finally built up the courage to go back a few weeks later, the news came that her sister was dead. It was too late. She was even too scared to go to the funeral because she knew he'd be there. He'd killed her. There was no doubt in her mind, but the coroner's report had said that the fall from the cliffs was accidental and once again, the man got away with it.

Molly had found out eight weeks later that she was pregnant. It was the one good thing that came from the whole sordid situation - a beautiful baby girl, Evie. They had moved to the Lake District shortly after the birth when she'd been offered a cleaning job on a caravan site for the summer, and there she had met Tony Peters, a man who changed her life and gave her and Evie a second chance.

She constantly regretted leaving her nephew, but what could she do?

Deep down she knew there was much more she could have done, but through sheer selfishness and fear, she'd just wanted to move on in a new life and forget. She'd get in touch when he was older.

Molly sighed as she looked at the mass of paperwork and files staring at her. How on earth was she going to find him now? She was so confused and held her head in her hands as she continued to gaze, hoping for inspiration of some sort.

"Mum, are you okay? You look tired," Evie asked as she swept into the room.

Molly looked at her daughter and smiled. She was twenty-eight now and stunning. She also definitely had her father's features. With long black hair and beautiful blue eyes, there was no denying she was Richard Adlin's child. Not to mention her intelligence. She'd always been extremely clever. That was also all her father, and although she knew nothing about him, Molly could see the questions in her eyes becoming more intense every year. They'd kept the whole thing private. Tony Peters was her father as far as she knew and a perfect father he was.

"Just a bit tired, love," she replied, standing from her desk and turning around.

"What are you working on?" Evie asked, looking at her quizzically.

Molly shut the file in front of her and closed the desk. Drawing the key from her pocket, she locked it tight and put her hand on the wood.

"Nothing, darling, just something that's unfinished. Let's go and have a cup of tea and you can tell me all about your new job in London."

They left the room to head to the kitchen. Molly turned and looked at the desk with tears threatening to spill. She was so sorry and just didn't know how to make it right, but she had to do more to find him.

"I will find you, Nicholas Adlin. I promise I will," she mumbled quietly, staring back at the desk.

"What did you say, Mum?" Evie asked as she looked over her shoulder.

"Just muttering to myself, darling. Nothing to worry yourself with."

She composed herself for a moment, sniffing back the tears that were forming before she left the room, closing the door softly behind her.

Chapter 9

Elizabeth

I sit at the kitchen table, looking at my reflection in the mirror. I've been trying for a good hour to bring my eyebrows under control and I'm failing miserably. I just can't concentrate on anything. The day at work was long and hard and I was distracted, messing up various orders and putting confectionery custard in the pastries instead of crème anglaise. I irritated myself so much that, eventually, I gave in and told the girls I was going home at four o'clock. Since then, I've been sitting here at the table, trying to work out how to deal with my current predicament.

The phone call from Alex completely threw me. Actually, the phone call wasn't from him at all. His very efficient PA called to tell me the car would be picking me up at my apartment on Saturday at 7pm. I went from confused but deliriously happy to feeling like I was heading to a business meeting in minutes. Now I'm really not sure what to make of any of it. If he wants a date, why isn't he picking me up himself? This isn't exactly roses and kisses, is it? Who sends a driver to pick up their date?

The whole idea is just bloody ridiculous.

Sighing, I leave the mirror and walk to the kettle to make myself some tea. In two days I will be seeing him again and I haven't got a thing to wear or the faintest idea what I should do to myself to feel confident enough to deal with him. Maybe I'll just keep it casual in jeans or maybe a skirt. That will make me comfortable at least. It's not very elegant though, and he is probably used to elegant. I have no idea how to achieve that in the slightest. God knows.

I throw my hands into the air, asking for some sort of divine inspiration. No one replies.

The door slams behind me as Belle enters, shouting into her phone.

"I don't care how many times you ask, Conner. This just isn't going to happen." Pausing, she listens. "No really, you're just being too pushy." Pausing again and giving me a frustrated glare, she rolls her eyes. "I tell you what, you come up with something that is stunning enough to knock me off my feet and maybe, just maybe, I'll consider saying yes." She pauses "Well you're persistent, I'll give you that." Another pause. "And that is just pornographic, quite revolting actually." And another. "Right, well, before you embarrass yourself further, I'm ending the call. Bye." With that, she presses the end button. "Good God, that man just will not accept that I'm not interested." I smile and look over at her with a giggle as I get to the teapot and grab two mugs.

"Just say yes, will you? We both know you fancy him rotten," I reply sarcastically.

She smirks. "I've told you before, I do not!"

"Right," I say, loading the cups with sugar and milk.

"Right," Belle confirms as she storms to her bedroom.

I can't stop the giggle that follows her.

We make ourselves some tea and retreat to the lounge to chat about the week's events and issues. Stretching her sore muscles, Belle talks about needing a massage and how she probably needs a holiday as well. She's right. In fact, we both do. I can't remember the last time we ventured outside the country or even took a bit of time off. We've both been so busy that somewhere along the business building timeline we've failed to relax.

"We should go on holiday then," I say.

"We should. Let's sort that shit out for the New Year. Get the laptop and we'll book now while I think about it," she replies without opening her eyes.

"Okay, first though I need to talk to you about something. I need your help," I reply, wandering over to get some Aspirin from the kitchen.

"Really, what?" Belle opens her eyes and looks at me with interest.

"I'm having dinner with Alexander White on Saturday and I-"

"You're what?" Belle splutters, throwing her tea over the carpet. I smirk and grab a towel as well as I walk back across to her and hand her the little tablets.

"He invited me to dinner and I don't know what to wear," I reply as I get on my knees to mop up the tea.

"Beth, what are you saying? When did he...? Why didn't you say anything? And will you stop mopping up the fucking tea," she says, leaning forward and snatching the towel from me, narrowing her eyes.

"Well I didn't know if it would come off and I didn't think it was real to be honest, but it's going to happen and now I'm just so nervous and I don't know what to do with myself. I've been messing up everything in the kitchen. I can't concentrate, and the way he looks at me, it's just so disorientating and I can't think straight around him and..." Definitely rambling again.

"Whoa, calm down and tell me all about it. In fact, hold on a minute. Teresa will be here in ten minutes and we need to get the wine out. I can't believe you didn't tell me. Is this why you've been murdering your eyebrows?"

"Yes," I reply as she heads to the fridge to get wine.

"Bloody rain! I hate it," Teresa exclaims, storming through the door. We both stare at her in near shock at her timing.

"What?" she says, immediately pouring her wine and then wandering into the lounge to sit.

"Well, honey, Beth is about to tell us something very interesting. You'll want to hear this and so do I. Off you go, little sister," she says, slumping back into the sofa and raising her brows.

"Really? What's going on?" Teresa questions as she tucks her feet under her.

I proceed to tell the girls the truth about the meeting I had with Alex and what really happened. I'd fibbed a bit and told the girls that I had simply dropped the bracelet off with Louisa Trembell. They've received emails since then confirming new catering orders so no one worried that returning the gift had offended him in any way. I tell them about the intimate moments and rather interesting questions and then tell them about the phone call from Louisa.

Teresa is now open-mouthed gaping at me. Belle is smiling and blowing me kisses. Neither of their responses is going to help me in any way at all but at least I've shared.

"Well done, darling. It appears you have bagged yourself a millionaire... or billionaire. I'm not sure which. Scrummy though. A bit

Charlotte E Hart
SEENING WHITE

unfair of you if I'm honest as I saw him first, but hey ho off you go and all that," Teresa chides.

"I doubt that, honey. He probably just wants a fling or something." I smile shyly and snuggle deeper into the chair.

"I think this deserves a shopping trip on Saturday then and don't worry, honey I'll sort out your eyebrows," Belle says. I glare at her, trying to tell her in no uncertain terms that I am at least capable of that. She laughs at me.

"Actually, I have a much better plan. The Thompsons have just cancelled their lunch tomorrow because of the rain. Don't worry; they're still paying us. They don't hold us responsible for the weather but they've moved it to next Wednesday. I said we could fit them in. Why don't we just close up shop for the day and go to the spa and then do some shopping?" Teresa says.

"What? We've never shut the shop before," I burst in, completely shocked by her proposal.

"Well, you've never had a date with Alexander White before, have you? I think that deserves some rather special treatment, don't you?" Belle says pointedly.

"Okay, well listen. How about I phone Tom and ask if he'll cover for the shop front. You haven't got any big orders, have you? And there are plenty of pastries available," Teresa questions.

"I don't know. I don't think it's worth shutting up the kitchen for. I mean really, ladies, a quick shopping trip on Saturday will do just fine."

"It most certainly is. I am the eldest and I say we do it. I can rearrange the appointments I have. You will feel like a princess for this date and I will get my massage."

"Right, I'll get on the phone, call my dearest brother who hasn't got anything better to do anyway, and book it. I wonder if we can get into that new place. Apparently it's wonderful. I heard on the grapevine that it started out in the North West somewhere. Still a bit quiet so we might have a chance if I get straight on it." Teresa jumps with joy and heads to her bag.

Apparently I have been railroaded. She, of course, does her thing and unbelievably, within twenty minutes, with a few freebies thrown in from Scott's, we're in. She's booked three haircuts, three sets of nails and three waxes all before lunchtime, giving us plenty of time for clothes finding in the afternoon. They're both overjoyed with the thought of it. I am not in heaven at all as I watch them discussing my date because they simply don't understand what he's like, and although they would probably handle it better than me, I can't help but feel that if they were in my shoes, they wouldn't be quite so enamoured by the reality either.

~

Hoffi Studio is by far the swankiest place I have ever been for a haircut. I normally go to the lady on the corner of our street. This place is gorgeous and so far removed from what I'm used to that it's just scary.

I now stand here feeling completely at odds with my surroundings. The words awkward and ungainly spring to mind. Belle and Teresa simply waltz into the sleek white interior and collapse on the sofa, talking about what type of nails they will be wearing by the end of the day. I'm not even sure I realised different types of nails existed, so I sit self-consciously on the end of the red leather sofa and look around the multitude of rooms. Beautiful women lounge around in their high-end clothes, perfectly made up, with a confidence and poise that seems to radiate from every pore on their flawlessly polished skin. I cringe inwardly at my dull hair and lack of make-up. I don't stand a chance. What the hell am I doing here? Trying to impress Mr. White, that's what.

Bloody ridiculous.

"I'm leaving," I state, getting up and grabbing at my bag.

"What?" Teresa exclaims far too loudly. Both of them look at me.

"I can't do this. I don't even know why I said yes to him. It's just stupid. As if he would ever be really interested in someone like me. Look around you. These are his women, not me." I start for the door.

"Elizabeth Scott, get your arse back on that sofa immediately," Teresa states with a fury not often heard in her voice. I slowly turn and start to protest but am yanked into a quiet corner.

"No! You will shut up and listen. I have been your friend for a long time now and I have listened to your sister try to give you some confidence. You blatantly disregard her good advice every time. You will not do this again. You are absolutely the most beautiful woman I know. You do not need any of this to stand out in a crowd. The grace and composure that flow from your demeanour when you stop over thinking everything is astounding and if I had one ounce of the traits and qualities that ooze out of your being every day, I would be a very happy girl. Stop beating yourself up about whatever it is you're beating yourself up about. You have every right to date Alexander White and he obviously thinks so too," she says in a low tone so no one can hear. I look at her agog, having never seen her like this before. "And furthermore, I will not let you screw this up because you feel you are not worthy for some stupid reason. You know nothing about him apart from what you've read and learned from spending an hour in his company. Did you enjoy it?" she continues with seething eyes and a tapping foot.

"Yes," I reply quietly, looking at the floor. I feel very nearly put in my place.

"And he you?"

"I think so."

Teresa picks up my chin with one finger so we look directly at each other, well me down to her anyway. She softens her tone a little and smiles.

"Then just be happy and go with the flow. We are here so you can relax and be pampered. If that gives you some much needed confidence then great, but the last time you saw him you were wearing jeans were you not? And he still wanted to see you again, didn't he?"

"I suppose so," I reply, looking around the room nervously as some women perk up their ears to hear what's happening.

"So stop overthinking and just enjoy it. Please," Teresa pleads, "And don't look at them. Fuck them. They're not going on a date with Alexander White, are they? You are. He chose you," she says with a smirk and an elbow nudge to my ribs.

"Okay," I say in a small voice as tears brim in my eyes. I sniff them away and look at my best friend with a smile. In normal Teresa style, she throws her arms around my neck and pulls me into an enormous hug. I feel myself hang on for dear life and try to compose myself. If I'm going to allow this to happen then I'm simply going to have to learn to let go of my fear and enjoy it, because that's what it is really - fear. Whether it's because of him or not I have no idea, but I decide in that moment to just be myself and see what happens. I mean, he can't be that bad, right?

"O.M.G! O.M.G! Look at these fabulous women. Girls, come surround me and stare at these visions of sexiness."

A very gay and very wonderful man is staring at the three of us intently, gesticulating at his staff and barking orders for hair colours and facial treatments.

"Ladies, I am Sebastian, and this is Hoffi, and you are about to be blasted with the most amazing service you've ever had. Not that any of you need it. However, we aim to tweak the last nuances of perfection for you," he screams with delight and enthusiasm.

Clapping his hands sharply, he directs each of us to a different girl and we go our separate ways.

The next few hours fly by in a calm and relaxed fashion and I find myself enjoying every minute of it. The damn waxing is very painful but the results are at least astonishing. Teresa's little chat has hit home and somewhere in the last hour I have finally decided that enough is enough with the self-deprecation shit. He wants me. He made it clear. All I have to do is follow his lead and see where we land. It will more than likely end with me being devastated but as long as I don't get attached to some stupid emotional response to him, I'll be fine.

"Stunning. You are utterly complete and I am finished," Sebastian comments in his overly camp tone. Opening my eyes, I look at myself in the mirror. I kept them closed the entire time and told him to do whatever he wanted but not to cut too much off the length.

"Wow," I say. I have nothing else. The man is a genius.

"Yes, indeed. Your hair is too fabulous to work with and I just had to tweak it and... ta da!"

The cut has taken my hair from all one length with some long layers to a stylish and sexy, wavy creation. The natural red is suddenly gleaming through the brown layers as if it's on fire and it feels like pure silk to touch. I haven't a clue how he's done it but it's impressive all the same so I swish it about and watch it bounce.

"I love it," I exclaim. "How did you do it?"

"It's an art, I know, but really with hair like this, I didn't do much at all. Take some of this." He tosses a bottle at me. "And some of this." He adds another one. "And you must use this once a week." Another bottle lands in my lap.

"Right. Thank you," I reply, looking at the bottles in confusion, not having a clue what to do with them. The girls will know.

"You, my darling, are done. I am utterly ecstatic. My work here has been exciting. Book in with Claire for a six week appointment. Love you." With that, he air kisses me on both cheeks and saunters off to his next client, throwing over his shoulder at me, "Just fabulous darling."

We leave the studio laughing and studying our various shades of nail polish or hairstyles and are all very ready for a bite of lunch and a glass of wine, so we head down the street to the bistro on the corner and find a table. Enjoying a leisurely lunch, I find myself smiling and giggling like a schoolgirl at our conversations. The morning has been surprisingly refreshing and rejuvenating. It has put us all in a gloriously good mood and we are savouring every minute of the time we have together on our day off. I make a mental note that the three of us really need to do this more often as I smile over at Teresa and Belle who look radiant and carefree. I have to admit that's how I'm feeling too.

"Okay, let's shop," Teresa says as she gulps back the last of her wine.

"Yes, definitely. What are you thinking of wearing, Beth?" Belle asks.

"I don't know. Do you think it's casual? He is cooking after all."

"I think that means a skirt - a flirty skirt. Or dress. What do you think, Belle?" Teresa questions.

"Don't know, but I've seen a top in that new boutique on the high street. Let's go there first."

We put our money on the table, leave a generous tip and make our way out the door and along the street to the shops.

"I cannot believe he's cooking. I didn't know men like that could cook or even wanted to for that matter," Teresa exclaims, walking along.

"I know. Maybe he's trying to impress," Belle responds with a wink as she links arms with me.

"More like he doesn't want to be seen in public with me," I laugh. Both Belle and Teresa stop in their tracks and stare at me in apparent disbelief.

"I can't believe you said that," Teresa snaps as she abruptly turns me to face a shop window.

"Look at your reflection, Beth. Really look at yourself."

"Okay," I say warily, looking at my reflection.

"You must see that you are gorgeous," Teresa says, slapping me around the back of my head.

I do look better than I did before; I have to admit. My face feels toned and the eyebrows have added a more refined sophistication to my heart shaped face. My hair is sleek and glossy and somehow I seem to have gained an elegance I've never noticed before, but it doesn't feel like me. I frown at the thought, feeling like I've been transformed into someone I'm not convinced I'm comfortable with yet. Maybe that will change in time because Teresa is right, I haven't ever looked this good before.

"Okay," I say again. I still have nothing else to actually verbalise on the subject.

"Enough, Beth. Do you hear me? Enough now," Teresa says sharply as she slaps me around the head again. Belle responds in kind by slapping me on the other side with a giggle.

"Okay, so now that shit is sorted, what about underwear?" my dearest sister says in a very dirty voice. I roll my eyes as they both grab my arms and drag me across the street towards a lingerie shop. I have no hope. This will be a very long afternoon.

Chapter 10

Elizabeth

Standing in front of the long mirrors in Belle's bedroom, I look at myself. This isn't a Beth I recognise. This is a divine creature that has been modelled and sculptured to within an inch of her life. Belle and Teresa have worked tirelessly on my make-up and hair, and the outfit I presently wear is wonderful. My hair is piled up in a very neat up-do and the make-up is incredibly sexy, dark eyes and sultry lips matching my hair to perfection. I love it. I also hate it.

The outfit that has eventually been chosen isn't my first choice but the girls have pushed me to go with something a little more flirtatious than I wanted. The dark teal dress wraps around my body like a second skin. It's asymmetrical in its cut and finishes just below my knees. The neckline is straight across from collarbone to collarbone accentuating my breasts, and its three quarter length sleeves make my arms look long and lean. Thankfully, the scant amount of black silk underwear that I have been forced to buy is well hidden and can't be seen through the material, thank God.

I have to admit, I look remarkable and very not me at all. I will definitely stand out in the crowd looking like this. The look is finished off with a pair of suede, teal, three-inch heels that I loved on sight but worried that I wouldn't be able to walk in. Teresa had promptly told me I'd be sitting most of the time so I absolutely must have them. I've opted for very little jewellery, simply going with my mother's small diamond studs in my ears and the very beautiful diamond bracelet Alex has given to me, which he will be given back the moment we've finished dinner, regardless of how lovely it is wrapped around me like a second bloody skin. Why do expensive things work like that?

"Something's not right," Belle says, standing behind me also looking in the mirror.

"Yes, I know what you mean," Teresa agrees, holding her chin.

"Pull the hair down. You don't look like you."

Belle starts to take the hairpins out and then simply scoops up the sides into a clip, letting the length of my hair fall down my back in wavy spirals. I'm immediately put at ease about my appearance. I instantly feel softer and calmer for some strange reason as if the up-do had made me into some sexy siren I just didn't possess inside.

"Perfect," they both chime.

"Do you really think so? It's not too much?"

"You look beautiful, understated but ready for anything. Besides, you never know where you'll end up. He might take you out after dinner," Belle says.

"Oh, I hadn't thought of that," I reply, watching Teresa swan out of the room.

"Right, you can borrow my winter coat and Teresa's got your bag sorted so unless you've got anything else to get ready in the next fifteen minutes, may I suggest you get a drink in you," Belle says as she heads out the door.

"Do you have any condoms? I've got some you can have if not," Teresa shouts from the other bedroom. I gasp in fear. The very thought disturbs me. The immediate vision of his eyes and his body weight against me makes me raise an eyebrow at the possibility. I shake my head and try to refocus.

"I will not be sleeping with him, Teresa. I don't even know him. Good God, what do you think I am? I need to know someone first," I exclaim, forgetting the company around me and my potential indecision regarding the subject. Shit. "I mean, I know you two can and that's obviously fine but it's just not for me. You know that."

"Right, Beth, I'm sure when the mood's right and you've had a few drinks and he leans into you with those eyes and fingers and probably very hard abs, you'll find it somewhere in you to say, *no, Alex I wouldn't dream of it*." She starts laughing as she wanders past the door into the kitchen. Bitch.

"I will. I do not have sex with people on a first date," I almost shout as I follow her.

"Well, just in case you do, could you give me a text if you're not coming home, sister dear?" Belle says laughing, pouring a shot of vodka and handing it to me.

"And have you powdered your bits? You know, down there?" Teresa asks as she puts condoms in my bag anyway. Oh for fuck's sake.

~

I caress the luxurious leather of the seat with my hand as I'm whisked towards Mr. Alexander White. The black, sporty looking thing is immaculate and smoothly glides along the dark London streets as I sit nervously and wait for whatever is about to greet me at the other end of this journey. Andrews was at the front of the foyer doors at exactly seven o'clock as expected, and nodded, opening the door for me without saying a word. It felt mysterious and slightly foreboding, and now I feel as if I'm in some sort of James Bond novel, being taken to certain death like a spy.

I start giggling to myself as my vivid imagination runs wild at me again, and try to contain the fit of hysterics that is threatening to erupt. It could be madness or simply nerves, but really the whole scenario is comical. I take a deep cleansing breath and try to calm my nerves. It is, after all, just dinner with someone I actually seem to quite like as a human being so far. He's charming, witty and intelligent. I try to push aside the thoughts of his very naughty words and the flirtatious behaviour that put me on edge last time I saw him, but the inappropriate thoughts are still lingering around just waiting to be reawakened.

The smell of his spicy aftershave lingering in the interior of the car finds its way to my nose and I inhale again, breathing in the aroma that is Alex. So mesmerizing, I would know it a mile away. When it meets with the images of him in my mind, I close my eyes and feel like I can almost taste him. Those beautifully sculptured lips and those hands grasping the back of my neck as he pulls me tighter and... Christ, I can feel my heart rate thump rapidly at simply imagining the moment he holds me and kisses me.

Oh yes, I am in complete control. Not.

The car seems to swim through the very lively traffic as if it has a divine right to access anything and anywhere it wants to go, which is straight through central London and on toward Mayfair it seems. It never slows or speeds up. It just keeps gliding toward my unknown destination, intent on getting there with some kind of forceful dignity, not unlike the man himself, I suspect. I haven't got any idea where he lives and remind myself to text an address to Belle when I arrive, just

116

as the large imposing houses of the very rich seem to begin looming over me. I stare out at them, gulping back the fear that is now creeping its way back up my throat, then realise that the car is slowing as we enter the Kensington district. I immediately do that faffing thing with my hair and bite my thumbnail in the hope of calming the panic, and then I see where we're heading.

Oh. My. God.

Andrews pulls into a driveway, and the wrought iron gates seem to swing open of their own accord. The car continues along a short gravel drive and slowly comes to a stop outside the pair of dark red front doors of a very large Georgian house. I sit and observe the worrying yet beautiful building through the tinted window. What the hell am I doing? I am suddenly flustered beyond even my belief and can feel myself recoiling in terror at the intimidating structure that stands before me. That's how it feels - sheer terror. I am not ready for this at all. I consider telling Andrews to take me home when I hear his door open and close and then recognise the clunk of my door being opened. Well it's too late to back out now.

"Miss Scott, welcome to Catton Manor."

He holds a hand out to help me get out of the car and I'm suddenly stood under a portico outside a very ominous house - *his house* and I'm going in. *Shit. Shit. Breathe, Beth. Just keep breathing.*

Andrews opens the door and I'm met by the most stunning and warming interior I have ever seen. It isn't at all what I expected. I expected a sleek and glossy space with very modern furniture and white walls. The sort of place you see in the high-end magazines. The sort of place that is just like his apartment. This is, while enormous, very homely. The tiled floor of the hallway is old and elegant and the walls are a deep burgundy colour complementing the floor. The high skirting boards and picture rails are painted white, contrasting beautifully with the masculine colour. There are various gilt framed artworks hanging and huge modern vases of flowers on the two hall tables, which stand either side of the wide sweeping staircase in front of me. It curls its way up to the second floor and a burgundy carpet finishes the look off to perfection while the heavy ticking of a large clock sounds through the quiet space, giving a timeless appeal to the whole area. Andrews continues to walk in front of me as I hear my own footsteps clicking on the floor behind him and then I hear music

117

coming from somewhere ahead of me – a soothing sound that calls to me. I smile quietly. I've heard it before. My father played it over and over again when we were young and for the first time in the last hour or so, something feels comforting. Ottis Redding's Sittin' On The Dock Of The Bay is soothing its way around the house smoothly from wherever it is that we are heading. I couldn't have asked for anything more calming.

"May I take your coat, Miss Scott?" Andrews suggests, holding out his hand.

"Yes, please." He takes it and hangs it in a nearby cupboard.

Fidgeting a little, I smooth down my dress.

"Andrews is that you? I'm in the lounge." *His* voice comes at me over the music. It's rich like velvet, causing my knees buckle a little.

"Sir, Miss Scott has arrived," Andrews replies.

"Wonderful," he says, and then he walks around the corner.

Shit. I'm speechless once again. His presence hits me like a battering ram. It's absolutely not fair at all. All thoughts of *in control* have been handed over to him in an instant because I'm panting again. Stupidly. I yank my ridiculous combusting effect back into myself and blow out a small breath in the hope that he hasn't noticed.

"Elizabeth," he says quietly as he gazes at me with his hands in his pockets.

He takes his time lazily caressing my body with his very blue eyes and eventually rewards me with his breath-taking smile so that I can start that panting thing up again. Shit, I'm flustered and my heart is hammering, and I have no hope knowing what to say. *Remember your manners, Beth.*

"Alex, nice to see you too," I reply, a touch of sarcasm at his blatant perusal of me. "Your home is beautiful." There. In control. Situation handled. I can do this.

"Mmm," he responds, still looking, although thankfully this time at my face.

"Sir, if you need me at all, please call," Andrews says as he moves away from us.

And then we're alone, and he just continues to look at me, smirking with those eyes of his. I'm falling into them with every next breath, still panting.

"You came?" he says softly and rather oddly. My face screws up, stopping my ridiculous panting.

"You invited me. Why would I not come?" I reply, slightly confused.

"I thought you might change your mind."

"Really? Why?" I ask. Where is this going? And who would ever change their mind about seeing him anyway?

"No matter, you're here now. Please, come in."

He smiles, finally moving aside and ushering me into the lounge.

I glance around as I enter the room. The same burgundy is on the walls, but this room does have a more modern feel. The entirety of the vast back wall is made of glass doors, which obviously open onto the garden. The numerous couches and chairs are either dark brown leather or have a William Morris pattern, and a certain style radiates throughout the room that has a sense of charm and manliness, reminding me of an Old English Gentleman's Club. At the centre of the room sits a coffee table with an intricately carved chessboard ingrained in it. The game is apparently still being played because the cut glass and very modern pieces are in match positions. I stare down at it with a smile and wonder who it is that he's playing with. The room somehow manages to twist and turn through the ages with modern art hung in strict rows and several modern glass sculptures, but the traditional feel is still embedded. It's truly gorgeous and feels like someone's home unlike his apartment.

"Do you like it?" he asks.

"Very much," I reply, wandering around the room touching things. "I love the mix of old and new. You love your art, don't you?" I say as I nod toward the row of modern paintings.

"I buy primarily for investment but some of it is interesting."

"Oh, that seems a shame. Art should be cherished, loved even," I reply, wondering why he would bother having it at all, then thinking about that small boy in the rain in his apartment. I wonder who it's by and remind myself to Google it at some point. "Who are you playing with?" I ask, inclining my head toward the chessboard while still looking at the paintings.

"A worthy adversary," he replies from behind me. I turn to see him about two feet in front of me. Shit. He puts his large hands on my waist and pulls me closer to him.

"Elizabeth, how would you like to play this evening?" Too close. Very close. Can't breathe again, and what does that mean anyway?

"What do you mean?" I reply, taking a step backwards and trying to create a little room between us. His brow instantly furrows as he tightens his grip, apparently refusing to let me go.

"Well, we could pretend this is all very formal and then we could get to know each other slowly over a few glasses of wine while sitting at the dining table, or you could kick off those exquisite heels and relax on the sofa while we loosen up and enjoy each other's company. I will do this properly if you want to, but I'd much rather just unwind with you and see where things go."

I pull back again and try to untangle myself from his very rigid body. He frowns a little at me but does at least let me go this time, so I look him over for a few seconds. He's dressed in a very smart brown jacket, a blue shirt and smart jeans with brown brogues. He looks just like the model I had first imagined, stylish and tasteful, formal and yet relaxed somehow, but that very sexy devil is very definitely still dancing in his eyes as he watches me looking him over with a smirk on his stupidly erotic mouth.

"Oh, right, well I guess whatever you prefer. It is your house and I'd quite like to see the real Alex White."

"Good," he says as he shrugs off his jacket. "If there's one thing I can't abide, its pretentiousness." Smiling and moving toward me again, he pushes me backwards towards a sofa playfully. My face must be a picture of expectancy as those visions develop again.

"Sit," he says. Actually, it seems more of a demand from his tone, so I do. Well, as gracefully as I can manage, given my heels and the very low sofa.

He crouches down in front of me and lowers his hands to my knees. I stare at him uncertainly as he slowly runs his warm hands down my legs until they reach my shoes. I feel myself shuddering with anxiety as my heart begins its hammering again. What is he doing?

"Nervous?" he says softly. *God yes.* But as I gaze into those eyes, something seems to hook onto me, something that tells me to just trust him and let him guide the way. I have no idea if it's his air of superiority or simply the fact that I can't take my eyes off the wide shoulders hovering so closely in front of me. Or maybe it's his hands that seem to make my legs look oddly protected somehow.

I blink across at him, feeling like I've been drugged and trying to process how the contact is actually making me feel.

"Yes," I reply, with a slightly edgy giggle. It's ridiculous, I know, but the man is completely overwhelming and I seriously can't think.

Slowly, he removes my shoes and gently traces his fingers over my ankles. I'm so captivated by the way he moves his hands over me that I stop thinking completely for a minute and just feel every stroke of his faintly calloused hands as I watch him watching his fingers journey across my skin. Then I abruptly realise that it really feels far too good having his hands on me for the first time, so of course I absolutely can't stop my mind from wandering to thoughts of what other things those hands are capable of. I stiffen beneath his touch a little at the various images I'm confronted with. He chuckles at me and withdraws with an amused expression. He can obviously read minds as well.

"You shouldn't be. You look breath-taking and I'm humbled to have you in my home," he replies, slowly unfurling his frame to stand and walks across the room. My shoes go with him, his fingers carrying them until he places them on the side table next to a very expensive looking glass horse sculpture. "While these are beautiful, I want you to feel perfectly at home and I don't know about you, but I do that better barefoot." He reaches down and removes his shoes and socks. "Feel free to remove your dress as well if you want, or I could do it for you." He winks and throws me a true panty dropping, Alex White smile. It's beautiful and I immediately laugh. It turns almost hysterical. This whole thing is beyond strange - the car, the bracelet, him, me, this house. I'm losing it, and tears are welling up in my eyes because I'm laughing so hard.

He looks at me quizzically with a very cute crease in his forehead.

"Okay, I know it was a good line but I don't think it was that good," he states, frowning at my inane laughter, which I have now thankfully dimmed to a slightly smaller giggle.

"Oh, Alex, it most definitely was a good line, and you have managed to make me feel completely at ease in your home. Thank you." I laugh again. He shakes his head but his grin returns with show stopping effect.

"Fantastic. Now, what would you like to drink? And would you prefer to eat in here or in the kitchen?"

"Anything white?" I ask, a sense of irony offered, as my inner confidence somehow emerges and reminds me to just be myself and see where it goes.

"Absolutely," he says, rolling up his sleeves and smirking at me.

"And definitely the kitchen. Mind you, I haven't seen it yet. Is it as awful as the rest of the house?" I giggle and wave my hand around the lounge.

He barks out a laugh. "Oh, a sense of humour I see. Superb. I love a woman with a good sense of humour. Lovely to finally meet you, Elizabeth," he says, the loveliest of smiles creeping over his face. It's almost shy somehow and my knees buckle at the gorgeousness of it.

"Why thank you, Alex. It is a pleasure to finally make your acquaintance." I smile in reply as I watch his blue eyes warm and dance humorously back at me.

"Come on." He motions, stretching a hand toward me. "I hope you like fish?" I take it gingerly as we walk towards what I assume is the kitchen.

~

By the time we have finished eating, we've probably discussed hundreds of topics and I'm completely myself. Unbelievably, he has continued to act like a charming, excited schoolboy and has continuously complimented me and seems to be doing everything in his power to make me feel comfortable. It's working. The food was delicious and the wine, which has flowed extremely freely, has been wonderful. Who knew a man like this could cook? And fantastically, at that. He's told me of his love of cooking and that although he rarely gets the chance, he always gives Mrs Jenkins, his housekeeper, the time off if he's home so he can have the kitchen to himself. We've talked about books and art and business. He's told me of his love of the outdoors, sailing and snowboarding seem to rank quite highly on his list of the best things to do. He's asked varying questions about my past but never pushed me far enough to make me uncomfortable. He's the perfect gentleman, funny, informative and genuine. I feel very happy and very relaxed and also really quite drunk. It's slightly worrying but not so much that I'm not picking up my next glass of wine.

"The bracelet does look wonderful on you, by the way. I'm glad you kept it," he says as he reaches out and runs his finger over the bracelet, briefly touching my skin again and sending more shivers racing along my spine.

"I didn't keep it. I gave it back but it magically appeared in my bag. You must have fairies in your apartment," I reply with a sardonic smile.

"Yes, they are pesky little critters, aren't they?" He winks. "Come on, let's go through to the lounge," he says as he lifts his very appealing frame from the table, takes my hand and leads me from the table through the door and into the hall again. While walking, I notice a room on the left with a soft blue glow coming from the half opened door, and a huge wall of books dominating the side of it.

"Wow, that's quite a collection you've got in there," I exclaim as I stare in awe at the masses of leather bound books. He stops and turns around.

"Oh, that's the study. Go on in and have a look if you like," he says, gesturing toward the door and placing his hand on my back gently. More shivers race across my skin as I glance back at him and then walk in.

My jaw drops at the sight of it. The room is huge and filled with books. It looks like an old fashioned library. Perfectly crafted bookshelves line the walls with library steps leaning up against them. The room smells of paper and leather, and the large desk at the end screams of businessman, several stacks of papers arranged on it. Rather quaintly, a pair of glasses also seems to have been abandoned there.

"Wasted really," he says from behind me.

"Really? Why?" I ask.

"There's never enough time for reading or relaxing. Feel free to spend time in here whenever you're about. It would be nice to see someone use it to its full potential."

"You imply that I'll return, Mr. White," I reply, giggling and looking back towards him across my shoulder.

"Well, you will, Miss Scott, because I will tell you that I want you here and you will do as you're told," he says rather severely as he moves around in front of me. He brushes his fingers into a lock of my hair and drags it around to the front of my chest, eyes narrowing a little as he lets go of it and drops his hand.

And there it is. In a split second, the atmosphere is fully charged and demanding. He's made it so, and electricity has ignited around the room. His fixed gaze is guarded, emotionless and searing. He appears to have snapped into killer mode and there isn't a thing I want to do about it, even if I could. The Alex from the lift has returned and suddenly, and rather confusingly, I'm happy to have him back. My breathing starts its unbelievable panting and my fingers begin to tingle with something unknown. He takes a step toward me so I slowly back away, bumping into the stacked shelves. I have no idea why I'm retreating, but I'm hoping it's self-preservation or something. He stops and seems eerily still as if he's frozen time around him somehow, or around us.

"You will not run from me, Elizabeth. Stand still," he demands - *yes, demands*. My eyes widen at him but I do, shaking in fear or excitement. I'm really not sure what I feel but I definitely feel hot and flustered again. "Do you want me, Elizabeth?" he asks quietly but directly, looking me over. My face falls to the floor, probably in embarrassment. "Look at me when I ask you a question. Don't ever drop your gaze unless I tell you to," he orders. It's a snapped tone I haven't heard before, disconcerting in its growl, but gut-wrenchingly erotic as well.

"Alex I... Umm, I..." I'm stuttering like a fool as I look up to meet his eyes, because shit, where the hell has this come from? And do I want him now?

"No, Elizabeth. Just a one word answer - yes or no. This is the last chance you'll have to leave," he states calmly as he continues his perusal of me.

"Yes." I could have lied but frankly, what's the point? The man is gorgeous, and regardless of my self-disgust, my inner slut is still panting for him.

"Yes, you want me or yes, you want to leave? Say it, Elizabeth, and louder this time."

He fixes his now predatory eyes on mine again, the corner of his mouth turning upwards just slightly. Oh god, such ridiculously sexy eyes. I suck in a breath and pause for a moment, looking straight into them as they draw me into him. They're so cool and calculating, merciless in their stare, and my skin is suddenly on fire, my breathing ragged with nerves. He knows he has me on edge and he's enjoying it as he looks back at me, completely in control of this moment. Unfortunately, I have no doubt what my answer is.

"Yes, I want you," I answer breathlessly.

He stares for a few seconds as if breathing me in, his face softening just slightly, that crease appearing again and then there's a sudden shift in his demeanour. His stance becomes harder and taller, his angular jaw clenching and a frown forming. Something flashes in his eyes and then he's in front of me, pushing me back against the shelves forcefully. He slowly brings his hand to the front of my neck and pulls my face to meet his. Every part of his heavy body is pressing against me, strong, lean and powerful. It's the most erotic moment of my life. I stop breathing and wait, pinned under him for whatever it is that's coming next.

"Are you ready for me, Elizabeth? Can you do this with someone like me?" he growls in my ear. Can I? Christ, I don't know. I'm not backing away from this though.

"Yes," I whisper, hoping to hell that I actually am.

He surges his mouth against mine and grasps my neck so tightly I can hardly breathe, but I melt into him and return the kiss passionately, revelling in his lips and his touch. My dress hitches up roughly, his knee forced between my legs and pushing against my groin to lift me onto his thigh. Our mouths and tongues explore with a vicious desperation I've never experienced before, and as I remove my mouth to take a breath, he immediately drops his head to my neck, sucking and licking his way across my collarbone. Moving his hand from my waist to my wrist, he pulls it sharply above my head and holds it tight against the books.

"Oh, God," I sigh in complete disarray. The force on my wrist is almost bruising in its grip but feels beyond good for some strange reason.

"Fuck, you are the most delicious woman." He groans as his hand drifts to my thigh and backside, squeezing tightly and pushing himself against me harder, grinding into me, still biting. "Christ, I knew you'd be good. I won't do this now, not yet. You're incredible and I want to, but..."

"Alex please." I'm begging, remarkably, for what I don't know, but I'm definitely feeling the build of an orgasm as he continues to grind into me. Overwhelming heat rises up through my body as he moves his mouth down to my breasts and lightly bites against my nipples through the material of my dress. It's irresistible, making me squirm and begin tingling at the sensation. "Oh, God." I breathe out again as I feel the clenching effect between my legs. They're the only words I have as he continues to rub his thigh against me, my crotch blatantly rubbing back against him.

"Are you going to come for me, Elizabeth?" he whispers in my ear. "I can feel that tremble I was after."

"Alex, please," I beg again. I've never been more ready. I can't even begin to fathom my begging so I give in to my body and let go.

"Would you prefer my hand down there?" He growls, increasing the force of his thigh against me. "Do you want to feel me inside you?" I fall onto it, more pressure driving me onwards as I continue my rhythm and climb towards my bliss.

"God, yes... Please... I'm so close," I beg again, feeling his hard length pushing against my hipbone as I tip my head backwards and he increases his hold on my neck. It's so tight, and then tighter, squeezing his fingers around my throat and making me feel slightly delirious somehow. *Yes.*

"Make yourself come on me. Use me. I want to hear you moaning for me." He moves his mouth back to my breasts and bites my nipples hard with his teeth and mouth, pulling and then releasing in the same rhythm as my rubbing against him. It's too much. I close my eyes and let my orgasm take hold of me. "Christ I want to fuck you," he says into my neck, biting my jaw and forcing more of his body weight into me.

"Yes. Oh, God yes. More. Yes." Complete abandon begins. Stars and white lights shining brightly behind my eyelids like I've never seen before, as I tumble into the most incredible feeling of my life. He growls at me and holds my weight aloft, still rubbing his thigh against me to keep the sensation prolonged.

I cling onto him as he quietly nibbles at my neck, enjoying the vibrations running across me, then realise that I'm still digging my nails into his back. Slowly releasing my hand and nails, I start to ease back and let go. He grabs me back and holds on fiercely.

"Just stay still a while longer," he says, rubbing his groin lazily and kissing my shoulders, thumb rubbing back and forth across the skin on my wrist. "I just want to feel you some more."

I wind my fingers into his messy hair and gently stroke the back of his neck while I let my own breathing calm. That was the most amazing orgasm of my life and I'm very happy to stay still longer. Maybe I can try regaining my own balance and composure while enjoying my dull throbbing core. I can also try to not think about the fact that I've done what I've done and why the hell I've enjoyed the physical assault of it quite as much as I have. I've never been one for rough before, and that was definitely rough. Very rough.

"That was by far the most provocative thing I have ever been a part of. You are captivating to say the least, Miss Scott," he exclaims into my neck, still kissing me and letting his tongue roll around my collarbone.

"Mmm," I reply languidly. I can't speak. What could I say? Who cares.

I reach down to stroke his leg with my hand and move it towards his groin, wanting to reciprocate this whatever it is. He instantly releases my wrist and grabs at my hand to stop me, gently bringing it to his mouth. He kisses and sucks each finger while bringing his eyes to meet mine. They're soft again and relaxed, but still oh so piercing. The other firmer man has gone but I can't help wondering when he'll return.

"No, Elizabeth, this has been yours and yours alone. While I've enjoyed your arousal and pleasure, another time will be mine," he says, a soothing voice coming from his lips as if calming a wild horse. "You're not ready for me." What the hell does that mean? Not ready? I am very ready I'll have you know. In fact, did I not just make that plainly obvious to him?

Feeling a little confused and irritated by his belittling dismissal, and more than a little embarrassed, I make a move to extricate myself from his arms. He takes a step back and gives me some room, looking at me with a raised brow as I shove my dress down. I make to quickly

127

leave the room - to where, I don't know, but I'm suddenly feeling ridiculous and uncomfortable again.

"Elizabeth, where are you going?" he asks calmly as I turn to the door.

I don't hesitate. "Home. I think it's probably best," I clip as I continue walking.

"Why would you want to leave? Haven't you enjoyed yourself?" he asks, obviously confused.

Good. So am I.

I feel myself swing round to face him before I even think about it. I'm angry, or maybe it's frustrated at his patronising tone. Either way I can't seem to avoid the words that are forming.

"You... You do that to me, and then you dismiss the moment and tell me I'm not ready? I... I can't believe I did that. I'm just so... So ..." *Furious, embarrassed, overwhelmed.*

He's smirking at me again, standing there in all his beautiful glory, arms crossed on his chest as he casually leans against the shelves, the same shelves he just had me against. I turn and start to leave again, furious for unknown reasons given the best orgasm of my life.

"Elizabeth, turn around and look at me," he says in that demanding voice of his. I take one more step. "Now, Elizabeth. I won't say it again and you don't want me to lose my temper," he scolds with a slightly more serious tone. "Or do you?" I slowly turn to face him again.

"Good girl. Now, walk towards me and when you reach me, get down on your knees," he says. What? This is not expected. Is he fucking serious?

He quirks an eyebrow at me as if giving me an ultimatum. It's apparently not an invitation, more of a direct order. I have no idea how to deal with that statement, but as I slowly walk towards him, not knowing what drives me, I try not to over think my behaviour. It seems I can't keep myself from him. His presence is overpowering me somehow. Perhaps it's magic or something, or maybe those pesky little fairies, or maybe just those damn eyes pulling me forward. I could just be after another one of those orgasms if I'm honest.

"On your knees." My knees buckle, oddly interested in the thought as I sink to the floor, still looking at him. An absurdly wicked gleam flashes across his mouth, his body kicking off the shelves as he keeps his eyes fixed on mine. "Well done," he says, lowering himself to crouch at my level as I watch him move. "Now, I think you'll find, Elizabeth, that *you* did that to *yourself,* using my thigh as an anchor, and the reason I said you weren't ready for me is because of these," he says, looking to his right. I follow his stare and there, dangling from his elegant fingers, are a pair of steel handcuffs.

Umm, what the hell?

"Oh," I reply, staring at them with an open mouth. He chuckles.

It's really not funny.

Chapter 11

Elizabeth/ Alexander

❝Oh," I say again, rather stupidly, as I swing my eyes back to meet his briefly and then back at the handcuffs. His jaw-dropping smile is still in place. I have absolutely no words for this moment at all. I can feel him assessing my reaction, and unable to look at him, I continue to stare at the shiny steel things swinging in front of my face instead. They're quite erotic really, hanging from his finger like that, looking all interesting and odd. Strangely enticing but abnormal in this room for some reason. Maybe they're not - well clearly not for him anyway.

I don't know how much time has passed with me on my knees, just looking at them and trying to process all the things they might mean to me or to him. Handcuffs, really? Do people really do that? Something tells me this probably isn't a mild interest for him.

"Well, at least we know you can kneel comfortably for a while," he states casually with that damned quirky smile of his, rising from his crouched position and gracefully walking towards his desk. He slides open a drawer and places the handcuffs inside, shoving it closed with a slam. I instantly feel oddly bereft at the loss of them, my eyes staring at the drawer. Where did he get them from, anyway? Have they been in his pocket the entire evening? And why are they now living in his desk of all places? I think my mouth is still open so I close it and try to formulate words. Not a sodding thing springs to mind.

"Actually, I prefer rope but it all means the same thing. Do you know what it means to be submissive, Elizabeth?" he asks indifferently, as if talking to a colleague. No, absolutely not, and I don't want to thank you very much, regardless of the rope or handcuffs that his clearly devious hands have been holding.

"To be a servant," I reply, starting to get up from the floor.

It's all I've got to give with my non-existent knowledge of the subject. And given my aching knees and the fact that I'm not going to continue with this kneeling thing any longer, I can't find a better response anyway. I'm also still seriously wracking my brains as to why the hell I've been on my knees in the first place.

He moves toward me quickly and offers me his hand, never removing his cool eyes from mine. Those beautiful hands suddenly look very ominous to me so I get up without his help, which earns me a very serious frown.

"No, that's not what it means." He sighs. "Please, let's go through to the lounge. I need to- No, I want to talk with you about something," he says as he seductively brushes my arm with his finger and takes my hand in his quite possessively. Mr. Relaxed and Charming has returned, it seems. I'm not sure who he thinks he's bloody fooling.

"Okay," I reply, feeling a bit unnerved but actually quite intrigued nonetheless.

"Go on in and sit. I'll get the wine. It's only ten thirty and I think I need to explain myself before we go any further. If you want to, that is." He moves off toward the kitchen, kissing my hand as he lets go of it.

"Yes, you do," I whisper to myself, heading towards the sofa, because seriously, what the hell is this conversation going to be like? I've just had the most explosive moment of my life and now he's going to hit me with, *"By the way I'm kind of perverse and I'm really not interested in anything remotely straight laced."* Fabulous. Just what I've always wanted in a man.

I hear him coming along the hall. The bottle clinking against the cut crystal glasses and the soft padding of his feet are an temptation to what's coming around the corner. In he walks, every woman's dream. Every time I see the man, my heart almost triples in speed. He's spectacular, masculinity personified, that strong, toned body and those long lean legs, his face worthy of every magazine. Frankly, his mouth alone probably sends most women mad with desire. I currently know that feeling well, regardless of how much I'm trying for relaxed. Jesus, I feel like fanning myself again and it's in this moment that I realise that whatever he's about to say won't stop me from wanting him, or wanting to please him. He has me, completely. He might not know that for sure himself yet, but he does. It's ridiculous. I'm ridiculous, though I expect most women are around him.

Pouring the wine, he passes one to me and takes up position on the other end of the sofa facing me. He gestures for me to put my feet up onto his hands so I do.

"Do you like your feet being rubbed?" he questions randomly.

"Doesn't everybody?" I reply.

"I don't. There are only two places I don't like to be touched and that's one of them," he says with a wink.

"Oh. Am I supposed to ask about the other one? Are you ticklish, Mr. White?" I reply inquisitively with a giggle.

"You can if you like, and no I'm not." He smirks and presses into the ball of my feet with precision. *God, that's good.*

"Where's the other one?"

"None of your business." He beams at me and it's glorious. I'm useless around him.

We both laugh and it seems to ease the tension a little, albeit I still feel myself short of breath and a little anxious. It's still ridiculous. The man's a sodding Adonis. Who like handcuffs.

"You're quite the master at it, aren't you?" I say, leaning my head onto my hand.

"Master at what?" He looks slightly puzzled at my sudden change of subject.

"Resolving a situation, easing a mood, changing direction to get where you want to be successfully. I watched you in the boardroom and now here. You're a genius with your persuasive techniques." *See, Mr. White, I can be intelligent too.*

He chuckles and returns his attention to my feet.

"It's what I do, Elizabeth. It's what has got me where I am now. Without it I wouldn't have achieved all this." He waves his hand around the room impassively. "Well, that and a good friend anyway. I've learnt that it is far easier to manipulate than to force. Albeit sometimes it can't be helped, and I do enjoy doing something forcefully," he states bluntly, a twinkle in his eyes as he takes a sip of wine.

"Obviously," I say, raising my eyebrow at him.

"And there's that humour again that I adore so much," he replies.

"Who's the good friend?" I ask with a spit of jealousy twanging in me. *Where did that come from?*

"Just someone who's known me a long time, who understands the way I am."

I sigh. What should I say now? I take a sip of my wine and wait because whatever's coming next, I'm sure that he'll find a way to say it more successfully than me.

"My world is very different to yours, Elizabeth. I'm inviting you into it, but I'm sure it is nothing like you've ever known," he says, eyeing me through his lashes as he lets go of my feet and travels his hands towards my calves. "I want you to be a part of it, but I'm not sure what you're expecting of this, of us?"

"I'm not sure what I'm expecting. I haven't really thought about it too much," I blatantly lie. "What have your other girlfriends expected of it? Of you?"

He sighs and grips my calves tighter. "There have been no other *girlfriends,* as you so quaintly put it, Elizabeth," he states.

"What, none?" I reply, clearly rather bemused at a lack of girlfriends.

"Well, I suppose there have been a few that have lasted longer, but nothing of any significance to me in that sense," he says, as he drinks some more wine, quite unapologetically.

"You're telling me that you haven't had any serious relationships in your life, at your age?" I ask, disbelief evident in my tone.
"No, and I'm not that old, thank you," he scolds.

"How old are you?" I ask, suddenly aware that I don't even know.

"Past thirty. That's all you're getting out of me," he responds with a smirk. *Okay.*

"Oh, right. You mean you haven't been in love? At all?"

"No, Elizabeth, and I'm in no rush to be. I am... difficult." He stares, bold as brass. I'd say so.

"Sounds it," I reply, sipping my wine. "I'm not sure what it is that you want me to say. It's not a very tempting invitation, is it?" I'm quickly starting to feel a little despondent again. "What do you want of me, Alex? A quick session as and when you feel like it without any hope of something more lasting?"

He immediately starts rubbing my feet again soothingly, clearly recognising my irritation and tension, and as he pushes the pads of his thumbs into the balls of my feet I can't help sighing out my pleasure. My eyes close and I lean my head back against the sofa.

"Better?" he asks, a half laugh in his voice. Clever sodding bastard.

"You can't remove from my mind what you've just said, Alex. You still mean the same thing," I return, my eyes still closed. Those hands are amazing. I start to imagine them all over me. Good god, he's only rubbing my feet and I'm hot and bothered again.

"I haven't ever before met a woman who has been so mesmerizing to me, so enthralling that I've invited them into my home, let alone cooked for them." My head shoots forward, eyes opening. "I've surprised myself and now I'm not sure how to proceed." I look at the uncertainty in his eyes. He frowns over it, looking at me watching him. "I'm very exacting in my standards and lifestyle, Elizabeth. I don't bend to the will of others or suffer fools gladly, and I have no idea what a relationship involves. I haven't ever wanted to know." What on earth do I say to that? It's plainly a lie. The man's stunning. How could he not have had a woman here before? Although he has no reason to lie to me. I'm lost. "And I won't take back anything I've said. I never do."

"You've never had a woman in your home before?" I ask, still utterly astounded by that fact.

"Please, don't speak yet. I'm trying to be very candid with you and tell you as much as I can so you can make an informed decision on what you want to do. I have particular preferences that you are obviously now reasonably aware of, and I have issues that make me unyielding in my behaviour. I am absolutely unworthy of any truly decent woman's attention," he says quietly, slightly discomfited as he watches my reaction. "I don't want you entering into a situation where you aren't fully aware of what you're getting into."

He's honest; I'll give him that. I gaze back, having no idea what to say.

"Right, so you're saying-"

He cuts me off as he drops my feet abruptly, stands up and paces about a bit. Remarkably, he looks a little unsure of himself and as I realise how unusual this is for him, I begin to relax back into the sofa again, smiling to myself and simply waiting for his confessions.

"I don't know what I'm saying. I do know that ever since I first saw you, I have wanted you, desperately. You fascinate me and I don't want to let you go. You're the most beautiful creature I have ever seen and you revolve in my thoughts constantly. The small amount of time we had in the study only furthers my appreciation, but I am not usually so..." he pauses and looks into space as if searching for the right word, "...preoccupied with a woman. I should ask you to enter into the kind of arrangement that I would normally have, but that would only serve my side and you would probably run a mile." My brows raise at him. He scowls and paces the other way again. "So I guess I'm saying that I would like to try something different, less limiting maybe," he says, finally stilling himself and putting his hands in his pockets.

Wow, that was definitely the most flattering thing I have ever heard about myself.

"Less limiting." I mouth the words softly. I have no idea what the hell they mean. "Well that's a lot for a girl to take on board. I think *you* will be a lot for a girl to take on board, Mr. White," I reply with a soft sigh as I smile at him. Clearly I couldn't have met an easy man, could I? Of course not, and I also have no idea what *different* means. Different to what?

"Yes, I have no doubt I will be, Miss Scott," he returns without any regret in his eyes, waiting for me to find something else to say. I haven't got much. Or maybe I have.

"Your particular preferences, as you put them... I've never... I mean, I haven't ever... Do you do it often?"

"Yes." No expression at all. It's not helpful.

"Why?" Because seriously I haven't got a clue what's so appealing.

He walks across to the coffee table and sits down in front of me with a lick of his very gorgeous lips, obviously sensing my interest in his proposal or version of a relationship.

"Look, I'm not one of the nice ones, Elizabeth. I'm not a man who'll caress my way inside you with featherlight touches and unfair promises of more. I am what I am." His eyes scorch at me with want and unapologetic desire. "So I want you to be very aware of what I'm suggesting, because I will be aggressive with you. Those preferences of mine can be particularly forceful, quite corrupt even, and more importantly, I'll expect you to take them from me."

Right, well that told me. Excellent. Confusing, though, given that he's been an utter charmer this evening so far. Surely he means on an every now and then basis. Clearly I can appreciate the *aggressive* bit - well, a little, if the study's anything to go by anyway, but what on earth does *corrupt* mean? This could be a very bad decision, one that my groin is currently making for me regardless of my brain's confusion.

"Do you expect subservience at all times? Because I don't think..." I have no idea how to finish that, so I tuck my legs up beneath me and gaze at him. His beautiful smile comes racing back to him.

"That wouldn't be any *different* for me, Elizabeth, and although I do know plenty of couples who live very happily that way, I don't think that's what I'm trying to achieve here," he replies cheerily, as if we're talking about ice cream or something. Jesus, who the hell is he? "I only want you to give yourself to me when the circumstances suggest it's acceptable and if it's what I want from you at the time. The rest of the time we'll attempt normal."

"Who will define when the circumstances are acceptable? And do you even know what normal is?" He chuckles, possibly at my interrogation, more than likely at my thumbnail chewing.

"I will, and I'll also expect you to comply. Fully. As for *normal,* no you're right; I have no idea whatsoever. That will definitely be your department." Right, so he is a complete control freak. Gorgeous, but weird nonetheless.

"Do you mind if I think about it?" I ask with a small smile as I consider the implications of what he's just said to me.

"How long do you want?" he says, narrowing his eyes and smirking a little.

"What? Do I have a time limit?" I reply, a little startled by his question.

He looks at me with a heart stopping frown that disables any defences I had in a second, and slowly inches his way forward like a lion stalking prey. My breathing hitches and my legs turn to jelly instantly. If I wasn't sitting, I would fall over. Not only is he jaw-droppingly gorgeous, but something about that predator mode has me thinking all sorts of disturbing thoughts, and for some reason, handcuffs suddenly don't seem so unappealing anymore.

"Miss Scott, you may take all the time you need, but I want to feel myself inside you very badly and I will get my way. If you decide against something more continuing then that will be your choice, but be under no illusion that I will have you. In several different ways, for varying amounts of time, and you will enjoy every second of it," he says, clutching me around the neck and pulling me towards his mouth. "You have no idea what I can do to you, for you, or what distances I'm prepared to go to to get what I want. Don't be so nervous of me that you deny yourself experiences that you've never dreamed of." I'm trembling. I know it's ridiculous but I can't stop it. His words, his face. God even his teeth look inviting, which is bizarre.

"Do you want me inside you Elizabeth? Do you want to try the goods before you decide? Let me show you some of what I can give you."

He brushes his lips over mine and I moan in appreciation. His growled response is followed by his tongue slipping into my mouth, pulling my body to his with delicious swirls and those teeth nipping lustfully. His arms increase their pressure and I melt into his kiss. Passion and need explode from the depths of me, and once again I know I'm his for the taking. He slows the kiss and pulls back to look at me. I'm completely breathless as I watch his eyes flicking between mine and my mouth. He slowly stands as if not to spook me and extends his hand.

"Come here," he says simply, and I rise immediately as if drawn to the flame in front of me. Not knowing what's coming next, I look into his eyes to try and answer my own question. He reaches a single finger to my chin and strokes it along my jaw, watching it move, unhurried and cool in his demeanour. "So beautiful. You're enthralling, Elizabeth. You are quite... indescribable."

He certainly knows how to charm a girl. I'm wet with craving, longing for his touch, and as I let my face melt into his firm hand, I stare up at him like a nervy schoolgirl. There are no words for this moment. It's all him. My mouth is uncooperative to say the least. To be honest, even my brain isn't functioning and yet my groin is clearly happy dictating my response. I might as well be panting in his face. In fact, I think I might be. "What do you want, Elizabeth? Shall I call Andrews to take you home or will you stay?" he whispers against my ear, moving his lips to my neck and pressing one of his large hands onto the small of my back. The other moves up my stomach, weaving it's way to between my breasts. "Say you'll stay with me."

He groans, pressing his groin into me. I should leave; that's what I should do. Run a mile as he said, not put myself in harm's way and somehow keep control of my craving, because it's stupid to think of anything more with him. He's Alexander White, for God's sake. All of that flies out the window as he lowers his hand and sharply yanks me towards him, his dextrous fingers gripping my backside almost to the point of pain. It's intoxicating and my thighs clench in anticipation. I have no choice at all in my decision.

"Yes," I breathe into his hair, grabbing at it like a woman possessed. All logical resistance has abandoned me.

"Good answer," he clips, and with that, I'm scooped up into his arms as he starts striding toward the stairs, leaving me feeling weightless and completely overwhelmed. What the hell am I doing?

He continues to kiss me as I glide up the stairs, presumably towards his bedroom, and I unconsciously realise that I've never been carried before. It's yet another erotic image that I'm completely overwhelmed by as we enter his room and he gently sits me on the bed. The moment I lift my eyes to his, he starts to remove his shirt, and oh wholly mother of God, the rippling muscles that greet my eyes are extraordinary. The strong hips and natural V make me shudder with excitement and appreciation. For a man past thirty, he's disturbingly fit. My fingers dig into the comforter on the bed as I try to regain some sort of control of my trembling.

This is it, isn't it? I am going to be taken by the sexiest man I have ever met and I can feel how embarrassingly slick with need for him I am as I watch him moving back towards me. His fingers are reaching for me. *Oh God.* My thighs clench again as I realise I haven't got a hope at control. I'm completely lost. He leans over me and pulls me back to my feet. I'm glad he did because I can't feel them at the moment. They appear to have abandoned me as well.

"I doubt we'll be needing this for a while," he says, smiling wickedly as he moves his hand to the zip on my dress. Thank God Belle forced me to buy that underwear.

Slowly pulling it all the way down, he pushes his hands inside and caresses the skin on my back. I shudder immediately at the sensation. His hands feel so beautiful against my skin, warm, firm and promising untold wishes. Nuzzling his face back into my neck, he drags his teeth along my collarbone and whispers, "You're perfect - simply

138

fucking perfect. Christ, what shall I give you first, Elizabeth?" I doubt he's actually asking me that question, more musing his own depraved ideas. Well I might as well know what I'm in for.

"Alex, don't hold back. Let me see all of you. I need to know what you want from me," I say aloud, surprising myself. Have I just given him permission to do whatever he wants to do? God, what have I let myself in for?

He drags the dress from my shoulders slowly and peels it from me then takes a step back.

"Turn around," he says firmly. Suddenly I feel very aware of my body and start to look to the floor in embarrassment. "I told you, Elizabeth, don't ever look down unless I tell you to. I want to see your eyes all the time. I want to see how much you crave me. Keep yourself focused on me. You have nothing to be self-conscious or embarrassed about. You are stunning and I am in awe of you. You have the control here. Take what you want from me tonight," he states with a tension I've not heard before. Was that nervousness in his voice? From him? Surely not.

I lift my head to meet his eyes and instantly see the craving he's talking of. His need for me sears straight to my soul, every straining muscle on show as I feel my insides grow stronger and he moves forward. One more pace and he's within touching distance so I raise my hands to tentatively feel the skin on his perfectly carved chest. I swear electricity jolts my fingers and I gasp as I look into his eyes again. He licks his lips and raises a brow, grasping my wrists firmly and pushing me back towards the bed.

"You have no idea how long I've waited for that," he growls, pushing me harder and forcing me onto the soft sheets behind. His body weight is everywhere before I know it, consuming me as each nerve ending shivers and shudders, igniting every erotic or indecent thought I've ever had. "Give me more of it, Elizabeth. Show me more."

~

Alexander

SEENING WHITE

He sat in the chair in the dimly lit room with a large glass of cognac and frowned. It was five in the morning and he hadn't slept. In fact he'd been sitting here for nearly an hour, just watching her sleep. She was here in his bed, sleeping. He'd never allowed a woman in his home, let alone in his bed before. This whole scenario was confusing the hell out of him. His eyes roamed over her body again for the hundredth time as he tried to find a fault. It seemed it just wasn't there to find, so he gazed over her long legs and tight arse again, licking his lips. His cock twitched. It was frustrating to say the least. He should just wake her up and take her again, but for some reason, watching her sleep was soothing to him.

She moved quietly and rolled over, which made him notice the dip of her waist curving into her long, elegant back. It was a simple movement but so mouth wateringly enticing that he very nearly went to her but gripped the edge of his chair and refrained instead. He couldn't even begin to process the way her face captivated his eyes, regardless of the torment he was currently feeling. It was as if she held the secret to happiness or something equally as disconcerting. Maybe she did. Was that even possible? And in any case, that happiness wasn't destined for him. He simply didn't warrant any form of love. He knew it and she probably would realise it too.

She was perfect, lying there like a fucking goddess with that tumbling red hair splayed across her creamy skin. He shook his head at the stupidity of his thoughts. No woman was perfect. There had to be a problem with her somewhere. He just needed time to find it, and in all honesty, he didn't know if he had it. She had been hesitant to enter his idea of a relationship. Of course she would be. It wasn't enough for her and he knew it. For the first time in his life, and regardless of how much they had done tonight, he was unsure of whether she'd still be agreeable when she woke.

She'd taken everything he had given her with complete abandon, and he'd been astonished by how well they'd fitted together. She'd moulded to him like a flower in the rain. Never had he had such a close connection with a woman. Fuck, he really was getting hard again just thinking about her screams in the throes of ecstasy. Her beautiful white skin and those tits that bounced with enthusiasm - a perfect handful each that were real, soft and warm. Nipples that were so reactive to his touch that he just couldn't stop biting them harder each time she moaned out his name. Christ.

The pleasure that had radiated through him when he heard her call his name was unheard of. Sure, plenty of women had screamed his name, but she had somehow meant it and he had felt it. Deep down, the sound of her voice had resonated in some way that he couldn't explain or express to himself. And when he'd finally pushed inside her, after an hour of making himself wait, and felt her warmth around him, he'd struggled for breath in surprise. He'd simply stayed still for some time to just feel her tightness encompassing him. The way she'd penetrated him with her eyes in that moment was indescribable and he'd damn near looked away rather than deal with the assault of her gaze. He could have sworn in those seconds that she knew everything, understood every emotion that he'd ever denied, daring him to keep trying as she grabbed his backside and pushed him further into her. Fuck, he couldn't get deep enough.

She was incredible and she'd fucked with a passion he'd never felt before. Her need for him had him yearning to please her in ways he couldn't honestly remember previously. His goal had never been to give another woman as much satisfaction as he might derive himself. Yes, he wanted them to be happy. Most of the time. Actually, sometimes he didn't give a shit but it was normally all about what he wanted and that hadn't been the case tonight. Tonight had not been about what he wanted at all. He hadn't even used restraints.

She'd shown she was pliable in more ways than one by allowing him to hold her down or push her to a different position. She didn't seem frightened when his touch had become stronger or more dominant. She'd actually seemed compliant, looking back on it now, and she definitely liked her throat being handled aggressively, thank fuck. Perhaps she was a little more experienced than he'd previously assumed. She certainly knew what she was doing with regards to his body. She'd held him at the brink too many times to remember, but then he'd given her permission and told her to take what she wanted. That's exactly what she'd done.

He had been entirely happy to just be with her and learn about her body. He'd relished every second of searching for what she enjoyed and where she needed him to be. Her nuances and differences were a fucking challenge to be revelled in. Worshiped even. He'd spent long periods of time simply exploring and licking his way around her, and Christ, she had tasted fucking good. So sweet, like nectar sent from the gods as his prize. She'd melted when he swirled his tongue over her and had made her come for the third time - so responsive and hungry for more as each moan of desire had pushed him further towards his own explosion. When she'd pushed him onto his back and indicated that she wanted to ride him, he'd let her. He hadn't wanted that for a long time. He normally didn't want anybody above him, yet with her, he'd allowed it, wanting her to stay on top so he could watch.

He'd been mesmerised as she'd taken his cock inside her and lowered down onto him, moaning with unadulterated pleasure and gasping as his size stretched her wide. He'd just laid back and enjoyed the ride, revelling in every dramatic glide of her skin on his. He couldn't keep his hands still for long, though, and had grabbed her hips and angled her perfectly to increase the pressure, sending her over the edge again. He'd been so enthralled in just watching her writhing about on him, that he'd exploded viciously inside her while those soft, soul tearing brown eyes pleaded with him for more, something more.

Eventually she'd snuggled into his chest, exhausted, and before long had drifted into a sleep that seemed restful and undisturbed. Snuggled? When the fuck had that word appeared in his vocabulary? Never before had he snuggled with anyone. In fact, it had only been a handful of times he could ever remember sleeping with anyone, and yet with her, he did and enjoyed doing so. Feeling her warm body moulding to his and her curves relaxing into his muscles, he'd felt something, some sort of relief or comfort.

He didn't have a fucking clue what it was but he liked it. He liked it so much he'd remained entwined with her to absorb it into his mind, but then quietly eased himself from the bed frustrated with the thought. He'd pulled on his jeans and walked to the kitchen to get a drink with every intention of doing some work, but he had felt a drawn back to the bedroom.

And so here he sat, waiting for her to wake and make her decision, whichever one it was. He wasn't entirely sure it would be the right one for either of them. Fuck this. Alexander White didn't wait for anybody. What was it that she had that had him so transfixed on her? He felt himself become irritated with his need for her and sighed to himself. He was no good for her and he knew it. Why he was even letting her believe there was a chance of something she deserved was a quandary because Conner was right. He treated women with a derisive tone. They were there simply to fulfil his needs. But she had completely disarmed him tonight. Her willing and compliant body. Her mind exuding a grace he needed desperately for some inexplicable reason. How could he possibly want more with a woman like her? He didn't merit any attention from someone so open and fragile. He would undoubtedly corrupt and damage her and she would be forever lost because of him.

Standing, he walked to the bed and pulled the sheets along her body up to her shoulder, watching her breathe peacefully for a few more moments. She was so beautiful, almost angelic, and his resolve shattered instantly as he realised he wasn't ready to let her go. He needed more time with her. Maybe she could find him somehow - find a way in and calm the storm.

He stroked a finger over her collarbone and she sighed, mumbling his name in her sleep. He felt his smile spread and then the wind left his lungs as he watched her mouth part and her eyelids flutter. He frowned to himself at the feeling, considering whether he might just be losing grip on his control, and turned to headed for the door. Checking the clock on his way, he noted the time and date. His thoughts lingered on the date - another significant day? A good one to remember? He wouldn't know until later in the morning when she woke, but he made a mental note to call Lisa tomorrow anyway and headed down the stairs with a strange smile on his face. It felt odd to him somehow, as if he'd never done it before, so he chuckled to himself and made his way along the corridor with a new sense of hope, or at least something similar.

On entering the kitchen, he noticed her phone flashing on the counter top. Who was so intent on reaching her tonight, or this morning at this hour? He swiped the phone to see a barrage of missed calls and texts from her sister. He frowned. Perhaps she was concerned, or something terrible had happened. He grabbed his phone and dialled Belle's number.

"Hello," she answered groggily, as if she was still sleeping. She probably was. Normal people did at this hour.

"Belle, this is Alexander White," he said quietly.

"Tell me she's with you?" Her voice was suddenly at full strength - fucking brutal actually. It amused him as he wandered over to the coffee machine.

"Yes, she's asleep upstairs," he replied, switching it on and grabbing a glass.

"Well, could you kick her fucking arse when she wakes up and remind her that some of us might worry about her," she said harshly. "uh... please?" He got the feeling please wasn't a word she used very often. She probably wasn't a morning girl either. That was going to piss Conner off no end.

His mind drifted to Elizabeth as visions of early morning showers floated through his mind.

"Cute. I'm really feeling the sisterly love," he said, chuckling. "No wonder Conner likes you."

"How do you know about-"

He cut her off. He was far too preoccupied with the woman in his bed to carry on with pleasantries at this time of day. "Have a good day Belle. I'll let her know you care."

Putting the phone down, he smirked and thought of his friend. He was asking for trouble with that one. He moved to grab the coffee glass and realised that another one had appeared beside it. He frowned and wondered how it had got there. He was either going mad or had subconsciously got another glass ready for her. Was that possible? Could he actually be thinking along the lines of this being normal somehow? It really wasn't. Nothing like this was normal for him.

It was fucking odd.

He frowned at the thought and put the glass back in the cupboard. His glass suddenly seemed lonely so he opened the cupboard again and put her glass back beside his. All sorts of images flashed through his mind as he gazed at the two glasses side by side, one of which disturbed him to the point of exasperation. He sighed then abruptly looked to the kitchen door as if sensing her. She wasn't there but regardless, the odd pull still was. Growling at himself, he moved his glass to the machine and hit the button as he stared at hers. He needed coffee. He'd get over this shit soon enough. Whatever it was, it was fucking with his head, or she was.

Chapter 12

Elizabeth

Feeling very well rested, I open my eyelids hesitantly and let the first rays of the day seep in as I begin to remember where I am. Alex White's bed no less. I push my legs towards the bottom of the bed and feel the footboard - the very same footboard I was bent over last night, in various different ways.

Smiling to myself, I let the sheets wrap around my body and turn to find the man I slept with. Or not. Where is he? I take a minute to get my bearings and lazily look around the room. I didn't have any thoughts about the interior design of Mr White's bedroom last night, as I was far too busy being seduced within it. I giggle at the thought. As if I could have concentrated on anything else when he was near me anyway.

The room is very large, more like a suite actually, and I gaze around it with my mouth agape. I don't know why I expected anything less really, but it's positively stunning, not unlike the man himself. It doesn't take me long to notice my dress draped across the stylish chair in the corner, almost perfectly matching the colour of the wall, and my brow rises at the coincidence of it. It's almost like fate - ridiculous, but not completely unheard of. I shake my head at myself and look around the room again.

There are two doors at the end of the room, past the sofa and coffee table that sit under the bay window, with another set of double doors to the side of the room. The whole scene oozes indulgence with its manly dark furnishings and gilt picture frames. Long, heavy curtains hang to the floor and pool elegantly, accentuating the skirting boards and picture rails, which contrast against the deep teal paintwork. The two chandeliers that hang low in the room twinkle with heavy crystal drops and seem to give that air of sophistication that only a chandelier can create. It's probably been done by some high-end designer to create that old feel. The result is very effective indeed, and very Alex.

It's definitely more warming in feel than the apartment, although the apartment did seem to suit his business aura - cold and calculated. It makes me wonder how many versions of him exist, because the man I spent most of the evening with wasn't like the man in the boardroom the other day at all. The word changeable comes to mind instantly.

Hoping one of the rooms is a bathroom, I hop out of the bed and move toward it, wondering what on earth I should wear. I snatch his shirt off the chair and shrug into it. His spicy scent lingers under my nose and wraps around me like a vice grip, enveloping me somehow. I go to the first door and find it locked so move onto the second. The door swings open and I glance around at the black and white marble bathroom. It probably cost more than our entire apartment. The black bath is so big it would fit four at a squeeze. What does a man do with a bath that big? However, it does look really rather inviting and I seriously consider it before shaking my head. I desperately need to pee and brush my teeth so I close the door behind me, do what I need to do and then start to search through cupboards to find toothpaste. I get lucky - right drawer first time, although I can't help wondering what's in all the other drawers and I feel my fingers itching to take a quick peek. *No, Beth. Be good, Beth.* Ha, that's laughable. Good Beth was apparently on holiday last night, because good Beth would have got her backside home and not acted like a damn floozy by staying the night with a man she hardly knew.

Squirting some onto my finger, I spy his toothbrush and figure he's had his mouth on most of me anyway so what's the problem in using his brush. Grabbing it, I very quickly brush and rinse, then glance at myself in the mirror. I am distraught and quite disturbed. How on earth am I going to face him like this? My hair is a tragedy and most of my make-up has worn off. My face is red raw from so much kissing and I didn't have the forethought to bring any make-up, because clearly I wasn't staying last night, was I? *Idiot Beth.*

I look very much like that disaster of a woman you see falling from a club at three in the morning - the one you can't help laughing at because she's such a wreck, but secretly you envy her because she probably had the best night of her life. Yep, that's me. Very slightly inebriated and most definitely had the best night of my life.

I may look like death warmed up but there's a twinkle in my eye that I haven't seen before, maybe ever, and I like it. Even if I am a complete hussy. I can't believe I stayed here last night. What I'll get from the girls is anyone's guess, and the fact that we didn't use any protection was just stupid. I'm definitely going to be getting shit for that, but the stilted conversation about condoms had made me feel stupidly at ease for some reason. *Ask him about the paperwork, Beth.*

Mind you, anyone who has paperwork about this sort of thing is probably clean, aren't they? *Stupid Beth.*

"Are you on the pill?" he said, his fingers torturing me slowly for the god knows how many'th time. I was pretty much about to explode.

"Yes," I screamed - exploding.

"I'm clean, I can prove it if you want," he said, moving his head back between my legs and swirling his tongue at me again. *"I want you bare, to feel the heat of you on me, to sink into you with nothing in my fucking way."* I was pretty much delirious with pleasure at the time.

"Oh god. Yes," was my rather breathy answer. *"Clean, yes... No problems there. How can you prove it?"* I managed to ask as he clamped his teeth down on my very sensitive sweet spot, causing me to arch my back into his mouth and almost instantaneously orgasm.

"Paperwork. Health checks," he muttered, moving his way up my body and finding his way to my neck. He hovered over me like a devil ready for more torture, sliding his hand beneath my backside to lift my hips. *"Too much to lose."* He growled into my neck again and licked his lips. *"Let me in, Elizabeth. I want you."*

"Okay," is all I managed to get out before he pushed his way in and blew my mind away from me... again.

Ask him about the damned paperwork.

Smiling to myself and shaking my head, I watch my eyes dancing in the mirror and imagine the moment when he first kissed me in the study and what transpired in there. *Wow.* And apparently I'm the first woman to have slept with him in his home, too. *Double wow.*

I look at the huge shower and sigh. That would feel too good to walk away from. He's not here anyway so I'm sure he won't mind. I'm going to have to face him soon and lord knows what the next conversation will be, so I damn well want to feel refreshed and ready for him. God, he might have changed his mind. I hadn't thought of that. Am I going to find him just so he can throw me out?

I'm definitely having a shower.

After turning and twisting various knobs, I finally work out how to work the enormous shower. I step under the waterfall, letting the warmth flood over my hair and body, and grab at the shampoo to massage it into my hair. The scent is clean and fresh with a hint of lemon or lime. Whatever it is, it's heaven, and I breathe it in like it's wild flowers on a sunny day.

I'm not sure how long I stand here letting the water cleanse me, my mind wandering through the events of last night, but God, it starts the trembling up again. He was breath-taking. I couldn't have asked for a more skilled lover. He gave me endless orgasms and was both masterful and gentle. I saw no perverse angle or anything that scared me, and felt completely comfortable in my own skin regardless of his chat downstairs. Okay he does have a tendency for being a little heavy-handed, but given that I actually enjoyed his authority over me, I don't see that as a problem at all.

I'm not really sure how he managed it, but I'd never been so reckless before. I was so aroused by him that I threw everything into him. He quite literally opened me up to anything and somehow forced me to abandon every inhibition I've ever had. After his revelations about what his *particular preferences* were, I remember being worried that it wasn't going to be enough for him, that *I* wouldn't be enough for him, but he didn't do anything to scare me off in the slightest. I narrow my eyes at my own naivety and think about the locked door in the bedroom. No man holds up handcuffs and then doesn't think about using them, and then it hits me as I realise that those hands weren't working at full capacity last night at all. Oh.

Suddenly a breeze enters the room and I instantly sense him near me again. It's odd but I seem to feel his presence as if he's calling to me somehow. The shivers run down my spine first and I rub anxiously at my arms and then abruptly feel my breathing change. My stomach starts its relentless churning and my nerves cause my legs to liquefy again as I lick my lips at the thought of him.

"Good morning," he says, sliding open the shower door and walking in. Oh god, the most perfect specimen of naked masculinity just walked into the shower and said good morning, and I'm seriously not tipsy enough to be calm about this. Shit. My eyes hit the floor instantly.

"Morning," I reply quietly, trying desperately to convince my legs to keep holding me up and not knowing where the hell to look.

"Are you looking at the floor again, Elizabeth? I thought we discussed this." My head shoots up in reply. Mr. In Control is apparently here this morning and not taking any shit.

"No, I was just..." His face stops me in my tracks. Pure sex is pouring off him in waves as he raises an eyebrow, pushes me backwards a little and steps under the water.

"Still so self-conscious - beautiful but insecure," he says to no one in particular, chuckling and grabbing me to him. "We'll have to work harder on that."

He is not in the least bit shy or embarrassed as he moves around me and caresses anything he wants, his body glistening under the water as muscles twist to various positions around me. The confidence soon starts to make me feel entirely different, almost awkward and inexperienced in his presence. I close my eyes and let him do what he wants, anyway, enjoying the sensation as he takes my breast into his mouth and bites at my nipples. This is a different Alex from last night, far more selfish and controlling. I sense instantly that I may well be meeting some of his *preferences* this morning, as he handles me roughly. I wince a little, which results in him chuckling again. He's no longer whispering sweet nothings in my ear or helping me relax into the moment. No, he's demanding I give in and allow him what he wants. This seems to be about me complying to a different version of him, and much as my brain might be struggling, my slut's jumping all over him.

Stretching his hand up to my throat, he grabs me and drives me back to the wall forcefully, moving his other hand down to my sex. I stiffen slightly, suddenly unsure how his frame of mind is going to change the sexual dynamic. I was happy with a bit of rough but this mood is making me nervous and edgy somehow, as if I'm giving him carte blanche to go for anything.

"Open up those legs, Elizabeth," he says firmly, moving across to my other breast and biting down harder. "Or maybe you want me to make you?"

"Oh god," I pant in reply as for some unknown reason, I instantly obey and spread my legs for him at the jolt of pain.

"Good," he says, almost to himself as his teeth soften slightly.

He drags his lips back up my body towards my mouth, pushing his body weight into me, and grinding himself onto me as he teases me with his hand. Panting hard and holding onto his shoulders for support, I begin to beg for him to touch me harder there or faster, I really couldn't care less. *Begging? How does he make me beg?*

"Please, Alex, I need to... Oh, please."

He lifts his head to meet mine and stares into my eyes. A feral look flicks across his features almost as if he hasn't seen me, yet quite unnervingly he still seems somehow completely in control of himself and me. I gasp at the vision and watch him, realising I can see it now, that part of him that houses his intriguing preferences is here in front of me. His eyes seem to have changed in colour to a darker blue and as his pupils dilate further, his eyes begin to look almost black.

"What do you need, Elizabeth? Tell me now or I'll do what I want and you'll do as you're fucking told." He growls at me, his fingers still drawing over my sex slowly. "I won't hold back much longer." I honestly can't speak. Who says that sort of thing? So I just gaze back at him with my mouth parted, panting again and waiting for whatever he's about to deliver.

Forcing my legs further apart with his thigh, he thrusts two fingers inside me immediately. I gasp and stare into his eyes, as he presses his thumb to my sensitive spot and begins to push his hand back and forth into a hard rhythm. It's vigorous and with no restraint, splitting me open for him, and his other hand begins tightening around my throat. I can't speak, once again I can hardly breathe, and oddly, I find myself enjoying the feeling of being held in position, almost used as a tool for his desire. He is absolutely in control of me and I'm flying high as his fingers work me faster.

His body moves fluidly as if he's done this a million times, his unyielding hands holding me completely in place as he pushes me with ease towards exactly what we're both craving. If this is him showing me more, it's beyond exhilarating and so erotic that I can't imagine ever feeling this kind of lust again.

"Is this what you need? Are you going to come all over my hand?" He groans as he grasps my throat again and stretches my neck upwards. "Do it soon because I'm going to fuck you so hard you hurt. Do you understand me, Elizabeth? I can't wait to sink into you again and fuck you raw."

150

Yep, that does it. I throw my head back and, "Oh god, yes... Alex... Fuck..." My scream echoes in the glass cubicle around us as I call his name over and over again and waves of pleasure roll across me. He doesn't give me a chance to look into his eyes or snatch a breath before he's lifting me toward him purposely.

"Don't let go of me," he says, growling again, a sneer passing across his mouth.

I grab onto him and wrap my legs around his waist. He groans with pleasure as he lowers me slowly, giving me at least a little time to get used to his size, stretching me wide. I gasp and groan at the sensation as he begins to move with brutally hard and fast strokes. Each thrust is punishing, forcing me back against the wall for more leverage. I can feel the tiles bruising me but I couldn't care less. I'm adoring his need for me. It makes me feel potent and sexy, lost or found. He's slamming into me so deep that it's almost painful, but oh so good. Each thrust is forcing me down harder on him and I can feel the familiar build of my orgasm again so urge him on faster. I've never experienced anything like this sort of sexual pain, or pleasure, or whatever it is. It's blindingly good and I'm not thinking again, just feeling and letting him guide me forward.

"Yes, Alex. Yes... Harder, please."

I'm tearing and scratching my nails into his back like a wild banshee. I have no idea where the hell this has come from but I'm not holding it back because it's euphoric, mind bending. My mind fogs as my body takes over completely at the pure adrenalin that's coursing through every inch of me. Pain. Pleasure. Brutality and aggressive handling. It all seems to wind me into a frenzy of need.

His grip on my throat tightens as he grasps for control and I feel my insides start to explode, tightening around him and contracting hard. The swell of him inside sends me spiralling into the first waves of bliss.

"No, Elizabeth, stop," he snarls at me. Stop? Sod that. I can't stop. I'm about to come again, hard, and I couldn't damn well stop if he ordered me to.

"God, yes. Alex," I cry, wave after wave of pleasure rippling through me to my core. My back arches forward into him, stars flashing before me as I release my built up tension and bite down on his shoulder.

"Oh, Christ. Yes. Fuck," he shouts, his come pouring into me with a force I've never felt as he leans his head into my shoulder.

He grabs me tight to him, shaking and panting and still grinding himself into me, releasing the last of his seed with growls of approval and groans of pleasure. My mouth hovers over his neck, still biting as if I can't get enough of his taste inside me. He groans, turning his head to give me better access, so I rake my nails across his back again and soften my teeth to gentle nipping. I have no idea where this siren has come from but I seem to be getting on quite well with her and he seems reasonably enamoured so I carry on, softly biting and running my tongue over his skin as we calm our breathing.

His face eventually shifts towards me and nudges my head backwards.

"Perfect," he whispers as he leans me against the wall and brushes his lips over mine gently.

He grabs hold of my bottom lip and sucks it into his mouth then gently pushes me into the most heart-melting kiss I think I've ever had. Soft, strong lips meander their way around my mouth, his tongue quietly seeking mine and teasing me as he releases my throat and travels his hand to the back of my neck. The move pulls me in closer, connecting us again, as he pulses deep inside me. God it feels good. Warm. Safe. I've never felt this before, this comfort in a man, this coupling.

We stand there for minutes, hours, I don't know. He's leaning on me, regaining his breathing as I hold onto his shoulders and gently stroke his back, my legs still wrapped around him. It's then that I remember seeing the tattoo on his back. I can't see what it is from this angle. I couldn't last night either. It's black writing of some sort. Sod it, I'll look at it later. I'm seriously too busy enjoying this moment to give a shit about anything else.

"I'm sure you will probably kill me at this rate," are the next words I hear from him. "Do you have any idea of the effect you have on me?" Oh. Good... I think.

"One night with me and you're done for?" I question teasingly, giggling. His eyebrow rises as he squeezes tighter against me, grabbing at a sponge on the wall behind me. He moves back and I get to see those wonderful eyes in full view again, a smirk of amusement lingering that makes me realise the other man has left and Alex is back again.

"I have little control around you, Miss Scott. I'm not entirely comfortable with that scenario. It is... confusing," he states, frowning while lathering up the sponge and moving it across me in soft circles. *He's washing me?*

"Oh, stop being such a grump. You can't live your life completely in control. Give a little of your power away every now and then," I reply as he moves the sponge between my legs gently, which is bloody hilarious given the battering I've just received. I can't believe he's doing this.

"A grump? Did you really just call me a grump?" he says, his lips curving upwards wickedly.

"Yes, I did." I raise my eyebrows in an act of complete triumph, challenging him, possibly stupidly if I'm honest.

"*You* will get your beautiful arse out of this shower and into the kitchen to cook me some food, before I really show you grumpy, Miss Scott." He swats my backside and continues. "Go on then, that's a good girl." I stare at him with an award-winning smile.

"Feeling weak from your exertion, Mr. White? In need of sustenance? I hope you're not getting too old for me?"

He instantly makes a lunge for me and I dash from the bathroom toward the back of the sofa, laughing like a schoolgirl as he chases me. Grasping at me with ridiculously swift hands, he throws me to the bed with ease and pins me underneath him. My wrists are clasped into one of his hands before I know what's happened, body rolled into whatever position he chooses. His hold is vice like. I couldn't move even if I tried, not that I want to. The vision of him on top of me again is disturbingly good, and as his muscles wrap around me like a constricting python, I sigh in pleasure at his weight. He moves his other hand to my chin and directs my face to look at him. He's so heavy on me that I wriggle and squirm a little beneath him, trying to get comfortable, but he tightens his grip and moves his knee to my crotch, causing me to flinch a bit.

"Sore?" He smiles a slightly evil grin. I'm not sure I like it at all.

"Yes, a little," I reply, trying to move away from the pressure. He increases the friction and moves his knee further into me, purposely causing more pain.

153

"Good. Are you certain that you are satisfied with our session? It really would be my pleasure to find something else to add to our entertainment for a few more hours. I have plenty of other things that will help enhance your pain." His stare is ruthless and slightly cold. "When I have you entirely, Elizabeth, when you have told me you will be mine with no reservation, you will be extremely sorry you thought of me as old. I can be relentless with my... affection for you." His face softens and warms again, almost as if he's surprised himself by his statement.

"Affection?" I squeak.

"Yes, I think that's a good word for it, don't you? I'm not sure I've ever used it before. I rather like it. Now, get to the kitchen before you distract me again." He dazzles me with his smile and jumps up, throwing his shirt at me and pulling on some jeans. "Oh, and by the way, I spoke to your sister and told her you were here."

"Shit, I forgot. How did you know?" I can't believe I didn't call her. She's so going to kill me.

"Your phone had missed calls on it," he says with a small shrug as he walks back towards me.

"You looked at my phone?" I ask with a frown. It pisses me off. I'm really not sure why.

"Yes, it was flashing. I wondered if it was urgent. I would have woken you but I thought you'd like the peace. Are you bothered that I looked at your phone?"

Am I? I don't know.

"No, it's just a bit soon to be so familiar. Would you be bothered if I looked at yours?" I ask with my hands on my hips, standing in his open shirt. Am I really about to start an argument about my phone with him? Especially when we've just discussed pain? And with no clothes on?

"Probably, yes," he replies calmly, smirking.

"Then why did you feel you could look at mine? It could have been something private?" Smirking? Really? *Arsehole.*

"I did it because I could, Elizabeth." He looks pleased with himself for some reason. "Actually, I was trying to be helpful and I assumed you'd have nothing to hide from me." His face wavers a little. "You don't, do you? Please don't make me suspicious. You wouldn't like me when I'm suspicious." His eyes narrow and anger flashes across

154

his gorgeous face. A sigh escapes me as I realise this is neither the time nor the place for a row, and quite oddly, he looks too damn inviting in his near angry state with all his gorgeousness on show for me to be able to be truly irritated.

"No, Alex, I have nothing to hide from you. Just don't feel that you can make decisions for me please." I close the remainder of the buttons on his shirt as dramatically as I can manage, staring directly at him, and move toward the door, leaving him looking slightly agitated and watching me like a hawk with prey in mind. "And where's the sodding paperwork?" I call as I make my way down the stairs, wondering if it really bothered me that much or if I simply needed to make a point early on. I will not be manipulated or completely controlled by Mr. White, regardless of his magnificence or incredible abilities in the sex department.

My bare feet hit the cold tiled floor and I feel him behind me. Soft, warm arms clasp my waist and spin me round toward him.

"Was that our first row?" His eyes smile at me. This is clearly his way of rectifying the situation.

"I think so," I reply quietly, still not entirely enamoured for some reason. Unfortunately, the man is still as stunning as ever. Nothing has changed in the minute it took for me to descend the stairs.

"I'm... I shouldn't have... I'm an arse. It was rude of me and I won't do it again. I'm just not used to this and I've never had to ask before," he says with some contrition. My eyes narrow at his acknowledgement of wrongdoing as his smile comes back in place.

"Right," I say haughtily.

"Are you still angry with me?" He starts kissing my neck. *Bastard.*

"Yes," I say as he runs his hand up the inside of my thigh. I can't think straight again. He knows exactly what he's doing. Manipulating sod. My core traitorously clenches inside as the irritating tremble begins in earnest.

"Don't be angry with me." I roll my eyes at him and laugh a little.

"How can I stay angry while you're doing that? You know exactly what you're doing. You're not playing fair."

"Why would I do that? Fair is completely overrated." He grabs hold of my hand, twirls me into a dance hold and proceeds to dance us along the hall to the kitchen, softly whistling a tune. Good god, he can dance, too? I laugh and throw my head back as we spin into the kitchen.

"Is there anything that you can't do? And what on earth made you think of that song?" I ask, recognizing the tune as *'The Recipe For Making Love'* and smiling at the thought.

He stops and kisses me. "Yes, a few things. *You* don't need to know about any of them, and I am a great fan of Harry Connick Junior."

Really? Probably one of the world's best crooners of love songs and Alex likes his music. That does not sit at all well with the *'Frankly I have no idea what a relationship involves,'* statement.

"Well, it seems you're the romantic type without you even wanting to be, Mr. White."

"I never said I wasn't a romantic, Miss Scott," he states, gazing at me as he continues our twirling. "I just haven't ever had a reason to act on romance before." *Oh, right.*

His phone is ringing by the time we reach the table and he lets go of me, kissing my hand goodbye as he grabs it and heads off back down the hall.

I head to the wonderful, obviously white countertop and start to look for the fridge. He must have some decent food stashed in here somewhere. Finding the door, I open it to find everything a good cook could want. Bacon and eggs for a Sunday morning, very appetising. My mouth starts to salivate as Alex wanders back into the room and drops a large red folder onto the table, still talking away on the phone to someone. I hold up the bacon to him and he smiles and nods at me. As I start opening and closing cupboards, he moves in behind me and pulls out a frying pan and switches on the high-tech cooker expertly.

"Hold on. I'll ask," he says, looking at me.

"Would you like to go to INK tonight?"

"Umm, I don't know. I said I'd spend the evening with Belle," I reply, putting the bacon under the grill. He puts the phone to his ear again.

"Yes, you heard. Christ, okay, I'll ask her again," Alex responds.

"It's a good friend. He's asking if you'd like to bring her along as well." His eyebrows rise in question and he pinches my nipple for full effect.

"Okay, I'll phone and ask her in a while," I say, rubbing at my nipple and scowling, which is sore enough, thank you very much.

"Okay, did you hear that? Either way I'll see you there at eight thirty. Yep, you too." He puts the phone down and leans over my shoulder, wrapping his arms around my waist.

"He thinks you're nice," he says as he kisses my shoulder.

"He hasn't seen me. How would he know what I am?" I say, turning the bacon and enjoying his attention.

"You must sound fantastic then. Besides, his instincts are good most of the time."

"I doubt someone can make an informed decision on someone based on their voice alone. Do you do business that way, Mr. White? A quick phone call to someone you've never met and the deal's done."

"Actually, I never do business with someone unless I can look them in the eye. It's the only way you can tell if someone's lying to you."

"Really? Always?" That's just stupid.

"Yes, unless I know them well."

He smiles and pushes himself into me as I crack the eggs into the pan.

"Well that's very distrustful of you. You should try a little bit of faith. Sometimes people might surprise you."

"Mmm, so naïve, Miss Scott. We will have to get rid of that. Mind you, I do quite like your innocence. It's quite refreshing. Stimulating," he says, pushing his hand between my legs again. I swat his hands away with the bacon grabbers and click them together a few times, narrowing my eyes.

"Down, boy. It's time for food. Go lay the table and show me where the plates are."

"Down, boy?" he repeats as if no one's ever said no to him. I roll my eyes at myself. Of course, no one probably ever has, and certainly not a woman.

"Yes, down boy. Food, plates," I reply, pointing my grabbers at the table.

"Yes, ma'am." He mock salutes with a smirk as he pulls some tableware out of the drawers and moves to the table, pointing at the bottom cupboard. I load up our plates and cross to the table, placing our food down. Looking out at the garden, I sigh and stare out to the huge manicured garden through the large French doors.

"It's very beautiful out there."

"Yes, I suppose it is. I don't go out there all that much. Only when I host the summer parties and what not. This is good. Where did you learn to cook?" he replies, digging into his food.

"That's awful. How can you not enjoy such a wonderful garden? I thought you enjoyed the outdoors? I miss an outside space. My mother and father love gardening. We used to spend so much time outside just pottering around."

"You miss them?" he questions, gazing at me, his eyes suddenly searching.

"Yes, I do. They're fantastic people and they've always helped us achieve our goals. I try to see them as much as I can but we're normally so busy. What about yours? Are they very proud of you? They must be," I ask, shaking my head at the stupidity of my own question. Who wouldn't be proud of him?

"My mother is dead and my father is... a waste of my time." He looks instantly annoyed and his face hardens.

"Oh, Alex, I'm sorry. I didn't know. I shouldn't have asked." I drop my gaze.

"Head up and look at me. You've done nothing wrong and you weren't to know. My mother died when I was about two. I don't remember her and I haven't seen my father in years. We don't communicate and I have no wish to. He's an exceptionally difficult man. I've got no other family or anyone to care about." He reaches out and strokes my face, his turning soft again. "You're only the second person to know that information and I am trusting you with it so please don't tell anyone else." He smiles warmly and returns to his food again.

Okay, that was intense. He's all on his own. No wonder he's completely in control of his life.

His phone starts ringing again. "Tell me about your life and family?" he says as he stabs his phone and frowns.

"I don't think that's very fair in the circumstances." His eyes harden instantly. Obviously that wasn't the right thing to say.

"Don't pity me, Elizabeth. Ever. Yes, my life has been hard at times, but I don't dwell on it. I move on and get something I do want.

If I hadn't had the childhood that I did then maybe I wouldn't have the present that I currently do. I focus on the future and try to forget the past. I don't need anyone's fucking sympathy or compassion so do not insult me with your kindness," he spits at me, irritation and anger lacing his voice as he shoves his plate away.

I immediately reel back from him and stare in shock at his scowl of annoyance. His fury is being thrown directly at me with a force that leaves me feeling slightly humiliated and a lot lost. What on earth did I say that was so wrong? I was simply trying to stay away from a delicate subject to make him feel at ease. I doubt I'll bother with that technique again. If there is an again, which I'm highly doubting at the moment.

"I think that's probably my cue to leave. I'm sorry if I made you feel awkward." I stand and make a move toward the door.

"Sit down," he says quietly.

"Excuse me?" I turn to him. Those eyes hold my gaze fiercely as he reiterates.

"I said sit down. Now." Sodding ordering? I think not, arsehole. My hands shoot to my hips.

"Alex, I don't know why you feel the need to vent your frustration on me but I did nothing to deserve it and I don't appreciate it." His eyes still pierce mine venomously. It's enough to make me look down again as a frustrated sigh leaves his mouth, which doesn't help stabilise my nerves at all.

"If I have to tell you one more time, I am going to get fucking annoyed. If you're going to have the balls to stand there and defy me by not sitting your pretty little arse down when you're told then at least have the backbone to look me in the eyes when you do it. I have told you never to drop your eyes from mine unless I tell you to and I mean it." He smirks - yes smirks - back at me as I draw my eyes up to meet his. "Good girl. Now come here and kiss me." I feel the small smile and frown hit my face at the same time and try to process how to react to it. He's an arse. That's clear, but a bloody beautiful one regardless, and how I'm ever going to keep up with these mood swings is a complete mystery.

Moving slowly to sit on his knee, he wraps his arms around me and breathes me into him.

"Please, don't do that again," I say quietly. He grips tighter and nuzzles his head into my neck.

"I'm sorry," he says eventually. "My past tends to bring out the worst in me. That's the very reason few people know about it, so don't take it personally."

"But I do, Alex, and I will continue to, so if it's some sort of relationship you want then you're going to have to try and be less, well... reactive about stuff." I look into his eyes, searching for contrition. "Or explosive or whatever that was, because it's not fair, you know. That was .." I don't know what that was. I'm rambling. Standard response.

"Okay," he says, still smirking.

"It's important, Alex. Don't dismiss it as a joke. It really isn't," I say, slapping at his shoulder.

"Okay, okay," he replies with his hands in the air. Something makes me think this isn't the last I've seen of his temper, but we'll move on for now.

"What's the folder for?" I say, trying to take the conversation to somewhere different.

"Paperwork," he says as he pulls it back towards us and opens it.

"I don't need your whole medical history, Alex," I say, refusing to look at it.

"Obviously not, but the piece of paper you do want is in here," he says as he thumbs to a section and opens it. "There you go. Thoroughly inspected, inside and out." I glance down at the medical report that was dated two weeks ago. Apparently everything was very healthy indeed.

"You haven't been with anyone in two weeks?" I ask, surprising myself at my own nosiness. His face falls a little. Obviously he has.

"I always use protection," he replies quietly.

"You didn't with me," I return, staring straight at him, looking for some sort of explanation and hoping he will calm my fears a little about our stupidity.

"No, I didn't. But you have my word that you are my first," he says, returning my stare, his eyes never blinking. "Can you say the same, Elizabeth?" Suddenly business Alex is in the room.

"Yes, I can," I respond immediately. Never once have I had sex without a condom, even in a relationship, which obviously increases my confusion as to why I am doing with him. I am only on the pill because of my bloody periods.

He continues to stare at me, probably searching for a lie. Well he isn't going to find it here.

"Okay," he eventually says as he smiles. "Then that's settled."

He pulls me into a very passionate kiss and then picks me up and makes his way into the lounge, depositing me rather crudely on the sofa. He stands there gazing down at me with a smile that is both charming and infectious, his jeans hanging low on his finely toned abdomen and his hair all messed up and sexy looking, and yes, that inner slut is instantly ripping my shirt off, or his rather.

"I don't think I've smiled so much in a long time, Miss Scott. I think you might be quite good for me, challenging, but good nonetheless."

"Well I hope so, Mr. White. I'm sure you'll be worth the effort." I giggle. God I'm pathetic. I'm really going to have to gain some control over my ridiculous stupidity around him.

He sits down next to me and we stare at the fire as he puts his hand on my thigh and lightly strokes his fingers back and forth. It suddenly feels so comfortable again, so right. Who am I kidding? He is perfect and I am absolutely falling for him. One night and a morning and I'm thinking about all sorts of absurd things. Even with his unusual preferences, which I know I haven't seen the measure of yet, I will probably give him anything he wants because I am totally hooked and there isn't a way out of it. As long as he wants me, I'll be here. I just hope he won't destroy me. After all, he is Alexander White, apparent God of the bloody universe and I am just... well, me. What on earth makes me think I've got a chance of keeping up with him is a mystery, but as I cuddle into him, I can't stop the glimmer of hope that this is real and that maybe I've found that special someone to cherish for the rest of my life, that maybe I've found the one, or that he found me.

"Elizabeth, why do you think you like being near strangled whilst you're being fucked?"

Okay, maybe I was a bit premature with that thinking.

Chapter 13

Elizabeth

"I can't believe you slept with him. You are such a hussy, young lady," Belle taunts.

She's been on at me about it from the moment I stepped back into the apartment. She just couldn't help herself and to be honest, I don't blame her. I have always been the more reserved one of the three of us. I've never slept with anyone on a first date and I'm never as outrageously flirtatious as the others. I tried to explain that he weakened my defences, but she simply shrugged it off and continued with her assault of jibes and jokes. Teresa's going to be even worse.

"Mind you, I don't blame you. I suppose he is quite a looker. Who's this friend he's bringing with him?"

"I have no idea, only that he said he's a good friend," I reply.

Obviously Belle has jumped at the chance of going to INK for the evening and we've spent the last two hours preparing and drinking wine while I wear the happiest face I've seen for ages. I keep noticing Belle smiling at me with a genuine look of love on her face. Much as I adore her, the sweetness of that smile is absolutely not her style and I much prefer the ever present mocking sneer that normally frames her lovely face.

"He seems to have impressed you, little sister," she teases. Impressed? Am I? I have no idea how I feel. The man gives me a whirlwind of emotions, but impressed is probably a good description.

"He is... indescribable, Belle. I just can't help but think he's like a dream - one I'll wake up from and suddenly find out that he's actually a monster." Her splutter of laughter causes my eyes to narrow considerably.

"Oh, honey, didn't you know? He is a monster. Well known for it apparently. However, while he's being wonderful to you, grab it with both hands and enjoy him. He took the time to call me, so he obviously cares to some degree. Perhaps this is meant to be, and you know how I feel about that sort of shit."

"I'll try, but he's so disorientating. I feel like I'm ten feet behind him all the time."

"You almost certainly are, darling, but that's only because you're highly unlikely to hold your head up and face him." She narrows her eyes at me as she taps the table.

"Funny, that's what he keeps telling me to do."

"Then I like him already, but you really must stand up to him, Beth. He won't like it and definitely won't understand it, but a man like that needs handling with extreme care and a firm hand every now and then. Now what time is he picking us up again?" she says, clapping her hands for effect.

"Quarter to eight."

"Right, well we better get you looking fabulous then."

"Belle, it's a Sunday evening and you know INK is far more casual on a Sunday. I am not going over the top in something too short." I glare and give her my best *not happening* eyes. I'm not sure why I bother though. She always gets her way in the end.

"No, darling, I was thinking skinny jeans, my blue heels and that fantastic strapless red and white number you've got. I've got that blue crop jacket you could borrow." She smiles, quite sweetly for her really.

"Oh, okay. I can do that. Hair up or down?"

"I say up and soft. I'll get my curlers. Go do your make up and I'll get more wine."

~

An hour or so later and we're finally ready to go, both of us waiting in the lobby. It's a little early but we've had some bookings to discuss so we've passed the time well enough. A car pulls past the foyer of our building that I don't recognise so I ignore it and continue chatting about the up and coming Jenkins party that's on for Thursday evening.

"Oh, how beautiful is that car?" Belle casually says as she looks at the matt grey sporty thing that has now returned in front of us. "He's going to be stunning whoever he is. Only the gorgeous ones drive Aston Martins. Who's in this building dating someone with a car like that?" I shrug. No idea.

It's then that I see the door open and a messy, very sexy head of black hair get out and stylishly walk around the front of the car towards us. My legs almost buckle. He's on the phone, which gives me a minute to admire him. If it's at all possible, he looks even better tonight. Oh god. I grab onto Belle's arm for support. He's wearing black jeans that fit snugly to those impressive thighs, a brown shirt and a short black wax jacket. Of course he's finished it perfectly with roughed up boots that are screaming bad boy at me. Could he be any more devastating? My stomach flips over. How can he possibly manage that when in the morning he will be wearing a ridiculously expensive corporate suit and probably be flying off to Singapore or somewhere? Christ, he's just beyond words.

"Well of course, it would be him, wouldn't it?" Belle sniggers beside me. I take a long breath and hold my head up, before he tells me off again.

He strides towards me, eating up the ground between us with precision and balance, never removing his eyes from mine as a soft, sexy grin breaks across his face. He pockets his phone and turns to Belle.

"Excuse us a minute, please." He throws his keys at her and nods towards the car.

"Well, lovely to see you too, Alexander. I'll drive, shall I?" she says, running toward the car, giggling. It's quite worrying and probably not a great idea.

He sweeps me up to him and smiles. He's holding on so tight, I think I might explode and it's all I can do to return his smile and gaze at him as my heart leaps out of my chest.

"You look ravishing. I am sure I've broken every speed limit getting here." He presses his lips to mine softly and dips me backwards into an exaggerated bow. I hang on and kiss him back with a passion I can't control, sexual torment assaulting my senses, and seriously consider dragging him up to the apartment and not going out at all. *Oh, get a grip, Beth.*

"Alex." I groan into his mouth, pushing him off me a little. "Much as I'm enjoying your affection, I'm not sure I trust my sister in your car much longer," I say breathlessly. "She'll probably leave us here and steal it."

"God, you feel so fucking good. I've missed you," he says, sighing, his hand grinding into my backside, not looking at his car in the slightest.

"Really? We've only been apart a few hours," I say in surprise.

"I know. Strange but true. I'm quite shocked myself." He laughs. "Did you miss me?"

Really, Mr, White, the tornado of so many hearts, asking me if I missed him?

"Yes, Alex, I did. Very much." I look to the floor timidly and he growls. My head shoots back up and I gaze at him again. This head thing is definitely an issue for him.

"Perfect, just perfect," he says, a soft smile gracing his face as he strokes mine. And here we stand, still having nothing to do with going anywhere and both of us thinking of anything but going out. He frowns suddenly.

"Is she really going to drive my car?" he says, looking slightly troubled. "She does know how to drive, doesn't she?" I look over his shoulder, turning him slightly and giggling.

"Looks like it," I say, pointing to a mad woman waving from the driver's seat. He grabs my hand and starts us walking towards her.

"Come the fuck on, you two. I have some drinking to do and a very fast car to drive," Belle shouts, squealing with delight. Well this will be interesting.

~

As we pull up outside INK, Alex chuckles through gritted teeth and unfurls his body from the car.

"I'm glad you enjoyed yourself, Belle, because that is the very last time you will ever drive my car or preferably anyone else's for that matter. You're absolutely insane and I'm not sure how we got here alive."

"Please, I hardly went above fifty. Too many fucking cars around for my liking. Please don't tell me you're an old man who potters around all the time?" She lets out a whoop of laughter. I giggle as he raises that eyebrow at her as she gets out.

"Elizabeth, I'll send Andrews every time you need to go anywhere. There is no way I will allow you to be potentially killed by your maniac sister for a minute longer." He grabs my hand, helping me out and gives me a stare that infers that he actually might mean what he's just said.

"Don't worry, she's not normally so dramatic in a car. If yours wasn't quite so nice, I doubt she'd have put her foot down quite so much." I snicker as I find the pavement and straighten my jacket.

"You like it?" he asks. Who wouldn't, for god's sake?

"Of course I do. It's fantastic. Much better than I'm used to." I grin. He gazes at me for a while; it's an odd look, as if he's remembering something.

"Keys, Belle?" he says, glancing at her. She chuckles again and hands them over, swinging herself around to walk toward the entrance.

His eyes return to mine and he yanks me forward for another kiss.

"Christ, you make me horny. I've done nothing but think about you all afternoon and what I want to do to you. I might just have to fuck you while we're here." His fingers curl into my thigh firmly as his leg nudges between mine. "Does that make you wet for me? Are you ready for more of me yet?" he whispers in my ear. I can feel him smiling at me and waiting for my answer. God, yes. Just looking at him makes me wet. He doesn't move, just stays by my ear, nibbling at my neck and holding me rigid. I can't breathe and the thought of doing something like that in public makes me almost fall over. I clutch onto him with an iron grip and whimper at the completely erotic image of him keeping his hand over my mouth to quieten the screams. Bloody hell, what is he doing to me?

I really need to find some form of grip.

"Come on, let's go in then, shall we? The night has just begun," he says, letting me get my balance and taking my hand again. His face is calm and relaxed, as if what he's just said has had no effect on him whatsoever. I, on the other hand, am a quivering pool of heat and tension. I have absolutely no clue how he manages that. It's as if he has an impenetrable force field around him, some ability to morph from one character to another in seconds. Frustrating isn't the word for it.

We walk toward the entrance to find Belle has already disappeared into the depths of the darkness. I flex my fingers in his hand to try and bring some life back to them as he clutches onto me tightly. He looks down quizzically at our joined hands for a few seconds and then relaxes his grip slightly as we approach the security guy. Mr. Doorman stiffens a little as Alex throws his keys at him nonchalantly.

"Take care of the car, Jaz," he says with no emotion at all.

"Sir," Jaz replies as he nods and starts to talk into his earpiece.

"I didn't realise there was a parking service here," I say as we walk through the door.

"There isn't. Jaz will have someone take it home and Andrews will pick us up later. I feel like having a drink or two," he replies with a brilliant, boyish smile. It's cute. I've never seen him look cute. I'm not even sure if the word's the right description to be honest. Maybe adorable is better.

"Oh, but how does he know where you live? And why would they do that for you? I mean, you must be a pretty loyal customer for them to go to so much trouble," I question, flummoxed by such a grand gesture.

"They do it because I pay their wages, Elizabeth," he says, casually glancing at the reception area. Of course it would belong to him, wouldn't it? *Stupid Beth.*

His arm wraps around my waist as he guides me cautiously through the throngs of people milling around and toward the sliding doors.

"Oh. You really are quite, what's the word I'm looking for? Diverse, Mr. White." Business tycoon and club owner. I don't know why I'm surprised. I get the feeling this may happen quite a lot, because I dare say this man is full of little shocks.

"Yes. I most definitely am." He winks and we walk through to the bar.

I am now feeling more than a little apprehensive. I've just learnt that not only is he the most glorious bachelor in the room, which frankly was making me nervous enough, but he also owns the building we're in. That's obviously the reason he was behind the bar with

Conner that night. Most women in the room are now staring directly at him or trying to do the subtle approach from the side. Every single one of them is giving me the most disgusted look they can manage without potentially offending Alex, and I am feeling like a little frightened sheep in the midst of some very overbearing wolves. Shit. Where the hell is Belle when I need her?

Alex squeezes my hand and looks down at me with something like concern in his eyes. I can't look at him. If I do he'll see the fear in my eyes and it'll show him how pathetic I really am. He'll see the dread and then realise I'm so not cut out for this world. For his world.

"Elizabeth, look at me. I know you're avoiding doing so," he says sternly. I don't. I just keep fidgeting. "Elizabeth, I'm not saying it again. If you want me to, I'll take you to my office and spank you until you learn to look into my eyes when you're told," he says, more quietly this time. My eyes widen at the comment, but there's so much authority in the threat I have little choice but to look up at him with nervous eyes. He frowns and reaches a hand to my cheek.

"Why do you feel so uneasy with me?" he asks. Him? No. Good god, not him.

"Alex, no, please. It's not you. You're wonderful. It's just..." I can't even finish my own sentence. I am so feeble that even I am disturbed by my idiotic behaviour.

"It's what?" he says softly, looking deep into me with those beautiful eyes.

"It's them," I say, nodding my head in the direction of everybody else. He looks instantly shocked as if a particularly strange thing has occurred. It really hasn't. It's just me being a moron as usual. Why didn't I drink more alcohol before we left?

"Has someone done something to offend you? I'll have them removed. Show me who." He swings around to follow my gaze. I swear I can see the hackles rising on the back of his neck.

"No, Alex." I sigh. "It's no one in particular. It's everyone. The wealth, the status of it all. I can't help but feel..." I start to drop my head and before I know it, his hand is on the back of my neck, forcing me to look at him. "I know it's ridiculous, but I..." His chest rumbles a throaty growl as he peers around at the other club goers, as if staking a claim on his territory, and moves his mouth towards mine.

"Keep looking around while I do this and notice the reactions from them."

His kiss is tender, loving even, and I struggle to keep enough wits about me to see faces as I fall hopelessly into his arms, but when I do, there are looks of utter surprise or even astonishment. I close my eyes, melt into his mouth and let him take me far away from their watch.

Eventually, he pulls back and smirks. It seems he's found his show amusing. "I've never brought a woman through those doors with me before. You're the only one. This place is my spirit, and I wouldn't dishonour it or myself with anything that was fake or undeserving. You, Elizabeth, are the most fascinating and enchanting woman I have ever met and of all these people, you deserve to be here the most." He frowns and looks down a bit. "Perhaps even more than me." I look at him in complete shock as he puts his hands in his pockets and gazes at me. Lovely as his words are, they're completely ludicrous.

"You don't even know me, Alex. You can't make those judgements."

"Oh, I do know you, baby. You are everything a superior woman should be and more. You're the reason why men like me hope and dream, knowing that we'll never be good enough for a woman like you while wishing that we could be. I am the unworthy one here, not you." He sighs and looks a little lost. "Look around you, Elizabeth. See the sharks for what they really are for once. I'm one of them most of the time." He looks as frightened by something as I am and I feel a snap of connection between us that impacts my heart with such ferocity it almost knocks me off my feet. I turn to look at the other people and notice most of them still staring with open mouths, all looking beautiful as they fling out indirect threats. "Sycophants and wolves, hungry for the next meal of money." I suddenly and quite unexpectedly realise that they are the ones in the wrong. He's right, and I can see it in every one of them so clearly with him beside me. They're all fraudulent in some way and I have no idea why I have been so uncomfortable in their presence before now. I turn back to Alex to find him gazing adoringly at my face with a small smile. Has he done this to me somehow? Already? I have no idea.

"I need a drink," he says. "That was emotional." So do I, frankly. Wow. Revelations.

I laugh as he grabs my hand and tugs me towards the bar, growling at anyone who dares not to move for him or maybe for us, then smile into his back as I hear Belle's voice.

"For fuck's sake, Conner, will you just give it a break for a few weeks? Good god, how do you keep the charm levels up so high for so long?" her voice snarls as his fingers leave the small of her back. "Why the owner of this fine establishment lets you in here to tarnish its good reputation is simply beyond me." I snigger as we come up behind them.

"The owner lets him in because he happens to be my good friend." Alex chuckles as he moves toward Conner and gives him a man hug. Good friend? *The* good friend? Oh.

"This…" Belle points a finger. "This is why you invited me here?" She stares at me. If he wasn't a good business proposition, I'm pretty sure she'd have laid into him with more gusto than that.

"Actually, Belle, I think Conner invited us here to meet him," I say, laughing and trying to regain some balance to her hostile approach.

"You knew, didn't you, Beth?" she hisses, narrowing her eyes at me.

"No, I didn't. I also didn't know he was friends with Alex or that Alex owns this place. I am in as much shock as you are. It is pretty cool, though. Frankly, I wish you two would just sort yourselves out and get on with it." I smirk at my sister's discomfort, hardly able to control the giggling that is rumbling around inside me as she glares in return.

"Well, I am appalled and a little distressed actually that you thought this was a good matching, Alexander. And you, sister dearest, will take that fucking ridiculous grin off your face." She huffs dramatically as she turns for the bar and sips at some fruit-laden drink.

"I really do believe you have her on the edge, Conner. It should only take a few more months and she'll be convinced of your natural wit and superhuman good looks," I tease him, smiling with mirth and trying to ease the tension she's created for no reason whatsoever.

Well, apart from the fact that she just won't admit she likes him.

"I think we all need a drink," he says a little grumpily as he looks at her back and shakes his head. It's cute. He really is quite besotted.

"That smile not working for you anymore?" Alex chuckles and slaps him on the back as he nods at the barman and does a two finger wiggle, which means something because the barman races towards the back and arrives back with an ice bucket and champagne. The label says Krug, obviously.

"Shut it, before I shut it for you," is Conner's response as he continues to watch Belle like a hawk. She's now decided to shake her arse in his face, as if she's forgotten all about him, so I narrow my eyes at her because she so likes him and is clearly going for some sort of game. As if on cue, Conner decides to play and leans over her back to whisper something in her ear. I have no idea what it is, but the dirty little smile that suddenly spreads across her face can only mean she's pleased, to some degree anyway. He chuckles and moves away again, leaving her giggling as he approaches me and smiles. "So, had any slippery fingers today, Beth?" I gape. What the hell does that mean? Alex very nearly spits out his drink behind me as he coughs around the glass.

"Conner, stop. Now." I swing my eyes to him and see the flash of anger that he tries to mask, quite unsuccessfully. Whatever the hell Conner is talking about, it's clearly some sort of joke, which Alex obviously doesn't find funny.

"Oh, chill the fuck out, man," he replies as he winks at me and grabs Belle's hand, who gawks in response but doesn't actually pull it away as he leads her across the room.

"Umm, what was that?" I ask, turning to look into his eyes. A wry smile greets me as he chuckles.

"He was attempting to wind me up," he replies, wrapping a hand around my waist and pulling me tight into his side. "Oddly enough, it seemed to work."

Oh, right. I still have no bloody clue.

~

The night progresses with an easy atmosphere and I watch the three of them all night, bantering and laughing with each other. There is probably nobody else in this room with as much money or clout as Alex, except maybe Conner. Actually, I have no idea, but I realise that I don't notice it on them at all. They ooze a sense of self-assurance that means they don't need to exploit their status or wealth in the slightest. As I glance at the other 'sharks' as he calls them, I can see

171

their neediness as they try to impress everyone else with tales of the latest this or the newest that. I feel myself growing more and more confident and holding my head up naturally. It probably helps that my head is really quite fuzzy and the champagne is slipping down my throat like water.

Belle and Conner are happily giggling like children. I don't know when that happened or what he did to change her mind, but I smile proudly at the pair of them. She is the probably the most *in need of love* person that I know, and every moment of happiness she receives is an absolute pleasure for me to see. Conner is so right for her and I can hardly contain my smile as I see her starting to realise it as we all chat. Although, I'm pretty sure she always knew it to some degree and was just avoiding it. Quiet, sly glances are thrown my way, the corners of her mouth lifting with every move he makes to convince her of his worthiness. I watch in awe as her flirtation levels increase steadily with an unusually reserved attitude. She's shy, and really, she doesn't need to be at all.

"I don't think I've seen him like that before," Alex whispers beside me, stroking my thigh and getting very close to the top of my legs.

"I know, but he is a playboy. You can see her point." I inwardly tense at my own comment. The man I'm with is as much a playboy as the one opposite me, possibly more so. I'm screwed.

"Yes, but he's never normally this attentive. He certainly doesn't normally laugh this much because of a woman and he's actually talking to her. I'm not sure I've ever seen that before." He smirks and kisses my cheek. "Are you having a good time?"

"Wonderful. It's good to finally see them getting on. It's been on the cards for months and I want to see her happy. She deserves some happiness." I frown at him, suddenly feeling very protective. "Can he make her happy? Is he really the bastard they say he is?" *Are you?*

"I don't know, if I'm honest. He's a good man and I've known him a long time, but whether he'll ever be able to settle down, I really don't know." He looks pensively at Conner and Belle for a minute or two. "I will say this, though. Once Conner's committed, he remains that way. Cheating is not his thing." He gives me a crooked smile.

"I'm not sure that inspires me with much confidence." I glance at Belle as she becomes more intimate and friendly, her hand on his thigh and his around her shoulder.

"Do you want to dance? I think these two could do with some space for a while," he asks me. My eyes shoot to his, breaking me from my internal battle.

"Really? Dance? You can dance? Most men don't dance," I ask, disbelief pouring from me. I know he can dance in the twirling style, but at a club? Really? Mind you, he certainly knows how to move those hips and it is his building.

"Well, this one does. It's why I own a club." He grabs me around the waist and launches me up into the air playfully, catching me with ease, then proceeds to shower me with kisses and drags me toward a very busy dance floor.

"Jesus, are you going to make some moves, man?" Conner shouts after us.

"Yes, I think I am. It's been too long." Alex quickens his pace while my own hips start their swinging around. I seriously can't help it. The music is so good and the champagne only heightens it.

I turn to look at Conner and smile. He lifts Belle's hand to his mouth and sweeps toward her. Thankfully she doesn't seem to protest as she wraps her hands around his neck.

Sweet, or maybe not.

Sweet has nothing to do with what happens in the next twenty minutes or so. Alex is probably the best male dancer I have ever seen, and surprisingly, he looks overjoyed with being in the middle of the thumping beats. His rhythm is passionate and right on the button and he seems to mould himself around the music as if this is what he was designed for. I feel the surge of heat through my stomach and groin, as he spends time pushing every inch of himself onto me and losing himself into the bass. His eyes are heavy and lust filled as he whispers all sorts of really rather intriguing things into my ear, most of which have me blushing beetroot red or simply not having a clue what he's suggesting. I've never heard a man use language that has made me feel so incredibly turned on, and I can feel myself becoming nervous for what he has planned. I am absolutely in over my head and I am so needy for him that I can hardly breathe, yet again.

SEENING WHITE

His hand wraps around my throat from behind in a grasp that tells me exactly where this is leading. His fingers flex firmly, causing my core to tighten, and suddenly I can't wait. I'm so horny that just the touch of his hand has me throbbing and yearning for more. I tilt my head back into his shoulder and feel him grinding against me in time to the music as my inner slut gives him every inch of her opening legs.

"Alex, please." What is it with this begging?

He gives me a wolfish grin and moves me toward the side of the floor. His eyes are pinned on something in front of him, as if he can see his destination and is pushing us there as fast as he can.

"You're impatient this evening, Elizabeth. I know exactly what you need. Are you ready for this?"

His hands suddenly grasp the backs of my thighs and lift me up onto him. I grab the back of his neck and hold on tight as he strides towards his target.

"Reach into my right pocket and get the card," he growls at me. I oblige and look at him. Actually, I might be panting, not just looking.

"Now what?" I ask breathlessly.

"Swipe it over that pad." He indicates his head toward a gadget on the wall by the side of a black door.

I do and it slides open, revealing a private area. It's like a cocoon of opulence and as the door slides closed, all the outside noise dies down and we're left with just our breathing and the dull thud of the outside bass thumping through the walls. He places me very gently to the floor and walks to the table. Lifting a small, white, iPod type gadget, he presses something and a secret cupboard opens in the wall. He grabs what looks like a burgundy silk scarf and moves toward me like a predator, slow, deliberate steps until he's in front of me. His face has become dangerously neutral and I wonder where the man from a moment ago has gone. All that sparkle has been replaced by nothingness, and the deepening blue eyes clearly mean only one thing.

"Elizabeth, I'm going to put this over your eyes and you're going to do exactly as I say. Don't question me and don't speak unless I ask it of you. Trust me to give you precisely what you are begging me for. Do you understand?" he states with a quiet composure that practically has me dribbling.

"Yes." It's all I've got, and I can't speak anyway because his mouth has been moving around words in that voice of his.

"Good girl."

He moves me into the middle of the room and turns me toward a glass wall. I know the dance floor is out there, but the wall is opaque to give privacy. He lifts the scarf and ties it over my eyes, and as the world goes black, I waver a little at the thought of being completely at his mercy. His hand steadies me as I nervously wait to see what happens next.

"Truly beautiful," he breathes over my shoulder as he skims his hands over them and down my arms. Just as I begin to get used to the feeling, he removes his hands and I hear his footsteps back away.

Silence, apart from the thud of bass which somehow seems to be resonating very loudly between my thighs and the rapid beating of my own heart which echoes in my head as I try to listen for any other sound.

"Take your heels off and then remove your top." *Oh, shit.* Okay, I can do this. Very slowly, I remove my shoes and then tease my top from my jeans, pulling it over my head, careful not to remove the blindfold. I hear the sharp intake of breath from behind me and smile to myself at my effect on him.

"Now peel those incredibly tight jeans down your legs, take them off and bend over," he growls at me. "And don't smile at yourself again, because you have no idea what's coming for you."

Okay, that makes me think a bit. God knows what's about to happen. Perhaps my inner slut should just take a back seat for a minute or two until she works out what's going on.

I reach down to start the tortuous task of trying to remove jeans sexily and push them down my thighs, which is clearly not easy. I complete the task quite gracefully, for me, and try to hide my smile as I kick them to the side. The pit of nerves in my stomach is rippling out to every part of me and I can feel myself dripping down my own legs with anticipation, so I bend over and touch my hands to the floor as commanded. Weirdly, it feels a little empowering, because regardless of how blind I currently am, I can feel his eyes roaming over my backside and drinking me in.

"Now move yourself forward two paces and put your hands on the glass." His voice is husky with need and suddenly more aggressive if that's possible. Playful Alex has gone.

I walk gingerly forward until I'm touching the glass. The thudding of the beat streams through my fingertips, the glass vibrating from the unwavering impact of the bass notes and resonating straight through me. I'm sweating and panting now as anticipation and expectancy fills my brain and floods my senses. The music slowly increases in volume in the room again, which only intensifies the vibration in my fingers.

I hear him before I feel him. I can imagine his face and that body glistening with the adrenalin that will be coursing through his muscles, the twist of his torso as his fingers brush down my spine and he moves them to my waist. He moves one large hand to my stomach and pulls me back against him. Christ, he's naked. When did that happen? His erection firmly presses itself into my arse as I squirm a little at his force.

"Do you feel how you make me want to fuck you? How hard I am for you?" He groans as I press back against him and he moves away. "Don't move Elizabeth. Stay perfectly still." I doubt that's possible. Next I feel him behind my ankles, gently tugging them apart wider.

"I want you to lower yourself down to your knees, keep your hands on the glass and your legs apart," he growls.

I do as he says hesitantly, not knowing what's coming.

The first swipe of his tongue ignites the flames within me. He grabs onto my thighs and buries his head between my legs, forcefully sucking on my clit through my panties and beginning the inevitable mind-blowing orgasm. My stomach clenches as he pushes my panties aside, delves his tongue into me and continues the torture in a hard rhythm.

"Oh, God, yes." I can't help myself. The feeling is divine, as if transported to a different place immediately.

Over and over again his relentless mouth and teeth bite and suck their way to my core and I feel myself building and building, higher, flying so high I can't bring in a breath. Oh god, I'm quivering and trembling and all my muscles tense as I gasp for air. The music vibrates louder somehow, pushing me faster and... Oh God, I'm there. His tongue dives in for the last time and I implode, with bright lights streaming through the blackness as his teeth connect again. The thud of the glass matches the throbbing inside me as I writhe on his face for that perfect spot, which he finds and clamps me to him.

"Yes. Oh fuck, yes. Alex..." I scream out his name and ride through the ecstasy that's skimming across every inch of me as I collapse onto him and moan out my gratitude.

"Hands on the glass, Elizabeth. You're not finished yet." His grunt is angry and full of heated desire as he pushes me back up forcefully.

He leans me back up against the glass and slides his hands back down to my hips. Grasping hold of my panties, he stretches the elastic and snaps them back to my skin. The pain is strangely hypnotic and I find myself pushing back against him, desperate for his touch again. He rips the side of them and I feel them leave my skin. The cold air hits my wet nub and sends shivers racing through me as his hot breath on my back and neck tease my skin mercilessly. Unfastening the clasp on my bra, he lets my breasts fall free and pinches at my nipples roughly as he pushes me forward until they touch the cold glass. They almost burn with sensation and I moan gratefully at the feeling. Then I feel his hand stroking me between my legs and forcing them open again.

"Are you ready for me now? Do you want me inside you? Answer me." He groans at my ear as he slides what feels like three fingers in, stretching me wide.

"Oh god, yes. Please, Alex." The sharp smack that suddenly hits my backside sends me reeling forward but he catches me before I fall onto the glass and brushes his palm over the sting. Warmth floods the area as I try to process the feeling.

"You're so wet, fucking delicious. Perhaps I should just make you come with my hand. The feel of you on my hand is exquisite, Elizabeth."

"Please, Alex, I need you inside me. Oh Christ, I can't breathe. Please." I'm begging so hard, desperate for him.

He removes his fingers from me and with the palm of his hand, puts so much pressure between my legs that he raises me upwards until my hands climb the glass in front of me for support.

Suddenly and with no restraint, he removes his hand, pulls my hips back towards him and plunges his full length into me, hitting my wall and making me wince in shock. The feeling is overwhelming and the power of his drive in forces my cheek to the glass, more punishing strokes pushing me further into it. His hand snakes its way up my back and towards my throat, causing the familiar quickening of panting to assault my airway. It feels euphoric, heady, and oddly, I need to feel him around my neck. I grab for his hand and put it to my throat in a show of unadulterated lust. I'm so close again as his hand closes around my windpipe that I lean my head back to give him greater access to it. His long fingers caress and stroke across it purposefully, eliciting all sorts of bizarre sensations from me.

"So. Fucking. Beautiful. You will see yourself as I do. Remember this," he says against my cheek as his other hand goes to my head and he unties the scarf, letting it fall to the floor. "Look at them, Elizabeth. Open your eyes and see," he growls at me. "Be so close to me that you don't care,"

As I open my eyes, I see that the glass is clear and I can see straight into every single person's eyes. I gasp in shock and recoil backwards towards him. He pushes back at me and replaces my hands on the glass as he surges forward again and presses my entire body against the window. Grasping at my throat, he places his thumb on my cheek and turns my head back to look at them. He slows his strokes and softens slightly, still forcing me to look. Feeling my hesitation, he moves his whole hard body against mine and softly grinds into me.

"You have more than they do. Experience how decadent you can feel when you just let go. Stay with me and let yourself go, baby."

My whole body begs for him to take me harder, to feel the pleasure and pain again, and as I realise they can't see me and that nobody is looking, I let my body relax back into him again as his fingers sink into my hipbone.

"Alex," I breathe. I have no fucking idea how I feel but his weight behind me, and the unrelenting throb in my core are beginning to fuel me forward again, to give in and just go with him.

Hunger, desire and pure lust sweep through me and I understand exactly what he wants me to see. Not to hide from self-consciousness and trust myself to give him everything, to go beyond the fear for him and to accept his opinion of me, of us, and his opinion alone.

"What do you want, Elizabeth? You have to tell me," he says quietly behind me as his fingers grip me harder. "Tell me. I want to hear you fucking asking me for it."

My thoughts collide with my need for him and I yield.

"Make me come, Alex. Show me more."

"Mmm, good girl," is his throaty response as his hand wraps around my stomach and forces me back to him. He slams into me with brutal, unremitting strokes and I feel him swelling deep inside. I keep my focus on the crowd, nervously watching their movements, but the unrelenting rhythm behind me is far more consuming and I start to lose myself in him again. The familiar build causes my legs to buckle and quiver. Only the pressure on my neck keeps me aloft, the persistent and unyielding grip on what is his. I sense his groaning behind me and close my eyes, letting him take me there with him. Passion and lust flow between us and I fall into some sort of darkness and light, some place I've never been before where everything is consumed by my body's reaction to him alone.

"Elizabeth, do it now. I want to feel you come with me." He growls low, like a caged animal.

And with one final penetrating thrust, the crowd disappears and it's just him and me in a sea of bliss and euphoria. Pulses and spasms ricochet through us both and he closes his arms around my waist and pulls me back to him, deeper into him. That's all there is. Just him kissing my neck and whispering beautiful words into my ear. Him keeping me close as we both enjoy the last of our mutual ecstasy, the last sensations of pleasure and adrenalin.

I'm in heaven and as I let my thoughts seep back to reality, I feel him soothing my neck and moving me back towards the seat at the back of the room. He sits and pulls me onto his lap, cradling me and stroking my hair as I continue to stare at the mass of unrighteous money-makers in front of us. I have no idea how I feel about what just happened, but I do know I've revelled in it, somehow found a new sensation in my mind and body that I wasn't aware of before now - some sort of detached space where it's only him and I. Is it heaven? Maybe it really is that mythical place where angels live, because they'd be able to do that shit no problem. Actually, I have no damn clue but I want it again.

"Do you understand where I want to take you?" he says, kissing my shoulder and brushing the hair from my face. I'm curled so tight in his arms that I couldn't feel any safer if I had an army surrounding me.

His embrace is all I need in this moment. His warmth and guidance is all consuming.

"Yes, I think so." He chuckles and kisses the top of my head.

"Mmm, I think you do, too."

Chapter 14

Alexander

Relaxing back into his chair, he rubbed the back of his neck, trying to relieve some of the damned ache caused from sitting for too long. The computer screen was still flashing back at him with renewed vigour as the barrage of emails kept pinging up. Sighing, he looked toward the floor to ceiling wall of glass at the end of his office. He wanted to be out there with her again. God, he was getting far too bloody slushy.

When he'd eventually woken up on Monday morning, after probably the best night's sleep he'd ever had, she'd gone. There was only a note left on the kitchen table to tell him that she'd had a wonderful time and that she would wait for him to call. She'd also left the bracelet in its box on the counter next to it. What woman didn't want diamonds? One with too much humility for her own good, perhaps? Fuck, that was so sexy to him, a woman he couldn't buy.

Drumming his fingers on the table and looking toward his phone, he contemplated calling her. It was Thursday, four days since he had last seen her, been with her. He hadn't called or emailed and didn't really understand why because he had wanted to, very much. She was in his thoughts constantly and no matter how hard he tried to dislodge her, he just couldn't. But was she really ready to see the world through his eyes and stand beside him? He desperately wanted her to, but something held him back. She was too innocent, good-natured. He didn't even have the right to show her the devious and often perilous game that he played with others. He certainly shouldn't teach her how to decipher the chessboard that was business and social engagements, how to manipulate and influence people, and how to be more in control of herself around all the fake and pretentious sycophants that invaded his world daily. Or should he?

He couldn't even contemplate her understanding or accepting his life before all this, so for the time being he would simply keep that away from her as he did with everyone else and hope she couldn't see it in him. He'd managed to hide it well enough for all these years and he hadn't been dragged backward too much lately. The occasional payment was needed, but most people owed him, not the other way around. He'd designed it that way. As long as he didn't have to lose his fucking temper around her, he could manage that side of himself fairly well.

He sighed again and rose from his chair to walk to the window. Why should she be pressured into his world? If she wasn't so bloody beautiful, he'd let her find a nice but dull man who would give her a quiet life. Instead, he was refusing to let her go and was only offering a world full of deception and lies, not to mention the sexual world he would be introducing her to. The thought of his own regrettable but ever-present past sent shudders of uncertainty and indecision through him as he wondered how she would react to that Alexander White. Nobody liked that man much. Christ, he didn't like him much and he'd created him. Still, he'd made a lot of money out of him.

More importantly, why on earth did he feel the need to express his own fucking emotions around her? It was pathetic. He'd even felt himself lowering his own head with thoughts of shame or disgrace when she had overwhelmed him with some level of grace and dignity that he hadn't believed was even possible in this life. For fuck's sake, why did she have to be so perfect?

Too damn perfect.

He also knew she'd be brilliant at the game he played. She already held people in the palm of her hand without even realising she was doing it. They fell for her charms because she was real, soft somehow, and giving. All he needed to do was help her see it. She'd match him flawlessly, but the moment he taught her and guided her, she'd also see the real him. She'd be inside him and he really wasn't sure if he could handle it or even wanted to. He'd been on his own for so long; he was completely in control when he was on his own and the thought of letting someone through his walls was fucking terrifying. Two people had been through those walls and even they had only been through them a little when allowed. Neither of them were female, and neither of them had evoked feelings from him quite as much as she was currently doing.

He pressed his hand to the glass and remembered her body in front of him as he'd buried himself inside her body and her inside his soul. The slick feeling of their bodies rubbing against each other in a film of glistening sweat, and the way she utterly surrendered to her own needs was beyond compare. Her long, lean legs that went on for a fucking eternity and the way her arse had arched into him with absolute need and desire. He'd never met a woman with such an innate and natural need to submit without entirely letting go of her own wants and requests.

She was no masochist and he would have to be careful, but she showed every sign of accepting his preferences. Fucking hell, he was getting hard again just thinking about it. That was also happening a lot lately - insatiable, relentless hard-ons. Just like when she'd dragged his hand up to her throat and he'd almost fucking exploded inside her.

Shaking his head again, he pinched his brow and huffed out a long breath. God, why hadn't he just ignored her and moved on to another woman? Some simple beauty who would just take what they were given and beg for more. Someone who wouldn't consume him and pressure him into this connection that she seemed to command from him every time she was near. Conner was right, he wasn't ready for this, didn't understand how to be open enough for it or how to relax and enjoy it without the irrational paranoia seeping in to haunt him again. How the fuck other people did this normal shit was completely beyond his grasp.

It puzzled him really. He was usually so totally disciplined with himself, and yet being with or thinking about her seemed to spark some unknown sentiment inside, something that made him feel out of control and if he was honest, slightly lost again. After all this time managing and keeping his anger and fear buried, why the fuck did he still feel the need to continue seeing her? Why would he choose to let someone too close, because she was and he could feel that, too. He'd had plenty of very attractive women and not one of them had had such an impact. Not one of them had come close to seeing the real man behind the businessman, The mask of one anyway.

He moved back towards his desk and picked up the phone. His default setting to deal with frustration or confusion was to get angry and discipline something or someone. What he needed to do was get his own house in order, shout some fucking orders around and get some results from his staff. Something was wrong with the Shanghai deal; he could feel it in his bones but couldn't put his finger on the problem. It just felt uncomfortable and he didn't know whether it was just his mood or a real problem. It was by far the largest deal he had ever tried to pull off and it would double if not treble his status and wealth the moment the contract was signed. He'd spent nearly a year double crossing, manipulating, persuading and inevitably paying so that he could be in the position he was now. He wasn't far away either. It should all be sorted by the New Year, but he needed to keep his eye on the ball. The one great thing about being such a fucking arsehole was that he was constantly on the lookout for the next fucking arsehole just waiting to steal his glory.

Swiping his finger across his phone, he dialled.

"Tate, where's that bloody revised contract? You said you'd have it here by two." He really wasn't that arsed; he just needed to shout at someone. Tate Westfield was by far the best contract lawyer in London. There definitely wouldn't be any holes in his work.

"Fuck off, Alex. You don't get to yell at me like one of your women. Besides it's only one thirty, you dick." Alex laughed at the retort. He had a great respect for Tate, mainly because of his complete inability to be subservient to anyone. They'd had a few arguments early on in his employment, but finally Alex had relented. His work was just too good to let him run to a competitor.

"What's got you all fidgety anyway?"

Another thing Tate was good at, reading people. He didn't need to see a person to know what they were thinking and he could also decide in a split second how to respond to a difficult situation.

"I'm not fidgety. I'm... perplexed by something."

"Right, well, could you either screw something or hit something and piss off. I have to get a contract sorted by two or my shit head of an employer will probably implode."

With that, the phone went dead. Ten seconds later it rang again.

"You okay?" Tate asked.

"Yeah," Alex replied, smiling and ending the call.

Fuck it.

Scooping up the phone and his suit jacket, he walked to the door and straight across the foyer toward Louisa, eyeing her legs as he reached her desk. Such a waste really.

"Sir, what can I do for you?" She smiled at him, her dark eyes peering over the top of her glasses at him with a calculation he had always admired.

"Have every department send me a financial report by tomorrow morning," he clipped as he turned for the elevator.

"Yes, sir," she said.

"I'm going out for a while. I need to do something." He smiled at his own enthusiasm.

"You have a three thirty with the Trenton Lawyers. Will you be back?" she questioned. Oh for fuck's sake, he'd forgotten another meeting. Christ, what was the woman doing to him? He stopped and turned back towards her.

"No, cancel it. Actually, don't. Tell Tate he can do it. I'm sure he'll find it highly amusing."

"Yes, sir. Anything else?" He looked at her for a moment.

"You look tired, Louisa. Why don't you take the afternoon off and spend some time with Gillian?" He raised an eyebrow at her.

"Umm, are you alright, sir?" she asked, surprise in her voice as she put her pen on the desk and stared at him.

"Yes, fine. Don't give me a chance to change my mind." She chuckled and turned back to her screen, tapping manically.

"Thank you then. That would be wonderful. I'll rearrange everything and be on my way."

"In fact, take tomorrow as well. I'll only be in for an hour in the afternoon and I don't need you until Monday." She peered over her glasses with a frown and a questioning eyebrow.

"Good god, sir, I don't think I've ever seen you smile for so long. Are you sure you're okay?" she said with a smirk at him. He walked off toward his private elevator and swiped his card.

"Have a good weekend, Louisa," he called over his shoulder.

"She is rather beautiful, sir. I'm glad to see you happy." He turned as he got in the lift and grinned at his PA's intelligence.

"Yes, Louisa, she is."

On reaching the entrance to the building, he saw Andrews pull up to the kerb and launched down the steps to the car, opening the door before Andrews even got out. *Launching*, really? God, he was acting like he had a schoolboy crush.

"Where to, sir?" Andrews asked.

"Barrington's."

"Yes, sir," he replied as he pulled out into very heavy London traffic.

~

Looking out of the window, he felt himself get a little giddy inside. He couldn't help but chuckle at his own immaturity. No one had ever made him feel nervous before and yet he couldn't wait to see her, to hold her again. Couldn't wait to see that perfect mouth that begged him to kiss her and those wonderfully sinful chocolate eyes that pulled him towards her, daring him to show himself and let her inside. He couldn't wait to get his hands in her silky red hair either and grab a handful to remind her what she wanted. The way she moved with such grace, it would be almost ethereal when she simply embraced herself and finally let go.

Pulling out his phone, he thumbed down to Sarah DeVille.

"Sarah, do you still have that diamond choker?" he said evenly.

"Hello, Alexander. Yes I'm fine, thanks. How are you?" she said in her clipped English accent.

"Do you still have it?" he asked again, little time for pleasantries.

"Yes, I do. Why?" she said tersely.

"Could you box it for me? I'll be there in about thirty minutes by the look of this traffic." He sighed inwardly.

"Is she a brunette or a blonde?" she asked, coldly.

"No, Sarah, this is entirely different. Could you just put it in something... elegant, beautiful? It's not part of a plan this time," he said, feeling protective for some bizarre reason.

"Why, Alexander White, has someone affected you in some way?" She barked out her aristocratic laugh.

He chuckled. He'd known Sarah a while and she knew him very well. He'd always liked her. She was incredibly devilish and sinful enough to fuck. Not to mention she was typically his type - blonde, curvy and tall. If she hadn't been married to Henry, he might have seriously considered her a good distraction and suspected she could have kept him entertained for quite some time, but he did have a few boundaries he wouldn't cross these days. Not many, but a few.

"I'll see you soon, Sarah." He laughed out loud as he ended the call.

He resumed his gaze out of the window and thought of Elizabeth. He really knew nothing about her. He'd been so busy wanting to consume her that he'd forgotten to find out what she liked or what music she listened to. Realisation hit him that he actually wanted to know. He really wanted to know, not because it would allow him to manipulate her, but because he was genuinely interested. Flowers, he wanted to get her some flowers but hadn't got a clue what she would like.

He pressed the button to open the window between himself and Andrews.

"Andrews, what flowers do you suppose a woman like Elizabeth Scott would like?" Andrews raised his eyebrow in the rear-view mirror.

"You're asking me, sir?" he asked incredulously.

"Yes, you're a man of the world and you've seen her a few times. I normally buy a woman the most expensive thing there is but that just doesn't seem to cut it at the moment."

"She seems to be a woman who would prefer some sentiment, sir. Perhaps some wild flowers picked from the top of a mountain. Showing her how far you would go for her favour."

"I never knew you were such a romantic," he replied, chuckling.

"I'm not, sir. I read a lot. But I fear you might have to be to retain such a woman," he replied quietly.

"Mmm, quite."

Alex closed the window between them and felt a stab of fear and panic hit him with force. Andrews was absolutely right, and while he could probably get by on wit, charm and sheer sexual dominance for a while, he knew the inevitable would come. She would expect more and he was unnerved enough already. She could be the one to consume him and hold his idea of a heart if he let her. He could feel it already, the slight loss of control and the confusion building within him. Could he be Alexander White and her lover at the same time? Was it possible to be so dispassionate about his world and yet passionate with someone at the same time? He had so much to show her and so much to keep her away from. He really hadn't prepared himself for this shit.

~

He walked through the door at Barrington's Jewellers and was hit with Sarah's beaming face at once, her long blonde hair hanging over her shoulder and her Scandinavian, deep blue eyes glinting at him. She walked towards him with a green bag swinging from her fingertips and a seductive twinkle in her eye.

"Sarah, as always you look wonderful."

"Wonderful? Alexander, that is not the type of compliment I expect from you. You make me sound like my mother, for God's sake." She smiled, putting her hand on his chest.

He stilled. He'd never found her touch unacceptable before. In fact, he'd rather enjoyed it given the cock twitching that normally ensued. But now, for some reason it felt awkward, wrong somehow. Taking a step back as quietly as he could while continuing to beam at her, he headed to the back room to pay for his purchase. Sarah DeVille was not someone to piss off. She could be very obstructive when she chose to be and she knew far too many people.

"Alexander, are you okay? You look slightly odd," she queried.

"Yes, very well actually. I feel enlightened."

"Really? Well she must be quite a treat for you." She sneered very slightly. Jealous? That wasn't what he expected from her.

"A treat is one way of putting it, I suppose." He laughed and continued to play. "So how are you, Sarah? How's Henry? I haven't seen him for a while." He quirked an eyebrow at her. She huffed and turned to take payment.

"Must you talk about him? You know how he bores me. Really, Alexander, that type of entertainment is beneath you," she said with more venom than he'd heard before.

"He's my friend and your husband. I think it's perfectly normal to talk about him, and really, Sarah, why are you so hard on him? It was only one mistake after all." He tried for empathy, probably failing. He knew damn well there'd been a lot more than one mistake.

She swivelled so fast he barely moved in time, but caught her hand before it slapped his face. Throwing her hand away and moving backward a few steps he glared at her until he saw weakness crease her forehead.

"What the fuck was that? Did you just try to slap me when I'm about to sign off fifty thousand pounds on a bloody necklace?" He felt like exploding at her but calmed himself as he stared at her angry blue eyes and waited.

"Oh, Alexander, for God's sake, when will you see it? Grow up and stop playing your silly games, because I can assure you, he is not. This is not a game to him. It is a rite of passage. He is not your friend. I've been waiting for you to figure it out, thinking you were smart enough, but maybe he really is that good. And he most definitely does not love me," she said quietly so she wouldn't alert any of the other shop girls.

"What are you talking about, Sarah?" he asked in complete amazement.

"I've said enough. You will have to do the rest yourself. I've already pulled all the strings I can to help you. He's suspicious of everything I do because he knows how I feel." She looked to the floor and sighed.

"Sarah, I don't understand what you're saying to me." He felt his anger and irritation at his own fucking incompetence building. What the hell was she talking about?

"Alexander White, you have a war coming and you can't even see it. Whatever or whoever it is that you've been doing, stop it now. You don't have the time for distractions or sentimentality. You need to be exactly the bastard you are if you're to find a way through this. He will not relent until you are crushed. Do you understand me now?" She stared in his eyes with such humility it shook him.

He took a moment to assimilate what she had just said. He felt the venom and bile rise in his throat and swayed slightly. His friend, one of the few he thought he could trust, was trying to ruin him? Why?

Eventually, when he had regained some focus and switched off the allegiance button inside him that he felt for Henry, he turned to Sarah. Why she'd fucking told him this was unfathomable but having directed his fury at a new target, he was at least able to soften himself for her.

"Thank you, Sarah. I don't know why you've told me this, but I am grateful. You've given me time and therefore power," he said, lookeding her over again for deceit. There wasn't any he could see so he conceded the actuality that she was telling the truth, as shit as that might be.

"I've told you this because I hate him, and because I... I don't hate you," she said, a beautiful smile lighting up her face.

Then he saw it. He'd never known before that she felt that way about him. She'd never shown him, but then she never would have. Even if she had done, he wouldn't have accepted it. It still would have just been a game to him because people's feelings had always been part of a bigger plan for him. She stared into his eyes, waiting. For what? A positive response? He simply watched her crumble as he processed the information again. Beautiful as she was, she was not of interest and however her feelings might be, they were not his problem, never fucking had been.

Moving toward her, he wrapped his arms around her in a comforting gesture, hoping to somehow make her feel better, not that he cared that much. He just needed her to think he did a little. And for all his indifference, he disliked these moments. They made him feel guilty - not a feeling he liked very much. She melted into him and inhaled deeply.

"I... I shouldn't have told you that," she stammered. No, she shouldn't, but it could be reasonably useful at some point. Actually, maybe he should fuck her now. That would piss Henry off when he eventually dropped it into conversation.

"You know I don't feel the same way, don't you?" He whispered the question, softly kissing her cheek. She clung on for a moment longer and then stepped backward out of his arms, wiping at her eyes.

"Of course I know. You, Alexander, will need someone better than me to free you of your demons. I expect you may have just found her. But please believe me, you must put her aside for now. You will need everything you have to deal with him." She almost begged to be heard. It appeared she really meant it. What the hell was Henry planning? He nodded and smiled, reaching out a hand to her face. She immediately stepped away and scowled at him.

"Don't. We have talked, but we won't be talking about this again." Her face was impassive and regal again. Gone was the emotion, and the crystalline cold face switched back on. His respect for her tripled.

"Okay, Sarah. Thank you again for your help." He smiled, feeling slightly pissed at himself for some reason. Soul-tearing brown eyes flying into his brain soon made him realise why. Nasty fucking games and damned emotions didn't mix. Fuck. Sarah nodded at him and led him to the door.

"Will we be seeing you at Henry's birthday party?" she asked with a wry smile.

"I think you know the answer to that question, Sarah." He smiled at her one last time then felt his gaze became cold and distant. She noticed and smiled back at his mask in approval.

"We'll see you there then. Oh, and thank you for the invitation to the Addison's Ball. We'd be happy to come." She turned and walked back into the shop, never looking back at him. As cold as fucking ice. He knew he'd never see her so weak again, probably never see her smile as radiantly either. Well, unless he needed something from her and had to pretend.

Staring at the door for a time, he listened to his heart beating slowly. He had some shit to sort out and quickly. Fuck, who was involved in this and who could he trust now? Fuck. Fuck. Anger and resentment filled his thoughts as he stormed to the car and grabbed at his phone.

How the fuck was he going to deal with this now? Much as Sarah's advice was probably spot on, there was no way he was giving up on Elizabeth. He was too involved to let her slip through his fingers because of his own stupidity. Trust and honesty between friends, that's what Henry had asked of him when the big deals started rolling in. What a complete dickhead he had been. How long had Henry been laughing at him and scheming? And what for? Fucking bastard.

No, he would have to find a way to build up the defences around himself for a while longer, to keep her out of this situation until he could give her what she would need from him in the long run. He wouldn't lose her. He simply couldn't.

Taking a deep breath, he thumbed through his phone, found Crantins number and called them. He ordered a bouquet of wild flowers with yellow roses thrown in and said he'd pick them up in ten minutes.

"Andrews, drive to Crantins and then to the park by Scott's. I need a little time to think."

"Is everything okay, sir?" he asked calmly in that normal military voice of his.

"No, Andrews, it's not, but it will be. Sarah's just made me aware of a few things," he replied with malice and irritation in his tone.

"Anything I can do or need to be aware of?" Andrews questioned. He looked at the man and wondered how much he might need from him this time. He'd always been there, never questioned a thing, and Christ, he'd been through some shit. Not that he knew about his past, but he'd certainly seen enough to suspect he wasn't just a businessman. He'd push the man's buttons if and when they were needed and Andrews would do his job swiftly and effectively. He briefly wondered if he'd kill for his employer. That would solve the Henry issue. He clearly had done in his previous employment. Fuck it, maybe he'd just do that himself.

"Probably. I'll let you know when I've worked out what the hell I'm going to do next."

He closed the window and reached into the small bar beside him, then, loading a glass with cognac, drank swiftly so he could pour another one, drank that one too and poured again.

How could his day have gone from light-hearted to abysmal in an hour? Henry was his friend, goddammit. The fucking bastard was trying to demolish everything he had, for what? He had no idea. However, if that was the way the little shit wanted to play then that was fine by him. He'd bring hell down on Henry if that's what he wanted.

This really would be a war to remember.

He needed to find out who was on his side and who wasn't. Tate? Would he be friend or foe? No denying he was a sneaky bastard; that's why Alex paid him so well, but he was also exceptionally intelligent. He would probably wait and see where the balance of power lay and then make a decision as to who his allegiance was with. Well, that wouldn't be good enough. Tate would have to prove his loyalty long before that.

He lifted his phone and called the one true friend he had.

"Alex, dude, what's going on?" Conner drawled.

"Are you high?" he clipped angrily. The man was a cocktail most of the time.

"No, man, just chilling out in the sun."

"What? Where are you?"

"Rome, in this cute little cafe, drinking the best fucking coffee on the planet and watching all the lovely ladies walking by. You should be here man it's-"

Alex cut him off as more frustration fuelled the already loaded rage. "If you're going to use my fucking house, you could at least have asked me. Are you on your own or do you have a skanky brothel with you?" he seethed, loading his glass again and staring out of the window.

"Christ, man, what's up your arse? You sound way too tense. Yes, I'm on my own, you dick, and don't fucking shout at me. You know how it pisses me off," Conner replied, lowering his tone to his trademark irritated level. Alex rolled his eyes, the man had never scared him, no one had.

Rome.

"I need to talk. I'm annoyed. I'll be there in the morning, so if you're going to have a fuck fest, get the place cleaned up and the girls out by ten."

"Jesus, okay. Touchy much?"

"Bye, Conner."

"See you in the morning, Mr. White. I'm sure looking forward to it, you cranky old shit."

Rome, his place of solace, of some sort of peace, and just what he needed to find his way through this new conundrum.

He'd owned the apartments on Via Veneto for a few years. When he'd landed a huge deal, he bought it as a quiet place to just be himself and slow down to some degree. He loved the buzz and the relaxed nature of the Romans, and the historic mood of the city seemed to soothe him in a way that no other place did. His social circle didn't mingle there too much. They chose Monte Carlo or some other such intolerable place to flash themselves around, so he wouldn't have to deal with too much crap, although there was always some. Thank God Conner had the foresight to need a break because it would have been the last thing on his mind, but now just the thought of being there was tempering the storm brewing under his skin.

Thumbing through his phone again, he sent a quick email to Louisa to tell her to ready the jet for him for the morning. She responded within ten minutes to tell him it had all been arranged.

Frowning, he looked at his drink and sighed. He couldn't remember the last time he'd had some time off. That in itself was fucking appalling.

Chapter 15

Elizabeth

Having thrown most of the contents of the Jenkins' salmon mousse into the bin because of its texture, I silently scream at myself. For God's sake, what the hell is wrong with me? Obviously Mr. White is what's wrong with me. Not one phone call since Sunday night, not a damn text, nothing. God, he really is the arsehole I thought he was. I don't know why I thought any different to be honest. If he was going to be so sodding predictable though, why did he have to make me feel so bloody good about myself?

I've got to pull myself together. We have a party to cater in about six hours and I'm not even half way through the meal. Okay, so it's only for ten people but it still needs to be perfect. Thank God I'm not serving tonight. I'd more than likely throw it at someone, I'm that sodding mad. The thought instantly brings strawberry mousse to mind so I snarl at myself and clank some more pots and pans around.

Moving the mixing bowl across to the sink, I stupidly stub my toe on the table leg and drop it on the floor.

"Fuck, fuck, fuck!" I shout at the top of my lungs. *God that felt good*.

Teresa comes running into the kitchen, brandishing a pastry knife and looking panicked. I'm not sure what the hell she thinks she's going to do with it.

"Christ, Beth, what's going on? Are you okay?"

"Fine, I'm just a bloody idiot, that's what I am," I spit out, slumping down onto the floor with my head in my hands.

"What's the matter, honey? Man trouble?" Teresa asks, sympathy radiating across her face. I so want to slap it off her for some unknown reason.

"Oh god, what have I done, Teresa? I've been such a fool." Tears are pricking my eyes and I know I'm about to bawl all over her. "I thought he genuinely liked me."

"Honey, he does like you. Just because he hasn't phoned for a few days, you can't go beating yourself up. He's probably in Korea or some other strange place. Give him a chance. He'll show up soon enough like a white knight. Excuse the pun," she soothes, calmly stroking my hair.

"Why no phone call then? Is it so hard to just message me?" I ask, trying desperately to hold back the tears that are now spilling out.

"Men like Alexander White don't think like that, sweetie. He never has to answer to anyone. I don't doubt he's thinking about you though," she says, smiling at me. What the hell would she know? Nice as she's trying to be, the man's just a bastard who has had his fun.

Sniffing up my tears, I pull myself onto my feet again and raise my chin.

"Well, that isn't good enough for me. If he wants some sort of relationship then he'll have to try a bit sodding harder than that."

"Good for you, girl. That'll show the little fucking shit. I don't care how much money the man's got, he's not entitled to treat you like you're not worthy. Who the fuck does he think he is? Dickhead. And what right-minded man has a friend like Conner anyway?" Belle chimes in from the doorway, smiling. "I mean, honestly, if that's who he's got as a role model, I'm not surprised he's being a knob. Fools, the pair of them. Unfortunately, Conner has a very large cock so I'll have to honour him with my presence again, but it'll definitely be at my request, not his."

We both stare at her from the kitchen counter, mouths gaping, and then burst into fits of hysterics.

"Really? Like massive?" Teresa questions.

"Yes, quite a stretch actually," Belle replies, chuckling.

"Well that's definitely one thing they've got in common," I mutter. Both their eyes shoot to mine.

"Bloody hell, I seriously need to get some action. It's so unfair," Teresa sighs, wiping tears from her eyes.

"Right, what's going down in this bloody kitchen? It looks like a bomb site," Belle says as she brushes some bread crumbs onto the floor with a look of disgust.

"I messed stuff up and I've fallen behind because I can't get that man out of my head. It's infuriating," is my meek reply as I continue chastising myself for my idiotic behaviour.

"Right, well, we better sort it out then." Rolling up her sleeves, she points Teresa toward the sink and grabs some salmon from the side. "Salmon mousse?"

"You're the best. I love you both," I reply with a tear.

"I wouldn't say that, honey. You've not seen the mess I'm going to make of the dessert," Teresa says, giggling as she begins throwing pans about frantically.

~

About two hours later, we're back on track and I'm beaming as I look around the work surfaces. Just about everything is prepared and all that's left is the champagne run. It's plain sailing from here on so I brush off my flour-laden black t-shirt and jeans and go to make a coffee.

Pulling out my hair net, I tie my hair back up into its high ponytail and head for the back room.

"What time is James picking it all up?" Belle asks. "And perhaps you should go out with him again. You know, he was rather lovely to you last time if I remember rightly."

James Bennett is a regular freelance chef who has done work for us since the shop opened. We went out on a date about two months ago, which was really quite nice. I'd been plucking up the courage to ask him out again when the inimitable Mr. White entered my life. Unfortunately, James no longer holds the same interest to me now. Rubbish as that might be. He's good looking, has sandy hair and soft eyes, around six foot, well built and we have so much in common, but since a rather more deviant pair of blue eyes has scorched me, I simply can't think about anyone else.

"He's coming at five thirty and it's three now, so I guess I should get across town and pick up the champagne. And yes, you're right, he is lovely but I'm not sure the timing's right anymore," I reply, trying to deflect her.

"Cool, make me one of those please, honey." She points at my coffee and twirls away.

"And me please," Teresa shouts from the front of the shop.

"Can nobody make coffee apart from me?" I shout sharply, trying to remember the last time one of them actually used the coffee machine.

"No, darling, you know I only pour wine and Teresa is bloody useless with the whole milk and sugar thing. Besides, yours always tastes better," she says, grinning her big sister grin. I snarl my mouth at her and hope I'm making a point. She laughs at me and flounces off.

"Umm, Beth, could you come out here a minute please?" Teresa calls timidly.

"Oh for God's sake, what's gone wrong now?" I practically shout, walking to the front of the shop and seriously considering pulling my hair out.

Shit!

I freeze as I round the corner to see Alex gazing at me from the counter with an enormous bunch of flowers that is just beyond words. I'm speechless, my mouth gaping like a bloody idiot as I take him in for a moment. He's head to toe in a midnight blue suit. Crisp white shirt, no tie. The whole look somehow making those cool blue eyes sparkle like diamonds at me. Either that or it's the black as coal hair highlighting them again. And oh god, the enigmatic smile. Like a ray of sunshine flooding my senses and dominating the small space around him. I can do no more than stare at him, practically panting with lust at the Adonis in front of me.

No, wait a minute. I'm mad at him. The arse didn't phone me for four days. My eyes narrow, the thought reminding me of his actions. *Stand up to him, Beth. Close your bloody mouth, Beth.*

"Hello, Elizabeth," he says with a beautifully raised eyebrow.

"Alex." I close my mouth and try to regain some control over my traitorous body.

"How are you?" he asks, quirking his head to the side and glancing at my neck.

"Fine, thank you. You?" I reply, my best unamused voice in full force. *God, he's beautiful.*

"I'm well, thank you. I wondered if you were free for a coffee." His own eyes narrow slightly at my hostility, a step forward in my direction.

"Did you? I'm afraid I'm a little busy here. Perhaps you should have called." I glare back at him, inwardly sticking my tongue out. He studies me for a second or two and slowly draws his lips up into a clearly very amused smile.

"Ah, I see. You're a little annoyed at me for not calling you, Miss Scott," he says, putting the flowers on the counter and moving closer, all the time walking in that way that means he's coming for me.

"Not at all, Mr. White," I reply, my voice dripping with sarcasm. "Whatever would give you that idea?"

I feel both of the girls retreat into the back room when they sense the storm brewing, Belle chortling to herself as she mumbles a "You go girl."

Alex briefly glances at the girls, taking in their reactions and then resumes his amused face at me.

"It was a mistake and I'm sorry. I've been... preoccupied." He's using his sexiest smile and I feel myself weakening at his reaching hands as he stalks his way to the hatch, cougar like.

"No. You stay that side," I say, pointing at the shop front. I absolutely must not let him touch me.

Oh god, please touch me.

"Elizabeth, let me touch you." He smiles again and keeps moving gracefully with his intent showing in every fibre of his body.

"No, I will not let you touch me because that would mean I forgive you and I don't, not for one minute, until you give me a decent explanation." I narrow my eyes again and set a stern face.

Doing well, Beth. Keep it up.

He lifts the bloody hatch anyway and brings himself within a foot of me, not touching me, just waiting with his hands in his pockets in that casually arrogant pose of his.

"Do you want me to touch you, Elizabeth?" he whispers, leaning in toward my ear. *Oh god, yes.*

"Absolutely not. You don't deserve it." I raise my chin, move a step backwards and look into his eyes again, trying for angry and folding my arms across my chest.

"I don't doubt that for a second, but that doesn't mean you don't want me to put my hands all over you, in you." My eyebrows shoot up at the thought. He keeps up his superior smile and closes the space between us again. I'm now close to being pinned under the bread slicer.

"When you've explained to me why you think it's acceptable to not call me for four days then we'll see what we can do to rectify the no touching thing."

I glare at him, hoping I'm getting my point across when really all I want is for him to kiss me, or slam me against the wall. Either would be good. My eyes narrow at my own pathetic inward response as I glance at his pocketed hands. It would be far too easy to succumb to those fingers, which are currently located very close to his quite delicious cock. Shit.

My eyes fly upward again in an attempt to regain some control.

"What are you doing for the next hour?" he asks, gazing at me.

"I have to go to Richi's to get some champagne for a party tonight," I clip as I remove my apron from my waist and think about trying to squeeze past him. It's probably not going to happen.

"Fantastic. Andrews can do that and we can go for a coffee then," he retorts as if nothing is going on.

"Alex, you can't just waltz in here and sweep me off my feet again. I am pissed at you," I almost shout, a new found attitude fortifying whatever uselessness was occurring.

"Again? Have I swept you off your feet already, Miss Scott?" His humour is not appreciated in the slightest.

"Yes... No. Christ, Alex, you've been an arsehole." I'm seething suddenly, ready to launch a tirade of insults at him for the behaviour. "I will not be played for a bloody fool."

"I appreciate that, and I will do my best to correct that issue, but we *are* going for a coffee and I *will* pick you up and carry you if I must," he states as he looks me up and down, hooded eyes lingering on every part of me. "I like this new feisty you." He winks at me, smirking still.

"You wouldn't dare," I hiss, my eyes widening. *He wouldn't, would he?* "And don't laugh at me. This is not funny."

"Please, you know very well I will and I'll enjoy it very much when you're over my shoulder. It'll give me greater access to your delectable arse." He raises an eyebrow in warning.

I hear Belle and Teresa snigger from the back. *Helpful, ladies, thank you.*

"I have a job to do and I'm going to do it. If you would like to come with me and explain yourself then you're welcome to do so." *Ha! Deal with that one, Mr. White.*

Both his eyebrows rise as he continues with the amused expression. *Arrogant bastard.*

Quick as a flash and with no warning whatsoever, he moves with lightning speed and throws me easily over his shoulder, his arm clamped over my thighs as he walks us out of the serving area and heads toward the door.

"Alex, put me down. You can't just do what you want with me," I scream, struggling in his grasp. I don't move an inch.

Belle and Teresa rush back to the front of the shop to see what's happening, Teresa with her mouth hanging open and Belle grinning like a fool.

"Elizabeth, you're coming for a coffee with me and that is my final word on the matter," he says commandingly, landing a rather painful smack on my backside then laughing to himself.

"Ouch!" I shout. "That hurt."

"Good, perhaps you'll go for the easier option next time then." He chuckles matter-of-factly. "I did ask you nicely." He laughs. Again.

"Girls, help me," I practically scream towards them, not sure what I want them to do or even if I want them to do anything anyway. "Put me down, Alex. I'm not a child."

Belle laughs hysterically and Teresa simply mouths, "White Knight" at me. *Well thank you so much for your support.* I narrow my eyes at them both.

As we get outside, he turns toward the car and addresses Andrews. Lovely, my arse in the chauffeur's face.

"Andrews, could you go to Richi's and pick up Miss Scott's champagne? Call me when you get back," Alex barks. "And have Antony call me if there are any issues."

With that, he turns and starts to stride along the high street towards the crowded streets of the city. I look longingly at Andrews hoping for help in some way. There's none forthcoming. He simply smiles and nods at me as if this is perfectly normal behaviour.

"Jesus, Alex, put me down. You cannot possibly think this is acceptable. It is not acceptable," I whisper, some venom muttered though my lips.

"Ask me nicely," he replies in an unconcerned manner, still continuing at speed.

"What?" Nicely? What the hell?

He stops stock-still in the middle of the pavement, hands clamping tighter around my thighs.

"I'll happily carry you all the way, because the more you struggle, the more I'll spank that arse. That will almost certainly get me absurdly aroused and then I'll have to fuck you in the nearest hotel I can find. I am already thinking about doing it anyway." The hands tighten even more, bruising the back of my legs and making me suck in a breath. "Believe me when I say that you are about to find out exactly what my preferences look and feel like, Elizabeth. So if you want to walk, you'll have to ask me nicely and you'll need to damn well mean it."

Is he asking me to beg for him to put me down when he's the one behaving like a Neanderthal? What on earth is this bizarre twilight zone I've been deposited in, for Christ's sake?

"You are the one being ridiculous here, not me," I quite firmly point out, struggling to get free again. It's not happening any time soon.

The direct smack that comes across my backside is immediate.

"Christ, that really hurt, you arsehole," I yell, feeling the sting radiating across my backside through my jeans. A second lands almost instantaneously, causing me to groan at the continued pain.

"Do not call me an arsehole. Do you want another one or are you going to ask me nicely?" I can sense his eyebrow rising at me. No, I don't want another one.

"Can you put me down, please?" I reply, quietly seething and just waiting until my feet are on the floor to give him the entirety of my venom.

"I'm not feeling the begging in that statement, and I love your begging, Elizabeth," he replies, cheekily rubbing his hand across the sting. "Try harder." I can't help but smile and roll my eyes at him as I stare at the floor and watch people gawping at us. The situation is becoming just a little bit amusing and my arse is feeling all warm and glowy for some strange reason.

"Sir, would you please consider lowering me to the floor so I can look into your eyes?"

That will definitely work for him.

His body instantly tenses for a few seconds and I feel him exhale. His fingers stiffen dramatically on my thighs, a low groan rumbling in his chest as he begins easing his grip just a little.

"Say that again, slower this time," he rasps out huskily. It's working.

"Sir, would you please consider lowering me to the floor so I can look up into those extraordinarily beautiful eyes," I reply slowly, using my sexiest voice and lightly brushing my fingers over his, quite unfairly at the moment, backside.

He releases my legs and slowly lowers me to the floor, exhaling a breath as he grasps the sides of my face in his hands and looks down into my eyes.

"You really are so beautiful, Elizabeth," he says, loosening his hold and just staring at me. "Do you have any idea how you make me feel?" No. Although if it's anything like my feelings at the moment that's got to be good. "I haven't felt anything for so long and... I don't know what is it about you, but you... Fuck it."

His lips meet mine in the most heart-warming kiss I have ever felt. Slow and yet so demanding, his tongue flicking at my mouth as if seeking permission to enter. I respond with my normal vigour and then stop breathing, utterly lost in the moment. Our mouths entwine in a duel of lust and passion, our bodies stuck to each other in a seamless union. His hard, muscular body presses into mine as he pushes me backwards towards a shop window, his hand moving to that place on my throat that lifts me to a different echelon as he grinds himself into me shamelessly.

Oh my God, I'd so follow him to that hotel right now if he pressed me.

Eventually, when we have finished our coupling session in the middle of the high street like a pair of horny teenagers, he takes my hand in his and leads me down the road towards a coffee shop on the corner. Several women smile at me, their hands fanning themselves at our little show. I'm not surprised because my inner slut is still thinking about hotel rooms and Alex's devilish grin at them clearly has the same effect as it does on me. My feelings of anger and humiliation appear to have totally evaporated for some unknown reason and once again he seems to have won me over. I'm really going to have to work on this staying mad at Alex thing.

He inclines his head towards the booth seat in the corner of the coffee shop and goes to the counter to order, seemingly knowing what I'll want. I have no idea how. Perhaps those pesky little fairies are hard at work again.

I sit and look out the window at the passing people going about their everyday lives. A family walks by and the little girl looks at me through the window, her eyes sparkling as she smiles and waves in that oh so cute way that small people do. Her mother rapidly grabs her hand and nods her head at me. I smile back and wave at the little girl with a sigh as I watch her dark curls bobbing away down the road, her mouth giggling as she jumps in puddles.

"Do you like children?"

Alex brings me out of my little moment by placing the tray on the table. I notice the double shot of espresso and what appears to be my regular drink of a vanilla latte.

"How do you know what I like to drink?" I ask suspiciously.

"There are no ends to my super powers, Miss Scott," he states casually. More like super fairies. "Children, do you like them?" I narrow my eyes at his superpowers but can't help glancing at the little girl again as she skips off down the road.

"Yes I do, very much. They have an innocent view of the world. They are what we make them, and I like that they are all about fun and freedom," I reply, smiling wistfully and reaching for my drink.

"They're most definitely what they are made to be," he mutters in a low voice, reaching for his coffee and looking lost in his own thoughts for a minute. Okay, childhood is probably not a place he wants to visit. *Change the subject, Beth.*

"So, what did you want to talk about?" I ask, my best happy voice in place.

"Everything and nothing. I just wanted to see you." He sighs a little. "I missed seeing you."

"Really? Because not phoning me for days is the best way to show me how much you miss me," I return with as much sarcasm as I can muster. He sighs and looks at his espresso, then out toward the street. Oh god, what is he going to say now?

"Elizabeth, I don't know how to do this," he says, a sad lilt coming over his features.

He's going to dump me. Great.

I look down at the table and fiddle with my coffee cup. His hand reaches toward my face instantly and he strokes my cheek with his thumb, tilting my chin upwards.

"Why do you look so sad?" he asks quizzically. "You were happy a moment ago. Did I do this to you?"

Okay, maybe he's not going to dump me, but I have no idea what he's thinking. I sigh and look back at him, trying to process my feelings.

"I look sad because you look sad, Alex. You're a puzzle to me. One minute you are happy, the next you're angry. Then you're sad and then you're playful again." I smile quietly, watching as his frown deepens. "I get lost in how I'm supposed to react to your moods. Couple that with you not phoning me and well... I'm just a bit lost in general," is my rambling reply as twiddle my fingers.

He looks thoughtfully at me for a moment before resuming his stare out of the window. I just continue to stare at his face, searching for anything to tell me how he's feeling, but his face is impassive and distant again, like his business mask has dropped into place and he won't let me see through it.

"Alex, you have to let me in if we're going to go anywhere from this point. I won't be treated like a fool who waits until they're called as and when you decide it's appropriate. I'm sorry. I just can't be in a relationship like that," I state calmly and quietly, leaning back into my seat and waiting for his response. "It's not enough for me."

"I know," he replies, still looking through the glass. "I'm just not sure if I can give you all you'll need though, and I don't want to see you hurt, Elizabeth. You're too wonderful to spoil." He sighs again and brings his eyes back to mine. "The thought of indulging you with my fucked up life is not something I'm feeling very positive about."

"Well, I guess you're going to have to try and convince me to entertain your rather *fucked up life,* as you call it, with an open mind and some faith," I reply.

"Faith?" He rolls the word around as if trying it out for size. "I don't think I've ever relied on faith in my life. It's not a very safe bet, is it?" He smiles as his head drops a little, such a hopeless smile it makes me want to hold him tight and never let go for some reason.

"No, it's not. So this is your chance to walk, Alex. I don't mind. I'm a big girl and we've had a wonderful time and-"

"What?" he snaps incredulously, cutting me off mid-sentence as his eyes shoot to mine. "Please, Elizabeth, no. I won't lose you. I've just fucking found you. I just don't know how to be the man you need. There are things you don't know and I'm just... I'm just fucked up." He lowers his eyes to the coffee table, frowning.

I take a few moments to study his face again and suddenly realise that he's as confused as I am by something. His arrogance and self-belief seem to have vanished in the last few minutes.

"Are you angry with yourself, Alex?" I ask tentatively, because I know I haven't done anything wrong.

"Yes, extremely, amongst other things," he mumbles, more to himself than to me.

"Why?" I ask, genuinely confused.

"Jesus Christ, you just don't get it, do you? All this you see, it's not really me - the pretty face and the money. I'm just empty beneath this. You have no idea what I am." He rakes his hand through his hair and growls, mostly at himself, I think. "You're a ray of light in a very cold and dark world, Elizabeth." He looks uncertain. It's uncharacteristic and slightly odd. "I'm an utter bastard to ask you to be with me simply because you deserve better than this, than me."

I lean back into my seat and stare at him as he exhales. Oh, right. Well that's inspirational, beautiful and desolate, what a great combination. *I so want him.*

"Well, that's good enough for me. If you can see it yourself then there's at least some hope," I reply, smiling and trying to ease the tension, his and mine. Well I hope there's hope anyway.

"Really? You don't think you're wasting your time?"

I honestly have no idea why on earth a man like this could think that of himself? Not only is he an Adonis but he owns a huge company and seems to be everything a woman could want in a man. Who would think he wasn't worthy of a chance? The fact that he happens to be funny, charming and incredibly fantastic in bed are all completely irrelevant, obviously.

"Alex, how could you be a waste of my time? You have my emotions in your hands. My feelings are what lead me, and you may be a lot of things, Mr. White, but I doubt anyone will ever see you as a waste of their time." I continue with the smiling, trying to lighten his mood a little. "Please don't doubt yourself. From what I know, you appear to be a good man and funnily enough, I appear quite like you."

"You have no idea who I am, Elizabeth," he says with a distant gaze, almost as if he's ignoring every word that's left my lips and is still intent on self-loathing or something.

"Then let me know who you are. Show me," I reply, hoping to hell that this isn't the end of something completely wonderful.

He stares at me for a time, not saying anything, his face resuming his expressionless gaze, but I can see barely there flickers of something crossing his eyes. Brows furrowed and releasing as if he's churning his mind through some kind of emotional battle. The corners of his beautiful mouth lift eventually and he smiles a lazy grin at me. Then, tapping his fingers on the table, he crosses his legs, leans back and brushes an imaginary piece of fluff off his jacket.

"I won't be easy, Elizabeth. Do you want to try enough to stay with me through the ride?" he asks, raising that damned eyebrow.

I simply stare and wonder. Can I keep up with him? Maybe he's right. This obscenely gorgeous and wealthy man is about to turn my world upside down and inside out. He's already admitted himself that he'll probably mess it up and that he doesn't want to hurt me. It isn't a great start, is it? I look down to my coffee, partly in despair, and then notice my watch.

"Oh shitting hell, is that the time?" I jump up and bang into the table, knocking over my coffee and literally throwing it towards Alex, again.

"What is it with you and throwing food all over me?" he says, rising and grabbing at a napkin, chuckling to himself. God, why is he always laughing at me?

"I'm so sorry. I have to go. James will be at the shop now and I have to meet him to tell him about the starter and... I'm sorry. I'm rambling again," I mumble to the floor.

Reaching for my hand, he pulls me toward the exit and as we hit the street, his smile floors me.

"I love your rambling. It makes me smile," he says, scanning the street. "Do you realise how rare that is?"

"Not really, no. You seem to do it a lot when you're with me," I reply with valid confusion.

"Exactly my point, Miss Scott. Exactly my point," he counters, continuing his beam.

We pick up the pace and we're back at the shop in no time at all. As always, he opens the door and places his hand on my lower back to usher me through, then spins me round to face him and lifts my chin to meet his gaze.

"Thank you for forgiving me. You don't know what it means to me."

"You're welcome. I may not be so merciful if it happens again though, Mr. White."

He gazes down on me with a slightly bewildered expression and brushes his thumb along my throat, briefly glancing down at my neck and then returning his eyes to mine. And there we stay for minutes, just looking at each other.

Eventually he sighs and looks towards the door.

"I have to go to Rome in the morning for a few days. I promise I'll call you as soon as I land."

"Okay," is all I can manage. Frankly, that one brush of his finger across my throat was enough to begin the leg trembling, let alone the continued stare heating me up all over again.

"Perhaps you could come and stay with me for a few days when I get back and we could catch up on some wasted time?" he asks in that way that assumes it's a foregone conclusion that I will anyway. He's right, to be fair.

"That would be lovely. I'll look forward to it," I reply rather shyly, thinking of all the things that the statement entails. His fingers find my face again as he softly kisses me, and I instantly melt under his touch as always seems to be the case, utterly losing myself in the moment.

All too soon he's backing away and opening the door.

"There you are, Beth. What is it you want me to do with this mousse?" James asks, sauntering into the shop front and looking all chef-like in his whites. Alex's head shoots round, a frown descending at James as he leans in to kiss me on the cheek.

"Hi, James. Just give me a minute, will you? I'll meet you in the back in five," I reply as I continue to look at Alex, trying to weigh up what's happening in his head. He's now moving back towards me possessively, as if staking a claim or something, and looking James over. James, to his credit, remains still and returns the glare with a determined sneer creeping across his normally casual face. It's actually quite impressive for such a laid back guy.

"Okay, do you need any help here?" James asks, continuing with his unmoving presence, seemingly growing a few inches in height and obviously feeling the irritation coming off Alex in waves.

"Why would she need any help, James?" Alex questions in that *try it if you dare* voice of his I remember from the conference room. He raises a brow and moves closer to me, his body is at full height and now growing too. I hadn't realised that men actually grow during battle. It's interesting. My eyes flick to James'. It's like a bloody tennis match.

"Well there's an overbearing arsehole growling all over her. I wasn't sure if she really wanted it or not," James responds, stepping toward him to block his advance. I almost giggle at his retort but Alex responds in kind by moving passed him to get in front of me and growing, again. I look between the two of them for a moment, realising what's happening and where it could be leading.

Okay, calm down, boys.

"The growling arsehole is becoming pissed off with the little moron who's making a fucking stupid mistake," Alex sneers. "Back off now, before I make you."

He's actually looking really quite scary now, dark somehow, as if he's another man or something. My mind reels with all sorts of very confusing sexual imagery at his new persona as I watch James deflate a little at the potential danger in front of him. *Oh, for God's sake.*

Moving toward Alex, I wrap my arm around his waist and attempt to pull him back with a warm smile directed at James. The wall of muscle beneath my hands doesn't move in the slightest.

"No, no help needed, James, thanks. We were just saying goodbye," I say with another smile. "I'll see you in the kitchen in a minute."

I really feel like giggling at the two of them parading like animals but I quickly reign it in. It's probably best not to and given my current core clenching I'm not even sure I could find a giggle if I tried.

James nods and sulkily walks off through the hatch to the kitchen. He can't help but give Alex a scathing look on the way though.

"He wants you," Alex says as he pulls me to him, watching his retreating enemy with narrowed eyes as James disappears around the corner. I smile to myself.

"Does he?" I reply, looking up at him and pressing my lips to his. His body is rigid. It's very appealing and reminds me yet again of all his potentially aggressive preferences. "Well I want you so it really doesn't matter, does it?"

"Of course it fucking matters. The little shit just pissed me off," he almost grunts in response.

"James is a good friend and an excellent chef. You've got nothing to worry about, so stop getting all grumpy," I say, patting his chest. His face softens slightly as he lifts my chin and kisses me again.

"He still wants you. I don't like it." He sneers again quietly, looking over my shoulder.

"Mmm," is my response. It really won't do any harm for him to think there might be some competition. Clearly there isn't any at all, but he doesn't know that.

"I have to go," he mumbles as he strokes my hair and kisses the top of my head, letting me go to walk to the door again. And then he just stands in the doorway with his back to me, one hand in his pocket and the other on the door frame. I look at him for a moment as he hangs his head and shakes it from side to side.

"Alex, are you okay?" I ask quizzically.

Tapping his fingers on the frame, I hear him inhale and then turn back to look at me. His breathing is suddenly heavy and his head's slightly lowered. It makes me take a step forward, considering what's wrong.

"Will you come with me? I want you with me." His eyes blaze as he slowly looks up and shakily blows out a breath.

"What are you talking about now?" I quirk my head to the side and giggle a bit. "I don't understand what you mean."

"To Rome, in the morning. I want you to come with me," he asks again. I hesitate, my mouth opening and closing at the thought. I can't go to Rome at the drop of a hat. I have things to do here, like working for a living.

"Umm, Alex, I don't think I-"

My sister rudely cuts me off as she saunters into the shop from the back door. "Of course she will go. She's always wanted to go to

Rome and the break will do her good. It's not like anything's going on here that we can't deal with." She smiles at me.

"Belle, I can't just go-"

She cuts me off again. "I won't hear another word. You will do as you're told, young lady," she bites as she shakes her finger at me.

"You sound like mum, you know?" I grin stupidly at her.

"Fuck off. I do not." She stares at Alex with venomous eyes.

"One more time, Mr. White, and I swear I will cut your balls off and nail them to the lion enclosure at the zoo. I am not fucking happy with you at all and you'd better be careful." She flicks her gaze between me and him, a smile coming again. "However, she's happy again and I'm sure you have something to do with it so you are just about forgiven."

"Thank you, Belle, and I have been told." He bows his head and takes a step backward in an old-fashioned gesture of politeness and compliance then turns back toward me. She snorts in derision.

"Believe me, you will not charm your way out of the next fuck up you make. I don't give a shit how much you're worth to our business," Belle snarls at him.

His whole demeanour instantly changes for the worse and I watch him quietly fume, as every fibre of his body seems to increase in size again. His eyes deaden in a heartbeat as he narrows them at her and I stare back at her with absolute astonishment. I can't believe she just put that out there. What the hell was she thinking? I turn back to Alex, hoping he'll control himself. Given the argument with James, he's already irritated enough and the thought of explosions between him and Belle is not something I relish. His stance seems charged and there's no hiding the brutal intent showing behind those rather cool looking eyes, as he looks her over in disgust. I'm not entirely sure I'm happy about it and feel myself tense beside him, not knowing where to put myself in the middle of this.

"I'll excuse your extreme outburst just once because of the current situation, and, Belle, you will never lose business from me because of my mistakes, but you may because of your own lack of respect, so be careful with your tone." He stares at her with an unfamiliar expression, something akin to a murderers eyes. "I'm not overly happy about it and will only be pushed so far."

He waits until she lowers her head before nodding. Apparently he's now happy with her acknowledgment of his authority. I'm not sure I'm happy about any of it, but knowing my sister as I do, she's played him beautifully. She's gained everything she needs from the moment and also knew just when to quit while she was ahead. He didn't even notice her sneakery. I seriously need to take some lessons from her.

He turns to me and his eyes soften. "You're lucky I'm so besotted with your sister. She's just too perfect for me to be truly angry at the moment. But please don't think that I can't see you smiling, Belle. You didn't win your little game in the slightest." Oh, he did notice then. "I'll pick you up at five thirty in the morning, Elizabeth. We'll be gone for three days so I'll have you home for Monday afternoon. Is that okay?" He asks, reaching for my hand. I swear my heart flips over in response.

"Yes. That sounds wonderful and I'm very excited," I reply, smiling my brightest smile.

"Good. I'm glad you're coming, too. I'll see you tomorrow."

Kissing my hand, he lets go and winks at me, then whistles his way out of the front door, lifting his phone to his ear. Talk about being swept off my feet... *Rome.* Shit, I haven't got a thing to wear. I swing my eyes to Belle and then back to the door, following his frame as he walks away. Her wardrobe is going to be seriously raided tonight.

"I think I was just put in my place," Belle says casually, not giving a shit.

"Yes, I think you were," I reply as I walk up to the door and peer down the street in search of him, butterflies still fluttering around in my stomach.

"Are you falling in love with him?" she questions softly as she watches me looking at the door. I turn from the window and wander back toward the back room.

"Who wouldn't fall in love with him?" I reply as I shrug into my coat and think about Rome. I'm going to Rome in the morning.

"That's not what I asked."

"I know. What do you want me to say? That I'm head over heels?" She shakes her head and grabs her jacket and bag.

"Be careful, baby sister. That's a whole lot of trouble waiting to be had that you've found for yourself."

"I know," I reply as we walk out the door. It's true. Much as I want him, he's told me himself and I'm not stupid. I can only hope that he means everything that's been leaving his very appealing lips, because I'm so close to being very much in love that it scares the living hell out of me.

Chapter 16

Evelyn Peters

E vie Peters stared up at the mass of glass and steel in front of her. The building was incredibly modern and screamed London at her with all the exuberance of the man inside. She'd moved down to London from Nottingham last week and had somehow managed to get herself settled into her new apartment in record time. Mind you, it helped that the enormous salary she was about to receive every month meant that she could pay for removers and un-packers. She'd found a fantastic apartment close to her new job, which meant she could walk to work each day and she'd been extremely happy to find out that she could afford the rent in such a desirable area all by herself.

However, now was the day she met her new employer and she was so nervous she didn't know what to do with herself. She'd actually been so amused with her own panic, she'd laughed out loud on several occasions. Passers-by must have thought her mad or pissed. Getting dressed this morning had been mayhem in itself. After throwing most of her clothes around the bedroom at least ten times, she'd eventually opted for a grey business suit with black heels. Her long black hair was up in a neat bun and her make-up was minimal chic. She'd grabbed her briefcase holding her beloved laptop and other gadgets, which she couldn't possibly live without, and headed for the nearest coffee shop.

She'd waited her whole career to land a job like this and now she'd done it. She just had to keep it, to impress a certain person so much that he wouldn't be able to run his company without her. What would she have to do to astound him? Play with him, that's what.

Her last job had been easy compared to what this guy was going to expect from her. She was the best software designer she knew and had beaten all of her peers with her intuitive knowledge of the systems she operated, but for some reason she just couldn't rein in her fear of meeting the inimitable Mr. Conner Avery. His genius astounded her. Sure, to the average Joe walking down the street, he would just appear like a fucked up rock star or something, but to her, he was simply the most dazzling mentor she could wish for. There was every chance he might see her as just another designer and that she just wasn't going to allow. He would see Evie Peters. She would make sure of it in any way she needed to achieve her goal.

He hadn't actually employed her directly. She had been head hunted by an agency on behalf of Bluetech and she'd jumped at the chance. Two very dull interviews later, she'd impressed the very incompetent Director of Design, Mr. Ian Lenton enough to get the job. With that came a very handsome salary and benefits package.

It was an absolute priority to show the man himself what she was capable of, and to do that, she needed to get close enough to him to let him see her rather extraordinary ability when her hands were on a keyboard.

She'd mainly worked on banking and security, but she could achieve anything given the correct guidance, and he was the man to give it to her. A blue haired, tattooed rocker who happened to be one of the world's most talented computer nerds, apparently he was also one of the world's most talented womanisers and Lotharios. If his looks were anything to go by, she wasn't a bit surprised. Not that he interested her in that way. He was a little too obvious for her liking. It was simply his mind and respect that she wanted.

If only her mum could meet him, she'd be appalled and scared to death. She remembered her conversation with her about the new position.

"What's your new boss like then, love?" she enquired sweetly.

"He's very experienced and I'm hoping to learn a lot from him, Mum."

"Is he a decent man, though? It's important that he's a decent man. As long as he has good moral instincts, you'll know your job's secure." she replied with a loving crinkle in her eyes.

God, her mum was definitely the sweetest woman in the world. She knew so little about the world of business and all the boring and complicated games that came with it. Evie herself had found that world really quite easy to navigate and had become indifferent to the complexities of negotiating her way through the politics of social interaction in the office. Given her mother and father's inability to function at such a scheming level, she never quite understood her ease with playing the game, as she called it. No one had gotten the better of her for a long time.

She'd been caught out once when first starting her career. Marie Thompson. The bitch had deliberately had her fired for something she hadn't done, just because Evie was better at programming and she'd felt threatened. From that moment on, she'd started learning how to play and hadn't looked back since. She'd become quite the master at it and no one had managed to better her yet. Albeit some new London variety would certainly be an entertainment for a while.

She felt herself giggling to herself at that thought and it seemed to release some of her anxiety.

Looking back up towards the mass of glass, she scanned for the fourteenth floor. That's where she'd be working, in an office of her own as a senior consultant. She would report directly to Mr. Avery on a weekly basis and would be expected to travel to the States regularly.

This was absolutely her dream job and she was so ready for it. So why the bundle of nerves in her stomach?

She glanced again at the vivid blue sign that signalled the entrance to Bluetech and took a deep breath, lifting her chin and smiling as she headed for the foyer.

"Good morning. How may I help you?" the peroxide blonde at reception said to her.

"Hi, my name's Evelyn Peters and I'm starting today on the fourteenth floor. I believe I'm to pick up my key card and paperwork from you," she replied in her most charming voice. *Never a good idea to piss off a receptionist. They hold more power than you think.*

"Oh, Miss Peters, yes. Please come with me. I'll take you to your office. My name is Terry Knowlson," she said with a professional lilt. Evie noticed her lime green nail varnish and instantly knew how to play this one.

As they reached the elevator, she waited for the door to open before she began.

"Terry, my word, where did you get that colour? It is just too fabulous." She indicated towards the revolting colour on her nails.

"Oh, do you like it? It is rather fantastic, isn't it? Harrods have it in on a promo deal. The girlies go there at the weekend to get all the latest new things." *Boring. So very dull and so predictable.*

"Oh, wow, well given that I'm new in town, you'll just have to fill me in on all the places to go and of course all the shopping around here." Evie fluttered her lashes. *Yes you can flirt with women, too. It's really quite effective.*

"Oh yes, you must join us one day and of course we all love a gossip about the main man upstairs, forever getting himself into all sorts of trouble. Mind you, he's so divine. I think we'd allow him anything. You should see some of his friends. My god, they're to die for. There's one, Mr. White, good lord, he's enough to set the heavens alight." She fanned herself for added effect. *Pathetic.*

"Well, I certainly can't wait to see that. He must be quite something," she replied with feigned excitement. *Really, most of them are arrogant arseholes with the accumulated brain cells of a gnat.*

"Yes, he's quite beautiful, and I dare say quite the handful if you know what I mean? Oh, we're here."

She stepped off the elevator and headed down the hall. Opening the door on the right, she ushered Evie into the room.

"This is all yours," Terry said, waving her hand around the vast space.

"Thank you for bringing me up here. It was very kind of you. Please don't let me hold you up. I'll be fine. I know you are probably very busy," Evie said, smiling her winning smile.

"Don't be silly. I'll grab you a coffee and then I'll disappear. Oh, by the way, Mr. Avery won't be here until next Tuesday. He's gone to Rome on business, but I was told to tell you to access his files for any information you might need. You have level six clearance, which you can get to via the server. Your code's in the card so you can get into most of his shared access. He also gave me that box in the corner for you to familiarise yourself with." She pointed toward the huge glass window and indicated the box sitting below it.

"Right, brilliant. You've been such a help, Terry. It's so nice to meet someone interesting on my first day." *Dumb arse blonde.*

"You are very welcome, Evelyn. It's nice to have a kindred spirit in the building. Most of the women here are quite corporate or geeky," she whispered and giggled.

"Well I'm grateful all the same." Evie giggled in return. *That's why I earn the money, honey. I'm corporate, you bloody idiot.*

"Right, so I'll drop off that coffee and then be on my way. You look like a milk and no sugar type of girl? Oh, and he's set a meeting for Tuesday morning at ten with you in his office. So that gives you a few days to get ready for him," she said, snorting with laughter.

"Okay. Is he terribly scary? I've heard all sorts of things," Evie asked, inquisitive as to her answer.

"Mr. Avery? No, just dreamy. A girl could lose herself in that body, for several days I might add." She fanned herself again. "He is interesting, though, never says what you expect. That's what I mean by preparing yourself." *Oh, perhaps not as dumb as I thought then.* "Oh, sorry. Listen to me waffling on. If you get lost or need anything, give me a buzz." She swept out the door in a flurry of what smelt like Chanel.

Evie moved to her new desk and sat down, looking around the office. Her office. Her really very large office. She pictured herself decorating it and moving in some plants. What on earth was she thinking about? She didn't have time for delicacies, and she needed to know more. She moved across the office and picked up the box. Dragging it back to the desk, she started to ruffle through the varying documents and folders. Boring. Easy. Irrelevant. Tedious. God, it was just more of the same shit in a different location. That was not the reason she came to this company. Might as well start as she meant to go on.

"Here's your coffee, honey." Teresa swanned in and plonked a rather disgusting looking mug of something in front of her.

"Oh thanks, Teresa, you're such a star." *Not.*

"Can I do anything else for you?" *Yes, fuck off.*

"No, thank you. You have been very helpful. Perhaps we can catch up on some gossip later though."

"Okay, hun. See you later." *Bye!*

She grabbed her laptop and logged on, simultaneously logging onto the company computer in front of her. After several minutes of familiarising herself with the internal server and systems, she drew up Mr. Avery's private email - naughty, but necessary for what she was about to do.

Logging back into her own system, she found the files and encrypted drives she was after and attached them to an email to him. This would either start her new career with a bang or piss him right off. She didn't care which; she just needed to make an impact, and when he received this email, if he could get into it, she would definitely make an impact.

Subject: Brown box of Dreary.
Attach: file xcc1143

Mr Avery,

Thank you for the position at your company. I hope to be a worthwhile investment for you.
Please see the attached, if you can.
As and when you have understood the unlimited talent you have just hired, please feel free to call me to discuss any potential projects you might have for me.

Kind Regards

Evelyn Peters
Senior Consultant
BLUETECH INC.

She hit send before she chickened out.

Right, well, she'd be fired or elevated to a very senior level by the start of next week. That was some of her very best work and she'd just given it to him with the hope that he liked what he saw. He could also just poach it for himself, but that was almost expected of a man with no moral compass at all. Clever? Yes, but a decent man? More than likely not.

She busied herself for the next three hours with the box of very dreary shit. Unexciting was not the word for it, but she at least had to ensure she'd completed it before she met with him. She ploughed through the monotonous crap until she'd finally had enough. It was time to go walkabout for a while and get familiar with the new building. She also needed a proper cup of coffee. She hoped that didn't mean leaving the building, but if it did, so be it. Just as she was leaving the office, she heard the bleep of her personal email and wandered back to the screen.

Opening the email, she gasped.

Subject: Imaginative

Miss Peters,

Shows promise.
Lacking in structure, but not too bad at all.
I look forward to our meeting on Tuesday, and don't worry, I have plenty of other boxes to keep you entertained.

Kind Regards

Conner Avery.

She frowned and blew out her breath. Well, she hadn't been fired.

But Christ, how on earth had he managed do that in under three hours while in business meetings? She'd seriously underestimated his talent. Maybe she'd be working a little harder than she originally thought.

Chapter 17

Elizabeth

• Are you ready for me?

The incoming text at stupid o'clock makes me jump.
Am I? God, I don't know. I've been awake most of the night and while I'm extremely excited, I'm also very nervous. It's also ten past five in the bloody morning. What the hell time of day is that to go anywhere?

• I think so.

I reply with fumbling fingers. *God, I hope so.*

Belle helped me pack last night and we downed at least three bottles of wine while we chatted about various Rome related topics and other things. Teresa also popped by, and before we knew it, we were all pissed as farts and cackling like a bunch of old ladies. I should have got a better night's sleep. I know this now, but I was so wound up by going away with him that I just couldn't settle. I don't even know a flight number that I can give to Belle, and I suddenly realise I don't know this man at all. I'm being completely swept off my feet and away from everything I know, allowing him to control everything around us. But no matter how much I try to tell myself I am being foolhardy, there's just something about him that makes me feel incredibly safe. Not in the emotional way maybe, but certainly in the physical sense. He will have the whole trip planned to within an inch of its life and I'm sure if it isn't precisely the way he wants it, someone will be swiftly fired. Actually, I'm sure the ever-efficient Louisa Trembell will have organised the whole adventure, probably in twenty minutes. It would be good to know what she looks like at some point.

My bags are packed and I've opted for my usual comfy attire, but have been persuaded by my ever present friend to "jazz myself up a bit," so I've applied more make-up than normal. I've also donned skinny black jeans and a thin, burgundy, cashmere jumper of Belle's. Actually, most of what has been packed into my suitcase is Belle's. I seriously need a shopping trip if I'm going to be spending any more time with the man.

So now I stand here by the door, staring at the ridiculously high patent brown heels of Belle's lying next to my comfy red Converse. Style or comfort? Fuck it. I will not have my entire world upside down because of him. It's bad enough that I couldn't decide on whether he'd like my belly button charm or not, so had spent at least fifteen minutes faffing around with different styles until I just went with my favourite and hoped it was okay. I'm still not sure he'll be into it but given he's covered his back in a tattoo, he can hardly be against it, can he? Maybe he will be. Who knows? Oh, sod it. He wants me, he's getting me.

I pack the heels into my bag and reach for my old, faithful converse. Lacing them up, I reach for my cropped brown leather jacket and pull my hair over the collar. I find myself gazing at my reflection in the hall mirror and tipping up my chin, really noticing my face for the first time in a while. It appears there's a confidence in my brown eyes that seems to be telling my inner self to grab life by the neck and shake the hell out of it.

"Alex," I murmur to myself. "Seems you do this to me."

Checking my watch again, I pull in a deep breath and grab the last of my coffee. God, I could do with a double shot of vanilla Latte right now, but there's no time for coffee shops. He'll be here in minutes and I can feel myself starting to shake a little. For once I wish it was the alcohol still in my bloodstream causing the shakes. It's not.

I let out that breath and head for the door, dragging my case behind me to meet him in the lobby, and wishing I could gain just a bit more of that Alex self-belief that he's so good at giving to me. Why does he make me so bloody nervous all the time? It's ridiculous, and quite unnerving. The thought makes me pop an extra strong mint into my mouth and check for my keys and passport again, not wanting to seem stupid when he gets here. They're both there in my pocket, just as they were ten minutes ago. I open the door, ready for my adventure and not in the slightest ready at all.

"Good morning, Miss Scott," he rasps huskily.

I yelp out loud, not expecting him to be leaning casually against the opposite wall from my doorway. He looks glorious with his legs and arms casually crossed, the sexiest smile creeping over his face as he watches me. I can feel my cheeks blush as my legs begin that ridiculous buckling beneath me. Good god, he is by far the most rewarding vision a girl could want in the early hours of the morning.

His graceful hand reaches toward my face and I shudder at the expectation of his touch.

"Are you so nervous of me that you always forget to breathe?" he asks quietly.

"Mostly, yes," I reply, because I just can't function quickly enough to lie.

"Well, we'll have to do something about that. I can't have you keeling over on me before we get the chance to play properly. I've got plans for you this weekend and you'll need all the breath you have for my dishonourable intentions." He rubs his thumb across my open mouth and then lifts my hand towards his mouth. Kissing it and then opening my palm and kissing the inside, he puts it to the side of his face and leans his cheek into it. "Don't feel uneasy around me, Elizabeth. Believe me, you're the one who has the upper hand here, not me. Although I will expect some give on your part for what I have in mind." Christ, I'm still not breathing. Does he have to be so beautiful? And what exactly does he have in mind?

"Right," is all I can manage because I'm seriously too busy trying to keep myself upright at the thoughts floating around my head. I really need to work on my responses.

He chuckles at me and moves to grab my suitcase.

"Come on, let's get to Rome. We have a lot to do and not much time to do it in," he says, taking my hand in his.

Well, yes, quite.

~

The journey is swift, and before I know it we're pulling through a set of steel gates. It's clearly not Heathrow. I have no idea where the hell we are.

"Where are we?" I ask, still sipping the vanilla latte that was miraculously waiting for me in the car.

"The airport," he replies quizzically, lifting that eyebrow.

"Really? Where's the terminal and everything else then?" I ask, genuinely confused.

"Oh, I see what you mean. That is a bit problematic, isn't it?" He laughs, a boyish grin lighting up his face.

"What are you laughing at now?" I lower my head to the floor and blush. "You're forever laughing at me." He tips my head to his and growls.

"Head up, always, unless I say otherwise." He turns my face toward the window and kisses my cheek. "God, you make me smile, Elizabeth. There is the terminal and everything else." He points out toward the tarmac and I stare in awe at the beautifully sleek grey jet that is slowly lowering its steps. Holy crap. He owns a plane? Of course he owns a plane, you bloody idiot. Why did I not realise this? How much bloody money has the man got?

"Oh God, I never thought you'd own a plane. Umm... Well done, you," I exclaim rather idiotically.

"I'll take that as a compliment. Do you like it?" he asks casually. I can feel his eyes on me as I continue to gawp at a tall, thin man in uniform walking down the steps.

"Yes, it's wonderful, beautiful. Umm, was it expensive?" I can't stop myself rambling. Of course it was expensive. I am such a basket case. Could I look any more ridiculous?

He chuckles. "Yes, it was rather costly," he replies, opening his door.

I reach for the handle but the door is opened for me and Andrews offers his hand. Before I can take it, though, Alex appears at his side, clasps on and escorts me to the plane with his eyes pinned in front of him.

"Good morning, sir," the uniformed man says, looking toward me and smiling.

"Good morning, Phillip. Elizabeth, this is Phillip Cramer. He is our pilot," Alex says, putting his arm around my waist.

"Good Morning, Mr. Cramer. I trust you know what you're doing with this rather impressive plane and that I'm in safe hands?" I try for nonchalant and chic to regain some sort of composure. Maybe it's working. Who knows?

"Yes, Miss Scott, and please call me Phillip." He smirks and offers his hand to help me up the stairs.

I feel Alex bristle beside me and turn, quirking an eyebrow at him. His demeanour is still cool but his eyes much less so. As I reach to grab onto Phillips' hand, Alex puts his in the way and lifts my hand from Phillip's into his own, clasping on again rather possessively.

"I'll help Miss Scott, Phillip. Please get ready to take off. Who is stewarding this morning?" he almost sneers. *What is his problem all of a sudden?*

"Of course, sir. Tara is on board already." He smiles meekly and walks up the stairs in front of us.

"What was all that about?" I ask as we climb.

"All what about?" Alex replies, his calm eyes back again.

"Your attitude change," I say in disbelief. Does he think I didn't notice? "Did he do something wrong?"

"You noticed that?" he asks in surprise.

"Of course. Your hackles were up as if you were about to launch at him, somewhat like your reaction to James yesterday. I could hardly ignore it. I doubt Phillip did either."

"Very astute, Miss Scott. I'll have to work harder at hiding my feelings from you. And Phillip will be well aware that he wasn't meant to ignore it. James will wait for another time." He smiles and then frowns a little.

"What have your feelings got to do with it?" I ask, genuinely bemused as we climb. He stops and turns my face to his.

"Everything, Elizabeth. He touched you. I didn't like it. Nobody touches something that belongs to me unless they're given permission to do so." He gazes at me, waiting for a reaction.

It probably isn't the time to go off on a tirade about me being personal property, and besides, I find myself actually enjoying the statement he's made. It makes me feel protected and cherished, somewhat bizarrely. Still, I narrow my eyes slightly.

"Mmm... But please don't hide your feelings. Interestingly you don't seem to be very good at hiding them anyway." I smile and brush my hand across his jaw. "From me, at least."

We stand for a minute and simply gaze at each other in the wind as I watch all sorts of emotions cross his beautiful face.

"You will be the death of me. I'm sure of it," he eventually says, turning and pulling me along behind him into the plane.

An incredibly beautiful blonde woman waits at the entrance hatch as we enter the plane. She's nearly as tall as Alex with a stewardess uniform on that hugs her curves very effectively. The smile she's wearing as she looks at him is sheer sexual magnetism. She's a predator who has most definitely been there before. Shit. Her eyes caress every inch of his body languidly, no intention of even glancing at me, as if such an effort is beneath her for some reason. Utter bitch is written all over her, unfortunately wonderful, face. I hate her immediately.

I look at Alex from beneath my lashes, quietly from the side, trying to gauge his reaction. His face is surprisingly impassive, almost bored.

"Good morning, sir. It's nice to see you again. I'm so sorry I wasn't able to make the last flight. I was in America with Mr. Avery," she says with a husky tone as she licks her lips. Really? She was with Conner. Probably slept with him as well then. Slut.

"No Problem, Tara. This is my girlfriend, Miss Scott. Please do your job efficiently today and give us some space so we can indulge ourselves fully," he replies rather harshly, squeezing my hand as he leads us through. *Go, Alex.*

I can't help the giggle that escapes my lips as I look toward her and her beautiful face turns slightly sour, and girlfriend? That's an interesting statement.

"Yes, of course, sir. Good morning, Miss Scott," she says through gritted teeth.

"Hello, Tara." I seriously can't manage anything else through my girly giggling. "Wow. This is spectacular," I exclaim, taking a look around the exquisite interior of the plane.

"This was my first real toy. I lavished every expense on her. I like to fly in comfort and it just makes the whole experience more pleasurable, don't you think?" he says with his hands in his pockets, waiting for my reply.

"I'm sure it does. I'll tell you the truth when we reach Rome," I eventually reply, still gazing at the luxury that dominates every inch of the space.

"Let's get you strapped in," he says, chuckling and smiling rather adorably at me.

He leads me toward two low leather chairs in the middle of the plane next to the windows, which face each other. A table sits between them, and as he pulls my coat from me and brushes his hand across my collarbone, instant hot prickles creep up my neck. I'm practically panting for him to kiss me but his eyes hold mine for a moment before he promptly pushes me backwards so I land rather inelegantly on the chair.

"Not yet. Soon, but not yet. I'm making myself wait, Elizabeth," he whispers in my ear, reaching for the strap around my waist. "You've no idea how hard it's been not to manhandle you already."

He stands and glances back at the buckle, nodding to himself before moving to the other chair and strapping himself in. I still stare at him with blushed cheeks and lust filled eyes, my breathing heavy as the air of sexual tension engulfs the cabin space around us. He simply looks across at me with his calculated mask on and presses the fingers of his clasped hands to his lips.

Eventually his look moves towards my mouth and he licks his lips. I immediately see the change of colour in his eyes. They're darker and far more intense, but that face remains oh so calm and expressionless. How can he think something and yet show so little?

Tara sweeps in and completely ruins our moment, so of course I drop my gaze to the floor.

"Are you ready, sir?" she asks in a breathy voice, still looking so very beautiful with her long legs and her fuck me eyes.

"Just a minute, Tara," he replies, not an inch of his body moving. "Elizabeth," he growls. I lift my head slowly to see the same fire in his eyes. Nothing has changed since she entered the cabin and thankfully his face is still completely focused on me. "Are you ready?"

I gaze deeply into his eyes and see only passion and desire for me, rather bizarrely. His question is acutely loaded. I know he is asking me to trust him and allow myself to gain from his strength and confidence. I need to grow a pair or something. I will not let the bitch intimidate me.

"Yes, I am," I say, looking toward her and frowning slightly, my eyes travelling to her face to study her reaction to my stare.

Remarkably, she withers away slightly and her eyes look toward the floor. I return my gaze to Alex and smile as he nods at me and winks.

"Then we're ready, Tara. Please tell Phillip to get going. Get us some champagne when we're up," he states, never removing his eyes from mine.

"Yes, sir," she replies, leaving the cabin with a very definite huff in her voice.

"You, Elizabeth. I'm only interested in you. You are the one who has my attention and all of it for once in my life," he says with an amused lift of his brow, as if he's just realised this himself. "If only you knew how rare that was."

"Okay," I reply rather inarticulately, a little overwhelmed by his statement and still somewhat distracted by my own libido.

"Why would you feel nervous around her? She's nothing compared to you," he questions as he tilts his head to the side and looks genuinely puzzled.

"Because she's beautiful, and because you've slept with her," I respond instantly, and Lord knows where I found the balls to say that. "It's intimidating."

He stares at me for a moment with no change to his expression whatsoever. I'm not sure if I'm expecting him to be remorseful or apologetic for his actions, but I am pretty sure I won't be getting either response.

"I can assure you I haven't slept with her. Fucked her, yes. Most of the world probably has, but that doesn't mean she's of any interest to me," he states casually. "And there is nothing beautiful about her at all."

How on earth can he be so indifferent about this? I close my gaping mouth at his harsh words and fold my arms. Christ, is the man completely devoid of emotion?

"You don't need to be so crude about it. She is still actually on the plane," I say nervously, looking around for her. He doesn't flinch, just keeps staring at me.

"I'm sure she knows full well what I think of her. If she doesn't then more fool her. I'm more interested in you, and if me telling you the truth helps you to understand how important you are then I'm happy to voice my opinion." His hand reaches out to mine and he brushes his fingers over it gently. "You should perhaps learn to toughen up to my attitude, Miss Scott."

I gaze up at him. "You should perhaps learn to be a little more compassionate, Mr. White. I doubt Tara likes your opinion of her and I'm not sure I do either," I reply quietly.

"Well then she shouldn't have opened her legs so readily, should she?" he responds as he draws his hand away from me and frowns a little. "And I never implied I was faultless, Elizabeth - far from it in fact."

My thoughts instantly fly to visions of our first night together as I move my eyes away from his gaze and look out of the window. I was that easy. Our first night in each other's company and I opened my legs in various different ways for him. Okay, it was the first time I ever did that sort of thing, but fundamentally I was no different than Tara. Maybe she thought she was important to him, too. Perhaps he said the same sexy words of endearment to her in their moments of passion.

I scrunch up my nose in irritation and look back across at him.

"It appears you have no respect for women who have sex with you on a first date," I say, hoping to God he finds an answer that will make me feel a little better somehow. He relaxes back into his seat, crosses one leg over the other and smirks at me. It's that laughing thing he does and my annoyance compounds further.

"I have the utmost respect for any woman who has sex with me on a *first date,* Elizabeth. But I particularly admire the date that has the courage to stay the night in my bed after I've told them some of the rather unspeakable requirements of my life - the same bed that no other woman has ever been in, as you well know," he replies with another twitch of his delicious lips. "You see, *first dates* are not something I'm very familiar with and because of that, such a thing commands a great deal of my respect. I'm afraid simply fucking someone is, by its own definition, just that - simple - and nothing that is simple or effortless requires any of my respect at all."

Oh, well that told me. My smirk knows no bounds at his acknowledgement of my importance. Maybe I do need to toughen up a bit. I still don't like his reaction to Tara, but I suppose he's right in a roundabout sort of way. Maybe that's the way all men think but most just never openly admit it. My eyes narrow at the now devilish smile

229

that's currently being thrown my way as he runs his damn tongue over his lips and waits for my reply. No, I'm pretty sure this man is a law unto himself.

The plane takes off without incident and Alex is walking around discussing something with someone on phone. I sip at the champagne that the rather pissed off Tara served, and relish in thoughts of Italy. The soft clouds rolling past the window seem endless and it reminds me of Belle and I cloud gazing when we were young, lying on our backs in the fields behind our house and making shapes out of the white fluffy billows of cotton wool floating around the sky. I grin at my own dreamy thoughts and relax back into the luxurious chair, still not quite believing I'm here.

"What are you smiling at? I love that smile. It comforts me." He looks to the floor and for a second, I think I see shyness cross his face, and then it's gone.

"Mr. White, are you looking at the floor?" I tease. I can't help it. It just seems so strange to see his domineering presence looking very slightly humble, if only for a second.

"Never, Miss Scott," he replies, smiling broadly as he turns toward a cabinet and pulls out a large green bag. He walks back towards the table and presses a small button on the side of it while looking at his phone. The table starts to turn over and I watch as it slowly reveals a chessboard.

"I thought we'd play a game," he says, smirking at me and lining up the pieces on the board, phone finally dismissed into his pocket.

"You don't know if I can play or not," I reply casually. *Oh thank you, Daddy.*

"I think you're trying to deceive me, Miss Scott. Your stance changed considerably when you approached the board at home. I think you're quite the player really. Regardless, we shall soon find out," he muses. "Besides, I'm changing the rules a little if you're open to suggestion?"

"Really, how?" I lift my brows at him.

"Well, when you gain advantage, you get whatever you want from me and when I gain advantage, the same applies for you," he remarks, still lining up the board and then pouring us more champagne. "Or we could just play safe. It's up to you." He smirks again as he sits down.

I can't help looking at his masculine jaw and mouth as he licks his rather erotic lips and taps his fingers rhythmically. It's like a sexual tempo being stirred up in my body as he somehow demands that I listen to his repeated cadence. My eyes draw to his hand as my heart rate increases again.

"Do you want to play safe, Alex?" I reply as sexily as I can muster because this I might have a chance of winning.

"Now I know you're teasing me, naughty girl. Do you like to attack or defend?" he asks as he stops his fingers abruptly. I shake my head at my mind fog and try to concentrate on the black and white squares. I'm damned sure he'll try to manipulate this situation to suit himself in some way.

Be prepared, Beth. Control yourself, for God's sake.

"I don't know what you mean. I've only played a little." I smile breezily.

"Well, I'll let you go first then, but I don't believe you for a moment. No one has such confidence around a board unless they can actually play. I expect a punishment will be in order when you've shown me your dishonesty." Excuse me? What the hell was that statement about?

We play for at least fifteen minutes before I make a deliberate mistake. I can't let him see my full game or he will probably beat me. I haven't played for years but it seems to be coming back to me very quickly. Worryingly, though, he does seem rather good. Why did I think otherwise?

"Really, Elizabeth, if you wanted to take your top off, you should have just asked," he says, deadpan.

"What?" I reply in confusion as my eyes shoot to his.

"You've just given me advantage, which I know you're well aware of, so off with the top. That's what I want for gaining my first lead." He inclines his head as if challenging me. Bastard.

"I'm not doing that in here. Anyone could walk in," I yelp, incredulously.

"You agreed to the change of rules didn't you? So off it comes. I want to see your beautiful tits while I play. You never know, the distraction might prove useful for you," he says with another one of those rather irritating, in the moment smirks.

"I can't believe you're making me do this," I stammer angrily, pulling at my top and then sitting there awkwardly. Thank God for a decent bra.

"Perfect," he says haughtily, staring at my now heaving chest. "Shall we carry on? And where exactly did that come from?" he asks with a smart arsed smile creeping over his face as he points to my belly button pendant - my one and only rebellious streak as a teenager, one I particularly love, and I so knew he'd bring it up. Why the hell I didn't wear it the first night, I do not know. I look down at the diamonds dangling from the charm.

"Do you have a problem with it?"

"No, not at all. It's lovely and will definitely be of use to me." My eyes narrow as I fiddle with said charm and wonder why the hell it could be useful. "Now, are you ready?"

Right, you bastard. Game on.

I force the play as best I can, but he's just too quick. He must be at least five moves ahead because I'm playing at three to four and he's slaughtering me. Time after time he defends and moves pieces to ensure his victory and another item of clothing is removed, along with any thought of winning. He counters everything I have and eventually I am left in just my bra and panties, while he sits there looking ravishingly exquisite in his blue shirt and black jeans, not an item of clothing having been removed from his body, much to my irritation. Interestingly though, I am no longer feeling awkward and frankly, the thought of being near naked around him is just too much. His constant glances at my body have made me hyper aware of the lust that is radiating through his pores and his darkening eyes have me quaking at the knees for him to finish the game or me. Either will be absolutely fine. As long as it ends up with him on me, I couldn't care less.

Then, finally, I see him deliberately reach for the wrong piece. He's far too good to have made that sort of mistake. He slowly looks up into my eyes and breathes out heavily.

"You have advantage, Elizabeth. What do you want?"

Sex oozes out of his ever-stiffening muscles, his breathing elevated and those blue heated eyes begging me to give everything to him.

"You," I reply without thinking, desperate for his touch.

"Then you shall have me." He reaches towards his king and topples it over.

"I have been beaten - utterly and without regret," he whispers softly, gazing towards me with some emotion crossing his face I haven't seen before. "Up you get." He stands and holds his hand out for me.

Lacing his fingers with mine, he guides me to the back of the plane towards a small corridor and then opens a door. He pulls me in and then kicks the door closed behind him, leaving me standing in the middle of a bedroom as he backs away and let's go of my hand.

"Elizabeth, I want you to do something for me. Do you trust me enough to do what I say?"

"Yes," I reply without hesitation. It's the most bizarre answer I could have given, bearing in mind that I hardly know the man, but for some reason I do trust him.

"Good, you should. Don't ever think I'll give you more than you can take. Do you understand me?" I nod in response as I scan the room a little nervously. "Never nod as an answer. Speak, unless you can't. We'll talk about hand gestures later. I have no intention of gagging you yet." He gazes at me for a minute and then moves to the side of the bed. "Do you understand?" *Gagging, really?*

"Yes." I smile and look towards him.

"Okay, go to that corner of the room," he says, pointing towards an empty corner as he pulls a length of rope from the bedside draw and removes his shirt. I back into the corner while he ambles his way towards me. God, he's breath-taking. I'm drooling watching his broad shoulders and rippling lean muscles moving around the space. His hands twitch around the rope as he gets closer. I feel my thighs clench and my heart rate quicken as the familiar stirring begins in my groin. Just looking at him is enough to make me come. He'll only have to touch me once and I'll probably explode.

"Have you been tied up before?" he asks as he twirls the rope around his fingers expertly, threading it and showing me just how familiar he is with it. I suddenly feel completely out of my comfort zone.

"No, never." I look gingerly toward the rope in his hands as he holds it out to me.

"Don't fight it or struggle against it. You'll cause yourself pain, and while I want you bound, I don't want you broken. Well, not yet anyway."

"Okay."

Looking directly at me, he grabs hold of something above my head and pulls down a long stainless steel pole that ends at his feet. Stamping on the floor by the base of it, a bolt miraculously slots down into place and holds the pole secure.

"I'm going to tie you to this by your hands and then fuck you in any way I please." My mouth opens to say something. He cuts me off before I get a chance. "At some point, your knees will give way, which will leave you hanging. That's exactly what I want from you. I want to see you stretched out for me with your head lowered either in exhaustion or respect. I really don't give a fuck which one." He stares at me, probably waiting for an answer, or maybe permission. I'm really not sure which.

I close my mouth and think, my fingers travelling along the pole as I reach out for the rope. It's quite soft for rope. I was expecting something courser. The thought of being restrained hasn't ever appealed before but with him, I'm so aroused that I'll probably do anything.

"Okay," I eventually reply, frowning at myself. I'm not even sure why I'm agreeing to any of this.

"Put your hands above your head," he says firmly.

I comply and he reaches above me. The smell of him so close to me as he brushes his body against mine is almost my undoing. His familiar spicy scent and the rasp of denim on my skin, as he pulls and tugs gently, is so enthralling that I forget to breathe out after each intake. I move my hands and wrists, testing my restraints. They don't move in the slightest and I look up to notice the rope around them has been threaded into some sort of thick cuff around my whole wrist. The look of it suddenly makes me feel a little panicky. It comes out of nowhere and I look to his eyes for some sort of reassurance. Those darkened eyes are instantly on mine, focusing my mind again.

"Shh, baby. Look at me. Keep your eyes on me," he says, stroking the side of my face soothingly. "You'll enjoy this but you have to let go and feel only me." I nuzzle in and nod my head at him again, feeling secure somehow.

He starts at my neck, smoothing his hands down both sides and putting some pressure on my collar bone with the pads of his thumbs, then kisses me softly, teasing my mouth open with his tongue and swirling it inside. Licking and biting at my lips, he pulls my body flush to his. I can feel the hard length of him pressing against my stomach but the helpless feeling of being tied is distracting me and I can't stop myself trying to struggle again.

His head stills as he removes his mouth from my neck.

"Elizabeth, stop struggling. I won't tell you again. I have other ways to teach you obedience if you'd prefer." His tone is stern, almost angry. I stop instantly because I have no idea where this version of him is leading. "Better."

His head resumes its course downwards towards my breasts, fingers moving my bra cups out of the way as he moulds his hand around one, kneading it roughly. And then lips travel, sucking it into his mouth and then biting gently at it. His right hand takes a leisurely path down my body as he transfers his mouth to the other breast and continues with his biting and licking. God, I can feel it building already. Heat is flooding towards my sex and I desperately want his touch down there, but his hand skates loosely over the material of my panties not giving me any pressure. I gasp at the impact of him being so close, arching into him to gain more weight from his hands, and then he claws his hand roughly over my thigh, back towards that aching nub.

"Please..." *God, touch me before I explode.*

He moves toward my sex again and this time presses harder on the material, cupping me while slowly moving his hand backwards and forwards.

"Oh god, yes," I moan loudly. He lifts his head and stands back slightly, watching me intently, still rubbing in an achingly slow rhythm. I can hear my own panting in my head as if I'm watching from a different angle, which seems to lull me to a strange place of softness. Images of those fluffy clouds fly through my mind as his hand continues and my legs wobble beneath me.

"Tell me, Elizabeth. Ask for want you want." His dark eyes sear into mine while his cool stance remains intact. If I could speak, I'd probably scream, but all I can do is gasp for air and hope he knows what I want.

"Please..." I can't find the words at all. I have never been so horny and the pressure my own body is creating is excruciating. He slowly pushes my panties aside and draws one long finger through me, lifting it to his mouth and sucking off my wetness. It's the most erotic vision I've ever seen and I swear, just once more and it'll be the end.

"So ready for me, so eager," he muses, returning his hand. He cups me again and presses his thumb directly to my swollen nub. Electricity sparks through me and I jolt forward into him. His lips quirk up as he pushes me away from him again to create distance between us.

"Not yet, baby. Hold it back a bit. Let me watch you squirm for a while," he rasps out, slowly rubbing his thumb around in circles, applying pressure and then releasing, applying then releasing. I can feel myself gripping the pole, barely able to stand already and yet he still continues the torture.

"I can't hold off. Oh, god." I pant out, closing my eyes and tipping my head back, trying to gain some control again. His intense eyes are too much for me. I desperately need to get away from them if I'm to have any hope of holding this back. His hand clamps my jaw and pulls my head level again, still moving his hand.

"Look at me. Keep your eyes open. I want to see your agony," he growls breathlessly. My eyes open to see the dark desire fuelling his as his hand works me mercilessly.

"Alex, please let me come. I can't..."

He pushes two fingers inside me and watches as I writhe like a temptress in front of him. It's too much. I can't breathe and him rubbing those fingers on my g-spot, now applying a slightly faster rhythm, is near mindblowing.

"Yes, oh god, yes. Please, faster." I moan in ecstasy. I'm nearly there - just a little bit more. My arms take my weight as my knees start to buckle beneath me. The rope rubs gratingly against my wrists, inducing a slight pain that only seems to intensify my need to come as my whole body stretches out and I grind down onto his fingers.

"You're ready now, baby. Let go for me," he says, scooping me towards him roughly and taking my weight in his arms.

Air puffs out of me at the onslaught, and oh Jesus Christ, the stars alight behind my eyelids as the most gut-wrenching orgasm travels the length of my soul and back. Every part of my body tingles and quivers and I swear I pass out for a second. I can feel his hand still rubbing, pushing me further into the pain and pleasure of bliss as he turns me round to face the pole.

"Hold onto that," he orders, pushing me roughly. "Don't let go."

While I ride out the effects of my shattering, he rips my panties from me. I hear a rustling of clothes and suddenly he's inside me. I lurch forward at the hard thrust as he hits my cervix from behind and slams in with such force, it takes what little breath I had away from me.

"Breathe, Elizabeth. There's more in you yet." I close my eyes and let the full feeling envelop me, the stretch so deliciously tight it's almost painful.

"Fuck, you're so tight. Say my name, Elizabeth. Scream it for me."

Grabbing my hips, he slams in again and again, and unbelievably, my body starts to react. I feel my insides tighten around him and the build of pleasure form in my core as he grabs hold of my neck harshly and tilts my head to the side. His arm loops around my waist to support me and he forges harder and harder until I'm nearly there again. "I can feel you. Fuck, you're so close again." Oh god he's right. So close, and his hand closing around my throat, applying that pressure I crave, spurs me on towards another bliss-filled place. "Hold it off. I want you to come with me."

He removes his hand from my throat and drags his fingers along my back languidly, slowing his rhythm and pulling himself backwards achingly slowly again.

"Alex, harder. Fuck me harder, please," I beg, pushing myself back towards him in the hope of speeding him back up. He groans with pleasure and tilts my hips slightly, pulling me back onto him with brutal intent. It's too much and the colours start darting behind my eyelids.

"Yes," I hiss through gritted teeth. "Christ, Alex, yes."

He slows his pounding again and splays his hand over my back.

"God, you're so fucking beautiful. Let me watch you longer. Slow yourself for me," he growls as he moves his hands to my breasts and pinches hard on my nipples, twisting them.

What? He has to be fucking kidding me.

I take in a deep breath and try to contain my orgasm by opening my eyes and focusing on my bound wrists. If I just stare at the rope, just focus on something other than the feel of him inside me, then maybe ...

"So tight, so achingly sexy. You are exquisite, Elizabeth, and fuck, I love hearing you beg for me. Do it again. Beg," he rasps out as he travels his hand back up towards my neck and moves towards my throat again.

"Please, Alex, do it. Fuck me." My breathing spikes instantly and I moan out as he starts to increase his rhythm, harder and faster, more, punishing stroke after punishing stroke slamming into me over and over again.

"You're just too fucking much."

"Yes. God, please make me come."

He pounds in again and grabs at my throat, lifting my head and pushing me towards the pole. I push back against him and feel him hit my core again. My orgasm starts with such force my knees buckle at the ache building to a peak of almost pain. Both of his arms suddenly wrap around my waist, taking all my weight, which allows me to just sense every mind blowing thing that is happening to me as he pushes me further into it.

"That's it, right there."

He groans into my ear as I feel him thickening and changing speed. My body falls apart around me, everything going numb. Intense sensation travels through the core of me. My legs give way completely and I collapse into his arms, lights flashing before my eyes. I have no fucking idea what's happening as I spiral out of control and vaguely hear him shouting my name in the distance. Warmth floods inside of me as he finds his own release and my brain fogs. Nothing else is here apart from the feeling of him inside me and the dull throb that's coursing through my bones.

What the hell was that? What did he do to me? Oh god, I can't even tell my muscles to work. Shit. Something's wrong. I slump back into him and before I know it, the ropes are removed and I'm lying on the bed with his arms pulling me to him. "Sleep, baby. You were perfect."

Chapter 18

Elizabeth

"Sir, we're half an hour out - on time and ready to descend. Would you like us to circle?"

"Yes, Phillip. Thank you." I hear Alex murmur, his arms tightening around me from behind as he nuzzles into me. "Are you awake, baby?" he whispers.

"Yes, I think so," I groan beside him. "What did you do to me? I feel like I could sleep for a week. Did I pass out?"

"It's the altitude, and no you didn't pass out. I'll have to work you harder in future. You were rather more robust than I thought you would be. You were remarkably pleasing." He chuckles, pulling me towards him again, pushing his morning glory into my back, or afternoon glory. What time is it anyway? I'm struggling to remember the day.

"You are kidding me, right? I still can't move and you're up for round two," I mumble, and what the hell does remarkably pleasing mean?

"Oh, baby, you have no idea how many rounds of you I'm up for. It's your own fault. You shouldn't be so damned gorgeous." He kisses my neck and moves a hand to my thigh.

"Oh, well. When you put it like that. How long do we have?" I push back against him and wriggle a bit, giggling like a bloody schoolgirl.

"As long as we need. I'd circle this jet all day for a few more minutes with you. I've never enjoyed just lying with someone so much," he says, a small sigh coming from him as he nibbles my shoulder.

"You certainly know all the right things to say to a girl, Mr. White. Ooh, turn onto your front a minute," I say suddenly, jumping up onto my knees with renewed vigour.

"What? Why?" he replies, quizzically.

"Because I want to see your tattoo." I smile brightly. "I keep getting glances but I've never really looked at it for long enough. I am not often behind you now, am I?" I say, raising my eyebrow.

He rolls over and I straddle his back. Looking down, I see one word stretched across his shoulders in black and grey.

"Belligerare," I mutter softly as I run my fingers over it and frown, not understanding the meaning. Scanning further down, I realise that the rest of it is simply lots of numbers and dots that start in the middle of his left shoulder blade and run across to his right. The numbers are a kind of Sanskrit style and all in black, about an inch high for each number. At present it reaches about halfway down his back and the last number ends just at his spine.

"It's beautiful. What does it all mean?" I ask, wandering my hands over the numbers.

"I wondered when you'd ask. All the dates are something of significance to me. Turning points in my life, you could say - good and bad." He turns over and gazes up at me softly. "I like you up there." He continues smiling and reaching up to grasp my hands.

"What does the word mean?" I ask.

"To wage war," he murmurs, dragging a finger down my body from my neck. "Latin."

"How apt, Mr. White." I giggle as I look down at him with something close to adoration. Such a beautiful man - the sort of man who would have his life tattooed on his body to reinforce his memories. "Why would you tattoo the bad dates?" I ask quietly. "Why would you want to remind yourself?"

"They have made me who I am as much the good ones. We learn by our mistakes, do we not?" he replies, a puzzled expression forming again.

"Yes, I suppose we do." I still don't understand why he'd want to remind himself, but he has a point of sorts.

"You know meeting you is of significance to me. You have no idea how precious you are. You seem to linger inside me with some sense of new meaning I didn't believe possible."

I look down towards his stomach muscles. I don't really know how to react to what he's said, wonderful as it is. Is he really putting me on such a pedestal?

"Elizabeth, what's wrong? I was hoping that would go down a little better than it has," he says softly, tipping my chin back up.

"No. God, Alex, you've done nothing wrong. Those words were wonderful, beautiful even. I just don't know what to say. I don't want you to think I'm something I'm not. Whatever it is that you see in me, I don't understand it. You could have any desirable woman you want and I just don't get why you think that I'm something special. I'm not. Really. I'm just Beth Scott."

He lifts himself up to me and wraps his arms around my back, kissing my lips softly and pushing my head upright with his mouth. When he looks into my eyes, I see warm blue oceans gazing at me adorably with a smirking mouth. More bloody laughing? Great.

"Elizabeth Scott, don't you see? You're achingly beautiful, funny, intelligent, and you challenge everything I've ever known. You have no idea how mesmerizing that is for me or what it means. If I can even dare to hope that I deserve some small part of you then that is worth everything I have," he says, stroking my face and pulling my lips to him again. His passion pours into me through a scorching kiss and my emotions flow back towards him. I'm feeling so lost in the moment that I'm barely containing the tears that are threatening to fall from his declaration of something more, and as he moves his hands to my waist and splays his hands over my ribcage, I sense the word *love* enter my brain. "I had no idea you would captivate me so," he whispers in my ear.

I run my fingers through his hair and pull his head to my chest and there we rock for a while, just holding each other while I try to find something as beautiful to say in return and control my tears. There's nothing in my head that comes anywhere close so I just hold on and let him breathe into me quietly until suddenly he pulls back and stares at me with narrowed eyes.

"You lied to me and I didn't punish you," he says, smirking. Okay, moment gone, obviously.

"What? When?" I reply hesitantly, still not comfortable with this punishment thing.

"Where did you learn to play chess? You're really very good," he asks, releasing a beaming smile. My core almost combusts in response as for some unfathomable reason I imagine more ropes.

"Oh, my dad. He used to compete a bit. I started learning when I was about five. Belle never got the bug. He plays a lot like you but a little more defensively." I giggle at the thought of a defensive Alex. Probably not going to see that in a hurry. "He'd like you. You're just his type of opponent," I reply.

"Well, I'll have to thank Mr. Scott when I meet him," he says nonchalantly as he brushes hair off my face and twirls it in his fingers.

"What?" I very nearly shout, open-mouthed. The thought is a little worrying to me.

He chuckles at me. "Only when you think it's appropriate, baby, but I'd like to meet your family. Although, I hope they're not all as hostile as your sister," he says, frowning. It's my turn to smirk.

"She's just protective. She loves me," I whisper, rubbing my hands across the bumps and ridges on his stomach.

"It's not hard to see why. Who wouldn't?" he mumbles. My eyebrows shoot up. Is he suggesting he does? "Come on. Let's get showered and dressed. We've got to get to the apartment and I've booked the opera for this evening. Do you have anything to wear or do we need to go shopping?" I dismiss the stupid thoughts of love and think of my suitcase instead.

"The opera? Wow. God, I don't know. What does a girl wear to the opera? I've never been before."

"Well then we should definitely go shopping. I want you to feel comfortable if it's your first time. It can be very intense." He frowns slightly. "Now, about that punishment, young lady."

With that, he rolls me over onto my back and nibbles at my neck as he grinds his hips into me. I'm instantly horny again. It's ridiculous.

"I thought we were going to shower," I say with a smile as he makes heavier contact with me and pulls a nipple into his mouth. Clearly not then.

"Mmm..." he replies, reaching out to the bedside table and pressing a button on the panel.

"Phillip," he barks. I giggle. It's so unlike the voice I heard a few seconds ago. He holds a finger to his lips to silence me. It doesn't work and I continue as he tries to hold a straight face.

"Yes, sir?" My giggling escalates and his hand clamps over my mouth.

"Circle again would you?" He grins wickedly at me and licks his lips, beginning to tickle me, so I scream into his hand as he kicks the covers to the floor and watches me squirming beneath him.

"No problem, sir."

Growling, he makes his way down my body, pushing my legs apart roughly and mumbling something to himself about devils and angels. I can't contain my giggling fit but as his hands suddenly grab my hips and yank me down the bed to him, I somehow manage to restrain myself.

"You won't be laughing in a minute, Elizabeth," he says as his teeth connect with my thigh.

Good god!

~

Rome traffic is unbelievable. The limousine that collected us from the airport was, of course, the ultimate in luxury, which is something I'm coming to expect from everything concerning Mr. White. But driving in Rome is a little more dramatic than anywhere else on the planet. The car hurtles around every bend, honking its horn constantly, and before I'm aware what's happening, Alex has dragged me onto his lap, holding me in a protective clasp against him.

The Colosseum comes into view and I stare in awe at its magnificence while we wait in traffic.

"It's stunning," I remark. It's really all that needs to be said about something so ancient and big. It's very big. How did they even make that back then?

"Yes, I always smile when I see it. It can't lie about itself or deceive you about what it was made for. For a city that thrived on the politics of the people, it seems amusing that it also delighted in the death of the people," he muses, laughing to himself.

"I'm not sure the death of people is something to be laughed about, Alex," I reply, digging him in the ribs and chuckling at his mock pain.

"Death is what made Rome what it is or what it was. The Emperors and senate unleashed more death than the world had ever seen before. With that death came order, enormous wealth and unlimited control," he states with a small shrug as he gazes out of the window. "I have a home here because of the historic nature of the city and its influence. It's how I do business."

"Your business deals with death?" I question, in astonishment.

"In a manner of speaking, yes, I suppose it does. I buy companies that are failing slightly or are simply available, destroy the worst parts of them and then sell sections of them on for profit. If something appeals enough, I keep it and turn it around into something more enterprising, but otherwise, I act only with regard to the balance sheet."

"Don't you feel morally obligated to help them out at all?"

"Why would I do that? Moral obligations have no place in business. Neither does guilt by association." He stares at me expectantly.

"Well surely with your guidance and backing, companies that were failing could start to succeed again," I state, feeling slightly angry that someone could be so harsh and remorseless, but then he's already shown me that with Tara, hasn't he?

Christ, I might be falling for an utter bastard.

"Elizabeth, the world just doesn't work that way. Would you have me make less money and aid unprincipled people to continue to make more? I give plenty of money to deserving charitable concerns. Please don't ask me to become yielding with regard to arseholes who couldn't give a damn about their responsibilities or civic duties."

"I suppose I see your point. But I'm not sure how you sleep at night when your job consists of so much negativity." I feel myself huff a little at his attitude as he pulls me tighter and strokes my hair soothingly, tucking my head under his chin.

"No sleep for the wicked," he mutters into my hair. I can hear his frown and wonder what makes him think he's so bad. Maybe he is. What would I know?

We sit silently for a while as I watch the visions of Rome all around me. Alex continues to stroke my hair and stares impassively out of the window. All the time he's seemingly lulling me back into his charms effortlessly, and I feel my body relaxing into his breathing, as he kisses the top of my head. How could I be mad with a man as beautiful as him? He tightens his hold and I tilt my mouth up to him and let my lips meet his with everything I have.

Wrapping my arms around his neck, I move to straddle him and I feel him stirring beneath me deliciously. He moves his hands to my backside and pulls me forward onto him with force, pushing himself into me and grinding slowly. The contact immediately sends shivers along my spine and I moan out his name as my brain negotiates just getting him out and doing it in the car.

"So eager, young lady." He chuckles. "I assume you're not mad anymore." His eyes darken and he starts to kiss my neck. Pulling my jumper out of the way, he nibbles his way to my nipple and lavishes it with attention.

"Oh, Alex, please..." I'm practically begging him, again. It's getting ridiculous. *Get a grip, girl.*

"You'll have to wait, Elizabeth. We are almost here," he rasps, still sucking at me. "Besides, a little waiting will do you good. Just keep thinking of all the things I'll do to you later."

"Mmm..." I can't think. All I can feel is the delectable tingling in my core as he continues to rub against me and I let the tension increase.

He abruptly lifts me off him and dumps me ungraciously on the other seat as the car glides to a stop, grinning at me in obvious delight at the effect he's had on me. Bastard.

"Honey, we're home," he sings, jumping out of the door like a bouncing schoolboy.

Well, this is a new version of Alex. I watch him hurry around the car, leaving his more severe presence behind as that open smile hits the Italian air. I smile. He really does look relaxed.

"Welcome to Rome, baby," he says, opening my door and helping me out. Quick as a flash, he lifts me into his arms and starts striding towards a large set of wooden doors. "I love it here. It's my place to relax and just be me." I wrap my arms around his neck and smile at him some more, love swelling inside me. I am in so much trouble. The man is seriously a magnet for my heart.

He puts me down on the floor about a foot from the door and opens it wide. Gasping, I step inside. The most charming courtyard I had ever seen twinkles in front of me. Abundant flowers of all colours litter the walls and a large fountain bubbles delightfully in the corner. The sounds of the busy traffic and street outside are instantly dulled as he pulls the heavy door closed behind us, and I watch the driver take our bags into a doorway. I stand for a moment and gaze around at the utterly enchanting scene in front of me. A large terrace with an elegant table and eight chairs stands underneath a canopy of vivid red flowers, and the sound of the water cascading from the fountain creates a magical feeling inside of me.

"It's breathtaking, Alex," I whisper, wandering toward a purple flowering plant and fingering its soft petals.

"It is, isn't it?"

He folds his arms around my waist and we both stare at it for a while longer. I can feel him smiling into my hair as he kisses my neck softly and reaches toward the plant. He plucks a flower and tucks it behind my ear. "Although I think it is more so now that you're here." I turn in his arms and run my fingers along his jaw. He's still the most appealing thing in here, regardless of the fairy tale world around me.

He takes my hand and leads me towards the open door to the right of the table and we walk into a large, marble covered kitchen area and through to a lounge. The stylish ambience is oozing with Alex and it's obvious he's poured his heart into the place. It's nothing like his London apartment or his house, though. It's lighter somehow and has a breezy feeling to it that shows the carefree side of him. I exhale at the thought of a less intense man. Gone is the modernity of the apartment or the heavy masculinity of his house. This space feels elegant and charming, with a certain relaxed and cheerful manner. Pale greens and creams dominate the interior. Luxurious throws and cushions blend effortlessly with the antique furniture and artwork hanging, all of which have that timeless European feel that welcomes you without dazzling too much. I'm still gazing around when the air is devastatingly shattered.

"For fuck's sake, you piece of fucking shit. Jesus fucking Christ! I will not let her beat me," comes bellowing around the corner, and then we hear an almighty smashing sound down the corridor somewhere. I gasp and scuttle towards Alex. He simply looks to me and smirks. It seems he knows something I don't.

"I think someone's a little pissed off." His brows rise as he inclines his head to the doorway.

"What? Who's here?" I ask, smiling in relief that it isn't a burglar or something.

"I forgot to tell you. Conner's here," he says, chuckling as he links his fingers with mine. "Shall we go and investigate?"

We head toward the noise, around two corners and then peer around the entrance of what is clearly Alex's study. The sight of a very red-faced Conner banging his head against one of those rolling ladders - the ones they use for high bookcases - greets us. Looking at his very smashed up laptop on the floor, I'm giggling instantly, but as he swings his head round and growls at me, I recoil, having never seen a look so feral from him before. I honestly feel my legs buckle a bit and try to hide behind Alex.

"Any reason why you're throwing your piece of shit laptop at my very expensive books?" Alex says, trying very hard to control his laughter.

"Fuck off!" Conner seethes, taking a step toward him in a very intimidating prowl.

Alex holds his hands up in defence. "Calm the fuck down, Conner. There are ladies present and I don't want to have to drop you on your arse before I've at least said hello and had a drink. And by the way, this is actually my house." His demeanour seems to change a bit as he stiffens and pushes me further behind him. Is he really nervous? I am.

Conner glares at him ferociously and then glances down at me as I peek around at Alex. His eyes soften a little as he steps forward, but that irritation still seems very firmly etched in to me. Alex pushes us back a little out of the doorway.

"Are you calm?" Alex questions, wrapping his arm around me and pulling me into his back protectively.

Conner shakes his head and reaches up to his neck, clicking it from side to side, and then takes another step forward as his eyes change and his stance softens. Alex immediately lets go of me and moves forward. God, what is it with these men and their instant mood changes?

"Yeah, man, I'm cool. Beth, I'm sorry. I didn't expect you. Alex knows this shit. You shouldn't have had to see that. I'm sorry. I'm just a bit... frustrated."

"Lovely to see you too, Conner." I beam around Alex's shoulder. "And here was I singing your praises to my sister. I may have to rethink that having seen your temper." I continue my giggling again.

"Dude, get out of the way. I need the squeeze of a good woman," he says, pushing Alex aside and swinging me around. I actually see Alex smiling and heading back into the lounge as Conner carries me toward him and dumps me on the sofa. Obviously Conner's allowed to touch me then.

"I think I need a drink or six," he states, walking to Alex and hugging him.

"I think coffee's in order first. Then you can tell me what that was about. I haven't seen you that worked up for a few years. Elizabeth, what do you want?" He lifts that bloody eyebrow and I can't help laughing at the innuendo flowing from those sexy lips. Coffee is not the first thing on my mind, if I'm honest, but nodding at the machine, I sit back and watch them interacting.

They're like brothers moving around each other. Alex seems completely relaxed and stands leaning against the worktop listening intently as Conner relays his irritation at some new female employee who has sent him a program that he can't access. He's had to lie to the woman to save face. My giggles burst to the surface again. It gains me another Conner glare.

Looking at Alex sends a warm swathe of pure heaven through me as I gaze at the gorgeousness of him. His lean muscular thighs attaching themselves to that rather glorious arse, his fitted shirt rolled up at the sleeves to expose his muscular arms. Broad shoulders leading up to the most beautiful and somehow boyish smile. His jovial nature and huge grin at his friend's misfortune is an aphrodisiac that I am failing to dampen in myself. Mind you, any of the versions of Alex seem to bring on the threat of an orgasm. I don't know why I am surprised.

I saunter into the kitchen area to retrieve my coffee and head toward the courtyard.

"Am I to assume from that conversation that you have been beaten by a woman, Mr. Avery?" I chuckle walking past him.

"Beaten? Absolutely not. Just delayed slightly. But Jesus, her work is out of this world. I have never seen anything so... So... I don't even have the right words for it." He huffs as he kicks the cabinet in clear frustration. Alex grabs at me and pulls my back to his chest.

"Well, looks like we all need to go shopping. You need a new laptop and you need a new dress. Do you want to get changed or are you ready to go?" he says suggestively as he pushes into my arse.

"Ready when you are. I can't wait to see this city." I smile and turn my head to kiss his nose.

"Got to love a woman that is ready and compliant as soon as she's told." Alex smirks.

"Alex!" I gasp and lower my blushing face from Conner's gaze.

"No, no, please don't blush for me, Beth. I like seeing him like this. It's quite intriguing. You certainly draw out a more emotive side of him. There's this weird touchy thing going on." He laughs and moves across the kitchen to get his jacket. "That's something I have never been privy to."

Okay, he's never seen Alex touching anyone before? That's just odd. Given that he's never had a girlfriend before, though, I suppose it's possible. But he's definitely had women before. He must have touched them, for Christ's sake.

Alex chuckles beside me and pushes me towards the door at my confused frown.

"I told you, you're very precious to me - significant," he whispers. It still doesn't clarify a bloody thing but I beam back at the words and kiss him.

"Are we leaving at any bloody point?" is Conner's rather irritated interjection. I slide my arms from Alex's neck and giggle at Conner's turned back. It's cute that he was trying to give us some space. Alex seems amused by it as well as he slaps him on the back.

Just as we're about to leave the courtyard, Alex's phone rings and interrupts our laughing. He looks at the number and frowns, clearly hesitating and trying to decide whether to take it or not.

"You okay, man?" Conner asks on the way to the courtyard doors.

"Henry," Alex hisses, seething with undisguised anger. I have no idea who he's talking about but evidently it's an irritation of some sort.

"Cool, what's the problem then?"

"I need to talk to you about that." The phone stops ringing and Alex walks up to me and puts his hands on my face, lowering so he can look into my eyes.

"Elizabeth, I have to call him back. There is something I need to... assess. Would you mind going with Conner until I can catch up with you?" he asks tentatively.

"No, of course not, Alex. I'm sure your hunk of a friend can keep me well entertained while you're busy." I smirk, and then wink.

"Did you just wink at me?" He growls slightly.

"Yes. Have you got a problem with that, Mr. White? I do hope not as I'm absolutely not spending my time arguing when I have a date with Rome and a rather wealthy, cute six foot four inch blue-haired genius. Who knows what we might get up to?" I wink again for added effect and smile.

"You've got to love a woman with taste," Conner muses from the side, slowly backing away nervously. "She sure knows how to push the buttons, man. You cool?"

Is he actually nervous? It was only a joke and from what I can see, Alex looks fine - a little stiff perhaps, but fine. Bloody confusing men.

"Yes, she does. Trouble is, she's so damned adorable that I'll have to let her get away with it. For now anyway." He smiles and kisses me. "Cute? You think that's cute?" he says, pointing toward Conner.

"Yes, I think he's an absolute charmer. Always have. I also think he's a good man. I like good men. They're *morally obligated,* don't you think?" I smirk and glare slightly. That'll hit a nerve.

"I think you two better be on your way before I change my mind. And believe me when I say that that man has fewer morals than you might think," he says as he turns toward Conner.

"Hey, I'm actually fucking offended by that," Conner replies with a frown. I'm not sure what I should think about who's the bigger moral arsehole of the two.

"Well, you'll both have to prove your moral worthiness then, won't you?" Both heads shoot to me. I smile sweetly. Alex frowns and turns back to Conner.

"Se le succede qualcosa, ti uccidero," he says, narrowing his eyes.

Wow, he speaks Italian.

"Morirei per non permettere che le succeda qualcosa, ma questo lo sai gia," Conner replies in a soothing voice and nods at Alex.

Wow, he speaks Italian, too.

Conner nods and bows at me, offering his arm. "Shall we go then?" he says in a terribly English accent as I kiss Alex and he rubs his thumb along my jaw.

"Be good. I'll catch up as soon as I can. I'm sorry, Elizabeth," he says, retreating back into the house and looking a little sad.

"Hurry, I don't want to be without you for too long. I might get withdrawals or something," I reply loudly, trying to lift his mood again and blowing him a kiss as I walk through the doors with Conner. Nothing appears to stop the scowl that develops, though.

"What was the Italian about?" I ask the moment we've left.

"He told me he'd kill me if I let anything happen to you," he replies, deadpan.

"Don't be ridiculous. He did not say that," I return incredulously.

"Believe me, Beth, that is exactly what he said. More importantly, he meant every single word of it. He is not a man to take lightly and my broken jaw had first-hand knowledge of that a long time ago."

"Oh..." What else can I say?

"Now, where to first? How about the Piazza del Spagna? You said you wanted shopping so that's where it's at. There are lots of pretty little things there. There's also some quite nice shopping. We'll go on the scenic route."

"Conner, you're incorrigible." I smirk. "And please remember you're trying to win my sister. You'll need me onside for that, I think."

"I know, but you love me anyway. Everyone does." I can't stop myself from laughing at his boyish charm.

As we wander along the small streets, Conner fills me in on the history of the city. He's quite the authority on Rome and tells me the story of the place in intricate detail while constantly pointing out historic monuments and landmarks. The beauty and tranquillity of the quieter areas lulls me into a wonderfully relaxed frame of mind as I stare in awe at the historic buildings with their gracefully faded façades and blackened edges.

After about an hour of walking, I realise I have been so lost in the glory of Rome and Conner's voice that I haven't remembered to call Belle and tell her that we arrived safely. I dig around in my bag to find my phone. Shit. I haven't even remembered to turn the bloody thing on.

Turning it on, I see ten missed calls and a few texts.

"Oh bollocks," I say rather ungraciously.

"Problem?" Conner exclaims in a slightly worried voice.

"I haven't called Belle. She is going to be so pissed at me."

"Ah, I see. Yes, she can be rather lethal with that tongue of hers. Mind you, I quite enjoy it. Why don't you sit your pretty arse in that coffee shop and I'll call her? I've missed her amusing wit and I'm sure she'll be happy to give some of it to me." He points to a chair and reaches for his phone.

"So what's going on with the two of you anyway?" I say, smiling up at him.

"I'm trying to persuade her that I'm in love with her and she's being her normal fucking obstructive self, so I am being... persistent." He smirks and moves away to make the call.

God, he's in love with her? That's interesting.

I watch for a while as his animated hand gestures and facial expressions show his pleasure and then displeasure. Bless him, she does give him a hard time.

Ordering two coffees from a passing waiter, I cast my eyes at the Pantheon in front of me and feel my whole body give in at the warmth of the Roman sun blazing down on me. I close my eyes and daydream of Alex's hands gently stroking my hair, all the time running my own hands across my throat and thinking of his fingers. Jesus, just thinking of his touch has me squeezing my legs together and moaning.

Quite abruptly, a slightly strange sensation sweeps over me and I shut my eyes tighter to try and focus on it, but as soon as I do it disappears into my brain again so I shrug it off and relax, and then a familiar scent hits me.

"Un altro caffe qui per favour."

Keeping my eyes closed, I smile and savour the sound of his velvety voice breezing past my ear as his lips meet mine. Even in Italian, his tone is exquisite. The words roll from his mouth with a low and forceful tone. I'm sure if I open my eyes, women will be fanning themselves all around me. The instant our mouths meet, my body feels like exploding. Electricity sparks and he pulls me up to him in an embrace that would have any girl panting with lust. It's disturbingly good, and his hand grasping the back of my neck as he devours my mouth with his only heightens the sensation.

"I had forgotten how enjoyable voyeurism could be. I've never been so tortured by such a tantalizing display," he whispers. "How wet are you?" He grazes his hand toward my thigh. "Should I find out right here?"

"I'm glad you enjoyed the show." I laugh, slapping him away as I lay my hand softly to his face. "But no, don't you dare." He smiles and turns his head to kiss my palm. It's a sweet gesture and I grin at him stupidly, adoring the moment.

"I missed you," I say softly.

"I'm glad. I missed you, too," he replies, slowly moving his hands down my arms and lowering himself onto a chair. I'm pulled into his lap before I get a chance to sit on my own chair.

"Has Conner been good to you?" he asks, quirking his head to the side. "Nothing inappropriate?"

"Conner has been wonderful. He is currently getting an ear bashing from my sister," I reply, nodding toward a somewhat defeated looking man sitting on a step. Alex frowns a little.

"He's quite preoccupied with her," he muses. "What is it about you Scott women?"

"I have no idea. You tell me," I reply on a shrug as I watch Conner's blue hair get up and wander around again, almost with a life of its own. He's causing quite a stir in his own way as I notice all the ladies looking him over and licking their lips.

"I've bought you something," Alex says from beneath me, completely changing the subject.

"Really? What?" I ask, closing my eyes to the very lovely sun again and leaning back into him.

"It will be at home later. Needless to say, you will no longer need to go shopping, and as I don't see any bags here, I assume you haven't already bought a dress." I can feel the smirk into my neck as his lips kiss just below my ear.

"No, we got waylaid by Rome and Conner's really rather in depth knowledge. Why have you bought me a dress?" I ask as I open my eyes, slightly miffed but also bizarrely happy.

"Because I can and because it reminded me of you. You will have to indulge me a little, though. I have a game to play if you are amenable to requests." His eyebrow raises and I narrow mine in return.

"Is everything a game to you, Alex? Is that your life?" I try to smile but then feel my frown spread at the thought of being a game to him myself. It instantly deflates my happiness, lowering my head.

"Yes, Elizabeth. It just seems that you are the only worthwhile one I have had for some time."

He doesn't flinch, doesn't move, just sits and stares at the people milling around him with that impassive smile. A game. Is that how he sees us? I think not. I'm just about to launch some kind of comeback when his mouth opens again. "Lift your head. We really need to work on that poker face of yours. You're far too easy to read."

What the hell?

"I don't even know how to respond to that. A bloody game? I thought you liked me for me."

"I do. I was trying to get a reaction out of you for effect," he says, still looking forward and brushing his hand along my thigh gently. I'm now even more clueless as to what on earth he's trying to say. "You really are far too honest for your own good. It won't work."

"Okay, what the hell are you talking about?" Because he's absolutely going off on a tangent, and I do not understand in the slightest.

"Those sharks, Elizabeth. They'll devour you and your decency."

"Are you suggesting I need protecting from someone?" I ask, slightly exasperated at this constant need to guide my emotional responses. "Because I'm quite capable of-" He cuts me off.

"My point is that you need to guard yourself more adequately. The people in my circles will exploit your good nature and harm you in the process, then possibly me, and that I can't have." He turns and gazes at me, reaching for the back of my neck. "I want you in my life, Elizabeth, and that means everything that comes with me. Most of it is not very appealing, to say the least, so I need to know that you can stand by my side and hold your own against them, all of them."

Oh right, well that was kind of sweet, I suppose, in a roundabout sort of way. Why he's frowning so seriously is utterly bemusing.

"So you're saying I need to lie more? I'm not entirely sure I can-" He cuts me off again.

"I'm saying you need to perform. You need to pretend, manipulate to some degree, to play a game just as you did on the chess board." I scrunch my nose up in response as he chuckles at me and squeezes his fingers into my neck.

"Oh right, well I suppose I can do that, maybe, well, sometimes." His blue eyes dance with amusement, as he quirks a brow and kisses my hand.

"Good, I'll enjoy the show."

I have no fucking clue what he's talking about in all honesty, but I smile a little in reply and decide to give up thinking about it too much. He lives in a very strange world, to be fair, and perhaps he's got some sort of point. Conner begins to amble back towards us with what can only be described as a thoughtful expression covering his handsome face. I can't begin to imagine what my sister's just put him though.

"Sorry to interrupt the lovefest," Conner says as he reaches us and smirks at Alex - who is still kissing my hand.

"No problem. How's the sister?" Alex replies cheerfully. It appears all serious conversation has now left the plaza. Back to light and breezy then. I absolutely can't keep up.

"Intense. She says hi and hopes you have a good time. I am now a little fucking hard and will leave you to your day. I need a drink and some software. By the way, I've called Antonio so I'll stay with him tonight. There's some party somewhere that I apparently *have* to go to. I'll come by tomorrow afternoon to talk about Henry," Conner says, chuckling and waving as he wanders off towards the taxis.

"Thank you for this afternoon," I shout after him. He turns and bows.

"You are most welcome, Beth. You were a pleasure to be with and a delight to look at." He winks and looks at Alex with an amused expression, which is definitely meant as a wind up.

"Stai attento, Conner. Non mi piace il tuo tono," Alex says firmly, clearly not amused, yet again. Christ, and he talks about me being an open book. What did that Italian mean?

"Smettila sciocco, lei ha occhi soloche per te," Conner replies as he chuckles and walks off. Whatever it was, Conner thinks it's funny.

I need to learn Italian.

Chapter 19

Alexander

He reached into the drawer and reluctantly removed his bow tie, sneering at it in disgust as he did so. He'd spent the last hour talking on the phone with Louisa and a few other business associates regarding the Shanghai deal. Some interesting remarks had been made that had led him to believe that Henry was indeed after destroying that particular opportunity. Of course, no one had made a direct suggestion that Henry was up to no good. That would be similar to committing suicide for most of them, but with a few well-directed threats of malice here and there, he'd been able to at least get them to indicate that there might be some issues that needed his full attention. Now, having pointed him in the right direction, he could start to see Henry's line of fire. He had to give it to the man, he was a smooth operator. It seemed he was nipping at the heels of three major acquisitions that were directly linked to the biggest deal of his life, and if one crumbled, the rest would probably tumble like dominoes.

It wasn't going to fucking happen any time soon.

However, the priority was that now he needed to find new funding to keep the deal moving forward and he had to find it quietly. He'd have time to work out the whys later, but he needed cold hard cash now, and fast. There were only a few sources that could lend that sort of money. One would not be forthcoming as he'd had a brief encounter with the CEO's daughter last year and treated her quite indifferently when she had claimed pregnancy. It was, of course, a hoax but still, Mr. Robert Dillon was not impressed and had told Alex in no uncertain terms to remove himself from his office and to not come back again regardless of the financial gain. A moral businessman... Who would have fucking thought it? The other London and American based financiers were simply too close to Henry one way or another and he'd find out almost immediately if Alex was trying to get different funding. No, he needed someone from outside of the

UK, preferably someone unknown in land development. The problem was, most of them were tied up in other deals and that was just bloody irritating. Twirling the tie in his hands, he looked down to see that his fists were clenched so tightly that his knuckles were white. Releasing the fucking thing, he dropped it to the floor and let out a long breath while stretching his fingers.

Why had he booked the damned opera? Now he'd have to spend the entire evening struggling to breathe.

"Do as you're fucking told, you little shit, or I'll drag you in there myself. You disgust me. You deserve to rot in there. Look at you. You're pathetic. You'll always be useless. Do you want me to make you do as you're told? You know how I enjoy it," he'd said, removing that fucking tie.

He shuddered at the memory of his father and lifted his chin to look in the mirror. Fuck, why couldn't he just get past this? It was only a tie, for Christ's sake. He'd quietened every other painful memory and taken control of all the other issues that haunted him every day. Why not this one? He'd made sure that nobody noticed over the years. He simply opted for the no tie approach. Even in the most prestigious of business events, he could get away with it. If you have enough money, you can get away with anything. However, black tie events were different. He simply stuck out too much. That and the fact that they wouldn't even let him into the opera without one. Wankers.

Staring at himself, he thought of the woman dressing in the next room and breathed out her name, a whisper of hope on his lips. Could she distract him from it for the evening?

He walked to the dresser and picked up the bag he'd prepared earlier, then, draping the tie around his unbuttoned collar, he wandered to the dressing room in search of her.

He very nearly fell over as he entered the room and had to lean against the doorframe to contain himself. She stood there in front of the full-length mirror in the dress he'd bought for her. Her luscious red hair was piled elegantly atop her head with softening tendrils falling around her face, sage green satin encasing her curves and pooling elegantly at her feet. Her breasts rose from the bodice gracefully and her long, elegant arms floated along her sides like some sort of divine fucking angel sent from the heavens, just for him. Christ, he should take her now, this instant. His dick did all the thinking as usual where Elizabeth was concerned.

"Elizabeth, you look good enough to eat. In fact, I might later." He chuckled. "Come here. I have something for you," he said, motioning his hand from the doorway.

She turned and swayed towards him with her ever challenging and condemning eyes pulling him forward, begging him for those emotions and feelings she was so open with - the same ones he told her not to show this afternoon. The fuckers would destroy her if she showed even a hint of decency. Especially a certain green-eyed one. He wasn't about to let that happen any time soon. He'd keep her emotions just for him, not that he deserved them, but he wasn't about to let her share them with anyone else.

Keeping his feet planted, he resisted the urge to go to her. She couldn't see him yielding to her, regardless of this strange damn effect she was having on him. His chest ached for some reason. Was that an emotional response to her? She smiled and lit the fucking world up as her hands reached for him.

"Mr. White, I see you're not quite dressed yet. Beautiful, but not quite finished." She giggled, fingering his shirt collar and licking her lips seductively. He inwardly groaned, imagining her mouth around his ever-hardening cock and smirked at the thought.

Reaching for her hands to stop her, he then forced himself to drop his own to his sides. If anyone could manage it, she could. Her soft hands trailed along his throat and as he felt it constricting, he gazed into those chocolate brown eyes with their never ending lashes. Why did he like that, her hands at his throat? It made no sense whatsoever. Slowly, the button closed on the collar as he continued trying to lose himself in her. She was so hypnotizing, her voice drifting around his mind as she talked to him while he concentrated on her face. He couldn't hear a word she said, but lowering his eyes, he looked at her mouth and imagined it moving its way down his body, nibbling and sucking. He liked it when she bared those delicate teeth and bit into him. How he was going to make it through this evening without ripping her out of that five thousand pound dress, he had no idea. Maybe he would. Fuck it, he could always buy another one, and the image of her moaning out his name as he tore it from her body was beyond satisfying to say the least.

"There. All done. Mind you, I think I might have preferred the rugged undone look," she said, patting his jacket and moving back to the dresser.

What? He reached a hand up to his throat to feel the bow tie. Christ, he hadn't even felt her doing it. He'd spent years trying to put a tie around his neck without panicking and almost passing out, and she had managed it in a minute? He moved to the mirror to see the finished effect. "Perfect," he mumbled quietly, frowning at his reflection.

"What did you expect?" she said with her hands on her hips. Fuck, he loved her little temper. He'd enjoy quietening it just as much at some point.

"I didn't expect anything. I have learnt not to with you. You keep surprising me," he said, lifting the corners of his mouth. "Now I want you to wear something else."

"What else could I possibly need?" she said, putting in her diamond studs. He pulled out the green box and moved toward her, placing it on the dresser.

"This. Open it," he almost stuttered. Was that nerves he heard in his own voice. For fuck's sake, grow up.

"If this is some other overly priced gift, Alex, I don't want it. I think the dress is wonderful and thank you, again, but really, I won't accept anything else from you," she stated firmly, crossing her arms across her lovely chest and pushing those tits up higher. "You do not need to buy me. You are all I need." Her eyes softened.

He felt his knees buckle a little. Did she really just say that? Who the hell said that sort of shit? What planet had she fallen from? Christ.

"Elizabeth, I do not want to buy you, simply to give you something beautiful. Also, it is part of the evening's entertainment, which I'm hoping you will enjoy immensely."

"Oh, okay then. But if it's too much, I won't keep it. I swear, Mr. White, you will not change my mind on this," she said sternly with a smile.

She reached her hand to the box and flipped it open. Her hands flew to her mouth as she gasped in shock at the array of twinkling diamonds on the choker before her. He smiled. Her face lit up like a million acres of stars and he couldn't help but chuckle at her. As much as she tried to hide her delight, it was still there. She turned her head and stared at him, still with her hands over her mouth.

"Alex, that is definitely too much, and I'm not..." she started.

"Elizabeth, shut up. I'm telling you that you'll wear this tonight and any other night that I want you to. Do you understand?" he stated, staring at her. Fuck, she looked cute. "Turn around."

She complied instantly. He could get used to this. She was becoming instinctively submissive, most of the time anyway. Actually, not that much at all, but he liked the small moments of it nonetheless. He took the elaborately tiered choker and fastened it around her long, elegant neck, leaving the platinum chain hanging down her back.

"Lovely, now pull up your dress to your waist. There is one more thing I want you to wear."

Slowly, she pulled up her dress with a shocked expression as she looked over her shoulder at him and revealed that fantastic arse. He gazed the length of her legs. The lace tops of the hold ups had him groaning and he barely withheld the growl as he took in the heels. His cock almost damn well jumped out of his trousers as he hooked his fingers into her panties and rolled them down to the floor, tapping her ankles so she'd step out of them. Grabbing in his pocket, he pulled out the *entertainment* and dangled it in front of her like a lure.

"This will be rather intense for you and I'll only remove it when I'm ready."

"Anything you want, Alex," she said in a whisper. Fuck, he nearly exploded just from that statement alone. What the hell was it about her that made him stop breathing every time she said his name?

He pulled the platinum g-string up her legs and straightened it so that the roughened patch lined up with her clit. Sliding in the side latches so that the fit was tight on her hips, he pulled the chain from the back of the g-string and threaded it through the back of her dress, attaching it to the choker, then moved to face her. Fucking incredible.

"Much as I enjoy the visual, I'm not sure the Opera's ready, so drop the dress. How does that feel?" he asked waiting for an answer, regarding her face as impassively as he could - difficult, given his raging hard on.

"Interesting," she replied. "Cold."

"Oh, don't worry, you'll warm up soon enough. Try moving around," he replied, chuckling with devilment and twirling his finger in the direction of the room. He watched as a cascade of emotions flashed across her face while she walked. Every step she took put pressure on her throat and on her clit so he focused his eyes on her mouth as she gasped at the sensations. Feeling his very fucking uncomfortable cock twitch again, he changed his stance a little. The sudden overwhelming urge to throw her across his knee and spank the living shit out of her was unbearable. Or maybe fuck her... He couldn't decide which but the thought of some more painful entertainment was definitely taking root in his mind. She took a deep breath and looked him in the eye.

"I think I'm ready," she said with a slightly glazed expression. God, he loved that look. Sub space would be threatening her again this evening. She'd almost gotten there on the plane and how she'd managed it, he didn't know given her inexperience but she'd find it soon enough. It was there, just waiting for her to find it. Then he could really start enjoying her. She'd be ready then to take what he needed to give her.

"Mmm, I think you are, too," he replied with a wicked smile.

Very ready. Well, she would be within an hour or so.

~

"What are we here to see?" she asked as they climbed the stairs to the Opera.

"Tosca, by Puccini. Are you excited?" he asked, grinning like a bloody fool again.

"I don't know how to feel with this... umm... underwear on. I'm struggling to stand up and walk straight," she replied with a very appealing blush.

He chuckled. "Well, you'll be able to sit soon, Elizabeth. Mind you, I think you might find that just as excruciating." He winked and grasped onto her hand. "If it's too much, I can unhook it."

"No, I think I can manage a while longer. Don't worry, Mr. White. You'll soon know when it is too much for me to bear." She giggled deliciously and gazed at him warmly.

"I'm sure I will." He gave the chain a playful tug and pulled her toward him, cocking her neck backward. "I've never thought of collaring someone but now it seems so much more appealing, Miss Scott."

"Collaring? What does that mean?" she asked with the most innocent of looks, purring as the choker tightened. Fuck he loved that sound. He'd heard it a thousand times from different women but never before had it drilled into him so deeply, affecting something other than his cock.

"That conversation is for another time, I think," he replied as he kissed her and wondered what she would make of the actual meaning. He assumed it wouldn't be at all favourable to her.

As they made their way to the private box, he studied the crowd, looking for anyone who might interrupt his plans for this evening. He saw a few couples that were worth his time and quite a few who absolutely weren't. His eyes locked with Luciana Rivalotti and he knew trouble would be coming soon. She was the world's largest bitch but her father was also one of the wealthiest men he knew and he couldn't afford to piss him off. He had made the catastrophic mistake of fucking her about a year ago and she had hounded him since. She was undeniably beautiful on the outside but she would eat Elizabeth for dinner if she got into a conversation with her. Well, they had to start somewhere and he supposed if Elizabeth was going to have to deal with his shit, this was probably the best place to start. He watched as Luciana moved across the room towards them like a lioness in heat. He turned Elizabeth to him and kissed her.

"I'm sorry," he said as she looked at him with confusion. Here we fucking go.

"Alexander, my darling, you should have called to let me know you were in town. How I've missed you. The place is overwhelmingly dull without your exquisite face to look at," Luciana almost screamed, announcing her presence before them as she placed her hand on his chest. He felt Elizabeth's eyes narrow at him from the side.

"Luciana, how lovely to see you. Please, let me introduce my girlfriend, Elizabeth Scott," he said, pulling a very tense looking Elizabeth to his side and moving an arm around her waist in the hope of soothing her somehow.

"Hello, Luciana, nice to meet you," she said, offering her hand.

In typical Luciana style, she completely ignored her hand and returned her gaze to Alex while stroking his chest. Fuck, this was not going to go well. He felt the tension increase in Elizabeth's body and turned toward her, expecting to see her head lowered, his hand moving to the chain on her back intending to give it a tug. Instead, she looked back at him with a new smile and returned her eyes to Luciana.

"I'm sorry, is it not customary to shake hands in Rome? I thought it the done thing the world over but if you would rather I kissed you, I will certainly oblige. You are, after all, a very attractive woman. I'm sure you understand that in my present company, I am always happy to oblige anything that is out of the norm. This little trip is becoming a revelation for me. Alex, what will you show me next?" she said as she dazzled them both with a mysterious smile that immediately brought Luciana's mouth open in shock. Did she just say that? He couldn't speak, his impassive gaze momentarily lost as he took stock of the utter brilliance of her statement. She had been pleasant, rude, sexually aggressive and contemptuous in one fell swoop. Rather than be simply astounded, his hackles reared their very ugly heads as his gut instinct took over. Too fucking intelligent. Regardless of how innocent she seemed, that was quite possibly the work of someone who knew exactly what she was doing. His eyes narrowed a little as he watched her new smile glide across her face with breath-taking effect, and where the hell did that come from? She turned her charms back toward him for a moment and he saw the familiar little blink of her eyes that somehow quietened his normally very astute paranoia. He was wrong. She'd just delivered a good performance by chance. She probably learned it from him in some way.

He chuckled to himself at his own foolishness and looked back at Luciana, who was still stood there open-mouthed. He'd never seen the bitch so confounded and mused interrupting their little dominance dance, but was simply too intrigued to see how she would continue her little game. He turned to Elizabeth with a raised eyebrow as she swung her beautiful face back to Luciana with another smile that would bring the devil to his knees. It almost did because he swore he felt his own knees buckle a little. That was highly fucking unusual.

"Luciana, really, this has been wonderful, but we must be going. I have never seen Tosca and I do love Puccini. I hope you enjoy your evening. Perhaps we could meet somewhere for a drink at another time? Compare notes," she said with a slightly sarcastic tone as she looked at him briefly then returned her head. *Ouch, that fucking hurt.*

Luciana nodded at her and tried for a relaxed smile, then for the first time, removed her hand from his chest and took a step backwards, apparently acknowledging Elizabeth's presence.

"Yes, we must. It has been an enlightening introduction, Elizabeth. Alexander, you must visit soon. My father would love to see you again," she said. Ah, back to reality. The bitch returns.

"I'm sorry, we're leaving on Monday but maybe when we visit next," he replied coldly, continuing to gaze at Elizabeth with a feeling of pride welling up inside him. He never thought her capable of this and yet it seemed she was really very good. A chance retaliation, maybe, but at least he had something to work with now and he could see her abilities. Flawless was a fair description. What she would think of his previous life was still a problem, but if he knew she could handle his present then perhaps they could work out the rest.

"Good evening then. Enjoy your time here, Elizabeth. I very much look forward to seeing you again soon. I am glad Alexander has found someone so... fascinating. I'm sure we could have a lot of fun together," Luciana said with a genuine smile. Fuck, she'd done it. She'd passed muster with Miss Rivalotti. Unbelievable.

"Good Evening, Luciana." He nodded, placed Elizabeth's hand in his and walked toward the box, listening to her mumbling, "I fucking doubt it bitch," under her breath. He couldn't stop the beam of happiness that spread across his face. That's the woman he was beginning to know.

"Well done," he whispered in her ear.

"Thank you," she said, giggling. "Quite fun, this game of yours."

"Oh, Elizabeth, that was your game completely, and you just made an exceptionally well positioned move." He beamed down at her and felt his heart jump. "Perfect. I couldn't have played it better myself. Now, how's that g string doing? Would you like me to do anything for you?"

"I would very much like you to ease my suffering, Mr. White, but I think your little contraption actually aided my game," she replied with a devilish smile.

"Being denied something is often the key to achieving more, Miss Scott. You'd do well to remember that."

~

The elegant box was off to the right of the stage on the first level. They stared down at the masses of other guests and politely nodded at waving hands and the other, subtler, nods of some of the more discerning associates Alex knew well - the ones that pretended to like him when in fact they hated him.

"Is your life always like this?" she asked with an irritated expression as she gazed at the crowd and smiled at someone.

"Yes, Elizabeth." He understood her implication - the complex pleasantries of social participation and the constant threat of knives in backs, protocol and all the bullshit that comes with it. To be honest, it was a damn sight easier before all this. Just being and reacting held a certain relaxation to it, regardless of the implied work associated with his previous career choice. Ugly as it may have been, there had definitely been a finality to circumstances that simply wasn't available in this world.

"When do you get any time to just be at peace with yourself, to enjoy who you are and what you've achieved?" she said, rubbing her warm and sensuous hand along his jaw. "You deserve so much more." He didn't deserve a fucking thing, certainly not her.

He felt his eyes darkening at her and moved to kiss her with a passion he'd only recently found. Suddenly aware of his surroundings, he pulled back and instead gave her a brief, chaste kiss. They couldn't see how precious she was. They would use her against him if they knew. He looked into those indulgent eyes that were pleading with him for honesty and commitment. Twisting his neck from side to side, he reached a finger to his throat to loosen the collar a little and contemplated her words. When did he have time to just enjoy life? Never, that's fucking when.

"Why do you challenge me so much?" he said with a smirk.

"It's not a challenge, just a question. I wondered what the point of the wealth is if you have to pretend to be someone else all the time. It seems a little, well, stupid, that's all," she said with honesty dripping from her beautiful mouth.

"I don't pretend to be someone else. It is part of me. I like my games. They keep me focused and sharp. I also have a passion for making money so this is what I need to do," he replied as he frowned at his own words. True as most of it was, it could be a bit tiring at times.

"Really? Well, it must be very confusing to be so constantly juxtaposed." She smiled and turned to the stage as the curtains drew back. "Anyway, what is the opera about?" she said over her shoulder, leaning over the front of the box.

"Lies and deceit, manipulation and murder, love, betrayal and death. The story of a woman giving everything she has for the love of a one man," he replied, inwardly hoping she got the hint. She was going to have to deal with it all at some point. He only hoped she'd stay the course with him. Her back twisted in front of him as her shoulders shook with laughter.

"Oh, very apt. She sounds like one hell of a woman," she replied, giggling slightly. He gazed at her hair and instantly felt overwhelmed with sadness or guilt. He was a fucking bastard to even contemplate doing any of this with her. She'd never understand. Why should she?

~

As the final curtain was closing, he drew in a steady breath. He hadn't even noticed the opera because he'd been far too engrossed in her reaction to it. Her face and reactions had been constantly changing throughout the whole performance. She laughed, cried, swooned and at one point, she'd made herself come. He was surprised she hadn't begged him earlier. She'd done well to hold herself together as long as she had, and he'd rather enjoyed examining the subtle movements she'd made with her hips while pushing her throat forward on the choker. Listening to her ragged breathing, though, had been like setting a fire alight in him and he'd almost dragged her outside. He'd watched her the entire time. More fascinating to him than any production was the way she'd let every emotion roll over her features with no fear of recrimination, no thought that anyone was watching and would use her weakness against her. Perhaps it wasn't a weakness. Perhaps it was strength to not care what people could see. But it was his own reaction to her that surprised him the most. He felt

266

a strange need to not hide from her, to tell her everything about himself, including his miserable and violent past. He couldn't fathom the reasons why, just that she needed to hear the whole fucking truth from him. Was it way too early to tell her? Fuck, if he was her and heard the story of his life, he'd run ten thousand miles to avoid having to look into his soulless eyes. He'd never told anyone about his father - well, two people knew some of it but not the entirety. And then there was AP and the employment he'd fallen into. She'd never understand that, would she? No, who would apart from the other fucking participants?

Soulless... Was he anymore? He rubbed at his chest as she leaned over the balcony and scanned the people below. It ached again, and for the first time in a long time, he could sense his heart returning to him. That's what the dull throb was, his heart. She was inching her way inside him and pulling something up from the depths of fucking nowhere. He just wasn't entirely sure that he could release it to her. Sure she was the most delicious woman he'd ever met and there was no doubting her unwavering integrity, but could she really be the one? The one to see him, just the way nature intended him to be? He highly fucking doubted it.

He shook his head and resigned himself to the fact that she just wanted the performance, the Alexander White that the world saw regardless of her pleading eyes and heart-warming smile. So that's what she'd get. He'd make the most of her affection privately, maybe even just fuck the life out of her and then get rid of her before she did any real damage.

His resolve was instantly shaken as she turned to him, smiling through her tears, and launched herself at him, kissing him with an unadulterated enthusiasm that left him feeling glorious and pure for the first time in his life. He wrapped his arms around her flawless body and squeezed tight as if he were scared to let her go. She released his lips and nuzzled her perfect face into his neck.

"That was indescribable, Alex. I've... Oh my god, I've never felt such emotion. Thank you so much for bringing me. I will never forget this evening. I'm..." she whimpered into his neck, still sniffing back the tears.

"Yes, mesmerizing," he softly whispered, stroking her hair and unhooking the chain. "I think you've had quite enough intense stimulation for one night," he stated quietly as he breathed in her perfume and embedded it into his mind.

She looked into his eyes and smiled a beam of a thousand candles at him. "Oh, I don't know. Maybe a few more intensities wouldn't go amiss. I wouldn't want to disappoint you." She raised her brows at him.

"Disappointing is not a word I could ever use to describe you, Elizabeth," he replied with a chuckle as he reached for her hand and headed toward the exit. "We have a table booked for dinner at an old friend's. Are you hungry?"

"Absolutely, I'm starving. Emotions do that to me." She winked. He smiled at her with warmth and cupped her beautiful face in his hand. If there wasn't a hoard of people around him, he'd show her exactly what his heart was currently doing to him. Perhaps he should give her a taste of himself, something she could understand about him. It was a small start but she was worth it. Maybe she would see who he wanted to be. "I love that wink of yours. Come on. There's someone I'd like you to meet."

~

"Ciao, Alex. Sono content che tu sia tornado in citta," Giuseppe said, wrapping his arms around Alex's back.

"Ciao, Giuseppe. Ce presento Elizabeth Scott, la mia ragazza. E la prima volt ache visita a Roma," he replied.

"Ah, well I'm sure Rome is enjoying her as much as I am. Elizabeth, welcome to my humble restaurant. Alex, you have done supremely well for yourself. I cannot remove my eyes from her beauty," he chided, looking over his shoulder as he took her arm and walked toward their table.

"Bada a come parli vecchia amico, lei e cosa piu importante nella mia vita," he said, raising an eyebrow at his old friend, suave bastard that he was.

"I do wish he'd stop launching into Italian when he doesn't want me to understand something. It's really quite disconcerting," she said with a smirk.

"Yes, it is rather rude of him. Well, he's just told me he's in love with you, if that helps ease your mind."

She spun around so fast that Giuseppe had to hold onto her to stop her tumbling to the ground. Did he really just say that to her? Fuck, he wasn't ready for this, not yet. And was he? It wasn't possible, was it? Stupid, sentimental Italian. *Think quick, White. Shit.*

Giuseppe just stood there with a shit-eating grin on his face. *Bastard.*

She looked deep into his eyes when she'd righted herself and searched for his reaction to the information. Of course he only frowned and felt his throat tighten, even though the tie was no longer there, still too lost for words to find a response. She saw the confusion instantly as he was clearly far too flummoxed to hide it, so he steeled himself for some sort of emotional retort. She lowered her eyes a little with a small giggle and then returned them to his. The fact that his confusion was amusing her actually helped him regain himself somewhat.

"I'm sure he'll tell me that himself when he's ready. However, thank you for your insight, Giuseppe. It was enlightening," she said, changing her focus to Giuseppe and smiling with warmth and affection.

Alex turned his eyes to Giuseppe and glared at him. He simply threw up his hands and laughed.

"You Englishmen amuse me so much with your feelings. Your inability to just go with it astounds me. Where is the romance, Elizabeth? If you were mine, I'd shout it from the rooftops," he said, continuing with his chuckling. Alex clenched his fists and wondered how to respond, given the complete balls up he was currently in the middle of.

"Giuseppe, ho dannatamente bisogno di Cognac e al piu presto," he snapped at his friend. What a fucking dick. What the hell did he say now? Giuseppe laughed and retreated to the bar to get some drinks as they sat at the table.

He found himself twiddling with the napkin and trying to do anything but look at her. Twiddling, really? For Christ's sake. He fortified himself and looked up to see the most enchanting eyes twinkling back at him, smiling and biting at her thumbnail. His cock leapt up to attention.

"Is there something you'd like to say, Alex?" she said, fluttering her long eyelashes. Was there? "Elizabeth, I don't know what came over Giuseppe. He's normally so... rational. And stop nibbling your damn thumb, it's distracting."

"Really? That's interesting," she responded, lowering her hand to her drink. "Why do you think he said that then?" she said, now smirking.

"I'm really not sure. Perhaps he's in love. Shall we ask him?" he replied, trying to deflect the conversation. "Here he comes now."

Giuseppe put the glasses of cognac on the table, looked at their faces and quite unhelpfully walked away after telling them he would bring their food over when it was ready.

"Alex, please, you started this little game of yours. There is no room for backing down now," she said, putting her lips to her glass. "This is very good," she said as he watched her throat swallowing the amber liquid.

"You are not a bloody game to me, Elizabeth," he replied, glaring at her. Did she really think that? Okay, maybe she was a little at first, but not now. She was far from a fucking game. He'd only been trying to provoke a reaction from her earlier, to show her how to control herself so that nobody hurt her.

"Oh, I think I am, Mr. White. I think you're trying to control me and manipulate situations to suit yourself, to only allow me to be myself when I'm alone with you and to not ask too much from you. You have encouraged me to become more confident about myself, so guess what? You've got it. I'm reasonably happy to play your game because I think you might be worth it, but with one stipulation."

"And that is?" He quirked his eyebrow. *She's negotiating?*

"That you tell me what you actually said to Giuseppe. That is all I want, just true emotions."

Of all the things she could have asked for, she had to pick the one thing he was struggling to give her. And she knew it. Oh, he knew what he'd said before was enough to let her know how perfect she was to him, but real emotions? Why the hell had he said those words to his old friend? He didn't even know what to do with his emotions, let alone give them to her.

She watched him as he gazed impassively at her. She sipped at her drink and gracefully tapped her long slender fingers on the table. Where had this woman come from? She was relentless in her lingering stare. He had definitely underestimated her. The weight of her eyes felt like they were draining the very core of him out. He narrowed his eyes at her. He needed to get some fucking control back and damn quickly.

"Elizabeth, we have only known each other a short time and I have told you how I feel. You know I will give you anything you want. You are more important to me than anyone has ever been and-" She cut him off.

"Spit it out, White. Exact words only, please." She grinned. She had him completely off kilter and she was loving every minute of it. He was so taken aback by her interruption that he almost knocked his drink over and couldn't help but lift the corners of his mouth as he imagined how many times he had made others feel this way. He picked up the glass, downed his drink and brought his eyes to hers. *Time's up, White. Get on with it.*

"I told him that he should be careful with his remarks, that you are my world. I suppose I insinuated that you are the most important thing in the world to me."

She gazed back with the most magical smile he had ever seen from her. Her eyes sparkled with happiness and the soft sigh that escaped her mouth was the most erotic sound he could ever remember hearing. So much so that he was damn close to throwing her over the table. He gripped onto it in the hope of stopping himself.

"Thank you, Alex. That was beautiful and I'm very glad you said it, both to Giuseppe and me," she said, reaching for his hand. He took it and grinned like a fucking schoolboy at her, feeling strangely lighter than air as the other more explicit visions left him. The sensation was unexpectedly satisfying and he found himself actually enjoying his own emotional statement.

"Have you both had enough time to extinguish the flames? Your pasta is almost certainly ruined but I am a fool for love," Giuseppe asked calmly as he wandered toward them.

"Yes, Giuseppe, I think we have reached an amicable conclusion to our negotiations," he said, winking at her.

"Yes, we have. Please, won't you join us? I'd love to find out how you two met," she said sweetly with genuine interest. His heart burned his chest. Christ, she really was perfect.

"I'd love to. Thank you. Shall we start at the beginning? How much do you want her to know, Alex?" he asked, clapping his hands and instructing a waiter to bring them some bread, olives and cold meats.

"As much as you'd like. She can know everything. But we're going to need a lot more Cognac for this conversation I think." He pinned her hand under his and stroked the back of it with his thumb.

She grinned at him and blew him a kiss. "But, Elizabeth, the man is known for his exaggerations so please don't believe everything that comes out of his over exuberant mouth."

Giuseppe's hand flew to his heart in a show of mock horror. He was still a theatrical son of a bitch.

"You wound me, old friend. Now where to start," he mused as he looked at the table as if searching for the memory. "Ah yes, well... The first time I saw Alex, he was stealing apples from my father's store room downstairs, a scruff of a teenager with an eye for mischief. I liked him immediately. My family did not, and from there, and regardless of the fact that he spoke no Italian at all, he seemed to have no trouble getting us into all sorts of danger."

He leaned back and watched as his old friend regaled her with over dramatised versions of events from his youth, some of which were true and others that were simply Giuseppe giving his all. Her body language was turned towards the man as he waved his hands about and enticed her with little snippets of information that she clearly lapped up, probably saving it for another time when she could ask for more. He knew it was coming, the inquisition she was slowly managing to make him accept, as if she had some right to know all about who he was. It was odd, but perhaps she did? He'd offered this to her, brought her here knowing his friend would tell her things about himself. Then he'd said he didn't care how much she knew, that she could know it all, and for the life of him he couldn't work out why the hell he'd said that. He'd probably take her to Pascal as well, where she'd no doubt gain more information. As long as she never met Aiden Phillips it would be fine. He could control everyone else.

"So did you really teach him how to pick pockets?" she said with a giggle and a wink. "Naughty boy."

Oh, for fuck's sake.

Chapter 20

Elizabeth

I wake to the smell of fresh bread and coffee - coffee that is very much needed. Three hours of talking and drinking Cognac into the early hours of the morning has had quite an effect on my sobriety this morning. I liked Giuseppe immensely. He was warm and affectionate and really very funny. The tales of what the two of them had gotten up to all those years ago was fascinating, if somewhat disturbing in places. I still can't quite come to terms with the fact that Alex had been poor, though - poor enough to steal? How did a man go from a young, scruffy runaway to the Alexander White that everyone knew today? It just seems impossibly bizarre. And why had he run away anyway? From what? And why Rome, of all places?

When I looked at him for a better insight into the details, he'd closed up on me. He knew what I was asking and had shut the door immediately without apology or regret. Why he couldn't just open up and let me in I didn't know. Maybe there was something in his head he just didn't want me to see, and given that there were few people who actually knew what I'd been told last night, I did at least feel like he was letting me in a bit.

Slipping from the bed, I wince a little as I feel the reminder of the evening's *entertainment* as Alex so pleasantly put it. Entertainment? It was bloody torture, but what sweet torture. My orgasm at the opera was ridiculously erotic. I've never had one of those in public before. I'd done everything I could to hide it from him but the g-string had just been too much to bear when I sat down. The gentle, constant pressure of the roughened surface on my most sensitive spot had been like an unyielding trigger, pushing me into pleasure quietly every time I crossed my legs, refusing to let me back away from it, and the choker had only intensified the sensation further.

SEENING WHITE

I'd imagined his hands on me as the woman had sung her heart out to a crescendo and then struggled to stop myself from collapsing back into my seat and showing him my rather frazzled state. No matter how much I tried to deny it, though, I was pretty sure he knew. I could see it in his eyes when he looked at me. They twinkled with amusement at my discomfort. Or maybe I was just so embarrassed by it that I felt he must know.

Giggling, I stand up and walk toward the bathroom.

Brushing my teeth and trying to assemble my hair, I remember the sex we had when we returned last night. He was tender and loving, not what I'd expected at all. He'd never been so emotionally attached during our love making before and I'd revelled in his touch. Soft hands had found their way to erogenous zones I didn't even know I had and he'd remained close and held me the entire time, and the time after that. Was this his way of opening up? Of letting me in bit by bit?

There had been no kinkiness, no commands and no discipline, just an Alex I hadn't seen or felt before. Whoever he was, he devastated me and left me feeling slightly more exposed than normal.

Not to say that I don't like the other Alex. He shows me things I didn't believe possible and I'm certainly expecting more of that version sooner or later. In fact, I've enjoyed that version of him a lot more than I thought I would. I'm finding myself wanting to beg him to do things to me, confusing as that might be. Those darkening eyes seem to tempt me into doing anything he wants with ease as a feeling of satisfaction wells up in me when I do as he asks. I never imagined this strange dominant world of his could be so playful. I'd always heard that you had to revel in pain or something equally unpleasant.

Dragging a black silk bathrobe from the back of the door, I set off to find him and my much needed coffee. Passing the hall table, I notice the time is after twelve. I can't remember the last time I slept until lunchtime. Mr. White, it seems, is wearing me out.

"Good afternoon, sleepy head," he says as I round the corner.

He stands against the counter cross-legged, holding a folded paper and drinking his coffee. In soft grey trousers and a white linen shirt, undone and rolled up to his elbows, he's every inch the man in those aftershave commercials that all women hope they'll have one day. His rippling stomach muscles and lightly tanned skin tantalise my eyes while his beaming smile enlightens my soul. I'm still in so much trouble here. If I didn't need the coffee so badly, I'd be fainting or fanning myself repeatedly.

"Good morning," I reply, smiling with joy at the vision before me and moving toward the coffee. "I can't believe I slept so late. Have you been up long?" I ask, filling my cup and taking a long satisfying slurp.

"Yes, unfortunately duty called and I've been on the phone most of the morning," he says dryly.

"Oh, poor you. This is the problem with empires to run and gazillions to make. There's no time to simply be. How much did you make this morning, dear?" I laugh at my own sarcastic wit.

"Well, if you count losing the opportunity to make around a million because of someone's incompetence then I suppose I've only made about one and a half," he says with a wry smile. "Mind you, it is only lunch time. There's plenty of time left yet." What? How much?

The coffee cup slips from my hand and I immediately spit my coffee everywhere as I gape at him and start choking. Coughing and spluttering like a bloody idiot, I feel his hand patting my back while I try to right myself and he helps me pull myself together.

"Are you okay?" he asks, chuckling quietly, probably at my absurdity. I would be.

"That's... That's an obscene amount of money. And it's Saturday, for fuck's sake." I now stand open mouthed, gaping at him. Who the hell makes that sort of money? What Saturday has to do with anything I don't know.

"Actually I'm rather pleased with myself. I just poached something from someone that should make me a great deal more if I get it to the right place quick enough." He grins and sips his coffee again, elegantly at that. I'm obviously a complete mess next to him. "Would you like another one?" he asks, inclining his head toward the machine.

"Umm, yes please," I reply, suddenly feeling incredibly inferior. I mean, I knew he was wealthy but I hadn't really thought about how wealthy he was. How rich is that? Shit. What am I doing here?

"Right." He moves to pour me another one. "Well, as I'm my own boss and we're in my favourite city, I suppose I should show you the sights today. Do you think I've made enough money to allow myself to turn my phone off for a few hours? You are the only person who's apparently allowed to challenge my resolve when it comes to work without me exploding, so what do you think?" he says, softening his eyes.

"Alex, I... Uh... You've just told me the value of your day. I'm not sure I can tell you if you can take the afternoon off. What do I know about the worth of your time? I have no idea how much could go wrong or how much you could lose in a few hours. What if something goes wrong and you blame me? And what about..." I ramble aimlessly. The thought scares the shit out of me.

"Miss Scott, you informed me last night that I was, how did you put it? Oh yes... stupid if I didn't enjoy my wealth, did you not?" he says, sounding like a very harsh barrister.

"Umm... Yes," I reply on a squeak.

"So you infer that if I don't turn off my phone, I may well look slightly ridiculous to you?" he continues. Shit, that's not what I meant.

"Well, I don't think I-" He cuts me off mid-sentence.

"Are you suggesting that you were wrong in your argumentative statement?" he states, eyes narrowing and moving toward me, smirking.

"No, I just meant that-"

"So you still believe that I'm stupid?" he interrupts as he unties my robe and pushes it aside.

"I didn't say you were stupid. Only that the situation was," I reply meekly. Fuck.

"And do you think that the amount of money makes a difference to the *situation*, Miss Scott? You're the one whose integrity seems split here. Should the amount of money I make or lose during my time out change my mind?" he asks, lowering his mouth to my nipple. Can't think.

"Oh, god, Alex." I moan.

"You need to start answering my questions under pressure, Elizabeth," he continues, lifting me up onto the counter and spreading my legs apart. "Perfect," he whispers, gazing at me and pulling his finger down my stomach towards my sex. *Good lord!*

Does he really expect me to carry on with this discussion while almost naked? How on earth do I answer him, anyway? A lightning bolt of brilliance suddenly hits me. Perhaps I can manoeuvre my way out of the conversation without losing face. He won't see it as long as I tread carefully and keep it sexy. It's not like he doesn't understand the art of manipulation. He'll probably be amused by my attempt, and given that we're going to have sex anyway, what does any of it matter?

"I think you should do as you wish, sir, and not that which you believe is expected of you," I say quietly. That should do it - sweet, respectful and turning the tables on him.

A moment in time passes where we simply gaze into each other's eyes. For my part, I'm simply wondering if he's noticed my ploy. What's circulating in his mind is anyone's guess but suddenly his fingers still just above my belly button and he lifts them away from me. I wasn't expecting that.

I watch as his eyes change. The edge of his irises slowly disappear to create almost black and then darkened blue begins to seep back towards his pupils, dissolving the earlier brightness and silently announcing a new arrival. I've at least managed to get away from the conversation, but his features now look black and disturbingly ominous. He takes a step back and stiffens slightly in his shoulders. It's a movement that seems almost natural to him and if I hadn't been watching him so intently, I wouldn't have noticed the change in demeanour at all. But as I see some emotion pass across his eyes, he appears to remove himself and then he's gone and another man stands in front of me.

His warm smile is now replaced by a detached stare and his casual, jovial tone has been relegated to some corner of his mind and I know I won't see it again for a while. I realise all too late that I may have overstepped some imaginary line with my ploy and that perhaps this new man is a little pissed off with me for even trying to out-manoeuvre him.

"Do you think you can beat me at my own game, Elizabeth?" he says, lazily rolling his stare over my body. He noticed, and is definitely pissed.

"I... I wouldn't try, Alex. I'm just not sure what you want me to say." I try for the empathy card, hoping it will diffuse him a little. I know I'm clutching at straws but visions of whips and gags are suddenly floating through my mind.

"Don't insult me, Elizabeth. You've shown your true colours already. You're more than capable of indulging my politics. Your manipulation knows no bounds, so maybe you're more than ready to indulge my other interests," he says with an uncompromising tone.

The man before me is suddenly so much bigger and more powerful than I have ever noticed before. It's actually a little scary. His demeanour is absolutely superior and his penetrating eyes burn a hole in my soul as a sneer forms on his beautiful mouth. I feel myself swallow and lower my head, feeling somehow ashamed of my little game and really very stupid. I may have won my battle with the bitch last night, but Mr. White is a lot harder to manipulate.

"And now she lowers her head." He sighs as he walks past me without so much as a sideways glance. "Keep it lowered and follow me."

I get down from the counter hesitantly to follow him to God knows what, rounding corners with no clue what's coming.

"Take off the robe and go stand next to the bookshelves," he demands while fiddling in his desk drawer for something. I do as he says, keeping my head lowered and grasping my hands in front of my thighs nervously as I look at the study floor. He walks past me out of the room and then returns a minute later holding the choker in his hand.

"Turn around." I turn and look at the books. His hand forces my head down again.

"I will not say it again," he says through gritted teeth. "I suggest you learn, fast."

He puts the choker around my neck and turns me to face him again. Muttering to himself, he walks to the other end of the study and kicks the rolling stairs up towards me then moves me about two feet over and tells me to go up two steps. I do, although my confusion and very nervous feeling are beginning to make me question what the hell I'm doing.

He moves up one step, attaches the chain of my choker to something on the shelves and then returns to the floor. I can feel his eyes on me as he stands beneath me and I'm about to lift my head and ask him to stop this when he shifts and goes back to the desk. My insides churn over again.

"Would you like your hands tied or free?" he asks calmly. "Be very honest. I expect you to say what you want, not what you think is expected of you." I can feel the irony of his statement hit me like a battering ram. My eyes flick up. His head inclines but his face remains stony and cold. It's randomly erotic in a nasty sort of way. I have no idea what I want but I drop my eyes again and think of his fingers.

"Tied." It's out before I know it and I sense my core clench at the thought of rope.

He moves quickly and thoroughly, securing each of my wrists with rope at two points on the shelves, leaving me positioned like a cross on the steps. Tension fills my body. I'm not sure if it's through excitement or fear but something just doesn't feel quite right about what's happening.

"Look at me," he states. I look up to see a long rigid whip in his hand. "The steps will move if you put uneven pressure on them. Try it," he orders quietly. I move my feet a little and slowly the steps move to the right. Pressure drags on my left wrist and my choker tightens. I gasp at the sensation and look back at him for some clarification as to what the hell is happening.

"Good, now you've got the idea. I'm going to make you come using this," he says, holding up the whip. "And you're going to control yourself because if you don't, the steps will go too far and you'll be left hanging. Actually, I wouldn't mind that at all, but the choker is worth quite a lot of money so best you don't break it," he continues, gazing coldly at me.

"Alex, I'm not sure I can do this," I say, lowering my head again and trying to find something to hold onto with my hands. There's nothing and I feel myself truly beginning to panic a little.

"Oh but you can, Elizabeth. You want it more than you know. Remember that you're the one who asked for this. *You* tried to manipulate me and *you* called this part of me out. If you don't want to continue at any point, just say stop. It's quite simple. Lower your head again," he says, tilting his own to the side. "Are you nervous?" Fuck, yes.

"Yes," I reply, staring back down to the floor.

He moves toward me and pushes his hand between my legs. "Wider," he demands, forcing my legs apart roughly until I'm on the very edges of the step. He pulls two fingers through my core and licks the blatantly obvious slick arousal from them. "Nerves seem to agree with you. Perhaps I'll go for nervous with you more often." He laughs a little to himself and pushes his fingers into my mouth. "Suck," he barks, so I do and the moment the taste of myself hits my tongue, I hear my own groan leave my mouth. He pulls his fingers out abruptly and backs away with a small smile.

The whip rises in his hand and gently lands in between my breasts. The tip of it has a long piece of silken rope hanging from it, which at this point seems to tickle a bit, and as he circles both of my breasts then drags it along my stomach, I sigh with pleasure for the first time. Soft tingling sensations shoot across my skin like a lazy wind blowing, which only intensifies every nerve in me and causes me to close my eyes and relax into the feeling. I'm not sure how long this goes on for, but I can definitely feel the pressure throbbing in my core as the swirling motions of the whip keep enticing a new wave of desire to heat its way through my body. The relaxing buzz in my groin begins to grow to a slightly uncomfortable ache and I feel all the weight in my body force down through my legs into my feet, almost planting me in place as I moan out. The whip unexpectedly leaves my skin and lands with some force on my thigh. My eyes shoot open.

"Ouch," I shout sharply, looking back up, but weirdly, the painful sting on my thigh actually begins to turn into a very pleasurable, warm burn. It's odd, stimulating. Strange.

"I didn't say you could enjoy yourself, Elizabeth. I will not tolerate manipulation from you and if I have to tell you one more time to lower your fucking head, I will strap it down."

His voice is angry now, resentful even, and I try to swallow the fear that's starting to claw its way up my spine. His face is still cold and unwavering in his reprimand and I nervously stare into his eyes as I suddenly realise the severity of my situation. I'm hung up for him and on display with no ability to run. Where has my Alex gone? This isn't a man I know or trust. Was one small gesture of defiance enough to send him over the edge of reason? This is supposed to be fun, isn't it?

From somewhere deep inside me, I pull up enough courage to try and find him again.

"Alex, you're scaring me a little here," I say quietly.

"There's no need to be scared, Elizabeth. You're just learning a very valuable lesson, and regardless of how you think you feel, you do want this, so you'll have to trust me. Do you want me to stop?" he says as he moves closer, turns the whip and slowly pushes the handle end inside me.

"Oh, God…" I cry out as he holds it perfectly still. Do I want him to stop? My body definitely doesn't. My brain's a bloody mess, though.

"Tell me to stop if that's what you want," he says, beginning to circle it around.

The feeling is exquisite and incredibly intense. I hadn't realised how close my orgasm was but the delicious sparks igniting every nerve ending again remind me of my impending bliss. I feel my legs buckling and the step moves to the left, stretching my right arm. Oh God, please. The choker tightens and I tip my head backwards and try to regain my balance. My thighs tremble as I pull the steps back towards the middle, the whip still circling and now pushing in and out in a steady pounding rhythm.

"Good girl. You will not come until you are told," he says softly, moving his head to my groin.

One long swipe of his tongue against my very sensitive clit and I'm losing it. My calves feel it first, and trying to hold myself together is agony as the step starts shifting sideways. The force on my wrists feels like torture and bliss rolled together, and the constant pull on my throat satisfies that unyielding new need to feel controlled somehow. No matter how much I try to fight it, the pressure that is wrapping my body is exquisite. He keeps pushing the whip and circling his tongue, his teeth finding my nub with bites of pain every now and then while I shudder and moan above him. I'm so close. The fear of earlier seems to have gone and has been replaced with arousal, flooding every sense. I know there's no stopping what's coming as my core begins to explode inside me, filling me with euphoric feelings of oncoming pleasure as it chases its way through my stomach.

"Do not come, Elizabeth," he snarls.

"Alex, I can't hold it back," I almost scream.

In one swift movement, his tongue and the whip are removed and his hand connects with my backside sharply, and then again. The abrupt smacking sensation instantly brings my mind and legs back together as the heat of my orgasm retreats a little, but the incredible burn that follows only seems to intensify my desire to let go completely.

"Oh god, that's good," I moan before I think about it and tilt my head back.

"You will hold it back until you are told to come. Do you understand me?" he growls.

I feel wetness slide down my legs as I tremble again and move the steps. I can't answer him. I can't think, let alone talk. I suddenly notice my mind drifting away as if I were looking down on myself, and yet every nerve continues to send a signal to my groin - *more*. The choker tightens again, causing the binds to constrict. The biting pain seems to have its own direct current straight down to my core and as I feel a breeze skim delicately across my body, it ignites inside me.

"Please, Alex, I want to come. I can't..." I moan, straining against the restraints.

I can't stop the moaning as I feel myself shivering from the beautifully intense sensations of the ropes. My eyes begin to roll back in my head and I tilt myself into the bonds, letting the biting and constricting blissful torture flow through my body. The steps shift beneath me and I feel my weight falling, but the unrelenting fire in my core carries on of its own accord, pulsing and throbbing so quickly that I give up fighting the step and let my body fall into the ropes and my explosion. Lights start flashing before my closed eyes and the world seems to go quiet. My frantic heartbeat is the only thing I hear as my limbs become weightless and the throbbing intensifies again. A calm serenity seems to wash over me as I let the world die away. I'm in a place somewhere between darkness and enlightenment and all I can feel are waves of pleasure rolling through me, seemingly pulling me to a place of heavenly peace, stretching my body and feelings to another level entirely.

Moments or hours pass before I slowly realise I'm being held up. My legs are wrapped around his hips and warm hands are soothing my back.

"You're safe. I've got you. I won't let you go." he whispers in my ear repeatedly with a tender tone. "I'm never letting you go." I slowly open my eyes and see a concerned Alex looking back at me, his hands tightening around me. "Hi." He smiles openly. "Just hold onto me for a bit longer. I can't get you out until you can stand," he says, kissing my cheeks and hoisting me up higher so the choker hangs loose on my neck. I sigh and look into eyes again, softer and less stormy. Lovely. Although, what the fuck just happened?

I move to right myself on his hips and the button on his trousers rubs against my very sensitive nub. I gasp as the familiar bite of oncoming bliss rips through me and my spasms start again. The thought makes me try to back off from him but he pushes forward into me again and smiles wickedly. Oh, Jesus. I can't do that again, can I?

"Yes," I hiss, moaning deliriously as I tip my head back.

"Look at me. Stay with me for this one, baby. I need to see you," he says, slowly grinding into me and splaying his fingers across my back to support me.

"I can't. Please stop me... Oh god, please." I groan, trying to find the energy to grip onto him and failing. I'm exhausted. There's nothing left after the first one and yet I need to do this again.

He moves his head to my nipple and bites down on it, sucking and swirling his tongue around as I feel myself pushing against his groin against my own will. Lifting his head again, I look deep into his eyes and let myself go again. So close. Heat begins to build through me and my rapture consumes me in seconds. Wave after wave of ecstasy rips through me again and again. My legs go loose around him, and I hear the groan of satisfaction coming from him as I ride the end of my orgasm and let myself fall into his embrace.

"So damn perfect," he mumbles, bending to kiss my chest. Panting hard, I try to slow my breathing yet again as he brings me back up towards him. "Open your eyes and look at me, baby. I need you to try and stand up so I can untie you."

Yes, ropes. I'd forgotten about them. But now he mentions it they are hurting me, scratching actually. He slowly releases his grip on my thighs and guides my feet back to the step.

"Steady, take your time," he says quietly. My feet wobble a bit but I nod at him and take my own weight. As the first wrist is released, an odd feeling sweeps over me. Is it anger or fear? The second is released and I rub at my wrists. A slight pain bites into me as I flex my joints out. Pain and anger, yes, definitely anger. How dare he do this to me? I am pissed. I frown and look at the floor while trying to control my emotions. Why am I so angry?

"You okay?" he asks from three feet away.

I look at the reddened marks on my wrists and lift my hands to the choker. My throat feels a little raw but also wonderfully sinful in an erotic type of way. I tilt my neck from side to side, trying to process my pain, pleasure thing. I have no idea what it is. Or if I like it or not.

"Take this off please," I ask shakily without looking at him. He does swiftly in typical Alex style and returns to stand in front of me, still three feet away.

"How angry do you feel?" he asks, chuckling. I lift my eyes to his. Very fucking angry. Why? I have no idea about that either, and is he fucking laughing at me? "Good. You did very well for your first time, but it will take a while to get your head around the fact that you enjoyed so much pain." Apparently jovial Alex has returned now and is being as condescending as usual.

Frowning again, I walk closer to him.

"You think something is funny, Alex?" I say, my palm twitching at my side. Am I really considering slapping him?

"No, baby, not funny at all. I just can't believe how perfect you are. I've never seen a more responsive or intuitive submissive. Your desire to please me, and yourself, is so ingrained you don't even know you're doing it," he says with his amused smirk firmly plastered on. "You have no idea of your potential." Potential? Arsehole.

My hand flies and connects with his face before I know what's happened. Boiling with rage, I stare at him. He doesn't flinch. He just takes it and continues to gaze at me in adoration. I feel my hand lift of its own accord to do the same again. He snatches at my wrist and gently pushes my arm back down as he pulls me towards him forcefully and clamps his arm around my back.

"Only once, Elizabeth. I haven't let anyone slap me for a long time and I suppose I deserved it, but don't fucking irritate me. I did push you a little, and I might be sorry that I scared you, but it needed to be done," he says with a smile, lifting my hand to soothe his reddening cheek. My anger softens slightly as he nuzzles and pulls me closer to him. "You are so beautiful. So fucking beautiful. I can't believe I've found you," he says softly, kissing my forehead and leaning me into him.

"Alex."

"Yes, baby?"

"If you ever make me feel afraid again, I'll be gone. Do you understand?" I state from his chest, trying to process what the hell is happening to me.

"Then we'll have to work harder on trust," he replies with a sigh, brushing the hair from my face.

"I can't trust the man I just met, Alex. He's not you." That man was some sort of monster, even if I did enjoy him. I think. Or maybe not. I don't fucking know anything.

"Yes, baby, he is. He's there all the time. I just haven't let you see him before now. If you look deep enough, you'll notice him more." He reaches for his shirt and drapes it around my shoulders. I shrug into it and he scoops me up into his arms and heads back to the lounge.

"But on the plane?" I question. He gently lowers me to the couch, kisses my lips and moves to the cabinet in the corner of the room.

"No, baby, that wasn't him. That was me assessing you. We need to talk about some things. I hadn't planned on doing it here but as I've just revealed a little of myself, I might as well get it out of the way and then you can make your decisions. Would you like a drink?"

He obviously doesn't wait for a reply because when I look up, he's standing in front of me with two large glasses of what appears to be brandy or something. He offers one to me and sits down at the other end of the couch. I pull my knees up to my chest and look to the floor, desperately seeking some inspiration for how I feel. Of course nothing is leaping to mind apart from confusion and something akin to sympathy for my own tormented brain.

"Drink it. It will help calm you down."

I swish the liquid around and gaze up at the fire. Do I want to know what he's about to say? Is this the end of someone I thought I was getting to know? I lift the liquid and down it. Definitely brandy, and god it's good as it heats my throat and eases my frazzled nerves. I hold the glass out and indicate that I want another. He chuckles and reaches for the decanter.

Pouring the wonderful liquor into the glass, he looks at his watch and then opens his beautiful mouth."What do you really know of Domination and submission, Elizabeth?"

"Not a lot, I suppose. I've never really thought about it that much," I reply in a small voice, swishing the glass around. He sighs and pinches the bridge of his nose as if something is, or is about to be, painful in some way. I can't help but feel a little satisfied about it given the last however long in the study.

"There are two types of dominant - good ones and bad ones. Good ones adore women. They worship the ground they walk on and spend most of their time trying to achieve a permanent state of pleasure and contentment for their subs. Or anyone else's for that matter. I'm not one of them, but then I've never had a reason to be." Great. I frown and keep looking at my drink. "So I'm going to tell you something that might make you understand me a little better. I want you to trust me to look after you and I think you need to hear this to do that. Hopefully if I trust you with this, maybe we can move on."

I look up into his anxious eyes and see a strangely uncomfortable and vulnerable looking man. My heart melts a little more, albeit my body is still too tense to be entirely devoted to his troubles. I do reach forward and take his hand in mine though. No matter how I feel, he is about to share something that clearly means a great deal to him and I want him to feel open enough to tell me about it. He leans back into the sofa and gazes at me for a few minutes, chewing the side of his lip. It's adorable and I smile quietly across at him. Maybe he's reconsidering? I run my fingers over his hand to encourage him to continue.

"My childhood was very difficult. I ended up fighting and getting into a lot of trouble. The police were often involved and for varying reasons, I ended up in care. When I was sixteen, I left and decided it was time to start over somewhere else. There was nothing and no one left so I took control of my own life," he says calmly.

"Rome," I muse, still running my fingers over his. He nods and lifts our hands to his mouth.

"I met Giuseppe as you know, who helped me to find at least some sort of normalcy to life. His family were kind and they gave me a home and a job, but I guess I was just too fucked up to accept it. I got into more and more trouble, leading him along with me, and sadly I didn't care. I didn't seem to know how to do anything about it anyway so I just got deeper into my madness. The day after my twentieth birthday, I left and never looked back," he says, sighing and refilling his glass. "Conner found me again a few years later in some high-end club in London, off my face on coke with some woman or another. My life had become a turbulent world of criminal activity and decidedly dubious encounters. I'd made quite a lot of money doing things I shouldn't have done and had a good reputation for being a very bad boy. He helped me find a path out of it and eventually a way to clean myself up a little - well to some degree anyway." He gulps back another large brandy.

"You said again," I question as I try to ignore the fact that he's just told me he's been a criminal and a druggie, and given his domineering presence, probably quite a good criminal.

I'll think about that later.

"What?" he replies, looking slightly startled by the question.

"Conner... You said he found you again?" I respond as I sip at my drink and look at him over the rim of the glass.

"Ah yes, I shouldn't have said that. Trust you to pick up on it. You're far too clever for your own good, young lady. That's Conner's story to tell. I'm sure he will if you ask him. But needless to say, I knew him before," he says with a mysterious smile and a wink as he pulls my feet into his lap.

"Oh right. Well thank you for sharing. You didn't have to and I know it wasn't easy for you."

"I haven't finished. Conner helped me find channels to relieve my aggression. He taught me what it feels like to be in control of myself and to determine my own future. I owe him everything. In a roundabout way he introduced me to my *preferences,* and from that I learnt to manage my anger. It allows me to organize my mind more... appropriately," he says, gazing at me for a reaction.

"Are you telling me that you need to do this sort of stuff simply to contain yourself or something?" And does Conner need it, too? Shit. Belle. She's not going to be up for that at all.

"Well, I rather enjoy it as well, but yes, fundamentally. I like the control. I need it. It keeps me sane and stops me from remembering too much." He smiles softly and runs his fingers up my legs. "But whilst I am a dominant, I'm not necessarily inclined to behave like a very decent one, and besides, I've grown tired of the term. It has become a little... restricting."

Restricting? I have no idea what that means. How can being a dominant be restricting in any way? Isn't that the point of the term *to dominate*, as in do whatever the hell you like? But hey, if it keeps him sane then I suppose it's a good thing for him. Is it for me?

"Right, so are you suggesting that to be with you, I have to accept that this will be part of our relationship whether I like it or not?" I say, removing my hand from his.

"Yes, to be in a relationship, this is what part of me will need from you," he states rather bluntly, looking toward my hands and tightening his own around my calf.

"No other explanation?" I ask, now slightly irritated for some reason at his lack of further information regarding the topic.

"No, not really. But I can tell you that you're made for this, for me. You only have to trust me and you'll find everything you never knew you needed." I frown and think of the last hour or so. Do I really want that sort of relationship? Did I enjoy the pain as much as he's indicating I did?

"Are you suggesting I'm some sort of masochist?" I ask with a twinkle of amusement at the thought. Beth Scott, caterer and cook, built for pain? Unlikely.

"I'm not sure I'd go quite that far yet, but fundamentally, yes. I think you're entirely compatible with what I want from us. I'm just not sure you're ready to understand it." I look at him with confusion again, pretty sure he's completely right but not really comprehending the overall meaning of his statement in the slightest.

He reaches forward and takes the glass from my hand. Putting it on the table, he waggles his fingers at me to suggest that he wants me closer to him. I slide over to him and look into those incredible penetrating eyes as he stares back at me with a smirk.

"Why did you just scoot over to me?" he asks, quite seriously.

"Because you asked me to," I reply with valid confusion.

"No I didn't. I indicated that I needed you and you responded without thinking, regardless of the fact that I've just put you through a rather intense situation. You knew I was angry and yet you still didn't tell me to stop. You see, in spite of your confusion, you wanted what I was offering." He smiles and draws his fingers along my jaw. "So please don't take yourself away from me simply because you don't understand everything yet."

"I... I don't *understand* what happened in there," is my quiet response, pointing vaguely in the direction of the study.

"No, you don't, but I do and I can help you with that. We just need time and we don't have it because my saviour will be here in ten minutes and I have to speak to him before he flies home."

"Oh, right," What else can I say to that?

"Look, have a bath, get dressed and we'll talk about it again later if you want. I'll tell you everything you need to know. I thought we'd go for a tour around the city. I have lots of places I'd like to share with you. Perhaps you'll be a little more relaxed then?"

Relaxed? There's not a lot of relaxing going on in my head at the moment. Okay, my body is completely lax but my mind is very much not.

I look at him for a moment and take in the smouldering man in front of me while he gazes at me, waiting for an answer. Beautiful from head to toe, he's everything a girl could dream of and more. But it seems to come at a cost and I'm really not sure if I want to pay it. I shake my head at my own ridiculous thoughts as I get up and head toward the bathroom. I don't know who it is that I'm trying to fool because the fact of the matter is that I'll let him take me further. I can't imagine those hands ever being away from me again.

"Elizabeth," he calls.

"Yes," I reply as I get to the bottom of the stairs.

"Turn around."

I turn around and see him leaning gracefully against the wall in the hallway, a dazzling smile adorning his stupidly sexy face and his shirtless, lean body glistening under the hall lights at me.

"It'll be worth it. You know that, don't you?" he says, easing off the wall and walking toward me.

"What will?" I ask. Good lord he's just stunning, and I can tell he knows it with every step toward me. Arrogant bastard, using his superhuman good looks to lull me into a false sense of security while secretly plotting to whip the shit out of me or something. I can't believe I'm contemplating any of this crap. The fact that my body's suddenly buzzing with tingly nerves again and my jaw is hanging open at his stalking manoeuvre is neither here nor there.

"Us," he replies, lowering his head to brush his lips across mine, barely skimming them.

He hooks his thumbs under the collar of my shirt and drags it over my shoulders. I feel my breath hitch and my heart rate increase.

289

Oh god, where's this going. We've only got ten minutes. Spinning the shirt over his back, he shrugs his arms into it, starts to do up the buttons and makes a spinning gesture with his finger.

"Go on then, off you go and have a good think. I'll want your answer by this evening." He smirks and slaps my backside playfully as I frown at him and turn.

"Ouch, that hurt," I squeal, quite pathetically really, and looking over my shoulder at him as he heads in the other direction. Those long legs glide purposefully as he swipes his phone from the table and chuckles to himself, annoying me with his superiority of my dishevelment.

"Not as much as the next one will now I know your tolerance for it," he replies as he turns the corner. My legs tremble again. What the hell is that?

Chapter 21

Elizabeth

M r White and Rome… What more could a girl want? After his meeting with Conner, he rushed me out of the door, claiming there was so much to see and so little time to see it. He was right.

We've walked hand in hand everywhere and I can't even begin to remember the names of all the monuments, buildings, plazas and museums he's showed me, but I do know I will never forget the visions or the feelings. One could never leave it behind because it is, by definition, divine.

Of course Alex has been charming, chivalrous and wonderful but he has also retreated from me a little. I can feel it in his hands, slightly tense and lighter in their grip. His eyes show less warmth, too, as if he's trying to keep me at arm's length for some reason. Whether something else is on his mind or he's simply thinking of my reaction to the earlier conversation I don't know, but I know I can't cope much longer without knowing more or just getting us back to the way we were last night.

We've stopped in a very expensive looking restaurant near the Vatican City to have coffee and cakes and are sitting at a second floor private terrace. The view is simply breathtaking and the surroundings are luxurious and decadent with a hint of that modern chic you see in all the glossy magazines. *Utter Bliss, albeit quite out of my normal comfort zone.*

"Do you want to go out this evening or stay in?" he asks casually, stroking my thigh with his fingertips.

I think about that for a while. Do I? I have no idea. I need to know more about what I'm letting myself in for with this man. There's no doubt that I trust him in some way, well sort of, but to open up my body to some sort of torture and risk my sanity in the process? I'm not so sure. Although, regardless of my hesitation in the matter, I somehow know deep down that he'll never really harm me. Not that I'm actually sure what the definition of *harm* is anymore.

"Elizabeth, are you still here?" he says again, pinching my thigh playfully. "What do you want to do tonight?"

"I want... No, I *need* more from you... About you, about your past," I blurt out abruptly, my brain obviously not managing to find a more subtle way of delivering that statement.

He stares out onto the plaza for a while as I gaze at him, studying him. Not that there's a lot to study because his face is absolutely expressionless, and with his sunglasses on, I can't even see his eyes to get a feel for what he's thinking. The corners of his lips slowly curl upwards.

"Look back over the past, with its changing empires that rose and fell, and you can foresee the future too," he muses, still looking toward the Vatican.

"Excuse me?" I reply, slightly startled by his random response.

"Marcus Aurelius was an emperor and soldier of Rome, a philosopher. That's his quote. Do you think that by knowing which empires fell around me that you'll be able to understand me more or see a clearer future for us? Do you want all the dirty secrets?" he says, turning his head towards me, his tone level and calm but with just a hint of something else.

Wow... He's quoting Roman emperors? Christ, does he have to be so bloody superior?

"I know that I need to feel you give yourself to me as much as you want it to be returned. There may be things in your past that haunt you and I don't expect you to tell me everything, but I do need to know that you're honest when I ask a question of you. That's the only way I can trust you to take me and my feelings forward. I don't doubt your ability to protect me physically, Alex, but I have to defend my emotions if you can't be truly honest about who you are." He sighs and turns back toward the street.

"I'm not sure what else I can give you, Elizabeth. I've given you more than any other simply to please you and help you see who I am. I've never lied to you and I don't intend to, but I won't answer something if I'm not ready to tell you the truth. I'm not sure my past would be very endearing to you and I won't risk losing you because of my history," he states, pinching his brow and looking troubled. "Can't you just accept the man I am today? My past is simply that, my past."

"Who you were defines who you are now, Alex. There are too many versions of you in the present tense. I'm confused as to which one of you I am dealing with most of the time and I would just like to know who I am meeting on a daily basis. I certainly want to know who I am meeting in the bedroom," I reply, giggling at my own sarcasm.

His shoulders began to shake and he full on laughs at my statement, a glorious laugh that has me grinning like a fool and falling in love a little more. Turning towards me and flashing me with a true megawatt smile, he takes my face in his hands and leans his forehead on mine.

"You are wonderful, Elizabeth. I love your honesty and incorruptibility. You can't imagine how refreshing it is to have someone remind me of myself every now and then. I must seem quite the enigma to you." He chortles, almost to himself. "Please believe me when I tell you that I want to let you have all of me, but I can't just magically erase the parts that are lacking. There are many things you do not want to know about my past. There are also things in my present that I can't tell you about. Not because I want to lie to you but because I simply want to keep you safe from certain elements of my life. You are far too special for me to risk your disapproval," he says as he kisses me briefly. He lets go and returns to his upright position, picking up his coffee and wrapping his lovely lips around the cup.

"I don't care about the parts that are lacking, Alex. I just want to know that you're honest enough to admit to them," I respond with a wry smile.

"Okay. So let's say I'll try your way if you try mine. Is that enough for you?" he asks, resuming his gaze at me across his coffee. "And you will always know who you're meeting in the bedroom, Elizabeth. He's basically the same man. It just depends on how you react to him." What?

"I have no idea what that means," is my thoroughly confused response. He's the one that changes into someone else.

"I became that way inclined because you challenged me and it pissed me off. Having said that, I did quite enjoy the ramifications of your confrontation so please don't stop on my account," he says, grinning like a naughty schoolboy.

"So are you saying that if I conform to your every whim there will be no more of whatever that was?"

"Well, you'll have to let me have a little fun, Elizabeth, and I absolutely do not want you to conform in any way, shape or form. What happened before was a punishment. Whatever happens going forward will depend on how happy you are to let me embrace my aggression with you," his says as his mouth turns up into a devilish grin that has me trembling with delight. My mind immediately starts castigating my traitorous body. It's confusing. Everything is with him involved.

"So you have differing versions of dominance as well then? The shower, the plane, the study?" He chuckles again.

"No, Elizabeth, I have one version of dominance but we're trying something different. Let's just say I'm building you up to something and hoping you'll understand when you get there."

The thought of more than has already been is bizarrely making my legs buckle despite the fact that I'm sitting down. I have no idea what he has in store but for some reason, my body wants more of whatever it is. I hang my head at my thoughts, feeling some sort of shame sweep across me. He growls, lifts my chin gently and looks deep into my eyes. I swear he reaches my soul with the intensity of his soft stare. Warm, blue eyes meet mine as his mouth quirks up a little.

"No, Elizabeth, not unless I tell you to. You've no need to feel ashamed or guilty about this. This is who you are. Nobody will ever make you feel uncomfortable again while you are with me, and if you are not then I'll have taught you to admire yourself more. You're doing so well. Just stop thinking about it so much and go with how it feels. Trust me to show you the way."

He continues with his hold on my chin until he's satisfied that his little pep talk has hit me square in the jaw and then moves back to study my face for any twinge of emotion. I wish he couldn't see right through me so easily. Is it even possible to read someone so quickly?

"I think we need a night out and a few drinks. Actually, I know I do," I say abruptly, changing the subject. He laughs and moves some hair from my face, tucking it behind my ear.

"And she says I'm changeable." He chuckles and kisses me quickly.

"What? I'm just answering your earlier question," I reply with a mock shocked face. "Do you know somewhere dark and loud where you can take my mind off my emotions?"

"I definitely know just the place for that, Miss Scott," he says with a mischievous wink. "It doesn't open until ten, though, so we'll go for dinner first," he continues as he glances at his watch, picks up his phone and texts furiously to someone. "Does this mean you're agreeing to my terms, Miss Scott?" he asks, looking at his phone.

"No, Mr. White. It means I'm in Rome and I'd like to continue my rather interesting experience for a while longer," I reply, looking through my lashes at him and batting them for the full on tease effect.

His strong jaw twitches as he reaches up to rub the back of his neck without looking at me and I watch as he draws in a long breath and blows it out quietly. Narrowing my eyes, I realise that he always does that when he's confused or nervous of something, rubs his neck. Probably why he doesn't gamble that much. Mr. White does have a weakness then.

"You are just as confusing, you know? Every time I think I've worked you out, you throw me again. It's really quite... disturbing. I've never been so perplexed by a woman," he says with a frown.

"Mmm... I'm glad you find me so bewildering," I reply, gazing again at the view.

"So am I, Miss Scott. So am I."

Finishing my coffee, I glance down to the street below us to notice a black limousine pull up in front of the cafe and roll my eyes at the thought. Why does everything have to be so damned expensive around him?

"Couldn't we have just taken a cab?" I ask without looking at him. "I assume that is yours?"

"Why on earth would we do that?" he replies with a quizzical tone. Clearly he doesn't get it at all. I don't know why I bothered to question it, to be honest. "Come on. Let's get home and changed for dinner," he says, pulling out my chair and offering me his hand. We descend the stairs rapidly and arrive at the car where a swarthy looking chauffeur holds the door open.

"Oh shit, we haven't paid," I ramble as I turn back to the restaurant in a rush.

"We don't have to. I doubt the price of a few coffees will break me." His face is confused. I return his expression.

"What do you mean? Is this an Italian thing I'm not aware of?"

"Ah, I see the confusion now. Look at the name above the door, baby," he says, pointing upwards and putting his phone to his ear.

"Bianchi," I announce in a crappy Italian accent. It still means nothing to me.

"It means White's."

He smiles and launches into a dramatic conversation with someone on the phone in Italian.

Well, of course.

~

I assumed that dinner in Alex's world would probably mean somewhere swanky. I was right. The atmosphere in here is very uppity and overwhelmingly glamorous. Not understanding the language has made me feel a little insecure again but Alex has somehow made me come back to him and feel light-hearted again.

"Don't you ever go anywhere normal?" I ask, casually, pushing my five pieces of food around the plate.

"What do you mean? I come here often. That's quite *normal,* isn't it?" he replies sarcastically.

"I mean fish and chips style normal, you idiot." My giggle bursts from me at his clipped response.

"I can't remember the last time I ate fish and chips," he muses, frowning and stabbing at some asparagus as he holds it on the fork and looks at me. "Makes this food look a bit stuffy, doesn't it?"

"I don't know about stuffy. It's very good. I just wondered if this is typical for you or if there's a more relaxed version of you hiding in there somewhere?"

"If you want the more relaxed version of me, I'm afraid you'll have to dig deeper than even I have for a while. I feel like I lost that man a long time ago," he says, no emotional response to his own statement whatsoever.

"Doesn't that bother you? Do you remember him at all?" I ask, looking into his beautiful eyes and trying to see the man underneath, the one behind the enigmatic smiles and rigid fronts.

296

"I don't try to remember him. He wouldn't have done the things I've done or seen the places I've seen, or made the money I have for that matter. He would have been sitting in some dive of a bar, snorting cocaine and fucking anything that moves. I hope I've moved on from that rather successfully."

Well that was blunt.

"Wow... So, no naughty fish and chips then?" I ask on a smile.

"No, no fish and chips, Elizabeth," he replies with a smirk.

"You could have both, you know?" I state, licking my lips, picking up a piece of carrot and frowning at it. "It's not all that naughty for you, is it? Or relaxing, frankly."

"Searching for yet another version of me, Miss Scott?" he asks, watching my mouth with those icy blue eyes. "I thought you were confused enough already."

"I'm just looking for the real man behind you, Mr. White. I think he's hoping to make an appearance soon."

~

I'm very glad that I've opted for a very special dress that Belle let me borrow for the trip, although there hasn't been a lot of dinner eaten because there isn't an inch of room left in it. The shimmering grey cocktail dress clings to every curve on me and the halter neck lifts and enhances my breasts to perfection. It's a little shorter than I'd normally go for, around mid-thigh, but something about Alex just seems to make me go the extra mile to please him and frankly, I can't stop feeling sexy as hell around him. The matching grey three inch sling back shoes lengthen my legs and make me feel incredibly elegant so I've left my hair down, put some curl to it and kept my make up very simple to soften the whole thing a bit. And anyway, what's the point of make-up in a club? It only slides off your face within twenty minutes.

The car is winding its way around the small streets of Rome as we travel toward the club. It's already eleven and I'm well on my way to being quite tipsy. According to Alex, a man called Pascal Van Der Braak owns the place. He's apparently quite the scoundrel across the European circuit and is very well respected for his connections and wild parties. He's warned me to stay close to him for the evening because of Pascal's complete lack of care when it comes to any sort of appropriate behaviour around women. He is, and I quote, "A complete sexual predator and someone who is used to getting exactly what he wants, when he wants it." Great.

Of course, he's also one of Alex's few good friends. Why would I have thought anything else?

He sounds just like the man I'm currently sitting next to. Unfortunately, this only furthers my nerves at meeting the man. One Alex in the room is definitely enough for me. No way I'm going to be able to cope with two because in all likelihood, the man is probably another completely explosive and unpredictable character. I know this because Alex only appears to have friends of that nature so it's completely obvious to me that I'll probably be an utter disaster when I meet the man. It's just what I need to feel relaxed and comfortable for the evening, not.

"Drink your champagne, Elizabeth, and relax. Really, he's not all that bad. Just play his games and you'll be fine. I promise I won't let him near you. Unless you want me to, that is. Do you?" he teases, smirking. My eyes shoot to his in surprise.

"What? You don't expect me to do anything with him? I mean, he won't expect it, will he? Because I can't do that sort of stuff and I-" He laughs and pulls me across the seat toward him, abruptly cutting me off with a rather passionate kiss.

"No, baby, you're mine and I'll let him know that. I really just wanted to see your reaction. He is quite the charmer though. I've never known a woman turn him down. In fact, I don't know many men that have turned him down either," he says, chuckling and reaching for his drink.

"Do you mean he's bisexual?" I reply, eyes wide open at this titbit. Not that I mind, I just haven't met many actual bisexuals and the dynamic confuses me a little if I'm honest.

"Oh, Elizabeth, he's all kinds of sexual. I doubt there's a category for what he is and even if there was one, he'd hate to be labelled with it," he replies while he gazes out of the window and drifts in his own thoughts.

"Oh. Right," I reply, downing my glass of champagne. "I'll have another then please," I say, lifting my glass and nodding toward the bottle. Clearly I'll need it to deal with whoever Pascal is.

"Good girl. Go steady though, you'll need a clear head for this place," he counters with a beaming smile as he returns his eyes to me, his black hair glinting as the street lights dip in the window. "I want you to remember everything about the evening."

"Oh, I thought it was a dance club. Isn't the point to get a little drunk and let go?"

"Well dancing does go on and it's definitely a club. It's just a different sort of club," he says wickedly, steeling me with a hardened, sex-fuelled gaze that has my panties almost combusting. "Your *letting go* is a prerequisite of entering the building."

"Right well, I'll be careful then," I say, watching him sink another large Cognac. Where the hell are we going? To the devil in his lair apparently. I'm not at all sure I'm comfortable with the prospect and nervously sip at my drink in the hope of quelling the rising panic.

"Good, just stay close to me and do as you're told. Now, take off that beautiful lace g-string you're wearing and give it to me." I stare in open-mouthed shock at him as he smoulders in the corner, swirling his Cognac around the glass.

"You expect me to go in there without any underwear?" I practically shout at him. "After what you've told me about the place and its owner?"

"I expect you to do as you're told, Elizabeth. If you want to challenge me in this, please be my guest. We're nearly there and the venue will offer plenty of tools for punishment."

I watch for any sign of possible joke in his face or amusement on his lips. There isn't any, just his divine mouth that calls to me for something more than I've given before, so I gaze at his perfectly dishevelled hair and his piercing blue eyes that dare me to defy him and consider his request. He's dressed in a black suit with a black, slim fit, open neck shirt that does nothing to disguise the incredibly firm physique beneath. The only splash of colour is a pair of gold cufflinks with a strange symbol embedded on them, hinting at something I obviously have no idea about. The effect in its entirety is striking, mysterious, undeniably delicious and not beyond the realms of Satan. He's also deadly serious and I'm going to have to make a decision - no panties in a strange place or punishment in a strange place? Oddly, I find the decision easier than I thought I would.

Leaning forward on the seat, I take another long gulp of my champagne and put the glass back into the console in a relaxed fashion, well, as relaxed as I can be around Alex. Then, reaching for my bag, I dab on some more lipstick while looking into my mirror. I look good and I feel sexier than I ever have before now. He does this to me somehow, gives me confidence to feel almost euphoric in my sexuality. So pouting my lips and smacking them together for effect, I close the compact with a snap and lean back into the seat, crossing my legs seductively in the process and gazing towards him with a look of complete defiance. His slight chuckle and raised brow as he licks his lips only intensifies my lust driven stupid thigh-clenching, which is still utterly ridiculous. I seriously need to get control of that at some point. No man should ever look that damn sexy. It should be law or something, and the instant visions of the things I'd let him do to me drifting through my mind do nothing to help me gain any sort of control whatsoever.

"You have been warned, Elizabeth," he says with a smirk.

"Yes, Mr. White, I have been well warned and I'm still refusing," I reply, hoping for nonchalant, probably not achieving it.

"There's no room for sentiment or remorse in there," he says, gesturing toward the window as the car glides to a stop. "Are you ready?"

A large black door stands outside the window with a burly man in a tuxedo standing at the side of it. Small gold letters mark the door, EDEN, and the same symbol that Alex has on his cufflinks lies next to it. I feel the panic rise a little but one look into his questioning eyes again and I know what I want. Him, and if that means entering the unknown, I'm more than willing to go. Just not entirely on his terms, but thankfully, my inner slut is feeling a little frisky and ready for anything.

"Yes, I think I am," I reply with a smile as I flick my hair over my shoulder. He reaches into his pocket and pulls out a diamond bracelet - my diamond bracelet.

Grabbing my hand smoothly, he links it around my left wrist and kisses the palm of my open hand.

"Yes, I think you are, too. Now, do not take that off. It will show them that you are mine and they'll leave you alone. Well, most of them will. I'll deal with the others if I have to. Do you understand?" he asks with a slight frown.

"Yours?" I question, because what does that mean? He doesn't own me, for God's sake.

"Yes. Mine. Do you have a problem with that?" he says, raising an eyebrow and encouraging a negative response. "You could always go in there on your own and meet those sharks head on. I'll very much enjoy watching the show."

Oh, I hadn't thought about it like that and I definitely want to have him close to me for what I think we're about to enter.

"Okay, I don't have a problem with that for this evening, but tomorrow may be a different matter entirely. I do not belong to you, Mr. White," I reply as I look him directly in the eye and hopefully counter his expression.

"Mmm... Feisty. You can't help but give me leverage for later, can you?" He laughs as he opens the door and leaves me alone for a second. I narrow my eyes at his figure as he wanders around the front of the car. I'm not entirely comfortable with the statement at all, or what it might entail.

"Here we go," I mumble under my breath.

As I step out of the car and accept his rather charming yet deviant hand, the cold wind whistles past me instantly, hardening my nipples.

"I like this dress, very thin. I can almost see through it." He smirks as he moves his hand to my backside, squeezing firmly and sliding it downward, teasing the inside of my thigh with his fingers and trailing it upwards. "Remember that whatever you see in here and whatever we do, my eyes will only be for you, Elizabeth. You are fucking irresistible to me. I'm already hard just thinking about what I want to do to you." He moves my hand to his crotch and I gasp at the rigid length that he pushes against it with a groan.

I look up into his hungry eyes and am about to say something when the club door flies open and a man is quite literally thrown out of the door. He lands with a crunch about two feet away from us. I stare down to see the man rolling over, clutching his stomach and squealing like a pig. Turning to Alex, I see a small smile cross his lips. He moves me back a few steps and then looks up to the door. I follow his gaze to see the most fantastic man stalk out the door. He looks like he's walked out of the eighteenth century, his dark hair tied in a short ponytail with a crushed red velvet suit adorning his lean body. Long black riding boots finish his look, with frills falling out of his cuffs like some sort of regency dandy. He's holding a black walking cane over his shoulder that has a gold top, which glints next to his dazzling green eyes, and a cigarette dangle from his lips.

He's stunning, like nothing I've seen before, almost pretty in a manly sort of way. Nothing like Alex at all, none of his solidity or breadth. He's more of a fantasy creature of some sort. He's around the same height, although leaner and far more angular in his appearance, but there's definitely an undeniable attraction because his whole being oozes sex and pleasure. He also knows it, and unfortunately I can't stop looking at him.

I watch in fascination as he wanders nonchalantly across to the man on the floor, unzips his trousers and pees all over him. While inspecting his victory and directing his pee, his eyes stray to my shoes and lazily draw their way up my legs. They stop briefly at my breasts as he licks his long lips then smiles and continues on to my face. His eyes hit mine in seconds and something about them immediately begins to hypnotize me. I feel myself getting lost in the liquid green pools of lust with no sense of my surroundings or thought of Alex. My mind rallies for a second as I try to pull myself together. Those eyes make me very nervous. He makes me nervous, so I instantly look down and then frown as I notice him put himself away and do up his trousers. Alex growls at my side and pinches my backside. "Head up," he murmurs, so I lift my eyes and look back at the man as he opens his unfairly captivating mouth.

"I have never seen such a morsel. My teeth are wet with want and I am so very hungry. Please, my dear, let me taste you - just one bite, maybe two," he says, moving toward me and reaching out with his cane to my throat. Alex grabs at the cane before it touches me and throws it to the floor as he moves in front of me. The man laughs. "Oh, Alexander, now you have me intrigued." He turns back to me. "You must be quite the indulgence, my dear. I have not known him to be possessive before now." His eyes linger, but he's distracted by the man on the floor, who is trying to stand. Taking a step back, he pounds the heel of his boot into his groin and leans down to whisper something in his ear while the man writhes in agony. The poor soul rolls over, picks

302

up the cane, pulls himself to his knees and then bows his head, holding the cane aloft for him. I'm in utter shock. It's like I've stepped back one hundred years to a different time. Some random thing is going on in front of me that I have no idea about. It seems there are a new set of rules to play with.

"Wonderful, Marcus. I'm glad we've had this little dialogue. Now go home to your beloved and tell her I will call her tomorrow. She may be more amenable now," he says, retrieving his cane and wiping it down with a handkerchief. I notice the man on the floor start to stand. "I never said you should stand, Marcus. You will crawl home," he barks at the man. The man nods and crawls down the street on his hands and knees. Oh. My .God. What the hell? My eyes follow him as he keeps crawling until he turns a corner and is gone from view. I snap my mouth closed again and look back at Mr Fantastical.

"Now, Alexander, my dear boy, how have you been? And why would you bring such a delicacy here if you're not willing to let me have her? It is too unfair of you," he says, never removing his eyes from my face. It's quite disconcerting because I can't stop returning his smile, which is naughty to say the least, possibly lethal.

"Pascal, you will do me the courtesy of looking at me when you talk to me or I'll throw you back into the dungeon. You know how much you enjoyed it last time," Alex replies from the side.

What? Where the hell am I? This is not normal. Mind you, nothing about Alex is so far. I really try for impassive but the man's slow licking of lips does nothing to stop my rapid heartbeat as he narrows his iridescent green eyes and turns to face Alex.

"Alexander, I would be happy to follow you back in there with my head bowed. You know how much you fascinate me. Such a beautiful specimen, don't you agree, my dear?" he asks, turning back to me with another radiantly disarming smile. "Please allow me to introduce myself as this uncultured moron hasn't had the decency." He dips to his knee and takes my hand. "I am Pascal Van Der Braak, and I am your host and servant for the evening."

Of course it would be him, wouldn't it? And servant? I doubt it somehow. The devil himself, definitely.

I turn to see Alex beaming with delight at me. "I think he likes you, Elizabeth," he says with a raised eyebrow.

"Good evening, Pascal. And yes, I agree very much," I reply as he kisses his way up my arm, and Christ, those lips are tortuous. I can't stop watching them move their way along seductively.

"Elizabeth, how very English. A rose amongst thorns. Do you bleed, my dear, when you are scratched? Or do you moan with desire?" he asks, now dangerously close to my neck. I still can't deny my trembling at his touch as I'm drawn back into those eyes again.

"Pascal, you are becoming a little tiresome already. Remove your tongue from her. I've told you she's not available to you. Would you like me to emphasize the point a little more physically?" Alex growls out beside me, his body in its casually aggressive stance. I'm completely turned on. I'm just not sure who caused it first.

Pascal immediately stills and let's go of my hand, then turning toward Alex, he moves as quick as a flash and is in his face in a second. It's almost super human speed. Alex doesn't flinch in the slightest. In fact, he looks bored.

"Alexander, you are delightfully spirited this evening and smell divine as usual, but do not push your luck, dear boy. I have half a mind to spank you for your insolence," he rumbles, running a finger along Alex's jaw and licking his lips again. I have no idea where to look, and can only assume that something sexual is going on that I'm not aware of. Actually, they might be bonding or something.

"Try, Pascal... Please," Alex retorts with a hint of anger looming. I have a feeling this has probably happened before and I watch on to see what happens next.

They face off for a few minutes. Pascal is almost growling with the sexiest of smiles adorning his intoxicating face as Alex appears to be doing that growing while retaining his impassive stare. I can't make my mind up whether they're about to fight or not so I start to lower my head. This clearly isn't going well. Then I think better of it and decide I'm not going to stand here for the evening while these two play who's the bigger boy. It's probably just a thing between them, some sort of dominance dance, and while it's interesting, and bizarrely sexy in some sort of way that I'm not able to process, I'm bloody freezing in this dress.

"Right, gentlemen, I am sure this is very entertaining for you both. However, I am a little cold and could do with a stiff drink. So could you drop the testosterone levels for a second and postpone your lover's tiff so one of you can lead the way to the bar?" I state with more force than I had intended as I land my hand on my hip.

Both men swing their heads around and stare at me. Pascal is the first to beam in delight as Alex calmly moves back towards me, grabs my hand possessively and kisses his way up the side of my neck.

"Perfect," he whispers. Pascal chuckles behind him.

"Yes, she is. Well done, dear boy, and quite different for you. Wherever did you find her?" he asks, returning to the door and beckoning at me with his hands. I'm really not sure I should take them. They look far too dangerous and inviting. "Come, Elizabeth, enjoy my playground. When you're bored with him do come and find me. I will be waiting. First, let me find you something stiff," he says, smiling wickedly at me.

I look at Alex for confirmation of how I'm supposed to respond to that. He smiles and nods, pushing me toward Pascal with his hand at my back but increasing his grip on my palm. Maybe I'm supposed to flirt a little? Who knows? The whole situation is weird. God knows Pascal is.

"Pascal, my hands are full for the time being and I'm more than satisfied with my current situation, but I'll keep your very enticing offer on the table. May I ask if you play chess?" I reply, smiling sweetly and hoping I can keep up with both of them for the whole evening.

Alex lets go of my hand and exhales as if I've passed some test that was necessary before entry was allowed. Was it? Or it could be nerves. But why would he be nervous of anything?

Pascal takes hold of my left hand and pulls it into the crook of his arm, patting my hand and pointing at the door with his cane. The doorman opens it and we walk through as he fiddles with my bracelet and gazes back at Alex for a moment, raising an eyebrow quizzically. I get the feeling that the diamonds sparkling on my wrist explain something I'm not aware of. Eventually the man talks again in that smooth European accent of his. I can't place it but it could be German under an Italian top layer, as if he's been here for a long time.

"Please don't tell me she's intelligent as well, Alexander. You know how I like them to challenge me. Oh, what fun we could have, my dear. I bet that smart mouth gives incredible head. I can just imagine bending you over a bench and..."

Oh dear god, who speaks like that in front of someone's boyfriend? If that's what he is.

"Pascal, once more and I will-" Alex warns from behind me. Well, here goes nothing. Time for me to perform, I think.

"Really, Pascal, must you be so basic? I've heard wonderful things about you and you're really not living up to expectations at all. I believe the terms Alex used were *astonishing* and *brilliant*, and that no one had ever turned you down. I'm afraid you'll have to work a little harder than that for me. Alex is, as you say, a beautiful specimen and I'd hate to lose something so precious because of something less worthy," I state, smiling and licking my lips out of nerves more than bravado, hoping desperately that it was the right tactic to go with.

Pascal stops and turns me toward him. His eyes narrow to an evil glint and his smile disappears as he lifts his finger to his mouth and frowns at me. It's deadly, almost crippling. I feel my whole body wobble a bit as his prolonged stare reduces me to an internal wreck in seconds. Christ, he's as good as Alex and I'm not even sure he's giving me the full effect. Shit, I may have gone too far. I mean, I really don't know anything about the man or what his version of a game is. What I do know is that I'm beginning to tremble again.

I feel my chin dip and then remember to lift it up. I can feel Alex's smile beside me as he fingers my hipbone then wraps his arm around my waist, pulling me back toward him. Pascal's gaze follows me so I try to keep my eye contact steady with his. Thankfully, Alex kisses my shoulder and strokes the back of his fingers along my arm, filling me with confidence, so I turn my face to his and beam up at him. He licks his lips and looks across at Pascal.

"Enough of this now. She's mine and you will stop. You've had your fun. Find someone else to play with," he says with a finality that we all feel and a smile that would captivate the gods.

"Astonishing, you say?" Pascal replies as he looks over my shoulder at the stunning man behind me with his eyes sparkling to life again. "Alexander, you bewitch me once more," he says as he returns his smile to me. "Really, my dear girl, you are truly beautiful and utterly tempting. However, it has always been him that I wanted. Why he continues to resist me, I do not know," he muses, taking my arm again and leading me along a corridor towards an inviting sound.

"Now, what would you like to drink, my darlings? I think we will have such fun this evening."

Did he honestly just say that? I've clearly entered some sort of twilight zone or something equally bizarre. Alex is relaxed and calm as if none of this is anything unusual at all. Well it might not be to him but it damn well is to me. The music in front of us somewhere is thumping away with a bass rhythm to die for and I listen to Pascal talking smoothly as he grips my upper arm and leads me towards God knows what.

"Champagne, please," I reply, because I really do need it, possibly lots of it. He smirks and keeps walking.

The door in front of us swings open and a stunning, raven-haired woman dressed in little more than a few leather belts and thigh high boots wanders towards us, her bright red lips singing along with the music behind her as she gazes at the floor, swinging a chain from her fingers. She's utterly beautiful and I immediately feel awkward and completely out of place. Her eyes notice our shoes, and as she looks up at us, she instantly drops to the floor on her knees and scuttles to the side to give us room to pass. Pascal brushes his hand over her head and chuckles as we continue onward. I turn to see Alex glance down at her. She stiffens considerably and nervously flicks her eyes to his then away again.

"Sir, it's good to see you back," she says. He looks up at me and smiles. It's one of his breath-taking, knee disabling, panty dropping smiles so obviously my core clenches and I look back down at the woman. Christ, is that what he wants from me? I can't do that, can I? Do I even want to?

The moment his fingers touch her head in what appears to be the normal greeting around here, my answer hits me square in the gut. I definitely won't be saying no to anything he wants from me this evening because that one touch on another woman was enough to draw every inch of jealously I have out of me. It's time to embrace whatever it is he sees in me and let him guide me towards wherever it is he's going to take me.

Chapter 22

Alexander

He watched intently as her sexy arse swayed its way along the corridor toward the doors of the club, those incredibly long legs gliding across the floor and that indecently short dress clinging to every curve on her body. He groaned and adjusted himself as his eyes lingered on her slender arm linked with his friend's as Pascal looked at her as if he were about to devour her.

He should be concentrating on other matters but his head was so wrapped up in his dick and his unreasonable emotions that he just had to bring her here. He would bind her, maybe suspend her, and have her in every way he could think of. Then he could get the ridiculous notion of something *more* out of his mind. Who was he bloody kidding? If that was the case, he wouldn't have cuffed her. He would have shared her with Pascal. He'd shared them all with Pascal and then tossed them aside to the rest of the mob after they'd both had their fun. She really had no idea who she was talking to and what depravity he was capable of. Good job to be honest. If she did know, she definitely wouldn't want to spend any time with Pascal at all, or himself for that matter.

His introduction to Pascal had been through a mutual acquaintance, someone of dubious intent that Alex no longer had much contact with, but that first meeting had been enlightening to say the least. Watching a man like Pascal tear open a woman with nothing more than a teaspoon and a candle in a small kitchen in Venice had been the most fascinating and absorbing moment of his life. He'd quietly gazed from the corner as the man had smirked through her open legs at him and asked him if he wanted to learn how to "enhance his appreciation of life." He'd nodded in reply and so it had begun.

Pascal had become his mentor in the D/s scene and he'd still never seen a better master of his art. Only once had he received a lashing to learn how it felt to be submissive, and it had been at the hands of Pascal. It was a night that he remembered vividly, and a night that he would not be revisiting any time soon. It had been necessary at the time and even vaguely enticing in a remote sort of way, but it was Pascal that would switch for the right person. Alex knew he most definitely would not.

He fiddled with his shirt collar and looked down at his unusually shaking hands. Noticing his cuffs, he smiled and shook out his hands. He had been given the cufflinks three years ago when Pascal had watched him reduce three subs to a beautifully begging disaster of tears with nothing more than a meter length of rope and his voice.

"Finish them," Pascal had said as he pulled up a chair in the centre of the empty room. *"You have thirty minutes. Make me proud."*

So finish them he did, thoroughly.

All of them had pleaded with Pascal to make him stop, and when his laughter had receded, Pascal had eventually let them leave. That had been enough to gain him lifetime entry to any club in their world and the title of Master. What that actually meant in the real world was still a fucking mystery but it had given him some semblance of order and a new introduction to the meaning of discipline. His brain had been given a way to organise itself and thankfully that meant he'd been taught a way to restrain his emotional response, which was usually violent or explosive to say the least. He chuckled as a memory drifted through his mind.

"You are the most entertaining of dominants, dear boy, but you really must work on your ferocity. Let it go. You see, you are entirely too pleasant in your demeanour and I know you have more to give than that. Perhaps you will do better with me at your feet. You will find that I do not break as easily as them," he'd said as he smiled and dropped to the floor in front of him.

Now, three years on, the only difference between the two of their more sadistic tendencies was that Pascal wouldn't stop when they screamed safe words at him, a trait he hadn't allowed Alex to follow. He had taught him to respect and treat his women with a care he never concerned himself with. Why the man had enforced such respect when he had so little was still a quandary but he imagined he would find the answer one day when Pascal allowed him in fully. The man was an enigma, with no sense of concern for himself or compassion for the world. Alex knew for a fact that Pascal didn't even have a safe word of his own.

"What is the point of a word, dear boy, when you place yourself in the hands of someone you trust with your life? If that one person can't see your end in sight then they might as well finish you themselves. Never put yourself in the hands of someone you do not trust implicitly. They will more than likely be your demise," he'd said as he looked up at him.

"But what if-"

"Get on with it, Alexander. I want to know how you feel on my skin. It is time you learnt to express yourself a little more honestly."

He smirked at the memories and looked across at the pair of them again. He'd never brought a cuffed woman here. In fact, he'd never been quite as possessive about a woman before, period. Of course, no one ever touched what was his without his permission, but he'd actually threatened Pascal when he got close to her. When he'd thrown that beloved cane to the floor and faced off with him, the intensity of his own emotions had surprised both of them. He knew how much that cane meant to his friend and it hadn't even registered until it was too late. He'd have to apologize for that mistake later. Damn, he hated apologizing, especially to his egotistical and narcissistic friend.

Pascal's reaction to the diamonds sparkling on her wrist had been both amusing and worrying. Alex had put them there for a very specific reason. The rules that Pascal himself had in all his clubs. The glance over the man's shoulder told Alex that they would certainly be having a conversation about it at some point. Thankfully, the slight nod was enough to tell Alex that he would keep his hands off Elizabeth, for the time being anyway. How long that would last was questionable but it should be enough for tonight at least. He had no idea what the conversation would consist of, given that he didn't understand the sentiment himself, but rules were rules.

1– NOT UNLESS ALL PARTIES AGREE.

2 – NO BLOODSPORTS.
3 – IF YOU DON'T WANT TO SHARE IT, CUFF IT, ON THE LEFT WITH DIAMONDS.

He frowned to himself and wondered if perhaps she would test the strength of their friendship. Pascal was not known for his lasting alliances and often walked over anything and anyone to get what he wanted, and he very much wanted Elizabeth. He'd known the man for a long time and saw his reaction instantly. If he was honest, he'd known he'd be in trouble before he even got to Eden. He knew Pascal would be as intrigued by her as he was. He could only hope that years of trust and friendship would make Pascal behave himself. If not, it would get very bloody in seconds. He had no doubt of it because he was willing to fight for her, even if it was his friend, and Pascal, well Pascal was a law unto himself and he wouldn't think twice about fighting just for the fun of it.

Still amused by his own reaction to her, he lifted his head again to see that perfect, angelic smile radiantly glowing at Pascal as he led her through the doors and towards the stairs. What was she going to think of this world, part of his world? Every inch of her begged for this, begged him to take control and show her what she was made of, and he intended to do exactly that this evening. As she pushed him to open up his soul, he would push her to give in to him more.

He hovered at the top of the balcony and watched as she descended to the bar with Pascal. Such beauty and grace, she outshone every woman in the place and he gazed in awe at her ability to stand out in a room full of practically naked women. Every part of him wanted her to be his, but each time she challenged him, it opened up yet another irrational emotion. He could feel them flowing through him, the same ones he'd kept buried for so long. Joy, delight, amusement and hints of a feeling he'd long since buried all hopes of. Unfortunately, with that came all the other ones - pain, anger, fear and shame, feelings he'd hoped never to revisit or have to deal with.

He focused on her face, took a deep breath and dragged his hand along the iron railing as he headed for them. Several people nodded at him and at least six women were on their knees before he'd even met their faces. Not one of them held any interest, only her.

The heat and comforting smell of evocative enthusiasm hit him as he gazed at the dance floor beneath him for a few seconds. The dull thud of the bass beat pulsed through his body and his shoulders stiffened in response to the situation around him. The classic salacious and brazenly explicit visions that surrounded the area focused his mind back to the reality of where he was. The grinding of the floor beneath him and writhing bodies being manhandled into various scenes or situations sent shivers of control to his brain and he rubbed his neck in anticipation, chuckling as he pushed through the crowd towards the stairs.

He watched for her reactions to the sights around her. She was soaking it in like a seasoned professional and showed no sign of nervousness or fear. Clearly she'd had just enough alcohol to feel calm around the fucking absurd situation he'd put her in. Even the dance floor full of naked depravity and debauchery didn't seem to faze her. What she did appear to notice were the doors. Her eyes kept flicking toward the eighteen different doors that circled the floor. He chuckled at what was behind them and pondered her reaction to their interiors. Would she be enlightened by her enthusiasm or confused by it? Perhaps it's just what she needed.

A shameless and sweet looking sub was kneeling next to her feet, looking peacefully to the floor while Draven Creed stroked her hair and talked to Pascal. For fuck's sake, Draven and Pascal. Could this night start off with any more lethal challengers than those two? Noticing Draven's eyes slowly study her body and draw across her face, he instantly felt his hackles rise in response, which was odd in itself. So sneering, he headed straight towards them. It was time to let others know who this woman was here with and the best way to do that was fiercely and with intent. He'd never bothered before, but then he'd never been interested enough to cuff anyone before.

Watching as the bastard completely ignored the bracelet and moved his body and hands towards Elizabeth, he knew he wouldn't get there in time to stop him touching her. Hate, panic and something deeper rolled through him as he saw her reaction to the impending fingers. She immediately looked uncomfortable and tense, afraid even. Gone was the calm she portrayed and something like repulsion darted across her features as she backed away and into Pascal. He simply grinned and wrapped his arm around her waist, pulling her arse into his dick. Bastard.

Rage bubbled its way to the surface and before he thought about the whys, he shoved and pushed at the crowd with force, trying to clear a path to her. He needed to get to her, needed to defend her, needed to feel her against him alone. *Elizabeth*.

He inwardly begged Pascal to do something to help her, or him. He wasn't fucking sure but as if sensing him, Pascal looked up and smiled broadly, nodding that imperceptible nod they had always used together. The cane was raised before he could blink, the wood of it smacking Draven hard around the head before he reached her face. The result was a very fucking irate Draven, raising his nearly seven-foot frame over Pascal in a bid for vengeance. It was enough to fuel the ferocity inside further, and seeing her pinned to the bar behind Pascal, looking scared to death with the little sub cowering into the side of her was all it took.

He didn't think, just reacted as the rage reached his fists and he got close enough. He sent a punch straight at Draven's face, knocking him to the floor before he got a chance to defend himself. The bastard deserved nothing less. He was an undisciplined fucker anyway.

"Do not fucking touch her," he stated, glaring down at the dick's shocked face and pushing his boot into Draven's throat. There weren't any other words in his head. That was all there was, because the thought of another man's hands anywhere near her felt like a knife in his heart. Not the normal irritation of something touching what was his, no, this was different somehow, possessive, almost protective.

He frowned at his own thoughts and shook his head as he felt a hand on his shoulder pulling him backwards. That familiar feeling of trust at Pascal's presence swept through him and he turned to find him smiling with that ever-evil glint hardening behind his eyes.

"Dear boy, you took your time. I thought I might have to claim she was mine, and fight again or some such nonsense. I am honoured that you would do battle for me but that is enough now. I think you have made your point quite effectively."

"It wasn't for you, Pascal," he snarled, still too confused by his own thoughts to communicate any further. He turned back to the threat instead, who was now getting up, and stiffened again ready for more.

Draven's head turned to him as he rose to his feet, clutching at the back of his head. "She's yours?" he questioned in surprise. "I thought she was Pascal's."

"Yes, she's mine," he said as he turned to look at her. "Don't make me show you how much she means to me, because I will, with fucking enthusiasm if I have to." Her beautiful eyes widened at his statement and his heart damn near exploded as she beamed at him. Everything else in the room disappeared from view. It was just her and these new feelings he appeared to be having. What the hell they were was mystifying.

He pushed past Pascal to kiss her. He had to kiss her. Never had he wanted to own something so badly, to show the world what he had found. Her face softened as his hands found the back of her neck and drew her toward him. Her warm mouth met his, flooding him with lust and desire as she melted beneath him, and he found himself locked in this moment with her. Wanting her, fuck he wanted her. He'd drag her to one of the rooms now, if he thought he could get away with it, and show her everything she meant to him. Need and something intensely emotional flowed through his body as he held her close and realised this was it for him. It was a moment there was no turning back from, a moment she'd caused him to embrace a feeling in. Never had he felt so close to something so utterly mind blowing and powerfully disabling in his life. In the midst of all that surrounded them, he realised that he was actually showing these people that it was him that had been found, perhaps even saved.

He moved his hands down to her waist, pulling her towards him and her fingers found their way to his face, softly stroking his throat as she began moaning into his mouth. God he loved her touch. It cornered his edges and soothed his version of a soul somehow. He wanted nothing more than to get her in a bed and show her the very heart of him, for what it was worth. She could have it all.

Sudden realisation dawned. This was all wrong. He didn't want her here, well he did, but just not at this time. It was too soon and conflicting. This scene around them of immorality and Machiavellian behaviour was strangely too sordid for her, unjust and untrue somehow. She warranted more than this for some reason. Not that he didn't want to play with her. He did, but just not with all these people nearby. All the Draven's leering made his feelings distasteful

314

somehow. Fuck, why had he brought her here? One potential touch from another man had elicited everything he was struggling to understand about himself. He needed to get them out of here.

He leaned away from her and gazed into her lust driven eyes, eyes so honest they screamed for affection and love.

"Well, my dear boy, that was quite the declaration of love if I have ever seen one." Pascal chuckled from the side. "I see now why you cuffed her, Alexander. I assume you probably did not know until this moment, though. Hmm?" The man smiled and nodded at her. Alex wasn't even sure if he liked *his* bloody eyes on her anymore.

He pulled her closer to him and felt the puzzled frown crease his brow, as his eyes drifted towards Pascal's and narrowed slightly. Love? Really? How the man would understand the emotion was incomprehensible.

"We need to leave, Elizabeth. I've changed my mind about being here," he said quietly, moving his eyes back to her.

She gazed at him for a while and softly blinked her eyes, the sexiest of smiles spreading across her face as she moved into him again. The storm inside of him calmed almost instantly for some unknown reason, puzzling him further.

"Why would you want to leave when you have so much to show me, Alex? I want to feel more of what you have to offer me. Teach me," she whispered, her lips lingering over his neck and sending a message straight to his cock. "I want to see all of the man I'm falling for. Show me who you are."

He stared at his friend over her shoulder and stroked her silken hair as he silently asked how the hell he was supposed to proceed. How did he continue what he had started now that these feelings were involved? Why the fuck he thought Pascal would have the answers was beyond him. The man had never seen a day's love with anyone.

"Alexander, you are sometimes so infuriating. Be yourself, dear boy. I know you remember who you are. Do not take it away from her. It will not work unless you give it everything you have. Believe me, I know," Pascal said as a look of sadness swept over his face. He abruptly tapped his cane on the floor after a second or two and smiled again. "Now, your suite is ready if you want it. Enjoy. That is all I will say on the matter. I cannot be seen to engage in this scandalous display of emotion a moment longer. It will ruin my façade and any future plans I have to humiliate someone."

Standing and reaching for her hand, he continued. "Elizabeth, it has been a pleasure. He will be worth your love should you choose to give it and if you don't, call me. I can't say I will be anywhere near as worthy but we would have fun finding out. No?" He handed her his card, nodded and moved toward Draven with a scowl.

Alex watched his friend-come-tormentor move away. What the fuck was happening here? Pascal had given her his card? To offer what exactly? Fuck. His eyes narrowed at the bastard's scheming brain as he turned back and looked at her confused eyes.

"What do you want from me, Elizabeth?" he asked with a tilt of his head.

"Eventually? Everything, Alex," she said with that mischievous smile of hers coming back. "For now, in this moment, I just want you to show me all that you can."

"Here, in this place?" he replied, waving his hand around and frowning. The thought fucking disturbed him. He'd never had a single kind emotion in here or feeling of any sort for that matter apart from control, and that emotion was not one he was feeling at the moment. Besides, he still wasn't entirely comfortable with what the hell was happening in his head anyway.

"Why not? This is part of you, isn't it? I assume it's why you brought me here." She licked her lips and kissed him lightly. "But if you feel you're not capable of making me do as you wish anymore then..." she said as she gave him her award winning smirk and placed her hands on her hips. He groaned and felt his dick jump to attention again. Feisty little minx.

He wasn't about to ignore her request now that she'd challenged him, so he threw her over his shoulder, slapped her glorious arse and pushed his way through the bar. Normally he'd drag a woman, or they'd simply follow behind with their heads lowered, but this was different. She was different, and the need to carry her overwhelmed him. He walked with purpose toward a passing waiter, who with one focused look kneeled on the floor and raised a tray holding champagne.

"Grab the glasses, Elizabeth," he called over his shoulder as he took a long drink from the bottle.

"Ooh, I think I like this version of you," she said, clasping the flutes. "Did that man really just kneel on the floor? Are we in bloody Narnia or something?" She giggled. It was fucking adorable.

"Don't giggle, for fuck's sake. You'll make me look like a fraud," he said, smiling at the floor as he continued walking, the crowd clearing for him.

"Well I think you might be, Mr. White," she replied, now laughing with abandon and squeezing his arse.

"I'll show you a fraud, Miss Scott. Grinding your backside into Pascal most definitely deserves some punishment," he said, sinking his teeth into her backside.

"Ouch, that hurt. Do it again," she said as she pulled his shirt from his trousers and kissed his lower back. "Where are you taking me anyway?"

"My room," he said, taking another drink from the bottle and turning right along the back corridor.

"You have your own room? Do you own this place, too?" she exclaimed. He chuckled.

"No, this is Pascal's venture, much to my irritation, and he makes a lot of money out of it," he replied, reaching for the door in front of him.

Pressing his thumb against the pad at the side of the door, it softly clicked open.

"I bet he does," she said as she continued trailing her lovely fingers across him.

He placed her on the floor, closed the door behind them and took the glasses. Then moving across the floor towards the table, he filled the two glasses and turned back to watch her. She stared at him for a moment and took a step into the room gingerly.

He gazed at her every expression as she edged her way forward, taking in her surroundings. She moved toward the four-poster bed and softly brushed her fingers across the black comforter, then traced her hand up the carved wooden post at the foot of the bed. Her hair shimmered in the low red lighting and the slight tremble in her legs as he saw her notice the cross at the other end of the room almost had him coming in his pants.

"St Andrew's cross," he said quietly as he approached her, holding out her glass.

"Oh, for restraining I assume," she said calmly, her eyebrow raised as she took the drink. He nodded and took a sip, slipping his hand into his pocket to adjust his dick.

She resumed her wandering and brushed her hand over the rack of various implements on display for torture and bondage. Her face was a picture of confusion and interest as she fingered each object with delicate hands and eventually stared at the ropes hanging on the wall with a smile.

"Why do you have so many ropes? I mean that long? I mean, why would they need to be so long?" she asked as she tilted her head and looked confused. Christ, that rambling was cute. Cute? What the fuck? He nodded upwards.

"Suspension. Look above you," he replied as he watched her reaction to the hooks and rings in the ceiling.

"Oh, right," she said with one of those adorable giggles as her hands returned to the table and poked at a ball gag.

"None of those are for you yet," he said gently as he noticed a slight frown on her face. She hesitated with her hand on a steel spreader bar and looked at him.

"How many women have you had in here? Or men?"

"I don't have a preference for men." He hoped she would stop at that. She really didn't need to know any more at the moment. Quite frankly, the vision of her small, pale hands on the spreader was just too much for him and he couldn't find anything else to say anyway.

"Has Pascal been in here?" He tilted his head. Her intuition surprised him. What had she noticed?

"No." It wasn't a lie. They always went to his room, or one of the others.

She watched him intently for a few seconds so he tried to remain impassive, but that was getting harder by the day with her. His cock twitched as she licked her lips and moved toward him.

"I think you're keeping something from me, Mr. White," she said with a smirk. "It doesn't matter. I was just curious. So what do you have planned for me while we're in here?"

Never had he felt so put on the spot in his life. He wasn't even sure if this was what he wanted or how he could do this and have feelings at the same time.

"Would you like my mouth wrapped around you while you think about it?" Her hand pressed against his cock as she reached for his belt. He hadn't got a clue where this woman had come from, but regardless he still growled at the thought and grabbed at her hands before she got the chance. No fucking way would he last ten minutes if that's how it started.

Right, get yourself together, White. Time to play.

He inched her backwards away from him and stood her in the middle of the room.

"I think you've had enough of this for a while," he said, removing the glass from her hand and placing it on the table. He watched her swallow as she realised the fun was about to begin. "Do you want the full effect, Elizabeth, or a more relaxed version?" he asked.

Her eyes drifted to his hands as he removed his cufflinks, unbuttoned his shirt and dragged it over his shoulders.

"I'll take whatever you think I can handle, sir. I'll trust you to know what I need." He chuckled in response and threw his shirt on the chair. Never once had she used the title properly before. He couldn't work out if he liked it or not.

"Take the dress off, Elizabeth, and give it to me," he demanded. Lovely as it was, he wanted to see what was beneath it more.

"Yes, sir," she said nervously.

He watched her unzip the dress and push it down her body seductively, then hold it out in front of her. He swiped it from her fingers, threw it to join his shirt and looked at her in all her glory. A grey silk bra and g-string were all that was covering her, and those fucking incredible legs ended in a pair of elegant sling backs. He'd never had such a divine beauty stood in this room. The vison made him groan inwardly, still unsure how to proceed.

"I'm going to put you on that cross, Elizabeth, and then I'm going to play with you so I need you to choose a safeword." She frowned, not understanding. "I mean a word that you will say if you've reached your limit. *Stop* will not be enough for me to hear you and you'll probably say it anyway, even if you don't mean it," he said, gazing at her face.

"Oh. Umm... Chess, is that okay?" she replied. He smiled and nodded.

"Perfect. There will be times when you want to say it but try not to until you can't bear it anymore. I'll stop the moment you utter the word."

"Okay." She nodded, biting her delicious lip and looking nervous all of a sudden.

Holding out his hand, he walked them to the cross and positioned her against it. Travelling his fingers across her perfect skin, he lifted her hands gently into the cuffs and secured the straps. "Open your legs wider," he stated as he reached for the bottom restraints. She positioned her legs and he couldn't help but notice the soft moan as he ratcheted the leg cuffs around her ankles. Smiling and licking his lips, he took a step back to admire her. "Breathtaking," he muttered as he moved over to the table. She looked utterly irresistible, every curve of her body moulding to the cross effortlessly as if she were made for this. Her calm demeanour surprised him but also heightened the erotic nature of the room. She closed her eyes and let her head rest against the wood, allowing her body to be bound without testing the effectiveness of the restraints. Complete trust. When had he deserved that from her? He'd given her so little assurance when it came to this side of him. He picked up a soft flogger and moved across to her.

"Look at me, Elizabeth." She opened her eyes and looked at the flogger. He moved forward and dragged it across her skin. "It won't hurt you. Just let yourself feel the sensation." She nodded and closed her eyes again. He drew his hand back and started the process of gently flogging her breasts and thighs. Her breathing immediately quickened and he watched as the rise and fall of her ribcage increased. She tugged at the wrist cuffs moaning and twisted her body slightly to try and alleviate the pressure. Fucking hell. Instant gratification poured across his body and he was suddenly desperate to feel how wet she was. She couldn't possibly be ready that quickly.

Grabbing at the sides of her panties, he ripped them from her body. Her eyes shot open, a small gasp coming out of her mouth before she moaned in torment.

"Alex, please..."

He reached down and found her dripping with arousal, ready for anything he had to offer. The slick feeling also made him realise his dick much preferred his own name being spoken by her.

"So wet for me, Elizabeth. Do you want to come for me?" he said, slowly inserting two fingers and moving them with slow deliberate movements. "Would you prefer my cock in here?" he continued, sucking a delicious nipple into his mouth and biting down on it.

"Oh god, yes, fuck me please." He chuckled and moved to the other nipple, teasing it with sharp nips as he drew the flogger up between her legs and put pressure on her clit. The strands of leather mingled with her juices as he continued his relentless slow torture on her insides.

"Hold it back, baby. It will be so much better if you keep control of it. Do I need to stop?"

"God, no, just ahh.... Oh fuck."

She near screamed as the beginnings of her orgasm took hold. He felt the moment when her legs started to give beneath her and her body fell into the wrist supports. He groaned and rubbed his cock against her thigh. Fuck, he was minutes away himself, and that wasn't fucking happening. He moved backwards and removed his hands from her, watching as she writhed in ecstasy on the cross. Her eyes snapped open as she felt his withdrawal and she frowned while regaining her footing, fighting with the cuffs violently.

"Please, Alex," she begged. Fuck he loved to hear her beg for it, and that damned snarl of impatient irritation was mesmerising to him.

"You'll wait until I'm ready, Elizabeth, he snapped, as he walked to the table and picked up the nipple clamps. Her eyes widened and she gasped a breath in as he pinched them together to show his intent. "These will help you focus a bit," he said as he removed her bra and put the first one on her. Her hiss as the first one bit down did nothing to stop his ardour, and he felt his now damned painful cock trying to break its way through his pants. The next clamp elicited the same response as he licked his way around them and moved his hand between her legs again. His thumb skimmed her clit and her head flew backwards as she moaned, almost collapsing into the cuffs. He rubbed in small circles and moved back a step to watch her grinding against his hand. Jesus, she was the sexiest thing he'd ever seen. He found himself wanting to make her come over and over again, not for his pleasure but for hers.

"Let go, baby. Come for me." Her eyes opened and she focused on his with an angry intensity he hadn't seen before. Pure, unadulterated desire swept across her features as she let her body give in to the pressure he'd placed her under. Her whole body began to shake in response and the erotic blush of pink travelled across her skin as she came violently onto his hand.

He watched in fascination as her breathing started to slow and she hung limply, her head lowered and her hair hanging around her cheeks. Beautiful was not enough of a word to describe the image of her strapped back onto the cross. His mind reeled suddenly with visions of suspension ropes and knots. Not many women had retained his interest enough for the patience and control it took to hang them up. Certainly not untrained subs like her, but his fingers itched at the prospect as he continued to gaze at her.

She took in a long breath, as her tongue licked full pink lips, and she started to take the weight on her legs again. Standing and twisting her head from side to side, she slowly brought her eyes up to meet his. The look that met him almost had him drooling with the desire to fuck her. Hooded eyes and a slow sultry smile spread across her face as she looked at the table next to him.

"Is that all you've got, sir?" she said huskily, keeping her gaze on his eyes, challenging him.

It wasn't what he was expecting, and he fought hard to keep his eyebrows from shooting upwards and his grin from breaking across his face. She wanted more, she could have it.

"No, Elizabeth it's not. Are you ready for more?" Her eyes focused on the bullwhip and he found himself questioning if he was able to do that to her. "You're not ready for it, Elizabeth. Don't push yourself, or me for that matter," he said with an edge of unease in his voice that he hadn't heard for a long time. He'd like nothing better than to see her all striped up from a good lashing, but she wasn't going to be happy with that amount of pain. She might be submissive, and he knew he'd found something special, but too much too quickly and this would end before he started it.

"If you think you're not ready, I won't beg you for it," she spat, an element of venom in the words. He scowled at her, unable to stop the rise of Dominance taking over. Where the fuck had this woman come from? It was as if the scene, the club, or the room had allowed her to become everything he knew she could be eventually, but he'd expected her want for pain to come much later. He should wait. He shouldn't do this. She had no idea what she was suggesting, but fuck the thought was tempting.

He walked closer to her and began to undo the foot restraints. Kissing his way up her leg, he paused at her sex to taste her. She moaned and tugged again at the cuffs on her wrists. "Let me touch you," she said with that anger in her voice. Submissive? Not a bloody chance. He was suddenly restraining a tiger and the thought 'switch' came to mind far too rapidly for his liking.

"No," he responded firmly. This topping from the bottom was fun but he needed to regain some control before he lost it completely. He continued onto her wrists and moved her over to the post on the bed. Turning her away from him, he pushed her roughly against the tall post and kicked her legs apart. She moaned again.

"Hands up above your head," he growled as he slapped her backside with more force than he'd intended. "You like it when I'm rough with you, don't you? Do you want it harder?" She ground back into him, presenting her arse for more.

"Yes, I want it all," she breathed out. "Show me."

He tied her hands to the post with the rope bindings and positioned her hands to a holding grip around the carvings. Tying her hair up with a band from the table and grabbing the whip, he dragged it down her stomach and pulled the length of it between her legs through her soaking core. She moaned again and shifted her stance to widen her endless legs further.

"You have to tell me if you want me to do this. What is your safe word, Elizabeth?" She continued grinding and didn't answer. "Elizabeth, safe word!" He felt himself shouting to get her attention, knowing that the moment he started this he might slip away. Nothing pleased him as much as a whip in his hand. The simple weight of it was already altering his breathing.

"Chess," she mumbled, pushing her arse against him. He noticed her fingers whitening with the pressure of her grip on the post. She was drifting, not quite aware what was happening, so he moved to the side so he could look into her eyes and grabbed her chin.

"Elizabeth, tell me you want this or we stop now." Her eyes glazed slightly as she fought to move her mouth. "Tell me!" Her face jumped back in response to the shouted order, then softened again.

"I want this. I want you, all of you," she replied as she turned back to the post. "Do it, Alex."

He removed the whip slowly and stood back away from her quietly, watching intently as she pulled herself up straight and looked over her shoulder at him. The smouldering look she gave him while having the front to wink and smile sent shivers through his entire body. Never had any woman had the balls to wink at him in a scene. He kept his face expressionless but as she turned her head and calmed herself for the whip, he couldn't help but smile.

He watched as she pulled in a long breath and lowered her head to the side of the post, bracing her shoulder against it. She was entering herself, trying to find her own private space in this moment, and he gazed in awe at the ability that came so naturally to her. It was captivating, enamouring. Enough so that he nearly lost where he was as he tried to remember to talk to her about it later. She probably hadn't even got a clue what she was doing to herself.

"We'll start with ten. You'll count them out loud. Do you understand?" he questioned, hoping to God that she wasn't about to run for the hills as she felt a small part of the man she was asking for.

"Yes," she said dreamily.

Drawing back the whip, he let it fly toward her with precision and softly land on her right thigh. She gasped, moaned incoherently and shifted her weight. "One. Harder," she ground out at him.

Pulling back again, he let the next one go with a little more vigour, basically to chastise the naughtiness in her response to the first. It landed on her left hip bone with a crack that had him growling instantly.

"Yes... Oh god. Two," she hissed as she flung her head back and released a breath.

He smiled at the vision and waited, ready to inflict more once he'd finished watching he writhe. The pain level she'd endure was much heavier than he'd thought, but then the need for it was quicker than he'd thought too. Maybe masochist wasn't so far away after all.

He let four more fly in different directions as he watched her bending and flexing her back, wincing slightly at the pain.

Unbelievably, she seemed to be drifting off into her subspace, though, studiously counting the strokes and pushing her groin against the post to increase her friction. She was close. He could see the slick evidence of desire dripping down her thighs as she tensed on a stroke and her legs quivered. He couldn't remember ever being so ready to explode while he watched someone receive a whip. His cock was throbbing with every movement she made, only increasing the need to fuck her aggressively, and damn soon.

The lash hit home on the seventh stroke and he heard her whimper in pain and stumble a bit. He hesitated and moved toward her. As much as he loved the look of her crumbling in front of him, he was oddly desperate to comfort her rather than produce more of it for her.

"Seven. Harder, you fucking pussy!" she screamed, a new venom lacing voice as she righted herself again and glared over her shoulder. The glower continued from her face as he stared, halting his step towards him. He scowled in response, ready to remind her what was happening here and who was in control.

"Watch your mouth, Elizabeth," he growled as he delivered the next stroke hard onto her shoulder and watched her flinch at the contact.

The stiffening of her whole frame, accompanied by the moan into the post, echoed pure lust throughout the room. It drove him mad, and the stripes on her back sent pulses straight to his painful cock. Darkness threatened to take over. He could feel it building inside. It wouldn't take much for him to be lost in her and that was something she definitely wasn't ready for.

She lifted one elegant foot onto the bed and wrapped it around the carvings, enabling her to push harder against the post. Jesus Christ, he wanted inside her, his cock almost bursting through his damn trousers at the sight of her. Everything was her at this moment. Hair, skin, the continued moans coming from her mouth egging him on for more.

"Eight," she moaned as the tail of the whip hit her square on the arse. "Nine," she screamed as he aimed and landed it again on her arse. "Oh god, please fuck me, Alex. I want you inside me."

He didn't need asking twice. Fuck being in control. He was undoing the rope bindings in seconds and bending her over the bed with such force that he stunned himself, roughly pushing her down flat with his hand on her back as he kicked off his clothes and moved himself forward to sink inside her. He paused for a moment to tease her entrance with his cock, trying to calm his breathing and savour the moment for as long as he could as he rubbed his thick length up and down her wetness. Deliciously wet. Fuck, this was going to be frantic and quick. He was on the brink now. The second he got inside her and felt her come, he knew he wouldn't be able to stop himself.

"So fucking perfect," he mumbled to himself while toying with her and grasping at her hipbones forcefully.

"Please, Alex, I want you inside me. Please don't make me wait anymore," she moaned into the bed, scrabbling for grip on the sheets as she trembled beneath his hands.

"Fuck, you're so beautiful," he replied, sliding himself inside her. So deep, so fucking deep. The sensation was mind blowing and his cock jumped in response as she moaned and groaned under him. A guttural growl escaped from his mouth. "Keep still, baby. I can't hold back if you keep moving," he panted. She didn't and he found himself fighting not to come immediately.

His breathing and heart rate spiked as he felt the now familiar build in her, and as she ground back against him over and over again, he closed his eyes and let the inevitable bliss begin. Reaching a hand around her throat, he pounded into her in a steady rhythm, letting the feelings of absolute pleasure sore through his body. Her muscles twitched around him and he could feel her coming as she screamed his name. The muscles clamped and milked him, spurring him on to come. He increased the pounding as he felt his own release build and slammed into her, pushing her up the bed. Grabbing hold of those exquisite hips and dragging her back, he lifted her upright to ease the friction on himself, then moved his hand to her clit to prolong her orgasm. She reached her hands behind his neck and turned her face to kiss him, her tongue finding its way to his in their moment of passion as he continued to fuck her relentlessly.

"Oh god yes, again," she purred into his mouth. Her core tightened again as he circled with his thumb and used his fingers to feel his cock pumping in and out of her. It was slick with combined arousal and it only intensified every fucking irrational feeling coursing through him.

"Now, baby, I won't stop this time. Come with me."

He let go as he heard her scream out his name again and shuddered at the intensity of feelings that flooded his senses as he exploded inside of her. It flooded inside her, claiming her in this scenario with more aggression than ever before. He panted, clamping his eyes closed and throwing his head back, and heard the animalistic groan that left his own throat as he collapsed on top of her on the bed.

"Mine," he mumbled into her neck as he came back to reality. "Tell me you're mine, baby."

She rubbed the back of his neck delicately and fingered his hair.

"Yes, yours," she whispered from beneath him, still trying to regain her breath.

"You're fucking incredible," he said as he kissed her languidly on the neck and eased the pressure off her to move down her body and look at her back.

Rather than the normal pleasure he felt at seeing the reddened stripes, he felt a twinge of something else. He frowned and tried to let the sensation process itself to some sort of conclusion. Nothing was forthcoming other than a constant, irritating niggle of confusion. Whatever it was, it was fucking uncomfortable so he lightly touched the welts and planted soft kisses along them.

"I've hurt you," he said, moving off the bed and crossing to the cupboard to retrieve the balm.

She chuckled, resting her head on her hands and gazing at him with adoration and something that looked possibly like love.

"Yes, Alex, but isn't that sort of the point?" He shook his head and chastised his own stupid behaviour. Fucking idiot. What the hell had he done? Striping her up like some other non-descript woman. She deserved better. He rubbed at the back of his neck and stared at her for a minute. She looked relaxed, calm. Christ, she looked happy even. In fact, she blew him a kiss and winked. Fuck, he loved that winking.

He walked back to her and sat down heavily on the black sheets.

"I don't deserve your humour, baby. I shouldn't have done it. I should have stopped you from pushing me. It won't happen again," he said, moving over her and carefully applying the cream. "This will feel cold for a minute or two but it will help with the pain." She instantly turned over and rose to kneel in front of him. Taking his face in her hands, she gently kissed him. Soft, warm lips chased the wind right out of him as he stilled in her hands and felt the emotion her mouth delivered. His mind quietened as her lips dissolved every negative image of his past. Peace drifted through his thoughts as he wrapped his fingers into her hair and dragged her closer, more, closer, deeper.

She eventually pulled her head back and softly placed small kisses along his jaw so he tilted his neck to get her to his throat. Fuck, he adored her mouth on him, especially there, where so much damage had been done. How did she do that?

She stopped and leaned back on her heels with a smile.

"Alex, I wanted to see you, all of you. I told you that. You didn't do anything I didn't ask for and I enjoyed it, so stop beating yourself up. Actually, I've quite impressed myself," she said as that mysterious grin took over her face. "I think the venue must have unleashed my inner slut or something. She's been about a bit recently." He chuckled and moved her back down onto the bed so he could continue with the cream as he felt his heart constrict at the thought of this woman knowing all of him, at her understanding the depths of his angry soul.

"You called me a pussy, Miss Scott," he said with a smirk as he kissed as much of her as he could. She was simply fucking delicious.

"Well, I was a bit worried you weren't giving it your all, that you might be hiding a more realistic version," she replied sarcastically.

He frowned and smeared a layer over her arse cheek as he thought about her statement. It was a concern. He'd have to build her slowly, train her and hope she found her way to accepting it, maybe even enjoying it. Because, no, he wasn't giving it his all. He wasn't even close, and that was, for the first time in his life, worrying to him. He had no idea how she'd react when he truly lost himself in her and showed her what he really could do.

Her legs shifted slightly under his hand, highlighting the other stripes over her lower back. What the hell was he doing? His life and past would destroy every part of her if she ever had to see the horror in it, let alone find a route through it with him. She didn't deserve this at all. She should be with a kind and normal man, someone who would adore her for the rest of her life and give her everything. Not someone who would drag her into hell in the hope that she could accept It.

He lay down beside her and let her drape one of those damned incredible legs over him while he slipped his arm under her and

328

pushed her head towards his throat again. She giggled and snuggled in. Fuck, she felt so right there, so comfortable, so peaceful, but it wasn't possible for him to give her normal. This part of his life wasn't fucking normal. Hell, he wasn't fucking normal.

He closed his eyes as he felt her hands threading into his hair and sighed as he considered his next move. Much as he wanted her, that guilty feeling kept hitting him in the gut for some unknown reason and he just couldn't choose between consuming her to the point of no return or letting her go. To find a better man, or at least a more decent one.

Chapter 23

Elizabeth

The jet touches down on the runway and I watch Alex furiously pacing the cabin, angrily chastising someone on his phone. The conversation has something to do with base rates and a Shanghai deal. I have no idea what he's talking about. What I do know is that his aggressive attitude is only fuelling mine to greater proportions. I'm pissed and it's all because of him and his constantly changing moods. They're stupid. It's that bloody simple. The dream of Rome is over and we are back to reality again. My time with him has been incredible but now we're home and I've been slowly feeling the old Alex return. Before this trip, I was more than happy with him but now I've seen the other version, the almost loving one, and I can't accept the more reserved one any longer. His barriers retreated considerably while we were away but it appears he's been very busy rebuilding them since yesterday afternoon. Well sod him, I want my version back, and I'm not accepting this bullshit from him.

I sigh in exasperation and look out of the window at the dreary London tarmac racing past us. It's chucking it down with rain, too, only highlighting the irritatingly sombre mood I'm in. Why would he hide himself away again? Did I get a little too close for comfort? And why bother telling me things that were important to him if he didn't mean to keep the information coming? I really felt the connection growing between us and I know he did, too. Regardless of that impassive face of his, I sensed the softer side of him. Even the vulnerable part made an appearance on occasion and no matter how brief it was, I knew it was there, hiding beneath the surface.

No, I'm not having it. If the night at the club has taught me anything it's to ask for what I want from him. He's absolutely been teaching me his own traits and I'm learning how to use them, fast.

The erotic pain and intensity of feelings he delivered to me at Eden were unbelievably sexy and completely overwhelming. I enjoyed everything, even the pain. Maybe it was the alcohol in my system or maybe it was the adrenaline from the whole ambience of the place and the people within it, but seriously, who would have thought I could orgasm from pain? Or that the pleasure found within those moments could be so mind numbingly good that I only wanted more of it?

He is absolutely right about what I am in the bedroom. His ability to dominate me is astonishing and I revelled in every second of it. I wanted him to push me and I wanted to be on my knees for him. I still do with all my very attached heart. But he's also shown me the self-belief I can achieve by learning from him in all circumstances, and as I sit here, I can feel the confidence encouraging me forward to ask more of him now. It isn't that I don't want the controlling behaviour or the dominant man. I do, desperately actually. I just need the man behind that as well, and him pulling it away from me is not helping me see any sort of future for us.

Pascal was rather enlightening with his "Declaration of love" statement, which I think even took Alex by surprise. Perhaps he saw something in Alex that I simply didn't. He clearly knows him well. Having said that, Giuseppe said the same sort of thing. Clearly they can both see something I have only received snippets of. Yes, he's said all the right things and we've had fun, but each time the connection gets a little too deep, he yanks it away from me. It's completely unacceptable of him and definitely not funny.

And Pascal, well he's a devil to think about at a different time. The man clearly has his own charms and demons flowing vividly through his soul, if he actually has one, that is. He certainly seems a very dangerous sort to play with but I think I held my own around him and I can't see why he would give me his card if he didn't like me. How relevant that is, I have no idea. And regardless of my confusion on the matter, I don't even know what I'll do with the bloody thing or even if I want him to like me. He appears to be a good friend to Alex so I suppose it's important. Again, I have no idea. I'm a mess and intoxicating green eyes are the last thing on my priority list at the moment. Alex is enough to deal with. The depths of Pascal are probably completely unfathomable. Although, there's no denying that

I like him. Well, I like the person I met that night anyway, whoever the hell that was.

I stare out the window and imagine them together. Intriguingly, there is something so very familiar between them. It's nothing like the brotherly affection Alex shares with Conner. It's something far more intimate, somehow more personal. How much has happened between them over the years? Their small, almost unnoticed nods and gestures, the way they look at each other, seems to be somewhat similar to that of lovers or maybe playmates, but he said he had no interest in men. He's so hiding something from me about that.

"Elizabeth, are you ready?" Alex asks as he gets in front of me.

"What? Sorry, I wasn't listening," I reply, standing and taking his hand. Such very wicked hands. My leg trembling happens again. It's still ridiculous given my current irritation with him. He chuckles and runs his fingers over the back of my hand.

"Dreaming of somewhere nicer?" he asks, smiling radiantly at me with that devilish upward curl of his. I gaze at him for a moment and wonder what to say. Do I continue with this charade of his retreating and me being okay with it? Or do I call his bluff and make him open up again? I might run the risk of chasing him off, which I really don't want, but I can't be with someone who throws up barriers constantly to keep me out of their thoughts. Yep, still pissed off.

"No, just a different version of you and a time we have now apparently left behind," I reply, smiling quietly as I move toward the door.

"Which one?" he asks with a grin. It's his lying one, his manipulating sod one.

I roll my eyes at him and grab my bag.

"I think you know."

I'm not even beginning to play that game with him over this. Whether he wants to admit it or not, he's let me in too far for me to not be able to see him trying to play his way around me.

"I have no idea what you're talking about, Elizabeth." Arsehole.

"Okay then, I'll tell you," I reply calmly as I look straight into his eyes, no fear of reprisal. "The one who doesn't run away from his bloody fears, Alex. The one who let me in a little and began to show me someone extraordinary. The one who wasn't afraid to let me see him for who he really could be." I'm right on this one and he knows it. I can tell by his narrowing eyes.

"What? Where did that come from? I am still here, with you. What are you talking about?" he says, rubbing the back of his neck and looking toward the floor a little. Liar, irritating liar. What a coward, bastard even. I bloody hate liars. I've had enough.

My anger explodes to the point of sod the consequences.

"Don't you dare insult me. You know as well as I do what you are doing. You have been distancing yourself since yesterday afternoon, probably because you feel like you've shown me too much of yourself, although I'm still not sure which of the many versions it is that you're afraid to let me see. You have taught me to bring my head up, so guess what, that's what I'm doing," I state with a firm tone. Arsehole. "You can have Andrews drop me off at home. When you have found the man I'm after again, you can come and get me, or not fucking bother because I'm not having half of you."

He looks at me with stunned eyes as I wrap my coat around me and start toward the steps. Ha, that'll show him. Bet no one's done that to him before. There is nothing sycophantic about me, Mr. White. "And if you're going to play poker with me, Alex, make sure your tell doesn't give you away," I continue, waving erratically towards his hand on his neck. "Do you even realise you give away so much with such a small gesture? Your reflex to your neck is always there at moments of discomfort. Why is that? You're not quite the hidden man you think you are, Alexander White. Not to me, anyway."

Sweeping down the stairs in what I hope is a dramatic exit, I see the car door open and Andrews reach the bottom of the stairs to help me off. I turn to see a very brooding and furious looking Alex still standing at the top of the stairs, and oh good lord, he's beautiful. His hair is being whipped around in the wind and those cold blue eyes seem to pierce me somehow, even from this distance. His hands are firmly planted in the pockets of his grey suit and he has the stance of a man with nothing but contempt for the world oozing from his demeanour. He's glorious, stunning and shit, what the hell have I done?

My feet itch to run back up the steps and tell him it doesn't matter, that I'll take whatever he's willing to give me. My heart longs for him to make his way to me and apologize for his behaviour, but I know he won't so I watch as he gives a head flick to Andrews, probably indicating that he's to take me home. I send him a sad smile, which he doesn't return and turn for the car again. I can't let him win this part of his game because there's no way forward if he doesn't let me all the way in.

"Are you ready, Miss Scott?" Andrews asks.

"Yes, Andrews, thank you."

He closes the door behind me and I tuck my legs beneath me on the seat, suddenly feeling incredibly tired and monumentally alone. What on earth have I done? I've lost him before we got anywhere and I've done it myself. I rub at my bracelet and watch the diamonds twinkling up at me, just like his eyes, beautiful and full of hidden depths.

Putting my head in my hands, I feel the tears well up in my eyes and before I know it, I'm sobbing uncontrollably, great heaving sobs of loss for something I'd barely found. What a mess.

~

The journey back to the apartment is over in a flash because the first thing I feel is someone gently shaking my shoulders to wake me up. I open my eyes to find Andrews sitting down next to me in the back of the car.

"Oh god, Andrews, I'm sorry. I must have drifted off," I say, sitting up and wiping at my eyes. He smiles and takes of his chauffeur's hat. It really is a lovely smile; he should do it more often.

"May I say something, Miss Scott?" he asks quietly.

"Yes, of course," I reply. He sighs so I tilt my head in interest.

"I know he's a complicated man and can be difficult to understand, but I've never seen him smile as much as he does when he's with you."

"Oh. Right. Thank you... I think," I say in response. Awkward much.

"Look, I hope you don't mind me saying this, but he Is liable to fuck it up if you don't give him some time to come to terms with the thought of falling in love," he says quietly, looking out of the window. I've watched the women pass through his life with no effect on him whatsoever and now that you've arrived, you've turned his world upside down."

Well that's insightful, possibly useful. I hadn't really thought about it like that.

"Andrews, I've never heard more than four words from your mouth. I'm happy to listen, although I hope the car's not bugged or something," I reply, giggling at the thought.

"No, I've turned it off. I would likely be sacked if he heard of this." A bugged car? Really? I giggle a little and look back at him, wondering what it is that either of us are allowed to say.

"Don't worry, I won't tell," I reply with a smile, resting my hand on his arm. "Thank you for the ride home, and the information."

"You're most welcome, ma'am," he says as he gets out of the car, puts his hat back on and unloads my suitcase. "Do you want me to take it up for you?"

"No, thank you. I'll be fine. Andrews, can you do me a favour though?"

"Yes, anything ma'am."

"Can you tell him that I miss him?" I say, not really understanding why I've just asked the chauffeur to say that sort of thing but feeling some sort of new friendly connection with him regardless.

"Of course ma'am," he replies, returning to his normal demeanour of stilted and poised now we've ventured out onto the road. "Goodbye. I'll watch you into the building."

"Goodbye, Andrews," I say, waving and hoping to god that this won't be the last time I see him.

~

Tuesday morning I'm woken by the sound of crashing in Belle's bedroom. I didn't see her the night before. We had a quick chat on the phone but she said she was out on a date and I was happy to have the place to myself so I could mull over the idiotic thing I'd done. That mulling consisted of me downing two bottles of wine and throwing my phone at the wall sometime around midnight, smashing it to smithereens. I looked longingly at the phone all evening as I watched crappy television and hoped he would call to talk, or text, anything to let me know he cared, but no, nothing, nada. *Bastard.*

The last thing I remember was falling into my bed, fully clothed. And that is where I stayed because now I am still fully clothed on top of my bed, staring at a half glass of stale wine.

"Belle, are you okay?" I shout, heaving my nauseated body off the bed.

"Yep, just throwing out some rubbish," she responds, chuckling.

I walk toward the door to see a rather sheepish and dishevelled looking Conner grinning like a lovestruck puppy and disappearing through the kitchen, shirtless.

"Morning, Conner," I yell after him.

"Late. Bye, Beth," I hear as the door slams behind him. I poke my head around the corner to see an equally lovestruck Belle sitting in bed, drinking a cup of tea and smiling.

"Going well then?" I ask, inclining my head toward the kitchen.

"Super, thanks. You look like fucking shit," she replies. Thanks. "Go get a cup of tea and tell me about your trip. I want all the details." I huff and wander off to the kitchen. "But I'd shower your sorry little backside first. You stink," she shouts after me. Thanks.

Ten minutes later, after a shower and some much needed caffeine, we are sitting in the lounge while I relay all the gory details of the trip - well, apart from the whipping bit, I'm not entirely sure my sister needs to know about all that. Thankfully though, we don't need to be in until lunchtime as Teresa is opening up and dealing with the deliveries, so at least we can catch up and put the world to rights to some degree.

"So you basically told him to get a life, find a brain and grow a pair," she states after the hour of my whining is completed.

"Yes, I suppose when you put it like that, I did," I reply with a smile, suddenly feeling a little happier about my reasoning.

"Well good for you. They're all fucking children. Honestly, sense does not appear to come with money at all," she says, stirring her fourth coffee of the morning, "How the hell they make it in the first place is a complete mystery to me."

"You and Conner seem good though," I say, grinning at her.

"That's because I'm not stupid enough to let myself become emotionally attached to him," she replies sarcastically, reaching for the biscuit tin. She's probably right.

"Belle, I think he really does like you. He was very complimentary in Rome. He didn't need to say the things he said about you, and honestly, if I thought Alex was saying those sorts of things about me, I'd be very emotionally attached." She narrows her eyes and turns back to me.

"Why, what did he say about me?" Ah, that got her attention - not quite so emotionally unattached then.

Two hours later, we walk through the door to a beaming but slightly harassed Teresa.

Delivery stock litters the back room and Belle and I set to work unwrapping and shelving all the new produce. It's good to be back in my kitchen. Rome seems like a lifetime away and for a short while, I find myself not thinking of Alex at all. Actually, time seems to fly by as the phones ring, customers walk in to purchase treats and I get on with doing what I do best.

I bake the day away, pulling inspiration from the goodies I discovered in Rome and creating a whole new batch of sweets and cakes. In fact, I astound myself and finally decide to sit down on the shop counter for a well-earned cup of coffee and chat with Teresa. It's about four o'clock and we're just about to clear the shelves of the remaining stock anyway so it's as good a time as any. We're not ten minutes into our conversation when the door opens and an entire florist shop's worth of flowers is carried in through the door. Men and women simply arrange the vases and bouquets around the shop like true professionals as Teresa and I stare with open mouths. All the colours of the rainbow are scattered around the floors and surfaces as the scent fills the air with summer, just about drowning out the smell of our cakes.

"Miss Elizabeth Scott?" a small and rather portly man asks as he looks at the two of us. I jump down from the counter and approach him. "I have been asked to give you this and these," he says as he hands over a small envelope and waves his hand around. "You must have done something rather wonderful. He bought my entire shop's worth."

"Uh... Thank you," I reply, slightly taken aback. With a small salute, he leaves and takes his team with him. Belle emerges from the back and frowns instantly.

"Oh for fuck's sake, does he think he can buy his way out of it?" she shouts. "When will they ever bloody learn? Why you are even entertaining opening that note is beyond me."

I take the note out of the envelope and scan the paper with trembling fingers.

I need to show you something. Please let me. I'll pick you up at seven. Wear jeans and something warm. You were right, you deserve better from me.

Ax

"What does he want now? Is this his way of fucking expressing himself?" Belle asks incredulously as she breaks off the head of a rose and chucks it in the bin.

"He wants to show me something," I reply, looking up at both of them.

"Well, you should go," Teresa says, sniffing her way around the flowers and singing softly to herself.

I look at Belle for her answer but she simply shrugs her shoulders and leaves the room.

"Belle, wait, I need to know what you think I should do," I say, running after her and reaching for her arm.

"No you don't, honey. I wouldn't do what you'd do. You're your own woman and you've landed a sodding difficult man. A beautiful one, yes, even I'll admit that, but a fucking bastard nonetheless. Only you know how to deal with him. I just want to see you happy," she replies with a tight smile. "If going with him makes you happy, then go." She clearly thinks I'm ridiculous. Maybe I am, but I can't stop the need to get to him.

"I love you, Belle. Please don't be disappointed in me."

"I could never be disappointed, honey, and I love you, too. Just don't bring him to the apartment until he's grown a pair. Maybe he just has, you never know," she says with a small chuckle.

"I need to go if I'm going to make it in time," I say, looking at my watch.

"Then go. We'll sort this shit out," they both say in unison.

"And don't take his shit anymore. Keep strong," Teresa says. Bless her.

I grin at them both like an idiot, grab my bag and exit the shop at breakneck speed in the hope of reaching the tube on time to make it home by six. I desperately need to sort myself out if I'm going to see him, and having smashed my phone up, I have no chance of calling him to let him know I'll be late.

Luckily, everything seems to be on my side for the journey home and I arrive at my apartment by six fifteen to find yet another enormous bunch of flowers outside the door - pale purple roses and another card. Picking them up, I walk inside and put them in the middle of the table while opening up the note.

I miss you too
Ax

Throwing my bag on the counter, I smile stupidly at the note and dart for the shower to clean off the day's flour and stickiness. I don't have time to wash my hair so end up with a French plait that's tucked up and pinned with a few grips. I apply some make-up and lip-gloss and reach for the wardrobe. He said jeans so I pull a pair of comfortable black skinnys out and team it with a light blue, thick jumper that I've only worn a few times. It's lovely but just too warm for everyday wear, more useful for mountains, and given the time of year and our night time outing, hopefully it should do the job. Walking through to the lounge, I'm pleased to notice that it's only six forty five, so I boil the kettle and pour myself a cup of coffee as I wait for whatever's coming.

Standing against the counter and blowing the hot drink, I give myself a few moments to think about what he wants to show me. What the hell would he want to show me? Talk to me, yes I can understand that, but show me? Andrew's words float through my mind. *"He's liable to fuck it up if you don't give him time to come to terms with the thought of falling in love."* Is that what this is all about? Has twenty-four hours given him some time to process things in his own mind? Well at least he's contacted me, at least he wants to try and sort this out. How he's going to do it, I have no idea about.

Three sharp knocks at the door bring me back from my dreamy little moment as I literally throw my coffee over the floor at the realisation that he's here, ten steps away from me, behind the door. The second I think it, my heart rate speeds up again and the tell-tale spike in breathing hits me. For God's sake, I can't even see him and I'm horny. *No, Beth, stick to your guns. Be strong.*

I walk to the door and open it, then almost fall over at the sight. A devastatingly gorgeous looking Alex stands in the doorway clad in black leather. He's head to toe in bike leathers with his black hair spiking out in that artfully dishevelled manner, filling the sodding doorway and looking at me as if he might jump on me at any moment. I'm entirely lost. My mouth is open and dry and I'm panting like a wanton hussy. It causes me to inwardly curse my treacherous body for overruling my head, but the man just shouldn't be allowed out in public. His cool blue eyes narrow at me as that wicked smile curves his mouth upward. The bastard knows exactly the effect he has on me and is most definitely about to use it.

I retreat a step in the hope that I can control the situation. I'm obviously very wrong. He takes two steps forward and before I know it, I'm pinned against the counter top in the kitchen and being lifted up onto it. His hands are everywhere as his mouth crashes into mine with a groan of desire or frustration. I'm not sure which.

"God, I've missed you. You have no fucking idea," he growls, running his hands up my back and pulling me into him as he pushes my jumper up. His mouth's devouring my neck before I know what's happening, his hips pushing into my groin with deadly intent. The feeling of his cold leathers against my skin sends shivers of craving through me and I absolutely know if I don't stop it now, I never will.

"Alex... Oh god, you have to stop," I eventually say, trying and failing miserably to push him away because of my own lack of bloody enthusiasm.

"No, I want you. I fucking need you. Let me have you," he replies, grabbing me more forcefully and pushing me down onto my back with his weight. His mouth lowers to my exposed stomach and he begins licking his way down to the button on my jeans, which causes me to groan because god, he feels so good on me. Then he gets the button in his teeth and starts to tug violently on it. My core tightens in response as his hands find their way to my breasts and he pinches me.

My mouth instantly salivates at the thought of sex and then I remember what I'm trying to achieve.

Get some bloody control of yourself, Beth!

"No, you have to stop," I say, grabbing hold of his hair and giving it a sharp jerk with both hands so he looks up at me. Those glorious dark eyes gradually rise up to meet mine with no sense of shame or slowing down. He just licks his perfect lips and runs his tongue over me again. I almost immediately change my mind and let him have his way. My panting is utterly ridiculous. It's so unfair but as he pulls me tighter against him and moves his hands between my legs, I somehow summon enough resolve to try my only other option.

"Chess."

His body instantly stills. Everything stills, and then his hands retreat as his eyes soften a little. It's not much but at least I've got his attention. He gazes at me for a few moments then stands and moves back away from me, holding out his hand to help me back to the floor. Okay, it's good to know this safeword thing works then.

"Spoilsport," he says, smirking at me. I quirk an eyebrow at him. "Okay, okay." He turns and holds up his hands as he heads back for the door, which is still open.

What? Is he leaving? No, that's not what I meant. Panic sets in. Shit.

"No, I didn't mean you had to go," I almost shout after him.

"I should hope not. I know I've been an arse but I hope I at least get another chance to redeem myself," he replies as he leans down, picks up a bag and shuts the door. I sigh in relief and then look at the bag quizzically as he places it on the counter top. "You'll need to put these on," he says as he removes a set of bike leathers and boots.

"Excuse me? You think I'm going to get on a bike with you. I've never been on one in my life," I reply in astonishment. My dad may love the things but that feeling does not run in the family in the slightest. He studies me for a moment and then exhales a rough breath while rubbing his hand through his hair in irritation.

"Elizabeth, do you want to know more about me or not? The choice is yours. I am offering you more because against my better judgement, I want you, all of you. I have never had someone give me so much bloody grief and yet still I can't get you out of my fucking head." Do I? I thought I was just being honest and .. "You confound me

341

and pinch away at something inside, and for the life of me I don't understand why, but I apparently enjoy it and want more of it," he says, lowering his head to the floor a little. He shoves those beautiful hands into his pockets, seemingly waiting for my response. I'm shocked, overwhelmed, elated actually and the grin that spreads lets him know exactly how he just made me feel.

"Oh... Wow! Well, that was quite a statement," I reply as I walk forward. He lifts his head to mine with a small smile. "I will happily do anything with the man that just said that." Gently planting my lips to his, I give him the sweetest kiss I can find and suck in his bottom lip as he wraps me up in his arms and takes in a long breath. "Although I'm still scared shitless about the bike." He chuckles.

"I seem to remember that nerves suit you well, Miss Scott," he says as he nips my earlobe.

"Very different type of nerves, Mr. White," I reply as I look at the boots on the table with a frown. I'm going to die. I know it. I absolutely hate bikes.

"Right, let's get you in this leather then. We've got a way to go and the thought of you wrapped around me is making me rock hard again. We'll never leave if I have my way," he says as he holds out the trousers and helps me into them. That would be preferable in all honesty.

~

Walking out of the building, I feel my legs trembling for all the wrong reasons. One of my friends from school was killed in a bike accident when I was younger and the thought of getting on that very fast looking thing is terrifying. When we reach the bike, he rearranges some straps on my rather uncomfortable skin-tight leathers and pushes my gloves into place. It's even more uncomfortable now, and him pulling a helmet down over my head and flicking the visor up like he's done it a thousand times still isn't helping my nerves.

"Comfortable?" he asks as he slips his own helmet on.

"I suppose so. As much as I can be," I reply uncertainly, still looking at the bike. Unfortunately, it hasn't miraculously changed into a car.

"Just wrap that incredible body around mine and hang on tight. It's nothing you haven't done before. There's just some leather in between us this time." He smirks and flips his visor down, simultaneously knocking mine down, too.

Swinging his leg over, he kicks the stand up and indicates for me to get on. So I do, gingerly, and then grab on tight. It's ridiculous, I know, but – scared.

"Are you okay?" he says as his disturbingly erotic voice comes through my helmet. I almost jump out of my skin at the unexpected noise.

"Wow, we can talk? Yes, I think so. Don't go too fast though," I reply in my best headmistress tone.

"Is there another way to go?" he asks as he chuckles and reaches backward to grasp my thigh. It's not a question. "Christ, you look so fucking hot in those leathers. I've got a mind to pull over somewhere and fuck you senseless in a lay-by." I can't stop the grin that spreads across my face, regardless of the fact that I'm shaking with fear. The thought is appealing to say the least.

"Umm, what do I do? Do I have to do anything?" He chuckles again and pulls me forward into his back. It's really not funny. Nothing is fucking funny at all at the moment.

"You know when I'm inside you and you somehow sense where I need you to be. You move to the place that feels closest?" Random, but hey the trembling is changing to a good thing at the very thought.

"Umm, yes."

"Do the same thing. Make yourself feel like you're part of me. Make me feel like I'm part of you." Oh that's sweet. Oh god, that's amazing. Did that actually come out of his mouth? Where did this version come from? Mr. Charmer has definitely arrived.

"That's actually a very amazing thing to say, romantic even," is my sighing response as I wrap around him a little more fluidly than the last grabbing technique and muse his softer side. He doesn't say anything, just starts the engine and taps my thigh. I couldn't care less because he said lovely things and that really is enough for me at the moment.

As we pull away, I lay my head down on his back and tighten my thighs around him. I can only imagine his devilish smile as he weaves his way through the traffic. His movements are so smooth that I find it easy to stay with him as we corner and he gently accelerates and decelerates. Obviously he's taking his time, letting me get used to the sensations, and thankfully, I can feel myself slowly relaxing around his body, that stupidly hard body that's still shouting "eat me" every other second to my groin. At one point, I feel him grab onto my hands and pull them tighter together, which for a moment I think is yet another sweet thing. Then I realise he must have taken both hands off to do it so I scream at him. He simply laughs at me. It's not funny in the slightest so I bump my helmet on his in frustration. This seems only to make him laugh more and speed up. That only intensifies the rather uncomfortable feeling I have that when we do reach some open road, we won't be going slow at all and then I notice the sign. It's the M1 sign, the sodding motorway. My heart rate increases tenfold.

"You'll love it, baby. Just relax. You're doing fine. I could always find a lay-by instead?" he says as if magically sensing my hesitation at the thought of going faster than this and trying to calm me.

"That's alright for you to say. You're the one in control of this death machine," I reply nervously, increasing my grip again. He chuckles and squeezes my thigh. It's still not funny.

"Have you ever not enjoyed something I've been in control of before?"

"Arsehole." It's all I've got. He seems to find that hilarious because his bark of laughter actually seems to make the bike swerve a bit. Okay, no laughing on board.

He hits the roundabout and then accelerates slowly for the ramp onto the motorway, heading north to God knows where. The bike begins to roar underneath us as I feel him shift gears and adjust his position a little. If I wasn't so scared, I'd be incredibly turned on because I expect the man looks like a god, although that's hardly anything different, is it?

"You ready?" His voice is slightly pitchy like an excited schoolboy as he starts to lower his frame.

"Yes, I think so. God, I hope you're good at this," I reply with some trepidation, adjusting myself behind him and clamping my thighs down hard as I try to get comfortable.

"Yes, I think you are too. Hang on," he says. I can feel the smirk he's giving me. He'll pay. I have no idea how, but I'll find a way.

He leans forward and picks up the speed as we head down towards the motorway. Luckily, clear open road greets us and clearly Alex uses it to his advantage at his earliest convenience. The moment the wheels of the bike come off the entry and hit the road, he hits the accelerator and the bike almost flies. I swear if it had wings, it would take off. My first thought is utter panic as I squeeze my eyes shut and bear hug him to the point where I'm sure he can't breathe. I don't even dare ask or look at how fast we're going so I just continue to hold on, hoping to hell that I can stay on. But slowly I start to relax into the motion and open my eyes, trying to focus on the sights around me that are whizzing past. The bike still roars beneath my legs and I began to realise that I'm smiling. I can't help it. The exhilaration of going so fast on such a ludicrously dangerous piece of equipment is ridiculously exciting and once I've gotten past the fact that I'm not going to fall off in a hurry, I find myself almost laughing. The feelings that hit my emotions are indescribable, yet another thing Mr. White has given me.

"Something funny?" Alex questions, obviously sensing my inner chuckle.

"No nothing, it's just bloody brilliant back here," I reply, giggling with delight as I wrap myself against him and smile stupidly.

"Want to go faster?" he asks, the apparent devil appearing once more. I can't believe it goes any faster if I'm honest.

"Oh god, does it go..." Before I finish, he opens it up and the bike finds more speed, stupid amounts of speed. I cling on for dear life and scream into his back as the growl beneath me intensifies.

I have no words. It's just, well... I still have no words.

We ride on for what seems like hours but probably isn't and then head off the motorway toward a town I don't know, so I ease my grip off slightly as the bike slows. Suddenly feeling remarkably confident in my abilities as a passenger, I let go of him and stretch my arms out to the side while twisting my neck around. The wind rushes against my leathers so I sit up slightly to ease my back, not realising I'm hurting until I move. The cramped position and my death grip on Alex have obviously taken their toll on my rather unfit body. It's ridiculous. I can take being whipped but not a few hours on a bike. I need to get fit.

"Don't worry. We're nearly there then you can stretch," he says in a terse tone, pulling my arms back around him. I frown at his double hand removing but it seems I'm not so nervous anymore. I'm more bothered by his voice. It seems a little distant. Jovial Alex has left the bike and has been replaced by another version it seems.

Ten minutes later, having driven through a few estates, he pulls up in the drive of a three storey, Victorian, semi-detached house in a quiet suburban area. He puts his legs to the floor and just sits there for a while with the bike idling beneath us, looking straight at the house. The lights are all off and it seems that no one's in. I have no idea what I'm supposed to do but the thought of getting off is far too appealing so I move to climb off. His shoulders instantly tense and his hand comes back to grab my thigh and hold me in place.

"Are you okay?" I ask quietly. "If you've changed your mind it's okay. We can leave if you want."

Silence. What the hell is going on?

"Alex, I'm going to get off the bike now." Still nothing. I slowly lean my weight on him and swing my leg over to hit the ground. They buckle slightly but the bliss that follows is truly orgasm worthy. I really could get used to this pleasure, pain, pleasure thing.

Pulling my helmet off, I stretch my body and wait for him to move. Still nothing. Okay, this is a bit weird now, so I walk in front of the bike, pull my hair out of the plait and shake it out, hoping that it might get his attention. It clearly doesn't because he's still sitting there, motionless, staring at the house. Right, so I haven't got a clue what to do. Should I go for the softly-softly approach or something? I can't even see his eyes to know what I'm dealing with here.

Reaching over the handlebars, I turn the key in the ignition and the bike cuts off. If I can at least get him off the bike it might help.

"Alex, get off the bike," I say as firmly as I dare. "You brought me here and said you had something to show me. So show me."

I watch as he slowly kicks the stand into place, pulls his helmet off and hangs it on the handlebars. When his eyes eventually meet mine, he's heaving in a breath and I can see him trying to contain his emotions. I don't know whether they're good ones or bad ones but I'm getting an odd sense of dread as I look at slightly cloudy eyes and a deathly still Alex. It's the kind of deathly still that makes you think something very bad is about to happen, or just did.

He leans the bike into the stand, unfurls his long body from it and steps off, and then unzipping his jacket, he pulls off his gloves and reaches into his pocket, pulling out some keys. Grabbing my hand, he moves us towards the door and unlocks it. I follow, not daring to say a word in case it stops him or makes him change his mind. What on earth am I about to see?

He walks in and switches the lights on. I find myself inside a very elegantly presented family home. It's full of the general niceties that a home should offer. A pleasant lilac colour adorns the walls, strangely similar to the roses he sent me, but the house feels cold and smells a little musty as if no one's been here for a while. He keeps hold of my hand and leads me into the hallway towards the stairs. When he reaches the bottom, he stops and kicks the first step a few times, then gripping onto the handrail, I notice his hand whitening under the strain he puts on it and watch his continued stare at the bottom step, which seems never ending.

"Are you okay?" I ask again, trying to look into his eyes. He looks strange and if I didn't know better, I'd say it was fear or trepidation, two traits I've never imagined he could even think of let alone portray or feel. The silence continues as he picks at a piece of wallpaper that's beginning to peel and rubs his thumb across the back of my hand. All I can do is hold on and wait, so that's what I do in the hope that speech might eventually arrive.

"I grew up here," he says coldly, taking a step up the stairs, his hand releasing mine as he moves away. "My father was... *is* a solicitor. He doesn't live here anymore." Okay. I'm not sure it's time to talk, so I don't. I just let him continue.

He stops halfway up and lets his fingers trace the wall around some scuffmarks. Frowning, he lets his hand drag up the rest of the wall as we keep climbing, then when we reach the top, he turns the corner and heads to the next set of stairs. I notice the wall colour change to a pale grey as he fills the landing in front of me and the ceiling height seems to have lowered, creating a more cramped feeling around him. The next set of stairs he climbs more slowly. In fact, he very nearly stalls at each step as if not wanting to go another footfall further. That sense of unease hits me again as we reach the top and he stands and stares down the corridor in front of us to a small, dark, wooden doorway.

I reach a hand forward to touch him but he immediately flinches at the contact and turns his eyes to me. I can't begin to process the emotion that's lying in them. They look empty somehow, lost even. I smile, hoping to get him back but he just turns back to the door and stands still again. Eventually, he sucks in a short breath and hesitantly walks towards it as I follow, wondering what the hell I'm about to see behind that door. Pushing his back flush against the wall by the door, he slumps down to the floor and pulls me down with him. I'm completely baffled so we just sit there in silence as he stares at the door over his right shoulder and I sit quietly on his left. I just hold his hand tight and lean into him. What else can I do? I have absolutely no idea what's going on or why we're sitting on the floor but clearly something is very wrong with that door, or at least the meaning of it.

"Do you want to tell me more or is this as much as you want to give? If it is, it's fine really," I say quietly, stroking his arm. There's still no response.

Another five minutes go by and we say nothing. He just stares and frowns. There's no tension in him anymore. He's just sitting and staring at the door, looking lost in his thoughts without a single movement from his body.

"He wasn't a good father. He hurt me," he says gently, still transfixed on the door. "He was forever hurting me."

My mind is confused for a second or two and then what he's saying hits me. He's saying his father was abusive, that he physically hurt him. My mouth drops open in utter amazement and then my heart launches out of my chest with such force I struggle for breath.

Shit. What the hell do I say to that?

I haven't got a clue what is that I'm supposed to do or say, so I wrap his arm around my neck and snuggle into him, hoping he will grab on. He doesn't. He just loosely drapes his arm across my shoulder and continues to stare as I listen to his chest hammering.

"He would drag me up here and then beat me until I bled. After that, he would put me in there and lock the door," he says calmly, pointing at the door. "I don't really know why he did it. He just kept saying I was useless and worthless. I don't think I'm useless, do you?" he continues, looking toward me for the first time with absolute truth pouring from his eyes.

Suddenly a small boy with a blood-splattered face sits in front of me and my heart tears in two. I instantly change position and straddle him to get closer. Running my hands through his hair and cupping his face in my hands, I move my mouth towards his and let my lips linger gently as I kiss him. It's all can do. I can't even think about what he's telling me so I sure as hell don't want him to. He doesn't really respond so I push my body flush against him and squeeze my thighs around him again, getting closer still and hoping that it's enough for him. Pulling back to see his glazed eyes, a flash of the picture in his apartment hits me square in the gut so I try to find the words to say that can make this better for him, or take it away somehow. There aren't any of any consequence, but I try anyway.

"Oh god, Alex, you are so much more than that. You are everything that's wonderful in my life. I can't believe you're telling me that you lived through this, with this. You didn't deserve it, any of it. You still don't. No one should have to go through that sort of stuff," I say, gazing into his blue eyes and trying to gauge whether I'm having any effect whatsoever. "He's an arsehole and you're a stronger man than he'll ever be. Look at what you've achieved. Look at what you've become."

He just gazes back with no emotion at all while his hands rest on my thighs and his mouth remains in that flat line. But I can see the emotion hiding in there now. It's the first time I've really noticed it so regardless of the fact that he's trying to keep it from me, I wrap my arms around his neck and pull him towards me. I grip on for dear life and squeeze him into me, pushing my body weight into him and encouraging him to hold on tight, to let it out if he wants to, and slowly his arms begin to tighten around me. The strength of his hold becomes so fierce that tears of sorrow start to bubble in my eyes for him as I continue clawing at him, hoping that I'm soothing something.

He buries his head into my neck and then suddenly pushes me away from him and looks at me, really looks deep into me. It's like an instant connection of something more emotional than before, more intimate somehow, and as I feel a tear run down my cheek, I know that we've just made a huge leap, that he's given me more than anyone else, ever. His eyes are glistening with unshed tears and it seems like he's trying to say something so I wait, searching his eyes for anything, but instead he just slowly leans his forehead onto mine and exhales a shaky breath.

My brain struggles to compute what it is that I'm supposed to say next. This beautiful, complicated man that sits underneath me in a damp hallway has survived something so abhorrent and unknown to me that I have no idea how I'm meant to make him feel better. He's showing me something so unimaginable and private that I feel myself being somehow ashamed of my own perfect childhood and loving family. I wanted more from him and this is what he has to show me, to tell me. He's giving me this so that I can try to make some sense of who he is today and why he behaves the way he does. I'm so stunned by it all, and humbled, that I simply can't find words for this moment.

Eventually I drag up the only words I think either of us wants to hear while I'm desperately trying to shield him from that fucking door. Anger and resentment rushes through me at what he had to put up with and suddenly, I just want to get him away from everything this place represents.

"Do you want to leave now?"

"Fuck yes," he replies, clutching me around the backside as he stands and walks us back towards the stairs. I can't help but watch as that door gets smaller and think of him locked in it as a little boy. Then the little boy in the rain creeps back into my mind. The picture in his apartment. It's yet another negative reminder of his past, not that there seems to be any positive ones. I sneer at the thought of his bastard of a dad and narrow my eyes at the door again as that venom rises back up in my throat. The thought causes me to surprise myself by spitting at it viciously over his shoulder. Thankfully, the lips I feel against my neck reward my quite disgusting and possibly irrational actions. It was revolting. But then so was his childhood, it seems.

Chapter 24

Elizabeth

"Can I use your phone please?" I ask as I look at him across his kitchen table, nursing a very hot cup of coffee. We arrived back at his just after ten and I'm freezing.

"Of course. Where's yours?" he says, pushing his phone at me.

"In a million pieces," I respond, searching through his contacts for Belle. He stands and walks into the kitchen area, grabbing some muffins and popping them in the toaster.

"Why?" he asks quietly. He's been like this since we got back, quiet. It's disturbing and so unlike him that I haven't got a clue what to say to bring him back to normal.

"Because you didn't call," I reply quickly and without thought. Given what has happened this evening, I see little point trying to hide my feelings or play games. He's shared something so precious with me that everything else around us seems to pale into insignificance.

"Oh really? A little pissed at me or hurt that I didn't call? It was your choice to walk away if I remember correctly," he says with his back toward me, his shoulders slightly slumped. That's something he's been doing a lot of since we got back, avoiding eye contact. I suppose I understand a little but it's beginning to annoy me.

"Both, and you know I had good reason," I reply as I text Belle to let her know where I am.

The toaster pops and he comes back to the table with honey and jam. We both begin to tuck into our muffins and eat in silence for a while. We haven't spoken about what he told me at all on the drive home and I was glad of it at the time. While a gazillion questions whizzed through my head, I needed time to process the information and try to understand what the hell I was supposed to do with it. What does that sort of start in life do to a man? How the hell did he make such a success of himself? And how on earth did he get through each day without crumbling into a pile of weeping dust? At least I now know why he went into care at such a young age and where the anger and control issues come from.

"Was it enough for you, Elizabeth?" he asks suddenly, completely breaking my quiet contemplation of his life.

"Excuse me?" I reply, looking up at him as he pulls me from my thoughts. Beautiful but sad eyes greet me with a slightly nervous smile creeping around the corners of his mouth.

"Is the knowledge of my past enough for you to understand why I distance myself? Why I choose to keep people away from me?" His icy eyes burn me a bit in their questioning and I struggle to answer him because I don't know how I feel about any of it.

"Yes," I reply quietly, looking back down at my empty coffee and wondering where else he's going to go. I still can't fathom how I'm going to deal with all this new information. I just know that I want it to go away for him and never have to see him in pain again.

"You know, I haven't been there for a few years. It's funny how it still looks the same. I always think it will change somehow but every time I'm there, I just see it through the eyes of a nine-year-old," he says as he saunters off to the machine and makes us both another coffee.

"You said your dad doesn't live there anymore so why do you have the house?" I ask softly as he returns and sits back at the table.

He chuckles and reaches for another muffin. "Call it self-torture if you like. He put it on the market about five years ago and I bought it, well a company of mine did. He doesn't know it was me. I just wanted to have it. It somehow felt wrong to let someone else live in it. I made him leave everything in it, apart from personal items." He shrugs almost apologetically for some reason.

"But why would you want to keep such horrific memories?" I ask, appalled at the thought of him forcing such negative images on himself. A bit like the bad dates on his back, this is obviously a recurring pattern for him. He sighs and throws his muffin back on the plate.

"Because they're my memories and they make me who I am. They remind me how to live and to never back down again. No one else knows what I went through or how pathetically weak I was then. From the moment I left that house, I became a fighter. I learnt to attack first and pay the consequences later," he replies with a wry

352

smile, as that look of confidence seems to seep back into his veins, thankfully. It's quite lovely to see again. "It wasn't until later in my life that I realised I could manipulate my targets rather than beat them to death with a club to achieve what I wanted."

I study his face for a few minutes, trying to formulate the right words for the question I want to ask. His brow is soft and he seems reasonably open to giving information so I decide to just go for it and deal with the possible aftermath. Asking him about his mental history probably isn't the wisest move but I need to know regardless.

"Alex, you weren't weak or pathetic. You were a child who deserved love not abuse," I say quietly. He instantly looks to the floor again. "You said no one else knows. Haven't you talked to anyone about it? Didn't the care home try to help you? A psychiatrist or something?" I ask, looking at his downcast eyes and inwardly begging him to respond favourably and not hit the roof. His brow furrows and as he lifts his head, he looks perplexed for a moment, as if regarding an idiot.

"Why would I want to talk about it? I found my own way out of it. Conner found me when I was struggling and pointed me in the right direction again. I don't think I've done too badly really, considering," he says, trying to brush across the point.

Twiddling my thumbs on my coffee cup, I respond calmly and try to keep him in a talking mood while gently maintaining my inquisition.

"You mean you've never actually had a conversation about your feelings regarding your dad and your childhood? No one has been there to guide you or give you some explanations, to tell you that none of this was your fault?"

"What are you trying to imply, Elizabeth? That I'm unbalanced or unstable because I didn't bare my soul and weep on the shoulder of a shrink?" he says with mock affront. I can see the hint of irritation looming in his eyes, though. I can also still see the emotion behind it. I just need him to keep that emotion coming and not close down on me. "And stop calling that bastard my dad. He is not worthy of the fucking title in the slightest."

"Alex, you can't make light of this. This sort of thing has a huge impact on people's mentality and the way they handle their emotions. I've been pushing you to give me something you might not even know *how* to give. I knew you found your feelings difficult but this type of damage could mean something completely different for you," I say as my mouth completely overrides any appropriate level of intelligence that I should have had. It's too much and the instant I look up into his eyes again, I know he's changed and I've lost him. *Stupid Beth.* His body stiffens and his quizzical frown has now transformed into the glower he uses when he's about to charge.

"I didn't take you there for your fucking sympathy, Elizabeth. I don't want it so don't you dare try that irrelevant bullshit with me," he snaps as he stands and begins to leave the room with loathing pouring off him.

"Wait, Alex, I didn't mean to..." I shout, running after him and trying to grab onto his arm. His body swings round to face me with such speed it nearly knocks me over, and I stumble backward into the dresser as he glares at me.

"You think because of your perfectly balanced fucking family you're more stable than me somehow? That you're superior in your ability to manage your feelings? Well fuck you," he roars as he towers above me. I immediately back up into the wall away from him, no clue what's coming next.

"No, I didn't mean to belittle you, Alex. I just..." I try to find what I mean but his overbearing presence and his furious scowl just leave me speechless. His body seems to increase in size again as his fists clench in anger. I flick my eyes to the floor as I sense the spike of adrenaline that's coursing through him while he moves closer.

"You just what, Elizabeth? Felt sorry for me? The poor little boy who got beaten up by Daddy? The weak little shit who couldn't defend himself? Fuck you. You can't even raise your own head in a room full of strangers without crying about it. How does it feel to be reminded of your own pathetic issues?" he shouts.

My mouth gapes and tears threaten as I watch him loom down on me. He looks so mad, his whole being barely holding onto any reserve as I stare up in shock. And then he turns, picks up a lamp and hurls it at the wall, smashing the ornaments from the hall table to the floor in the process. He seems to coil into a spring as he launches his fist into the wall twice and then bellows in anger or frustration, his eyes trained on the spot he just demolished. I back into the wall further and crumble to the floor, pulling my knees up to my chin and wrapping my arms around myself in fear. He's scaring me beyond

354

belief. I have no idea where he's gone but I'm now too scared to try and do anything about it anyway.

Blood is pouring from his knuckles and his breathing is so rapid I think he's about to explode as his face glances around at everything almost manically. I have nothing left to do but shrink back as far as I can into a hard wall and hope he calms down. Tears begin coursing down my cheeks and I can't stop the sniffing as I try to contain myself. His eyes flick back to me for a second and I rapidly look back at the floor in the hope of disappearing somehow, but when I dare to glance back up, his back is facing me and it's all I can do to keep myself from bursting into tears again. I look at the carnage of broken things in the hall in front of him and realise how vulnerable I feel in his presence. I've felt it before but not like this, and never this defenceless. Not knowing what to do next, I just sit and wait for him to do something.

Minutes go by as I wait for him to make his next move. Is he calming himself now or getting more agitated? His body seems less tense but his breathing is still shallow and his shoulders have no intention of dropping any time soon. Suddenly, he turns and storms back towards me, hauling me up from the floor by my upper arms so he can look into my eyes and forcing me back onto the wall with his strength, squeezing so hard I'm sure he's going to break something. I struggle in his grasp to try and break free but it's futile so I go limp and let him hold me there while he sneers at me and I start sobbing again.

"You want emotion from me? There it is. I've spent fucking years boxing it up so it doesn't ruin everything and a few weeks with you and I'm a fucking wreck again. I knew you'd do this to me. I saw it coming at me like a fucking steam train and I did nothing to stop it. Well no more. I'm fucking done with this shit. I don't need it or you," he shouts, releasing me with a forceful shove and heading down the hall for the door.

I stand shakily against the wall, gripping my now bruised arms and watch as he reaches for the handle, hesitates and then stands still again. His back is to me and he's either questioning himself or waiting for me to help him find a way through the mess we've created. Have I really done this to him? By asking him to open up and reveal himself, have I inadvertently unleashed the anger and hurt he's kept so well buried? I stare at his back in shock and confusion, trying to control my gasping and work out what the hell to do. If I have done this then I have to help resolve it somehow because I don't want him in pain. I don't want him to go, and I don't want this to end. I want my Alex back. I want him happy and carefree.

From somewhere deep down inside myself I found the courage to take a few steps toward him. He isn't done with this. If he was, he wouldn't be hesitating. Nothing about Alex hesitates, ever. It's just not in his nature. How do I find a way to make him feel comfortable again? This is the reason he is the way he is. He needs the control to feel balanced in his life and I've turned that upside down for him by pushing, stupidly having the audacity to question his way of doing it. It's a mess and his detonation clearly isn't helping, but I know I've got to try and put this right, regardless of scary Alex because I can't deny how I feel about the man in front of me.

"Alex, what do you want from me?" I say in a shaky breath, almost inaudibly.

"Some fucking respect!" His answer is immediate and harsh in its tone. He doesn't move. His chest still heaves in and out as if he could very well explode again at any given moment.

"You've had my respect since before I even knew you. You still have it. You get respect from everyone around you. What is it that you really want from *me*?" I ask again with a little more voice. His body visibly exhales a breath and his fingers stretch on his tight hands as he hangs his head a little and leans it against the door. I wait again, hoping that all of the above is a positive sign. Minutes go by with no response so I try again. "Do you want me to tell you how I feel about you?" I continue, taking another step forward and crunching the broken glass beneath my feet. His body tenses again as he hears me approaching closer and his head turns slightly, probably showing me his displeasure at my advancement so I stop immediately.

"No." His voice is still tense but there's a softer tone coming through now. I've got his attention at least and I don't think he's about to explode again. This might work and even though I'm not sure I want to do this yet, I have to find the words to show him how much he means to me.

"If I tell you, will you calm down enough to really listen?" I ask tentatively, hoping for a good reaction.

"No, Elizabeth. I don't want to hear it. I told you I'm done," he replies quietly through gritted teeth as he bangs his head on the door softly. A small smile kisses the corners of my mouth at his blatant refusal to hear anything remotely nice given the circumstances, causing my eyes to soften as my heart melts a bit more for the man in front of me. He suddenly seems like a lost little boy again.

"Why are you hesitating then? If you really don't want to listen, why don't you just leave?" I ask, waiting for a response. Nothing.

I take another step forward so that I'm only a few steps away and pull in a deep breath. He's given me so much this evening and I've almost ruined it with my lack of thought and reasoning. Still, he isn't storming off and he deserves so much better from me, so much more. This proud and fiercely independent man needs me to tell him how important he is to me, how much I need him and how much of an inspiration he is to me. If he didn't want any of this, he simply wouldn't have shown me so much and I refuse to let one argument kill everything that we can have because of his stubbornness or my fear. So he's going to hear it, whether he wants to or not and if the only way I can get through to him is to do this his way then he can have it his way.

Slowly dropping down to my knees, I assume a comfortable position and lower my head a little. I instantly notice his head move to the side the tiniest bit more and know that I've at least got his attention again so I smile a little and try to formulate enough words to keep it.

"When I met you, I couldn't understand why you were interested in me. You filled the room with such a beam of light that I felt I could do nothing but sink into the dark beside you and hope you might remember I was there. I couldn't understand what it was that you saw in someone like me, but now you've shown me someone within myself that I never knew existed." He still doesn't move, no indication to help me, but he's not leaving. "The short time we've been together has been the best in my life and you've given me so much to respect you for, so much to admire you for. You have no idea how absorbing you are to me and how much I want your attention and affection. Every time you come near me, I can't breathe. Every time you touch me, I feel faint and every time you make love to me, I feel like if I died in that very moment it would be worth every second." I breathe out, trying to find something that might make him turn. I don't know what though. "I'll give you everything I have, Alex. You can have it all if you want, but please be careful because you scare the hell out of me. You could take my soul and destroy it with one hand if you chose to, and yet despite the consequences, my heart is yours." I stare at his back, my pleading eyes worried about so much but not caring. "I want you to have it. I have never wanted anything more than I want you. I couldn't take it away from you now even if I tried, so take it with my blessing and do with it as you please."

I heave out the last sentence with tears brimming in my eyes and gaze back at the floor, hoping that I've made my point emotively enough and that I haven't just sentenced myself to the humiliation of rejection. If he wanted to hear my emotions then I've given all I have to give. My body is trembling with fear at the thought of him walking away and I hate that I'm still kneeling, but I have to see this through his way.

This could be it. My mind goes into overdrive. He might simply tell me to go and I will have no choice but to leave. He tried to let me in at his pace and my own stubbornness and stupidity has potentially ruined it for me. That a man like him was even thinking about revealing such personal information to me should have been enough for me. I should have backed off and let him show me everything else in his own time but instead I've been a fool and my stupid insistent need for clarification and more has destroyed his trust in me. I can only hope that my emotions are enough to make him see that this is still worthwhile and that everything we've achieved has been for a reason.

The air around me feels uncomfortably still as I continue to stare at the floor and wait. My knees are starting to hurt because of the cold tiled floor and the strange position for me is beginning to increase the pressure on my back. Three hours of being on a bike certainly haven't helped much either. I eventually close my eyes and take in another quiet breath while trying to take myself to the place where I went when we were in Eden, the place with no pain. That place was so relaxing and peaceful, like a little slice of summer meadows and warmth. I have no idea how I found it at the time but right now, I could do with finding it again.

So much time passes while he just stands there and I kneel with my head bowed, waiting and hoping. I should have been prepared for the fact that he would take his time, that he wouldn't make any move at all until he was ready, but I wasn't, and it is yet another reminder that I hardly know anything at all about the man I've just released myself to.

Suddenly I hear movement and then it stops again. I peek my eyes open a bit and look back at the floor. His feet are pointed toward me. *Well that's a start.* Taking three long strides he makes his way toward me and stops about an inch from my knees. Not daring to look up at him, I remain perfectly still and look at his boots. He nudges one between my legs until they're parted slightly and then he pushes a bit more until the toe of his boot is next to my groin. Looking down at the sight sets my damned heart rate off again and I grip my thighs with my fingers, trying to contain my ridiculously erotic thoughts given the situation.

"Better," he says in a commanding voice, the voice I know so well. Those eyes will be deep blue by now and his shoulders will be firm and inflexible. He removes his foot and walks to the lounge. I hear clinking and shuffling sounds as I remain in my position and wonder what's going to happen next. "Come in here, Elizabeth," his voice calls calmly. Oh thank god I can move!

Slowly shifting my weight, I ease myself up and stretch my legs out as I feel my back click in two places. It's pathetic so I make another mental note to get fit at some point. As I walk into the room, I'm rewarded with the glorious sight of him sitting in a wing-backed chair, facing the fireplace and drinking what is more than likely Cognac with another drink placed on the coffee table opposite him. One leg is crossed over the other in that timelessly elegant way that suits him so well and his chin rests on his fingertips as he presumably thinks about what he's going to do with me. His demeanour seems a strange mix of the dominant Alex I know and a more peaceful one that I haven't seen before. He's almost contemplative as if a little unsure of himself.

"Sit and have a drink," he says as he gestures to the chair and rubs his temple.

As I reach for the drink, I sneak a look at his eyes to see what I'm dealing with and find there's no darkened depth to them. His gaze is impassive and it leaves me feeling a little cold as I take a seat nervously. After a few moments, he speaks again while looking at the crackling fire.

"I'm not sure what you expect me to say about your feelings so I'm not going to say anything. I won't be cajoled into saying something if I don't feel like it so you'll have to wait," he says, holding up the glass and swirling the liquid around. *Okay.* "It's good isn't it? Le voyage de Delamain. It's got a quality that very few understand or appreciate, and sadly most people who can afford it rarely care about its particular taste. They probably don't look deep enough to give the flavour a chance to settle in their mouths and stimulate their tongues, or linger and show them its full capacity for gratification," he says with a small sigh of dismay. What the hell?

"Yes, it's very good," I reply in a small voice as I sip and wait, again. He continues to stare into the fire. Where in God's name is he going with this? Is he trying to tell me something with his little Cognac lesson? More minutes go by as he presumably thinks yet again about what to say or do next while I twiddle my fingers around the glass and try to not bite my thumbnail.

"Here's what we're going to do, Elizabeth. We're going to spend some time doing this my way. You will not question anything that I say or ask of you, and you will not intrude on my feelings again unless I give you permission to do so. You will not ask anything of me or try to manipulate your way around a situation that you don't approve of and you will not show any displeasure when the circumstance isn't to your liking. You will stay here with me as of Thursday evening for two weeks and at the end of that time, we will have another conversation about this. Do you understand or do you have any questions?"

I gawk at him with an open mouth. He hasn't moved his gaze from the fire and as he gulps back the rest of his Cognac and reaches to pour another one, I can't help but watch the way his strong jaw and throat work the liquid. He suddenly looks so bloody unreachable and in control of himself again that I find myself feeling very small and inferior around him, and is he honestly expecting me to agree to his terms? There's no bloody way I can do that, is there? I did just give him permission to take my heart and do what he wanted with it, but surely this is going to extremes, isn't it? I can see what he's trying to achieve but I'm not comfortable with it at all. Take out the feelings and you remove the problem? I doubt that's going to work with me involved in the scenario but maybe if he thinks it's worth trying then I should give it a go too. Obviously this is normal for him, but is he asking for complete subservience here?

"I have questions," I reply softly.

"You have three. That's all I'll answer so do it quickly before I change my mind," he snaps abruptly, his mouth sneering a touch. Okay, still angry then.

"I have to go to work-" I start. He cuts me off.

"Of course you do. Andrews will take you and pick you up every day. Such a wasted question, Elizabeth," he says with what sounds like contempt. "Next."

"I will want to see my sister and my friends. When can I see them?" I ask with conviction. This one's important.

"You won't see them outside of working hours. After two weeks, it might be different," he replies, still looking at the fire with complete indifference. Oh.

Not entirely sure what I should say to that answer, I decide it's more important to get down to the basic problem here, that being my heart and what he is capable of doing to it should he chose to turn into a complete arsehole, which it appears might be exactly what's happening.

"Alex, can you look at me please?" After what seems like an eternity, he slowly turns toward me, still expressionless but at least I can see his face. I need to see his eyes for what I'm about to ask. His beautiful blue eyes gaze at me. His lips part slightly as if he wants to say something but then he closes them again and swallows away his thoughts.

"If I do this for you, will you hurt me?" I ask with all the emotion I can pack into my voice, leaning forward towards him and imploring him to respond with some warmth to try and dispel my fears.

He doesn't.

"Physically? Yes. Emotionally? Probably. In all honesty, you'll just have to make up your mind if I'm worth the risk to you," he responds without a twitch to his impassive face, nothing to give me a chance of understanding what he's doing or why he's doing it.

Minutes go past as I look into his face, hoping for a sign of life or feeling. Nothing passes his chiselled features. This clearly is an Alex who won't be moved until he's completely in control again, a control that I took from him and a control that he's now asking me to give him

361

back. Moving my eyes back towards his lips, I watch as he opens them to speak, full lips so kissable and teeth that know exactly what they're meant for. I feel myself swallowing at the thought of what those teeth can do to me and that leads me onto visions of other very impressive images of him, so I scan his face once more and accept the inevitable. I don't even know why I'm thinking about it. It's only two weeks. How hard could it be?

"That's it. Time's up, Elizabeth. Will you do as I ask?" he asks with the first small smile I've seen in a while. He so saw me swallow. Arrogant bastard.

"Yes, with one stipulation. You will have to bend your rules if my work requires it," I reply with conviction. "I will not let this ruin my business."

"Agreed," he says sharply as he stands up and moves to the computer panel on the wall. Pressing a button, he speaks into it. "Andrews, Elizabeth is ready to go home. Could you get the car ready?"

"Yes, sir," comes the reply instantly. I look at him in shock.

"You want me to go home?" I ask in confusion.

"Yes. Spend tomorrow with your sister. Talk to her as much as you want. Go and get hammered for all I care. You have a free door pass at INK if you want it and I'll reserve a suite for you. However, be very aware that I will expect you to tell me what time you will be finished on Thursday so I can send Andrews for you, and the moment you enter that car, our terms begin. I would suggest you get yourself ready for them," he replies as he walks back to me and yanks me toward him with a sharp tug to my arm. Drawing a finger along my jaw, he pulls it towards my mouth and lightly brushes my lips with it. "Such a fuckable mouth," he says to himself as he moves his other hand to the back of my neck and forces my mouth towards his. "So soft and inviting." Gently placing his mouth on mine, he moves gracefully and with strong, supple strokes of his tongue, teases my mouth open, softly licking his way into my mouth. Increasing his hold on me and firmly moving my head to the side by my hair, he slides his tongue along my neck and I feel myself shiver at the contact. "So much potential to be harnessed and moulded." Kissing his way back up the other side of my neck, he moves back to my lips and lays an utterly exquisite lingering kiss upon them before pulling away and leading me to the front door. On opening it, we're met by Andrews waiting at the car.

"I'll see you on Thursday. Enjoy your time with Belle," he says frostily as he releases my hand and turns back to the door.

"Alex I..." he turns back to me and raises his eyebrow with an otherwise blank expression. I can't finish the sentence. I don't even know what I want to say. The passion has vanished in him and he feels cold and distant to me, like he has just switched me off and dismissed me. I stutter a little, trying to find a sentence to tell him how I feel but all the words just get lodged in my throat so I decide it's probably best just to get in the car and leave. "Goodnight."

"Goodnight, Elizabeth," he responds with a frown, as he turns again and walks into the house, slowly closing the door behind him.

Andrews shuts the door behind me and I snuggle into the seat. Gazing out of the window as the gravel crunches beneath the car, I watch the moon glinting in the sky and wonder what the hell happened this evening. In the space of five hours I have been through so many emotions I can't even remember what the first one was. Ah yes, excitement, then passion as he approached, then indecision about sex, then fear and eventually exhilaration about the bike. Then came shock and sympathy about his revelation, followed by yet more confusion and fear when I watched him explode at me, then the humiliation of thinking it might be over and finally chastisement as he told me the only way forward was his way. Lovely.

Wrapping my arms around myself, I lean my head against the window and wonder what it would be like to live in a world where emotions didn't have such an impact on every move you made, where you made decisions based only on what you wanted and didn't care to be interested in the opinions or feelings of others. Because that's the world that Alexander White lives in, isn't it? He chooses to regard people's emotions as inconsequential or irrelevant to his cause. He only uses their feelings to help manipulate them or influence their decisions to his advantage. Other than that, feelings have obviously become an irritation he isn't prepared to deal with or even acknowledge as relevant in his world. Yes, he's tried to open up with me and look where that's gotten him? He admitted himself that he felt as if he was an emotional wreck because of it, because of me. What have I done to him? How have I managed to break through the confinements in his mind? And how the hell am I ever going to manage to do it again now that he's shutting me out of it? That's exactly what these two weeks are going to be about. It's his way of regaining the control he desperately needs and readdressing his balance. He's going to use my inability to ask more of him to draw his own power back towards himself and away from me.

I smile as the car pulls by the coffee shop the girls frequent and I think of good times, times when my life seemed less complicated and more relaxed. Only a month ago I would have been simply enjoying life and not constantly thinking of the whirlwind that is Alex. It's worrisome given what I've agreed to now. When was the last time I just thought about work and really enjoyed a day in my kitchen without worrying about things or being consumed by him?

The car draws to a stop outside my apartment building and I move to open the door. Nothing happens.

"It's locked, ma'am. Wait, I'll come round," Andrews says as his door slams.

"Thank you for delivering me safely, Andrews," I say as he holds my hand and helps me out.

"You're welcome, ma'am," he replies with a frown, refusing to meet my eyes and turning his head from me.

"Are you okay, Andrews? You look a little worried about something?" I ask, genuinely concerned.

"I was about to ask you the same thing, ma'am but I thought better of it," he replies with a tense scowl and a huff of what appears to be frustration. What is he talking about?

"I'm fine, but thank you for thinking of me. I am just a little confused if I'm honest. I seem to be that way a lot lately," I exclaim, looking at the floor.

He shifts a little on his feet and turns his brown eyes on me.

"If he ever makes you really nervous ma'am, all you have to do is shout. I'm never far away," he says with conviction and a small sneer. Oh, that's what he's talking about.

"It was just a misunderstanding, Andrews, that's all. Please don't think anything of it." I can't believe I'm having to discuss this with him. "Where do you stay in the house?" I question, hoping to change the subject completely because it was hard enough to go through at the time let alone discuss again.

"I have a flat on the top floor, ma'am," he replies as he walks me toward the entrance to the building.

"Oh right. Well thank you again for getting me home. Goodnight," I say, pushing open the door.

"Goodnight ma'am," he replies with a smile.

He watches me until I get into the lift and then I see him walk away.

What the hell was that about? Why would Andrews have said something like that? Was he inferring that Alex could become a little too exuberant with his anger sometimes? Surely not after the childhood he had. Having said that, he didn't hold back when that Draven chap tried to touch me.

As I open the door and walk towards my bedroom, I notice Conner's laptop bag on the hall table and smile at the thought of my sister falling in love. It's about time really. Three years since that bloody bastard broke her body and destroyed her faith in men. If I ever see him again in my lifetime, it will be far too soon. Marcus sodding Renfield - even the name sends a horrific shiver of disgust across my skin.

Sighing, I wrench off my clothes and crawl into my bed, feeling exhausted and slightly terrified by the thought of everything that's happened today. Thankfully, sleep seems to pull me down immediately.

Chapter 25

Alexander

The irritating receptionist gawped at him with the look of a sex-starved hussy as he made his way to the elevator. She was quite a pretty thing really but she held nothing of interest for him. Positive she'd probably give him everything on a plate if he asked for it, he gave her a quick wink just to keep her interested and to let her think she'd have a chance someday. The moment he did it, he felt a nervous sensation prick the skin at the back of his neck. Was that fucking guilt? Okay, it was a sensation he was feeling a little more lately, but he couldn't ever remember feeling it with regard to a woman. Yes, other things, which probably did deserve the sensation, but not a woman.

He'd waited for her until midnight the night before, hoping she'd make an appearance at INK just so he could watch her, but she hadn't. He'd sat in his office all night long like a nervous damned schoolboy on tenterhooks, willing her to enter those double doors so that he could gaze at her stunning body, but he'd been left frustrated when she didn't appear.

What the fuck did he expect? He'd just ripped away the heart that she'd so bravely given - to him of all people - with trust and an absolute unwavering faith that he'd look after it. She'd knelt in front of him and graced him with words he neither deserved nor expected and he'd rewarded her by offering nothing in return, only his inflexible approach to the relationship he knew she was craving from him.

He'd be surprised if she even called him today. The phone he'd sent her yesterday morning had no sweet note attached to it, like he knew she'd want, just his card and *"Call me at three"* written on it. What a fucking arsehole. Why the fuck he was doing this to her was still a quandary, but it had been the only way he could think straight at the time. There was no denying that the possibility of less intrusive questioning was far more calming than the normal persistent force she used. Not that she appeared to do it to piss him off or cause more turmoil. It was just her way, her beautiful and angelic way of finding him, maybe even trying to keep him safe from the world and look after him. And fuck, he'd never felt safer than in those arms of hers, with her body wrapped around him. She pushed away the horror for a few minutes. To be there in that house and feel anything close to safe was fucking astounding. Did she even know she'd done that for him?

He sneered at himself and looked to the floor.

This shit was more than likely not going to end well.

The doors pinged open and he made his way through the blue and white foyer, slightly lifting his lips at the ostentatious sculpture of a laptop on its glass stand in the middle of the space. It continued to amuse him every time he saw it. Conner's ability to go over the top on just about everything was legendary and the sculpture just seemed to scream, "Look at me, I'm a fucking genius!" He was probably right but that was beside the point.

Striding across to Linda, he nodded at her as she smiled and waved her hand at the doors.

He entered Conner's office and found him on the phone, laughing and giggling like a child. He quirked an eyebrow at the new hairstyle with its spiky pink tips, drowning out his normally only blue hair. Shaking his head, he took a seat on the couch and dug out his phone. The bloody thing had vibrated at least thirty times in the ten-minute journey over here.

While busily emailing varying contacts and texting Louisa with orders and new account details, he overheard two words come from Conner's mouth that he thought he'd never hear again. *Love you*. His own frown and smile hit him at the same time and he couldn't work out whether he should acknowledge the statement or not so he simply continued with his thumbs and stared at the phone.

"Fuck off, you cock," Conner said with mirth a few minutes later. Alex threw up his head and glared at him.

"What the hell? I didn't say anything," he responded as a smirk rolled over his mouth.

"You didn't fucking need to. I could feel the hilarity pouring off you from twenty feet away," Conner said as he stood and walked over to the couch. Slumping himself down, he put his feet on the coffee table and tipped his head back. "Anyway, I can't help it. She's just awesome. I never thought I'd find someone who challenged me so much and made me feel intrigued permanently."

"Well I can understand that. It appears the Scott girls are rather good at getting under your skin and messing with your mind," he replied with a sigh, throwing his phone onto the table.

"Problems? Don't tell me you can't get it up? Nice suit by the way. Tom Ford, I presume? You always did look better than me in a suit, you bastard," Conner asked, lifting his head and looking toward him, grinning like a bloody idiot. This love thing obviously suited his friend just fine.

"Nothing I can't handle, and my equipment is working just fine, thank you," he said with a smile. "So what was so important that you made me come here? And what the fuck is going on with your hair? Pink? Really?"

"She said I wouldn't do it for her, so I did. It seems her little games are the only way to get her to acknowledge my seriousness about her," he replied while running his hand through his hair. Alex began to speak again but Conner held up his hand and silenced him as Linda entered with a tray of coffee. When she'd left and the door was closed, he wandered across to his desk and then returned to lock the door.

"Jesus, is there something covert going on that I should know about? Locking the fucking door? Are you expecting the police or something?" he asked in genuine bemusement. Given his past, it wasn't beyond the realms of possibility but he was pretty sure everything was currently okay, and why the fuck would Conner have anything to do with all that anyway?

He stiffened a little and narrowed his eyes as he watched Conner amble back towards him with an unusually nervous expression. It didn't bode well at all.

Conner sat back down and placed the brown folder on the coffee table. Sighing, he gave Alex some coffee and relaxed back against the couch.

"Do you promise me that you're not going to go all wanker ballistic on me?" his friend asked.

"Why? What have you done?" he replied with a frown, suspicion immediately flowing over his skin. He hated the feeling, especially where Conner was concerned.

"I haven't done anything. I think I might have just found something you need to know about and I'm not sure how you're going to react. We both know what an utter twat you are when you're all riled up and I'm actually quite in love with my face," he replied with grin. True, but he didn't need a fucking reminder, dick.

"Conner," Alex growled. "Just fucking say it, whatever it is. I've got two more meetings and a phone call to Shanghai to prepare for and you know how much I hate speaking to those damn lawyers."

"Oh, yes, and there's that temper I'm so fond of," he said with a roll of his eyes. "Well, I got to meet my new senior consultant a few days ago, you know the one who sent me that code I couldn't break? I did eventually, by the way, tough though. Anyway, the moment she walked into my office, I was gobsmacked. I honestly couldn't think and I ended up making an utter arse of myself."

"For fuck's sake, Conner, did you drag me over here to tell me about another conquest? Couldn't it have waited?" he shouted in frustration, cutting him off mid-sentence and moving to stand.

"If you'd let me finish, you snippy bastard, I'll get to the point. And no, this one is definitely not a conquest. I don't think I could deal with that shit at all. You see, the problem would be that I'd be fucking someone who looked just like you," Conner said quietly, screwing his face up a bit and edging away, ready for a defensive block. He watched the reaction with an inner chuckle. The man knew him well.

"What the hell are you talking about?" Alex asked with a very intrigued frown.

Conner simply nodded at the folder and indicated that he should have a look so he leant forward and opened the folder. The first thing he saw was his own intense cool blue eyes staring back at him. He felt the inward gasp of breath as he tried to process the rest of her face. Black hair tied up elegantly and a jawline that reminded him of his father. Her mouth had the same lines as his own but it was fuller and more feminine. He dragged his vision back up to her eyes. They were bewitching in their hypnotizing gaze, a gaze he knew so well, the one he used on so many people to entrance them. He noticed the small darkened flecks in the lighter blue and took in her softer brow line with that questioning rise of the right eyebrow. The same as his - the one that said, *"Go on. Try me if you dare."* She was him, obviously more feminine, but everything about her shouted that she was related to him somehow. It wasn't possible, though. He had no family, only his father and that son of a bitch never talked of other children. She looked younger than him and her skin was lighter but other than that, he couldn't deny that she could easily be his sister.

Leaning back onto the couch, he stared at the picture and frowned again.

"How you doing, man?" Conner asked nervously from the side. He chuckled at him and continued to gaze at her features.

"I... I don't know what I'm supposed to do with that. She could be anyone. People look the same as other people all the time," he said calmly, still regarding the photograph. Why he was denying anything was fucking preposterous to him.

"No, man, it's more than that. She just is you. The way she moves, the way she talks. Christ, she even questions me with the same distaste as you do. She is so unbelievably confident and self assured it borders on conceit, not unlike someone else currently sitting in the room. Honestly, dude, I was thrown by her as soon as she moved into the room. I mean, yes, she's incredibly beautiful and normally my cock would have been twitching instantly, but it was just too bloody spooky for words."

Alex's frown deepened as he wondered if it was possible that his father had an affair. He supposed it was. The man clearly had never had any form of morals with regard to the people around him.

"What else do you know about her?" he questioned, putting the photo back into the folder and closing it.

"Not a lot really. Her name's Evelyn Peters. She's probably as talented on a keyboard as I am, possibly better, which is fucking ridiculous. She comes from Cumbria or somewhere near there, and she's taken over my whole consulting department in a matter of days because she couldn't stand the way the department leader worked. She simply told me how crap he was by showing me some of his inaccurate algorithms and programmed some new systems with shit I hadn't even contemplated, so I sacked him and promoted her. She'll be a pretty wealthy woman soon with the amount I now have to pay her. I still can't believe she manipulated that much out of me," he said with a chuckle and poured some more coffee.

Alex stared at his friend for a moment, analysing his demeanour. He was impressed and that really didn't happen much with Conner.

"She's really that good?" Alex said, raising an eyebrow and thinking of the photo again, memorizing the facial features that mirrored his own at that moment.

"Alex, it's like she's a female version of you. Each bit of her glides together effortlessly and she just radiates a charm that blows me away. Actually, I'm a little bit threatened if I'm honest. You should see the way her fingers move over a keyboard. It's like she's part of the machine. A machine I wouldn't want to piss of any time soon, by the way. I swear those fucking eyes could even scold you if pushed."

Alex chuckled and tried to imagine what a female version of himself would be like. The thought made him smile and he couldn't help but be intrigued by the thought of meeting her or at least seeing her from a distance.

"Is she here?" he questioned, sincerely hoping she was.

"No, I made sure she wasn't, didn't want you bumping into each other in the elevator or something. That could have been a little fucking awkward, don't you think?" he said, standing up and moving back across to the desk. "It could be nothing but I thought you had a right to know, that's all."

"Yes. Thank you," he said quietly.

"What are you going to do about it?" Conner asked, sitting down behind his desk and squeezing his frustration ball. The bloody thing went everywhere with him.

Alex rubbed his chin for a few moments as he mused the best way to make a meeting happen. He realised he wasn't ready to actually meet her until he had more information on the matter, but he definitely wanted to see her.

"When's your Christmas party booked at INK?" Alex asked, knowing it was the perfect opportunity to be able to see her in real life and study the way she handled herself.

"Three weeks away. Why? What are you thinking?" Conner replied with a nonchalant smile.

"That I'll see her there," he said sarcastically as he rose and picked up his phone and the folder.

"Man, we'll all be there, I mean Belle and Beth, and you won't be able to hide yourself from her if you don't want to be seen," Conner said with a genuine care to his voice. Some part of him warmed to that emotion that Conner often delivered. Actually, it began to flow across him like water and he smiled at the thought of genuine feelings.

"I'll know by then whether there's any truth in it. If there is then the time will be right and if there's not then it won't matter, will it?" he replied as he made his way to the door. Hesitating before he unlocked it, he turned back to Conner and looked at him with something that presumably felt like brotherly love. His friend had saved him from a miserable life and now he'd possibly found him a family he never knew he had.

"I owe you a lot, you know? I don't think I've ever told you how grateful I am," he said, never removing his eyes from Conner's shocked face.

"Christ almighty, Mr. White, was that an emotion I heard there? Jesus, if I didn't know better I'd think Beth was softening you up." Conner chortled as he walked toward him, slapped him on the back and a pulled him in for one of those quick man hug things he was fond of. "It suits you, you know."

"What does?" Alex responded in surprise.

"Being happy. You should try it more often. I like this non-explosive new Alex," he said with a smile and a wink. "And thank you. You know how I like my ego stroked every now and then."

Alex inwardly winced at the mention of the word explosive and lowered his eyes to the floor. Conner was about the only person who could read shame when it was etched into his features, even when he was trying his hardest to hide it. It didn't happen often but occasionally these things did occur, even to him. And he was so furious with himself for scaring her on Tuesday night that the regret was firmly stuck inside of him, still eating away at him and making him question everything that he'd done.

"I have to go. I'll call you when I know more about Miss Peters. I might need more information from you about her," he said, turning for the door. Conner gazed at him for a moment and he could feel the question before he even spoke. *Oh, for fuck's sake.*

"What have you done, Alex?" Conner asked with a frown.

There was no point trying to hide it. Conner would see straight through his lies anyway and probably give him a mouthful for trying, so he removed his hand from the door and sighed, turning back towards his friend.

"I screwed things up a bit, that's all. I'm trying to fix it," he said with a shrug. "The rest of it is none of your fucking business." He tried to keep his eyes fixed on Conner's but the unyielding glare that met him felt unsettling and unusually, he found himself feeling strangely apprehensive as to what was coming next.

"Tell me you didn't sleep with someone else? God, you're a prick. I told you not to fuck her over. How could you do that to her? I knew I shouldn't have let you through to her. She is far too good for your perverted sense of acceptable. You really are a twisted son of a bitch," Conner sneered angrily as he shoved his hands in his pockets and continued to glare. His gut constricted slightly at being berated by his friend but he knew it was deserved. The only thing he could do was tell the truth.

"I haven't been with anyone else, Conner. I took her to that bastard's house, and then when she got too close to the fucking bone, I lost my temper. She didn't deserve it and now I am trying to do something to alleviate the tension," he stated. "Do you really think so little of me, that I would take the closest thing I've even known to perfection and destroy it for my own amusement?"

Conner's mouth twitched up into a smile and his stance quietened as his eyebrows shot upwards.

"You took her back there? Well shit, that's... Christ... Well, I suppose if you did that I don't need to worry about anything. But you have to see my point. You're not known for your monogamy, are you?" he said with a chuckle as his body visibly relaxed again.

"I've never had a reason to be monogamous," Alex countered with a smirk.

"That's just plain argumentative," Conner chided.

"Yes, I suppose it is," Alex said with a smile. "Now if you've finished with your damned lecture, I'd better go."

"Cool, just let me know what you need," Conner said, reaching around him and unlocking the door. They nodded at each other and then Alex ambled towards the elevator, noticing the gaze of a rather cute but probably dull brunette sitting in the waiting area.

"Miss Oliver, come in here now," Conner shouted fiercely across the room. The little brunette jumped up, swung her eyes off him and over to Conner. Alex turned his head back to Conner and raised an eyebrow. Conner smirked and winked at him, holding the door open, then lowered his eyes to the brunette's backside and followed her in. Alex chuckled all the way to the exit and made his way to the car.

Sitting in the car as they made their way back across town, he noticed the time. Ten past two, fifty more long minutes and he'd get to hear her voice again, that voice that simply melted into his soul and filled him with feelings of warmth and joy. The last time they'd spoken, he'd done everything he could to remove the emotion from his voice and to level the unconscious yearning he had for her. When she'd got on her knees and told him how she felt, it had hit him so hard that he'd almost lifted her from the floor and taken her to bed immediately. That a woman as superior as her could have fallen for him despite his faults was mind blowing to him, but to have shown her that he felt the same would only have escalated the feelings again and then there would have been more emotions to deal with. No, better to move the balance of power back towards himself so he could try and regain some sense of control over the relationship and more importantly, his own emotional response to it. Who the fucking hell did he think he was kidding? He was so desperate for her, it hurt. He could feel the heat burning through him at the thought of just touching her this evening and watching her fall apart for him. His thoughts were completely irrational, highly problematic and so incredibly consuming that every nerve ending buzzed with the possibility of the more she was offering.

Quickly making the decision that he couldn't be bothered with meetings, he emailed Louisa to tell her to cancel them and rearrange for a different day. He could do the phone call to Shanghai at home, but first he needed to contact an old colleague. Thumbing through his contacts, he found the number for Mark Jacobs and dialled.

"Alexander White, how the hell are you? Long time no speak," came the brutishly deep East End voice.

"Mark, I'm good thanks. Listen, I need your expertise with something," he replied.

"Righto. Whatcha got for me? Always happy to make another fat wage packet from you, and your assignments are some of the more interesting ones I take on," he said with a wolfish laugh.

"Two things actually. I need you to find some dirt on Henry DeVille, something that could break him apart if I chose to give it to the media. He's fucking good at hiding it so it won't be easy. Actually, you could just make it up. I don't give a toss. It just has to be something that you can make stick to him like shit," Alex said with a laugh. "And also, I need as much information as you can find on a woman called Evelyn Peters. She works at Bluetech. Conner will give you anything else you need regarding general details."

"Okay. No problem. When do you need the info by?" Mark asked. He could already hear the tapping of a keyboard through the phone. He smiled and wished everything was as simple as Mr Jacobs made it appear.

"Soon as you can. I'll have Louisa send the twenty this afternoon and the rest when you're finished as usual," Alex said, lowering the privacy screen between him and Andrews.

"No problem, mate. I'll call you by Monday at the latest. Cheers," he said as he finished the call. Alex chuckled and slid his phone into his pocket. He'd never met a more tenacious character than Mark Jacobs. They'd been acquaintances since before he'd become the man he was today, from the time when East End boozers and dirty money were more his cup of tea. Too many times they had been together in situations that pulled that fucking guilt flying back to the surface again, but thankfully, they knew just enough dirt on each other to be able to find a mutual respect of sorts. He rubbed his hand over the back of his neck at the images that assaulted him - blood, lots of fucking blood again. His fists balled at the thought so he flexed them out and imagined her mouth to focus on something more peaceful. It worked instantly and he sighed out another breath as he tried to process Jacobs without the carnage that normally associated itself with the man. He was an animal in all reality and a gun for hire. Regardless of that, though, he was also a fucking good investigator. If there was dirt, he'd find it, and if something wasn't right, he'd fix it. Alex liked him a lot, always had, even when the man's gun had been pointed at him. Well, he probably deserved it at the time. He was a bloody nasty piece of work back then. Aiden Phillips had a lot to fucking answer for.

"Home please, Andrews. Change of plan."

"Yes, sir," Andrews replied as he manoeuvred the car to the next lane. He frowned a bit, noticing again that Andrews had been uncharacteristically sombre in his tone for a few days. Maybe something was wrong. His brain quickly travelled back to more pressing matters, like Henry DeVille.

He'd started the ball rolling on finding a new source of investment and there had been a few positive interests, but once again his fate lay with Conner. He was introducing him to the American giant, Tyler Rathbone next week, who apparently had a shit load of cash and nothing to do with it. Rathbone had been buying Conner's designs for years and using them in his media corporation for various ventures and until now he'd shown little interest in property or land acquisition. Luckily, though, he'd spoken with Conner a few weeks ago about looking to the east and trying something new. Fucking perfect, although he'd have to go in at his most charming. Rathbone was known for being the hardest man in business and wasn't afraid to stamp all over anybody to get what he wanted. A man after his own heart. The irony wasn't lost on him at all. In fact, it was just the challenge he needed.

As the car glided down the road towards the house, his mind fell back to Elizabeth. What should he do with her this evening? He had to keep the pretence up for a while longer. He had to keep it emotionless and let himself work out if he could actually do what she wanted him to do. Their time together had given him a rollercoaster of emotions from the word go, and he had to find some damn control again before it all came tumbling down around him, before he curled up into a ball and cried on her shoulder like a baby about his fucking arsehole of a father and the life that haunted him daily. Frowning, he turned his attention back to the road and noticed Andrews sighing in the front of the car.

"Andrews, are you alright?" he asked.

"Yes, sir," he responded with a flat voice.

"Yeah, sounds like it. What's going on?" he tried again with a more authoritative tone, hoping it would do the trick.

"Nothing, sir. I'm fine," he snapped almost fiercely. Obviously it hadn't worked.

"Andrews, I'm not fucking around. I don't like being lied to and you are lying. I can hear it in your tone and you've been a miserable shit for a few days," he said calmly with genuine interest.

"It's private, sir. I don't want to discuss it with you," he replied as they pulled into the drive of the house. Parking the car, Andrews walked around and opened the door. He felt himself recoil a bit at the tone. He'd never heard Andrews be so brusque with him before and then his eyes narrowed. Was he hiding something? Distrust and doubt bit at him. Something was definitely not fucking right.

"Andrews, what the hell is the problem? Is it your family? Can I help at all?" He watched patiently as the man paced a bit and eventually pinched his brow.

"Do you mind if I speak freely, sir?" Andrews said on a sigh. Well this was fucking interesting.

"I think I probably do, but do it anyway," he replied with a small smirk as he put his bag on the gravelled drive and shoved his hands in his pockets.

"I have driven for and looked after you for six years now. You have been a good employer and I've no reason to say this other than the fact that I have come to care about you somewhat like a father would his son. I have watched you enjoy your money and never once have I questioned your behaviour or believed I had a right to, but... But I cannot watch you destroy something as precious as Miss Scott. She does not deserve your disrespect," he said, without removing his castigating stare from Alex's eyes.

He was completely taken aback, mouth fucking gaping open like a fool. Never had he been spoken to in such a manner. The only people who would dare were Conner or Pascal, and even they would have had the decency to avert their eyes a little. Well actually, they wouldn't in the slightest, but that wasn't the point. To have his bloody staff talk to him in such a way was completely unacceptable and disturbing the fuck out of him, regardless of the fact that he might be right.

"Did you just tell me off, Andrews?" he asked with cool eyes as his venom took hold. "Because I don't think it's any of your damn business what I do with the women I fuck."

He'd never seen Andrews move so quickly in his life. It was a blur of movement and before he knew it, he was pinned against the side of the car by his throat. Struggling to get free, he pushed at him and felt the panic rising as the fingers constricted, but Andrews wasn't moving and instead he pushed his entire body weight into him, giving him no room to kick his way out, then pinched his fingers tighter and effectively started to shut off his air supply. That is, after all, why he'd hired the forty-five-year-old ex-special forces soldier. He wasn't just a driver; he was probably the most ingenious and lethal fighter he'd ever seen.

"And there's the heart of the problem, Alex. You see, you don't fuck a woman like Elizabeth Scott. You protect her from everything and you thank your lucky fucking stars that she even dared to give you her affection. God knows men like us don't deserve women like that. You need to grow the fuck up now and start acting like a bloody adult or you will lose her and it will be the biggest mistake of your life. Or I suppose you could keep grazing your way through the whores and see which field you end up in," he sneered and with a final shove of his hand into Alex's throat, backed up and let go.

Alex stood there for a moment in absolute shock and wondered what the hell to do next. Fire him, yes - no, he didn't want to fire him. He liked him. He'd been there for so long that he felt like the man was the closest thing to family he had apart from Conner. Hit him? Yes. No, bloody stupid. Then the statement hit him again. *"Like a father would his son."* Did Andrews really feel like that? Fuck.

"Consider that my notice handed in. I won't watch you demolish her extraordinary beauty and innocence because of your own damn failings. You're a bloody fool if you don't grab what she's offering and beg for her love," Andrews shouted as he turned his back on him and walked into the house, presumably to pack his bags.

He stood confused for a few moments. What the hell was going on in his life? When did so many relationships in his life become personal? Why hadn't he just shouted at Andrews and sent him on his way? Or fucking hit him? And why the bloody hell did he now feel the need to go and talk to the dick about his relationship with Elizabeth? It was fucking odd. His whole fucking life was beginning to feel odd.

He walked in the house and listened to try and hear where Andrews was. A loud thump came from upstairs so he made his way up to find him. The flat on the top floor was right at the end of the top corridor and gave him plenty of time to listen to the irritated ramblings of Andrews. He chuckled a bit and pushed the door open.

"Andrews, what are you doing?" he asked as he watched him throwing things into a suitcase.

"Packing. What does it look like?" Andrews mumbled as he walked across to the bookcase.

"Well stop it for a minute, will you, and come downstairs. I think we could both use a drink, don't you?" Alex said as he walked out of the room and headed for the study. Glancing down at his watch, he noticed it said five minutes past three and there had been no phone call from Elizabeth. Fucking great. Could this day get any worse?

He slumped down at his desk and poured two large whiskeys, waiting and oddly hoping that Andrews would walk down the stairs without bags in his hands. Thankfully, within minutes he was sitting on the other side of his desk, staring at him coldly.

"Drink the fucking drink, Michael," Alex said, pointing at the whisky. "And while you're at it, calm down," he said, sipping his scotch and tapping his fingers. Andrews picked up the drink, downed it, slammed it on the desk and continued with his glare.

"Oh, for fuck's sake, I'm not going to beg you to keep your job. It should be the other way around, don't you think? A bloody apology wouldn't go amiss either, you great big oaf," he continued with a smile as he stared at the man. He couldn't recall ever seeing Andrews so mad before. Normally he was cool and collected while he beat the living crap out of people. Clearly Miss Scott had tapped quite effectively into his emotional side as well.

"I'm not sorry for what I said, but I am sorry for what I did. I just thought it might be the only way you'd understand. Violence seems to be what stimulates your brain cells the most," he replied in a monotone voice, clearly trying to regain some of his normal demeanour but making damn sure that the whole point of his attack was hitting home. Alex felt his brows shoot upwards and swirled his drink around for a while, trying to find the way to make this situation better. He still couldn't decipher why he was about to discuss his feelings with Andrews but decided that for once, he wouldn't try to second-guess the issue and just take a leaf out of Elizabeth's book and trust.

"I am a little lost with her. I took her somewhere very personal the other night and it confused me so much that I lost my temper," he eventually said, looking at his desk. Andrews sighed.

"Alex, I don't know all of your history and I don't want to. A little lost is fine. Embrace it. You should let every piece of yourself be open to her, give her everything she wants from you and don't regret a bit of it. She won't hurt you or punish you for your insecurities. She'll give you a shoulder to lean on and a face to trust amongst all your other so-called friends. She is quite exceptional and in the blink of an eye she could be gone," he replied with another sigh as he reached across and poured another drink for himself.

Alex's phone vibrated on the table so he picked it up to read the message.

> • **Sorry, disaster in the kitchen. Andrews can pick me up at 5 x**

He watched his thumb rub against the screen. It lingered on the kiss unconsciously and he smiled at his own reaction to her.

"She is rather special, isn't she?" he said quietly, still looking at the text. "I think I'm probably falling in love with her."

"Who wouldn't be?" Andrews said, laughing as Alex raised an eyebrow at him. Pushing his chair back, he moved toward the door. "I think my work here is done. I'll pack my things and leave in the morning if that's okay with you?"

"Don't be ridiculous, Michael. I don't want you to leave. I think you did exactly what was needed at exactly the right moment, even if I didn't want to hear it. I was about to do something that may have been detrimental and you just changed my thoughts on the matter. Mind you, I think you should probably take a holiday or something. You're far too tense and I actually quite like breathing," he replied and then frowned at him. "Have you ever actually taken a holiday?" he continued with a chuckle.

"Yes, two years ago," Andrews replied sardonically.

"Oh, that's just bloody stupid. Take the jet and go wherever you want for a week. Just sort me out a different driver, will you? I'll leave the details up to you. Liaise with Louisa. She'll sort you out with a hotel." Andrews looked back at him in shock. That was happening a lot, too, his own staff being shocked by something that came from his mouth. He smiled at the thought of her softening him up. Conner was right.

"Are you sure? I would have pinned you by the throat sooner if I'd known that this was the reaction I would get."

"Yes, go, but don't push your luck. Just because I have feelings again, it doesn't mean I intend to use them all the fucking time. Oh, and by the way, can you pick Elizabeth up from Scott's at five and bring her back here. She'll be staying for the next couple of weeks."

"Yes, of course. I'll wait for my holiday until after that then. I wouldn't want her with a stranger if you don't mind," he said, frowning a bit. Alex smiled at him and nodded. He couldn't bear the thought of her with anyone he couldn't trust either, and Andrews had certainly proved his loyalty to her this afternoon. It seemed everyone that she touched was in awe of her.

"Right, now that's over with, I have a phone call to make and some paperwork to do so I'll call you if I need you," he said, standing and making his way towards the stairs. "And, Andrews? I'll be quicker next time and more than likely rip your fucking head off so don't try that again."

"I've always known I'd only get one shot at it. This seemed an important enough reason for me to try my luck at it," he said with a damned cheeky smile as he headed out of the door.

Well fuck... What an afternoon, and now he'd got an hour's conversation with Chinese lawyers about the most significant deal of his life. Yeah, his head was definitely in the right place for that. All he wanted to do was bury his head and dick in Elizabeth and float off to that drifty place he found himself in when she was near, pulling him closer, deeper. Christ, he looked down to notice that his dick was in absolute agreement with his brain and decided that it was probably best to take a long, cold shower before his four o'clock with the Chinese.

Christ, what had she done to him? He needed to get his fucking head together before he blew this deal and humiliated himself even more than he currently was doing.

An hour later, he put down the phone, threw his glasses on the table and grimaced with anger and irritation at the audacity of the lawyers who had now decided that things were being handled less efficiently than they would like. Westfield had been a little lax with his deadlines and that had dishonoured someone of seniority in the Chinese government. That had then caused a lot of tension surrounding the deal, and therefore negotiations were now hovering between *"We're not comfortable with..."* and *"We'll destroy you if..."*

Only two things pissed him off to the point of no return and being threatened was one of them.

"Andrews, I'm going to see Westfield. I'll be back by seven thirty. Tell Elizabeth to make herself at home and that I'll be back as soon as I can." He released the button on the intercom and kicked the wall so hard it actually hurt his foot. Fuck!

Getting in the Aston, he floored it down the drive and called Tate. Was the bastard doing this on purpose? Was he in it with Henry? He hadn't got a fucking clue but he was starting to wonder about the merits of the man regardless. This political bullshit was fucking tiring. All he'd wanted was her smile and now he had to go unleash hell on someone he'd considered a friend of sorts. Tate's voice kicked in.

"Alex."

"I hope you haven't got company because I'm on my way over to kick your fucking arse all over the place. If I lose this deal because of you, I'll destroy you," he grated out and hit the accelerator again.

"Alex, I don't know what you're talking about?" the dick replied quietly, and a little too nervously for his liking. He was fucking hiding something, or lying purposefully.

"Well you're about to find out," he said as he ended the call and grumbled to himself. He needed to see his eyes. You could only ever see someone when you looked directly at them. That's where you saw the difference between deceit and truth, between lust and love, between hate and adoration. It's the one thing he knew with absolute certainty because it was the one thing he'd spent years perfecting. Nobody knew how much his own eyes were hiding and nobody knew the horror behind them.

The windows of his own soul were definitely too cloudy for others to read, and that's the way he wanted them. It's the way he'd made them appear.

Chapter 26

Elizabeth

S tanding under the huge shower, I let the water rinse away the day's dirt and smoke. The kitchen very nearly went up in flames this afternoon because of my own stupidity and now that it's done and sorted out, I can't help but laugh at my own ineptitude. Jesus, two-dozen trays of brioche and pastries were ruined as the old catering cooker finally gave itself the boot and died a savage death. Flames had erupted from the back of the ancient eight-ring burner mid-way through the afternoon and even though I knew exactly what I should have done, I just stood there, frozen. The extinguisher and fire blanket had vanished from my fire response trained mind and instead I simply stared at the flames licking up the wall and bizarrely thought of Alex, his face etching itself into my darkest fears. Belle rushing in at the smell of smoke and dousing the flames with expert precision was the only thing that brought me back to reality. I'm entirely sure the whole building would have gone up like a bloody bonfire if she hadn't saved the day.

Now I am here, standing in his bedroom, and this is where I will stay for two weeks, under his control and also under no illusions that that could mean anything he wants, he gets. His dominant nature and over-powering character shone through on Tuesday evening and I'm pretty confident about what I'll be receiving for the next week or so. What that means for the emotional side of the relationship is anybody's guess but I doubt I'll be receiving declarations of love any time soon.

Mind you, I suppose I have agreed to it. The anticipation of just the dominant Alex was just too bloody enticing to say no to and regardless of his words, I know he's still in there somewhere, hiding yes, but definitely still there. I just have to find him again. I haven't got a bloody clue how I'm going to achieve this goal, but I'll be damned if I'm giving up when he's shown me so much.

SEENING WHITE

Dressing myself in blue skinny jeans and a black shirt, I apply a little make-up and make my way down the stairs in anticipation of his arrival. Noticing the time is only a quarter past six, I decide that maybe I should start some dinner. Has he eaten? Is that even my responsibility? He had said he had a housekeeper but I've seen little evidence of her existence apart from a permanently immaculate house. Staring along the hallway, I notice a door along the corridor off to the right so I tiptoe toward it and decided to have a peek inside. I'm supposed to make myself at home according to Andrews, so what better way to start than to have a nosy around? I push the heavy oak door open and smile at what greets me. The room is beautiful, truly. Full of all sorts of musical instruments, the cello and violin sit neatly in their stands at the fireplace, the racks of guitars hang on the wall and the white grand piano stands elegantly under the window. Is Alex musical? There's no denying he can move and obviously likes his music, but I've never seen him play anything or even talk about it. The room does feel cold somehow, as if it's unloved or unappreciated. Maybe he doesn't come in here much. I stare at the grand for a few more moments and then feel my stomach grumble at me. Chuckling to myself, I retreat and softly close the door before the pull gets too strong to be able to refuse.

Walking through to the kitchen, I notice that the hole in the wall where his fist connected with it has gone and is now freshly repainted. The lamp that was smashed to bits has also been replaced and there is no evidence to suggest that an incident ever occurred. Jesus, things happen fast in the world of the wealthy. Is that how quickly one can cover things up, pretend they didn't happen, manipulate others around you into believing everything's okay? Probably, knowing Mr. White and his ability to diffuse all situations, but it's not, is it? Okay, I mean. It's different now and it's all because of that temper of his. I seriously need to get a handle on how to deal with that because shrivelling to the floor in a pathetic mess of snot and tears is not going to achieve anything, certainly not with him. Belle's words spring into my mind: *"A man like him will need a firm hand."*

Firm hand, my arse. The man needs more than a firm hand to stabilise that sort of fury. I'm not sure what that is, but showing him I'm scared of him isn't going to do me any favours at all, and I'm not anyway, well not really. Actually, I was the other night but not in a *'he'll hit me'* sort of way. More in a *'what the hell is he going to do next?'* sort of way. I need to do some serious thinking about how I handle this next two weeks. He can try it his way if he likes but we both know it's not going to be enough for any real type of relationship. Maybe he doesn't want one of those anymore? Shit, that's not good. What on earth am I doing? No idea.

Perhaps Andrews knows what I should do about dinner? Pressing the intercom on the wall, I tentatively speak, hoping I've hit the right button and am not about to set the house alarm off or something equally as stupid.

"Andrews, are you there?"

"Yes, ma'am, I'll be right down," he responds quickly in his typically efficient manner.

"No, no please don't. I just wondered if you know if Alex has eaten or if I should cook?" I ask, biting my nails.

"Oh, I umm... I don't think so, ma'am. Would you like me to call him?" he replies hesitantly.

"No, don't. I'll just throw something together. Thank you, though."

"Okay ma'am, call up if you need me at all." My nose scrunches up at the ma'am title. I really don't like it, and he certainly doesn't have to use it in every sentence. Perhaps I should just say something at some point. In fact I will. It's ridiculous, all this sir and ma'am stuff. Maybe not now, though.

Releasing the button, I make my way to the wonderful cooker and hob. Oh god, how I long for such an extravagant kitchen of my own. Running my fingers along the countertop and finding my way to the fridge, it suddenly hits me that I know so little about the man I'm staying with. I'm falling hopelessly in love and I don't even know what he likes to eat. Checking through the fridge, I find some steak and peppers, mushrooms and yes, some cream. Stroganoff. Brilliant idea. What man doesn't like that? Music, I need some music. I always need music to cook to. Now how the hell do I use this bloody speaker thing? Checking out the remote, I do some random stabbing at buttons until music starts spilling out into the room. Classical? That surprises me. I've never seen him as a classical sort of man. Liszt. Waves of beautiful and slightly melancholy notes linger one after another as the piano twinkles its way around the song. Laughing to myself as I remember the years of sitting with my grandma at the piano keys, I turn it up and let the music play on around me. Does he play the piano? I seriously need to find out more about him. I mean, he's just shown me how screwed up his childhood was and yet I didn't know that he likes classical music. That's all kinds of wrong.

Just as I'm putting the lid on the pot and opening the oven, I hear Andrews in the hall talking to someone. Peeking my head around the corner to see who it is, I glance at the back of a very well cut suit, and equally nice backside and instantly recognise him simply by his stance. The cane rather gives it away, too. My pathetic groin reminds me of other unsettling thoughts regarding the man so I quickly dip back around the corner to hide, then realise how ridiculous that is so look back again.

"No, sir, I'm sorry he's not here. If you'd called ahead earlier perhaps I could have told you before you came over," Andrews says calmly with a very rigid stance, blocking the doorway. Slowly that face turns towards him, irritation written all over it, quite beautifully at that. *Stop it, Beth.*

"Ah, you English people and your intolerable formalities. Why must I ask permission to visit my friends? I cannot be bothered with you enough to even wait for a response to that. You bore me. In fact this whole bloody country bores me," Pascal shouts as he throws his arms around dramatically.

I can't stop my face lighting up at the thought of a conversation with the man as I giggle to myself at his exasperation, so smoothing my shirt down and tucking my hair behind my ear, I wander into the hall and hope I can handle whatever comes next.

"Pascal, how lovely to see you again. Please, come in," I say as calmly as I can, given the utter sex bomb in front of me. It's actually a lot harder than I thought it would be. Both men swing their heads toward me.

"Do not tell me that you cook as well? That the divine fragrance coming from the kitchen is something to do with your delectable self? Beautiful Elizabeth, my rose. Why did he find you first? It is wholly unreasonable of him." Knocking his cane on the floor a few times, he gestures it toward the kitchen, barges Andrews out of the way and smiles with such dynamism that it almost takes my breath away.

Andrews scowls and moves toward us, apparently unhappy about Pascal entering the house.

"Andrews, I'll call if I need you but I'm sure we'll be fine until Alex gets back," I say with a grin as Pascal takes my arm and pulls me along with him.

"Yes ma'am, if you're sure ma'am," he replies with narrowed eyes and a nod. I'm not convinced he likes Pascal in the slightest.

On reaching the kitchen, Pascal launches himself at the pot and lifts the lid. Fanning his face with the smell of the stroganoff, I feel a smile of pride creep up my lips as I take a seat at the table. Cooking is the one thing I can do well. I'll be damned if it makes me feel anything but pride. Opening the wine and pouring two glasses, I can't hide my blush at his blatant sexual energy. The expensive cream suit that clings to his undeniably striking body is tailored to perfection and the matching pink tie and handkerchief are artfully positioned with the precision of a man who only accepts perfection. Not many men wear pink effectively, but he absolutely does and still manages to radiate masculinity from every fibre of his being. This is a more modern Pascal but the elements of old school charm are most definitely still flowing from his soul. If he has one, that is. He somehow reminds me of those roguish vampires that seem to be the rage all over the place at the moment and I giggle at the thought because it suddenly strikes me that he'd make an awfully good vampire, dangerous and clearly completely over the top. Perhaps he is one? You never know given these pesky fairies that seem to linger around.

"How are you, Pascal? Come, sit down and have a glass of wine. Alex shouldn't be long. He said he'd be here by seven thirty," I say quietly while fingering my glass and watching his lean frame gliding across the room towards a cupboard. He moves with accuracy around the space as if he knows exactly where he's going. He's obviously spent a lot of time here. Either that or the man just oozes precision and poise regardless of his location. That's probably true anyway, to be honest.

He retrieves a heavy glass ashtray and continues on towards me with a smirk. My sodding groin clenches at the vision. Shit.

"I am surprised, my dear. That is what I am. I am also rather amused that you are in his home. I have never seen another woman here and because of this, you intrigue me more and more by the minute. What do you have that consumes him so?" he replies, taking a seat and lifting the glass to his fiendish lips, those bright green eyes devouring me with his lingering stare.

"I think you'd have to ask him that, Pascal. I'm sure he'll give you as much information as he deems acceptable to divulge," I state, glancing down at the table and tapping my fingernails. I seriously have no idea myself at the moment. If I'm honest, I don't even know if we've got anything at all anymore.

"Ah, he is being a little obstructive, my love, yes? He is known for it, although not normally with a woman. He usually has no issue whatsoever showing his disinterest for their intrinsic flaws and inadequacies. Although I doubt there is anything remotely *usual* about you," he replies as he unbuttons his jacket, crosses his legs and lounges gracefully in that European way. Taking a cigarette from his pocket and lighting it, he inhales deeply and resumes his gaze through the smoke that he blows out. "Tell me, what did you think of my club? Did you have a good time in his suite?"

I feel the blush return instantly at the thought at what we got up to in that room and can't stop the smirk that crosses my lips. Pascal's fishing for details, though, and unless Alex wants to give them to him, I'm pretty sure it isn't my position to give away such information freely. These games of his, while strange, have rules. I'm not sure what they are yet but I'm not dropping myself in it anytime soon. Certainly not given what I've just agreed to with Alex.

"I think your club is wonderful, Pascal, a real revolution for the spirit. Do you have many or just the one?" I ask with genuine interest. *Well deflected, Beth.* He smirks and stabs out his cigarette as if he knows exactly what I'm trying to do. His look of amusement carries on regardless.

"Four so far, my dear. Rome, Berlin, New York and here. You will no doubt see them all in the months to come. I trust you enjoy the lifestyle or Alexander would not be so preoccupied with this little tryst of yours. I must say I am enjoying the view as much as he would be. Would you care to show me a little of your appeal? I'm sure if you just wrapped those exquisite limbs around me, I could use you fairly thoroughly for the evening," he says, reaching across the table and aiming for my hand with that imposing stare of his. If I'm honest, the gesture weakens my resolve a little, but I absolutely must not let him touch me.

I pull it back abruptly and raise an eyebrow, flattening my smile and trying for offended. I have no idea if it's worked or not but he does narrow those damned eyes at me.

Keep it together, Beth. Try and stay in control, for God's sake.

"Pascal, please don't degrade yourself to requests. It's beneath you, I'm sure, and I doubt you've ever asked pleasantly for something in your life. I'm his alone and you know that already. I think he made his feelings perfectly clear in Rome."

Good God, I sound like a seasoned professional at this BDSM thing, whatever the hell it is. Where the hell did that come from? Alex is clearly rubbing off on me to somewhat astounding proportions.

Pascal gazes at me for a while and then leans back into his chair again. That very wicked smirk hasn't even moved on his face as he considers my response. Eventually his face breaks into a wide soft grin as he refills our glasses, and holy hell, it's a beautiful smile. I can completely understand why women fall to their knees for him. My insides clench rather uncomfortably as I flick my eyes to his hands. They're probably very bad hands, possibly worse than Alex's. What the fuck am I thinking about? I immediately chastise myself for my own treachery as I think of the man who's coming home soon and raise my head back up to meet his amused eyes.

"Do you like my hands, my rose?" Shit.

"I... I..." I haven't got a bloody answer. Balls. He chuckles at me and licks his unfairly glorious lips, which continue to mesmerise me somehow. Jesus, I need to control this shit.

"I like you, Elizabeth, very much. You are loyal to him and so desperately sin worthy I forget myself sometimes. You are more than likely going to be the ruination of the finest dominant I have ever known. And please DO NOT tell him I told you that. He is conceited enough as it is and I doubt I could survive any more lust to pour out of my body for him. It would surely be the death of me," he says, another genuine smile and a wink following. That's unfairly beautiful too.

"Thank you, Pascal. I think," is my stupidly giggling reply. "Now have I passed your tests, or will there be more assessment to come? I'm trying to keep your friendship with Alex intact. I know he thinks highly of you and I'd hate to have him fly into another uncontrollable rage," I ask, trying desperately to stop my eyes from lowering to the table. The man simply makes me feel like a fraud in the room, as if he has more right to be here than me. He possibly does. Who knows what the pair of them have been up to over the years? Couple that with the fact that I can't take my eyes off his bloody mouth and I'm seriously considering running home where it's safer.

"We have been a lot of things over the years, my dear. I would like to think friends is where we have found ourselves now. As for you passing my examination, I am not sure I will be allowed any further investigations this evening unfortunately. I dare say I will try again, though, at some point," he replies with a very naughty smile as he nods toward the hall and raises his glass to his mouth again.

Footsteps echo and I lift my head to see Alex walking into the kitchen. I literally gasp in a breath at the radiance of the man. His wide shoulders are encased in a blood red shirt, rolled up at the sleeves showing off his muscular forearms, and his black jeans hug every lean muscle on his legs. I had almost lost myself in the sheer naughtiness of Pascal and it isn't until the raw masculinity that is Alex strides towards me that I realise just how deeply I love him. All of him, every different facet of him. He's engrained himself on my soul and there's no running away from it now.

His black hair is messy on top and his cool blue eyes twinkle at me as he approaches with devilish intent. He doesn't acknowledge Pascal at all. He simply grabs the back of my neck with a strong hand and hauls me up into a passionate and deadly kiss that has me weakening at the knees for him instantly. My core ignites, electricity seeming to swirl through my body and disable any form of defence I have. If he bends me over the table and asks Pascal to watch, I'll probably let him. Thankfully, he doesn't.

Easing his hand from my neck and releasing his lips from mine, he eventually pulls back and gazes at me for a moment. Those eyes tear through me as normal, right into the heart of me where he knows I can't hide from him. He moves in again, placing a small kiss on my forehead then releases me to wander across the kitchen to get himself a glass and another bottle of wine.

Pulling up a chair and pouring his wine, he leans back and stares at Pascal with his unfathomable smile. Minutes pass with nothing being said, just the two of them looking at each other over their glasses as if considering their next move in some sort of game. Alex's gaze seems impassive, but somehow vicious currents of something unknown surround his whole being. Pascal's demeanour is cool and completely unreadable. I almost say something and then decide it's probably best not to, given the current rather bizarre pissing contest that seems to be happening in front of me, which my core is still clenching about. Also that inner slut of mine seems to be flicking her eyes between the two and throwing far too many intriguingly explicit visions of torment my way. It's very disturbing.

Eventually, Pascal holds up his hand, inclines his head a little and speaks.

"Alexander, I concede. You have made your point, dear boy, and I see your mind will not be altered on the matter. However, I will say that I think you will have many tussles on your hands regarding this one," he says as he leans forward and knocks his glass on Alex's. I watch Alex's whole demeanour change as a genuine beaming smile erupts from his mouth and I almost faint at the sight of it. Glorious just isn't enough of a word for it. I've only seen that one a few times. I swear it's probably his authentic one and to be honest, absolutely my favourite. Why he's giving it to Pascal is a mystery, but I can't help my spat of jealousy about it.

"Well if I can top the master, Pascal, I shouldn't have too many problems with the rest, should I? And will you please stop calling me boy now? I haven't been your *boy* for some time," he replies with a chuckle, reaching across for my hand.

Warmth surrounds me the moment he does it, as if the other night has been removed from my memory and he's showing me some feeling again. Whatever he was planning on, or still is, thankfully he's at least going to show some form of emotion again as he does it. I look between them, not really understanding why the hell they have bothered with their little internal battle about me but enjoying the show nonetheless. I grip onto his hand to try and show him how much he means to me, and that he's got no reason to worry, but the sound of the timer ringing through the air disturbs the now peaceful atmosphere.

I clear my throat and stand, reluctantly letting go of his hand, and make my way to the cooker.

"Pascal, will you be staying for dinner?" I ask, turning to look at his face. He instantly raises an eyebrow at Alex, obviously asking for an invitation.

"Of course he will, as long as he can behave himself, anyway. You don't mind do you?" Alex responds for him as I turn back to the cooker.

"No, of course not. Why would I mind being surrounded by stimulating male company? I'd love to hear more about your lives," I say sweetly as I feel his arms wrap around me and sigh at the feel of them. I was so not expecting this show of emotion. "Why don't you two go into the dining room and I'll bring it through in a while," I say, emptying the rice into the saucepan. Frankly, I need a few moments to get myself together because the temperature in this room is getting way too hot for comfort.

"Thank you," he whispers in my ear as he kisses my neck, lets go of me and wanders into the hall. Pascal gets up and follows him out of the kitchen, winking at me as he leaves. I narrow my eyes and point the spoon at him, shaking my head. He licks his lips. It isn't good. The man is dangerous as hell.

Taking a few steadying breaths as I watch probably the two most attractive men I've ever met leave the room, I find myself leaning on the countertop to compose myself. How the hell am I going to deal with the two of them for an entire evening? Eden was one thing but to sit around with the both of them while they talk of old times and what they got up to in it is probably going to get me extremely hot and bothered. And I can't stop my thoughts drifting towards the bedroom, two pairs of hands grasping at me as yet more visions I've never even dreamed of enter my brain. Shit, this could be very wrong. I need to calm the hell down and pull myself back together. Then another vision hits me with full force, and my inner slut leaps about excitedly again.

I clearly have no control whatsoever.

I don't know how long I stand there but suddenly I notice the rice boiling madly and I snap back to reality. Have I really just been having thoughts of the two of them together, with me? Really quite inappropriate thoughts? I can't control myself around Alex, let alone Pascal as well. Mentally kicking my own backside and reminding myself of my own inexperience in these matters, I pull in a long breath and drain the rice. Besides, I'm sure Alex would kill any man that tried to touch me other than Conner if Eden was anything to go by, wouldn't he? Maybe he wouldn't. Is that why Pascal's here? Has he organised this? I was expecting dominant Alex this evening so maybe this was his idea all along. No, it can't be. He wouldn't, would he? I'm not doing it if he has. I couldn't, could I? Maybe I could. No, I couldn't, regardless of those intoxicating green eyes. Anyway, I haven't seen a sign of a different side of Alex yet, well apart from that peculiar little pissing contest which is apparently the norm between them anyway. No, he seems perfectly normal so far. Perhaps he's forgotten about his new version of a relationship. I shake my head at myself. Alex wouldn't forget such a thing. I'm utterly stupid.

Loading the two serving dishes with the meal, I walk down the hall to the dining room. Smiling as I hear the laughter drifting through the space, I turn the corner to see them playing cards or rather throwing them at each other with animated hand gestures. The table is big enough for twenty and the room is enormous. Luxurious curtains drape elegantly at the two massive windows and the two elaborate chandeliers accentuate the height in the room to perfection. To see the two of them sitting at the end of the room giggling like schoolboys makes me chuckle. These two are no doubt acting like children as they hussle and laugh idiotically at each other. I can't help but feel a warmth sweep through the room at the obvious affection they have for each other. My only question is how far that affection actually goes.

"Wonderful, our English rose has joined us. Alexander was just reminding me of his pitiable attempts at blackjack, and it is still, how would you say, ah yes... fucking awful. It is not a wonder he does not gamble for amusement." Pascal grins as they both move to take the food from me and lay it on the table.

"I don't gamble because I hate to lose anything I own, Pascal. You know how much the thought of losing something costly irritates me," Alex barks, smirking back at him.

"You, my dear boy, have never owned anything worth fighting for before now," he replies as he winks at me and pulls out the chair at the head of the table. I look toward Alex, wondering what his response will be. Given the current arrangement, I'm not entirely sure how he feels about me anymore. He's standing behind his own chair with his hands resting on the top, looking at me with an almost glazed expression, giving away nothing at all. He leans towards me and kisses me briefly.

"You may be right, Pascal," he replies, still with no expression as he sits and starts to serve the food out to both of us. I don't know what to think of that response but at least it wasn't negative. I glance up at him again and notice a small smile play across his lips as if something has amused him. It's probably me.

~

By nine thirty we are all sitting in the lounge. I'm curled up on the sofa, watching as the two of them sit across from each other at the chess table. Apparently this game has been going on for two years so far and neither of them is any closer to winning, even though to me, the board looks quite close to check if they play properly. I grinned like a fool when they took their positions. The thought of Pascal being Alex's "worthy adversary" had me giggling instantly. He definitely is. In fact, he's the only man I've ever met to rival Alex in the slightest.

At first I assumed it was Conner but now it's more than obvious. Having spent a relaxed evening with Pascal, he's shown he's a tactician through and through. His whole thought process is premeditated. Conner's actually far more of a "grab it and run" or "fly by the seat of his pants" type of guy.

Sipping my cognac and watching Alex, I find myself trying to determine his moves. He's absolutely aggressive in his play. His objective is to win the game by pushing his opponent and rattling him. Pascal's more thoughtful in his moves, precise, deliberate. He's not allowing Alex to rattle or manoeuvre him in anyway. He just continues to counter smoothly with a wicked glint of acceptance or something. I chuckle while thinking what a formidable force they would probably be if they ever tackled something together. It's actually a very scary thought and I have no idea why I'm giggling about it given my earlier thoughts regarding the both of them.

"Something amusing, Elizabeth?" Alex asks, not removing his eyes from the board.

"Yes. I was just imagining the two of you working together to achieve a common goal. I dare say you would both be a force to be reckoned with," I reply, smiling towards him.

"Oh, you have no idea, my dear," Pascal says, twiddling his long fingers around his bishop. Alex smirks and chuckles to himself, countering the move almost immediately.

"Where did you learn to play, Elizabeth? You have spent the entirety of this game complaining to yourself," Pascal enquires.

"My dad. He told me that I would need to understand chess to understand people. The more I learnt how to manipulate a board, the better I would become at influencing my own life," I reply as I watch Pascal move his knight. It makes me smile. It's a good move. Alex's brow rises at my comment as if something just clicked into place.

"And do you? Influence your life, I mean," he responds smoothly.

"I think you can only influence your life as much as others will allow you to. I have been happy making my way as I have and thankfully reasonably successful," I say, watching Alex move his queen sideways, his hand hovering a little longer than normal.

"I think you are naïve, Elizabeth. You cannot learn life from a chessboard. People are more devious than that," Pascal says. "This one is definitely more corrupt than most, spends his life scheming underhandedly and even he still loses occasionally," he continues as he nods toward Alex.

Standing and moving toward the table, I grasp both of their glasses and make my way to the bar to pour them another drink.

"I think losing is an essential part of living, Pascal. It's only when we lose that we learn to appreciate our losses," I reply, placing his glass next to him and moving to stand behind Alex, draping my arms over his shoulders he reaches up and squeezes my hand.

"Elizabeth believes that we must all harness our emotions to make ourselves more in tune with our inner selves. That we would be more rounded as individuals if we trusted more and embraced our feelings," Alex quips while brushing my arm with his finger and making his next move. I'm quite impressed he knows me so well if I'm honest.

"Really? My dear girl, I have never heard anything more absurd. I'm afraid we don't have the luxury of being emotional in our world. Besides, I can't think of anything more wearisome than fathoming my own feelings." Pascal laughs and returns his head to the board. He's clearly yet another tortured soul. My eyes narrow on him.

"Pascal, you only see the negative side of emotions. There is so much more to it than that. You have had a wonderful evening being with your friend. While the two of you have postulated and positioned yourselves, I have watched the two of you, read your emotions. Your defences have been down and all the while you have simply been relaxing. It has been wonderful to watch Alex really relax and while I do understand what you mean, I wish you could both simply be yourselves more and show the world who you really are."

"Elizabeth, I get the feeling you may be straying a little from our conversation the other night. Do not push your luck," Alex says with a frown and a more pressured grasp to my hand. Bastard. I must have hit a nerve. Pascal's gaze is thoughtful for a second and then suddenly it's replaced by a relaxed smile as he leans back and stares at me.

"You're lovely, Elizabeth, but quite wrong. Ours has been a long-standing game. I want Alexander in the most depraved sense of the word and he won't allow it, which I find a little exasperating and he finds highly amusing. It's the only reason we tolerate each other. Well, of course there are a few other reasons why he needs me, but I'll let him introduce you to them when he's acquiescent enough, and it appears he is not as yet, which is unfairly cruel of him." Alex snorts out a bark of laughter as my eyes widen at the whole sodding paragraph. I couldn't have got it that wrong, could I? No, I couldn't. They are definitely not just tolerating each other. They are far more than that to each other. And what the hell is Alex going to introduce me too that involves Pascal?

I'm really not sure I want to know the answer to that. Unfortunately, my brain seems to disagree as it launches new visions at me. I could growl at myself. Honestly, if I could, I might even whip myself to chastise my own naughtiness. It's completely unacceptable.

"Really? Well I'm a little tipsy, and what would I know anyway? I have simply enjoyed watching you be yourselves. Maybe I should leave you both to it," I say, leaning in and kissing Alex on the cheek. "I wouldn't want to trigger your negative emotions now, would I?" I continue as I wander towards the door, smirking to myself and watching Pascal's lips draw up in amusement.

"Elizabeth," Alex calls as I round the corner into the hall. "I haven't given you permission to leave yet. If you want to go, you'll have to ask me nicely," he says with a terse tone. What? Is he really

396

going to do this in front of Pascal? Hell no. In private is one thing. I am not having it with the king of debauchery sitting in the room. Mind you, I'm not exactly sure which one of them I'm referring to anymore.

Turning back into the room, I fix my eyes on his to see what I'm dealing with. Those cool blue eyes regard me impassively as he raises that damned sexy eyebrow to see how I'm going to respond to his order - *yes order*. How dare he? Lowering my eyes a little, I walk softly back towards the table. If he wants a game, I'll give him one to play with, idiot. Slightly scary maybe, but I'm still not having it. I flick my eyes across the board before I reach him and calculate as fast as I can.

"Would you mind if I went upstairs? I am tired and I dare say you both have plenty to discuss without me being here," I ask, watching from the corner of my eye as Pascal fiddles with his rook and smiles at the show. Could I feel any more humiliated? It's really not funny. In fact, I'm too full of irritation and unfair sexual frustration to deal with thoughts of embarrassment at the moment anyway so I glare at Pascal a little and then drop my eyes again.

"Better. You can go," Alex says, waving his hand toward the door and returning his eyes to the table. Really? Dismissed? I don't think so. Arsehole.

Turning and standing behind Pascal, I place a hand on his shoulder and stretch over him, narrowing my eyes at Alex as I reach for Pascal's bishop. Sliding it across the board towards him, I feel a smile cross my lips as I watch his brow furrow in agitation and his shoulders stiffen. Well fuck him. He will not beat me into submission, whatever the hell that's supposed to mean. He'll give me a little more respect than that.

"I think three more moves should finish him, Pascal," I say quietly. Feeling Pascal's chuckle under my hand, I let go of him and turn out into the hall again, making my way to the stairs. By the time I'm halfway up the stairs, Alex is at the bottom of them, exactly where I thought he would be, looking absolutely edible.

"You won't get away with it, Elizabeth. You *will* pay for that later," he says with a calculated smirk as he stands with his hands in his pockets, fierce waves of dominance radiating off his body. His eyes narrow at me as he watches me hold my head up in challenge. It even surprises me if I'm honest because the man at the bottom of the stairs is definitely looking a little edgy. I can almost feel his hands around my throat and my insides quicken immediately at the thought of what he might have in store for me. I take in a deep breath and continue up the stairs, feeling bizarrely excited about the prospect.

"Then I shall be waiting for you," I reply as I drag my fingers along the banister confidently and head for the bedroom.

Lying in his completely oversized bed, I contemplate the evening's events and what the result of my insubordination will be. Snuggling down, I feel my eyes fluttering closed as the warmth of the duvet envelopes me and Alex's scent wraps around my body, somehow drugging me into a sense of pure contentment. For someone who will be punished at some point, I feel remarkably relaxed about it, and unable to fight it anymore, I give in and let my body drift off into sleep.

~

"Elizabeth, wake up," I hear as a hand glides across my stomach. Gradually opening my eyes, I realise something's covering them. I try to move whatever it is but find that I can't move my hands. Feeling a little panicked, I pull at my arms and try to turn. They still don't move and neither do my feet. All I can feel is something grating against them and instantly realise it's rope. Shit.

"Alex?" I question, struggling a bit more against the rope, which is completely stupid of me because I know how well he ties those knots.

"Welcome back, Elizabeth. Try not to struggle too much. We wouldn't want to bring out any of my negative emotions, would we?" he says with a chuckle. I can feel the smirk crossing his mouth.

"What? What are you doing?" I stutter out breathlessly. My inner slut has clearly begun influencing my thoughts already.

"Punishing you for your little indiscretion, of course. Nice move, by the way. I was impressed. Are you still feeling quite so bold now or have you realised your error yet?" he replies as he pulls his hand down to the top of my thighs and then dips two fingers inside me.

"Alex I... Oh god, that's good," I mutter as his swirls his fingers around and then he pushes them in deeper with far more force.

"Is it? I'm glad," he says as he removes his hand. "How does this feel?" he continues as he puts something cold on my nub. The feeling is intense, almost painful as he increases the pressure and begins to circle it. I gasp at the icy feeling and try to recoil into the mattress but I can't move away from it. With my legs and arms spread, I can't find any purchase at all. Suddenly the cold thing is removed and his warm fingers are back inside me. Arching my shoulders a little I manage to grind down onto his hand. "Tut tut. Naughty girl. Stay still and stop being so fucking greedy or I'll make this far less pleasurable for you," he growls. I freeze instantly at his threat and try to relax again.

The ice is replaced and his hand withdrawn, over and over again. I can feel my orgasm building with his hand and then being obliterated with the ice every time. He pushes me back and forth like a toy, enjoying his slow torture over my body and revelling in his complete control over me. Each new cycle of movement with his devious fingers sending me close to explosion and then he rips it away from me again cruelly. I tug at the rope cuffs again brutally, trying desperately to get out so that I can gain some friction and just release my frustrated tension. This is most definitely punishment, and what's worse is it's amusing him. This is clearly his way of showing his power over me, what he can do to me.

"Please, Alex..."

"Do you want to come yet, Elizabeth? Is it hard for you? I love to watch you squirm like this under my hands," he says as his fingers return and I feel his teeth graze at my nipple.

"Oh god, Alex. Please, just..."

His mouth travels across my stomach as he licks his way to my sex and then his teeth catch hold of my nub, gently biting down and releasing as he blows a breath of air over me. *Yes.*

"Oh yes, please. Let me come," I splutter as he removes his fingers and mouth from me.

"Tell me you're sorry, Elizabeth and then beg me for it. Beg me to fuck you," he growls as he pushes his fingers back inside me and twists them around slowly, brushing that spot inside me but not putting enough pressure on it to let me come.

"I'm... I'm sorry. Please, Alex. I can't do this anymore," I reply as the ache becomes unbearable and almost painful. "I need to-"

"You can and you will until I believe you mean it. I want you to remember this. I want you to remember the ache that only I create for you. You're mine to do with as I please and you will not fucking annoy me again," he says as his tongue travels the length of my sex, delving in and then biting down on me, this time far more roughly and pushing me so close that stars threaten again.

"Oh fuck, yes. More... please. I'm sorry. You win. Please, just let me come," I scream at him as I strain against the binds and kick out viciously with my legs. My whole body is begging for relief from the torment he keeps forcing on me while he chuckles to himself at my suffering.

"Good girl. Now beg me to fuck you, Elizabeth. I want to hear you begging for it."

"Please, Alex. Please fuck me. Please make me come. Oh God, I need you. Please..." Thoughts and words are becoming redundant. My whole body is straining for release as his fingers and teeth continue with their little game of power. Every fibre of me is tense, like a coiled spring ready to explode. Just one more bite or lick or any sort of bloody pressure and I'll come, but he keeps withholding it. Desperation screams through my body as I shake my arms against the scratching rope again and feel the sweat pouring down my body.

Suddenly his hand is at my throat and one of my feet is free. My leg is hooked around his hip as he thankfully hoists my body weight to him and slides up against me. I can feel the end of him gently rubbing at me as his hand leisurely wanders down my restrained leg and releases it somehow. I quickly lock it around his back and thrust myself toward him, hoping to impale myself or something, anything, to relieve the intense sensation he's created.

"Calm down, Elizabeth. Stay still. I want to enjoy you," he says softly as he hooks his hands under my backside and lifts me towards him with ease.

"Please, Alex. Fuck me, please..." I shout, trying to still my aching body and failing miserably.

Painstakingly slowly, he guides himself inside me, inch by inch, stretching me wider, pulling out a little and then gently pushing back in again. Oh, God. I can't breathe. Desperate for him to drive forward harder, I kick at his back and use my strength to propel him forward. He drops me instantly and pulls out as he moves his hand to my throat, softly stroking it and gently wrapping his hand around it. He won't even do that with the pressure I need from him.

"You can't force me. It's all my decision. Now do as you're fucking told and stay still or I'll come in your mouth and leave you here with nothing," he growls in my ear, unnervingly quietly. "Do you understand me?"

"Yes. Please, just..." I pant out as calmly as I can.

Keeping his hand on my throat and increasing the tension slightly, he pushes himself back inside in an unhurried manner and grinds his hips against me leisurely. My breath catches at the sensation of being full of him as he gives me the pressure I need but still refuses me the aggression I want.

"Yes," I hiss in his ear. "Please, more. Harder... More," I ramble while trying desperately to stay still and not speed him up.

Pulling back and easing himself in again, he groans low in his throat and picks up his pace a little, increasing the force. I can feel the throbbing beginning and welcome it with open arms. His rhythm becomes more insistent as the deep pounding begins and I moan incoherently in response, knowing I won't be long and neither will he.

"You're so fucking perfect. Why do you have to be so fucking perfect?" he groans into my ear as he slams into me and kisses me with passion and fury. Our tongues entwine and our bodies mould into each other in almost frantic desperation, his hips slamming into me as I match his pace with a vigour and obsession I know I can't control. Our ragged breathing and moaning heightens every sensation in my body and spurs me on to my oncoming bliss as I reach my mouth for his again and am rewarded with his tongue catching mine.

"Yes... Oh god, Alex." One more thrust and I disintegrate in his arms. Spinning circles and stars explode in my mind and my body dissolves into a mass of liquid. I throw my head back, arch my back upwards and cry out his name. His body continues to buck into me as he drills himself further into me, deeper, harder, wrapping his arms tightly around my back and pulling me up to him as he erupts inside me with force and groans out my name..

His mouth finds mine again and as he gently kisses me, he reaches up my arms to release my hands. As soon as I can, I throw them around his neck and draw him down to me. Peeling whatever it is over my eyes off, I nuzzle my head into his neck, tighten my hold around his hips and kiss his beautiful shoulders. I simply can't get close enough for what he's making me feel for him. Safe, cherished, worshipped even, in a bizarre sort of way. All I want to do is love him and hold him and tell him how I feel, how he makes me feel.

"You are going to ruin me, Elizabeth," he breathes into the pillow, panting and trying to regain his breath. That wasn't quite the reaction I was after, and I can't stop Pascal's earlier comment entering my head because he clearly thinks that, too.

"I doubt I could ever damage you, Mr. White. I think you might be indestructible," I reply with a giggle, somehow questioning what I've said the moment it leaves my lips.

Rolling me until I'm astride him, he gazes up at me with soft eyes. "I like hearing you laugh," he says quietly as he pulls me down for another passionate kiss, brushing his fingers through my hair and rocking me forward on his still hard length. "I want to watch you. Make yourself come again for me." His intense stare is almost enough for me to combust on the spot and the feel of him twitching again inside me is enough to start pulling the familiar burn back to the front of my mind, or rather my groin. So slowly I start to move myself, and god I love being on top of him, gazing down at the extraordinarily erotic sight beneath me as his muscles undulate and his penetrating and lust-filled eyes stare straight into my soul.

Reaching around to grab my backside, he draws me towards him, dragging me along his entire length, heightening the feeling on my already raw nub and then pushing me back down smoothly while pushing upwards into me. His mouth parts and then rises into the sexiest smile I have ever witnessed from him as he closes his eyes and tips his glorious head back.

"Ahh, fuck yes." He groans. "More, Elizabeth. Give me more. You said you'd give me everything. I want everything."

Oh god, yes. Everything. I lift my head back and really start to ride him, reaching my hands to my hair and pulling it away from my sweat laden back as I feeling him rubbing that sweet spot inside of me. He angles his hips perfectly to meet me, thrust for thrust, and sends me spiralling towards utter desire again.

"So fucking beautiful. I love to watch you." He hisses at me through his teeth as I see his brow furrow and his muscles tense through his shoulders. His eyes scan my body intensely as he lowers them to look at us together. "The sight of you slamming yourself onto me is so fucking erotic. Watch it, Elizabeth. Look at yourself while you ride me."

Slowly lowering my eyes, I stare in awe at the sight that meets me. He's right. The vision is pure unadulterated sex and I groan at the feeling building inside me as I watch him moving in and out of me. I'm so close as the waves of ecstasy start to take over again. Those lights start to flash behind my eyes and my core tightens around him, igniting the impending mind-numbing state that he gives me.

"Come for me, baby. I want to hear you screaming for me." He growls as he drags me down to him and punishes me with three more beautifully brutal strokes.

"Alex," I murmur into his mouth as I fall apart all over him and collapse onto his chest. He instantly rolls me back over onto my back and stretches my arms above my head.

"More, Elizabeth." Oh, God. My head rolls back as he rises up and starts pounding into me again, drive after drive of unadulterated lust pouring from him as he keeps up his rhythm and wraps my legs around him. Unbelievably, my body begins to react again as his fingers tighten their hold on my wrists and his mouth meets mine. "You will give me more."

Christ alive, I have no idea how much more there is left to give, but his unrelenting stamina seems to know no bounds as he forces me further into the bed and increases his weight on me, binding us together with nothing more than our own skin and this need for each other.

"Oh, God. Yes..." I breathe into his mouth as his tongue swirls and heightens every emotion that I've got. Every thought of him as his body slams into me is consumed with love and closeness and connection and... "Yes, Alex. More."

"Fuck." He groans as his body tenses above me and he lifts himself away to look at me. I can't believe the emotion I see in those eyes as he continues to pound into me, so much so that I struggle to keep eye contact. "Don't look away. Look at me."

My whole being starts to shake as his hand holds my chin and forces my eyes to watch him. I'm so close, so very close. Every nerve ending is buzzing and as my core contracts around him for the first time, I watch the loss of control flash across his face while he growls out and narrows his eyes. That's it, my body explodes around him like the fourth of July or something. Never has it felt so close. Never have I seen the loss of clarity so clearly in his eyes. It's everything I need from him and I smile into his neck as he presses back down onto me and follows behind me, finding his own release.

"Elizabeth," comes drifting up at me as he kisses my neck and holds his hand on my throat like it's some kind of possession. It probably is, to be fair because it's all his. I'll give him anything after what's just happened.

Brushing my hair from my face, he lifts my eyes to his as he rests on his elbows and kisses me gently, a soft smile and a slight frown creasing his very beautiful face as he gazes down at me.

"You're like nothing I've ever found before. I feel like I can't breathe around you and yet I'm lost without you near," he says as he grazes my lips again, grabbing my bottom lip with his teeth and searching my eyes with his. "How do you do that to me?"

I haven't got any words at all as I stare into his eyes and try to process how close he's being. I'd expected nothing but a lack of feeling from him tonight, and yet he's delivering more than I've ever known. Every kiss and movement he's making, every breath and word he gives is screaming love at me and regardless of the fact that he's not actually saying it, I can feel it somehow, sense it in his eyes. So I can't help but fall into the moment and say the only thing I can.

"I'm falling in love with you, Alex. That's all I'm doing," I reply as I gaze back at him and his hands cradle my head softly. His exhale of breath as his mouth parts does nothing to help my nerves at what I've said but I won't take it back. It's far too late for that. It's the truth and I want him to know it.

Chapter 27

Elizabeth

I wake up and slowly open my eyes to the see the most exquisite vision of masculinity asleep next to me. Taking a rare opportunity to look at him unguarded, I can't help but smile at the boyishness of him. He looks so at peace with himself for once. Even though he gives the impression of complete control in his everyday life, I'm beginning to realise that most of it is a lie. Well, not a lie, but definitely a front of sorts. Sure, he's dominant in nature and obviously likes control, but there's at least a twinge of uncertainty in his organised mind, as if questioning his own worth in life for some reason. Clearly his bastard of a dad has really screwed him.

Fury boils up in my chest before I know what's hit me. What sort of man does that to a child? Why would a father think that is acceptable in any way? I can't fathom the very thought of it. How Alex has held himself together all these years and become a reasonably normal human being is completely beyond me.

Reaching forward to brush his hair from his face, I draw my fingers gently along his face and feel the stubble on my hand. He murmurs my name breathily from his lips and rolls towards me a little. My inner slut jumps for joy and runs down an imaginary hill, naked. He said my name in his sleep - in control, my arse! I have to find a way back in.

"Please let me back in," I whisper as I continue to stroke his hair. He mumbles something I can't quite hear and pulls the duvet towards him.

Quietly shuffling myself from the bed, I make for the bathroom and shower, thoroughly appreciating the feeling of my aching joints and sore insides. I find myself glowing at the thought of the precious moments of honesty and emotion he gave me last night. When I'll receive such praise again is anyone's guess given that we're not doing emotion for two weeks, so I take it and hug it tight to myself in hope.

Having bathed myself to death in that glorious shower, I creep back out and put on some clean underwear and one of Alex's shirts. His position hasn't changed. It's sweet, cute even, and I smile at the vision of him there. I look at the clock - eight thirty, good job I took the day off. I wonder if Alex has, too? It's unlikely that he's oversleeping. Well if he is, it's going to be highly amusing watching the flustered and panicking version of him so I decide it's probably best to let him sleep. He doesn't really seem to do enough of it normally anyway. I chuckle and leave the room.

Padding into the kitchen, I switch on the lights and flick on the coffee machine. Christ knows how you work the bloody thing but it doesn't look too dissimilar to the one in the shop so I should be able to deal with it.

Flipping the music on, I prod aimlessly until I source the radio and proceed to potter around looking for toast and honey. "He must have honey in here somewhere," I mumble to myself as I stretch to dig around in the top cupboards.

"I dare say you have plenty of sweet nectar of your own, my dear," I hear being growled seductively from behind me, very close behind me. Shit, why is he still here?

I swing myself around and find Pascal far too close for comfort. His eyebrow quirks as he reaches around me, brushing my thigh on the way with his groin and effectively pinning me against the countertop. He flicks the switch on the coffee maker up again and smiles rather wickedly, holding both hands on the surface either side of me. "You have to turn it up all the way up, Elizabeth, otherwise it doesn't get hot enough, and we all like it hot and steamy, don't we, my dear?"

My mouth hangs open, my eyes gaping at his seductive mouth. Is he really doing this?

Composing myself and realising my lack of clothing, I squeeze my way past him and pop the bread in the toaster, all the time keeping my head turned and trying desperately to stop the blush that is rapidly spreading across my face.

"I didn't realise you stayed last night, Pascal. Did you sleep well?" I ask, trying to turn the conversation back to the non-flirtatious type and move the hell on.

"Well, after I enjoyed the sound of your screams, I found my sleep a little restless to say the least, but I did eventually sleep peacefully after I had relieved myself of a little tension," he answers nonchalantly as he gracefully moves himself to the table and sits. Apparently embarrassment doesn't enter Pascal's thought process in the slightest. I'm so not ready for this. It's way too early to deal with Mr. Seriously Sexy and Naughty. God, I wish Alex was down here.

"Pascal really, I think that's a little too much information for me so early in the morning." I try for casual as I continue to potter about, desperately hoping he doesn't see me flustered. He cannot think he rattles me. I am so rattled by him, though, intoxicating man, and where the hell did he get that black suit? God, he looks good.

"I am sorry, my dear. I forget myself. I am absurdly naughty in the mornings. Forgive me please?" he says with a wry smile and a wink. "Your innocence is just too enticing."

"You are forgiven," I reply as I turn towards the coffee machine and frown. Innocence? How much does he know? I seriously have the feeling that I am not quite so innocent anymore. Was I even before this, given my disturbing thoughts regarding the pair of them? "What would you like?" I mumble out, suddenly irritated by his presence in the room, regardless of how picturesque he looks.

"Quite the loaded question, my rose." Fuck, I so did not mean that.

My head shoots round to find him grinning at me. Shit and buggery bollocks. His eyebrow is up as he chuckles at my gaping mouth again. "Double espresso please," he replies as he lights a cigarette and exhales. Jesus, I need to get a handle on this. Why can't I just be normal around the man?

Fumbling around a bit, I manage to sort out the espresso button and hit it with hope. Luckily the coffee drips beautifully into the small glass so I hit it again then abruptly decide it's a very appealing looking drink, quite chic really, so I sort another one out for myself and move across to the table, grabbing the sugar bowl on the way.

"What do you have planned today?" I ask as I load sugar into my glass.

"I have to pick out some new stock and then I have the enviable task of watching girls wrap themselves around, in, and then on various forms of equipment for the afternoon. I wish it were as exhilarating as it sounds but it can become somewhat tiring after a while," he replies as he lifts the coffee to his lips and gazes toward the garden. "I keep meaning to have these doors installed at home," he continues aimlessly.

"Pascal, you surprise me. Are you telling me that you're dissatisfied with your lifestyle?" I ask with a small chuckle. "And where is home for you?" I never have found out where he lives.

"My dear, when you have done this as long as I have, you find yourself searching for something a little more worthwhile, meaningful even. It's quite irrational really," he says as his eyes soften. "Unfortunately, watching you with Alexander last night reminded me of another time in my life that I rarely revisit."

"More is essential, Pascal. I don't think I'll ever be complete with anything less than more," I reply, thinking of Alex with a smile as I hug my arms around myself. His smile widens to reveal a genuine openness. It's quite lovely.

"Believe me, Elizabeth, you already have more. You may have to give him a little time to realise it though. He is such a stubborn soul, beautiful, but stubborn nonetheless," he says as he delivers a radiant boyish smile that shows me what he was before the Pascal of today. Gone is his mask of devilment or depravity, his eyes are almost kind and his demeanour is completely relaxed as he picks up his drink and drains the last of it. "I must go. I am already late. You are quite the distraction, my dear. I know what he means now," he says, rising from the table and straightening his tie.

Reaching for my hand, he places a kiss on it and moves towards the hall.

What? He knows what Alex means? What does he know?

"Pascal, please tell me what you mean by that. You know him so well and I... Look, please give me something to go on here. He gives away so little," I ask as I reach for my coffee again and sigh.

His eyes narrow a little as he stares across at me. I can see the wheels turning in his mind. What should he say? Should he say anything at all? Eventually he offers his hand to me, gesturing for me to get up.

"Dance with me, my rose." What?

"Pascal, there's no music. We're listening to the bloody radio." And dancing with him could be very dangerous, especially in this shirt. His smile flattens as his eyebrow goes up, showing his impatience. It's so much like the man upstairs that I can't help but smile to myself.

I giggle as I get up and move into his grasp. His body presses up to mine immediately as he gracefully positions me into his hold and begins to twirl me around. The feel of being scantily dressed and pulled up against him is undeniably disconcerting and I find myself trying to ease back a bit. He increases his hold violently, tugs me towards him again and leans into my ear.

"He gives you everything, my rose. He gives you his home, his bed, his solace in Rome, and whether he wants to admit it or not, he gives you his heart. I have never seen him so infatuated and it is not hard to see why," he whispers as he kisses my neck gently. "You are everything he needs and yet nothing that he wants. For him to realise this relationship, he will have to embrace his own inadequacies." Shivers spark across my skin as his tongue darts across me. He feels it, and as he digs his fingers into my waist and exhales, forcing me even tighter toward him as he lowers his hand. My bloody core clenches. I can't help it. "That is not easy for men like us. We do not do well with real feelings. They are limiting for us and we do so hate to be limited, Elizabeth."

I gasp at the feel of him hardening against my stomach and push backwards a little to try and create some space because I have to stop this. I must. It's ridiculous to be anywhere near this, let alone enjoying it. He spins me away from him and lets go of my hand, leaving me feeling rather confused by his actions, totally turned on to the point of no return, and yet somehow remarkably comforted by his words.

I stare at him, panting like a fool as he smiles wickedly and licks his lips. One wrong move and he will take me, here, in the kitchen. I know it, and he knows it. I have no idea whether to look him in the eye or stare at the floor but those green eyes are so consuming that I'm struggling, a lot. I am absolutely not in control at this moment. He's disturbingly tempting. It's like a sodding cloud of fairy dust is working some kind of magic. Vampires have that ability, don't they? That thought thing they do, whatever it is, is he doing that? Christ, I need a cross or something. Perhaps those fucking fairies might step in and save me, please.

He hasn't removed his eyes, not once, and I still can't breathe properly but I haven't looked away at least. Well, I hope that was the right thing to do. He eventually smirks and reaches for his cigarettes on the table.

"You are quite extraordinary, my dear. I am glad I have had my perverse moment with you. I have wanted to hold you for quite some time. It was worth every second of the risk but please do me the courtesy of not telling him. I fear I may get a severe beating from him if he hears of it." His brow furrows a little. "Actually, I might enjoy that so tell him if you like," he says with a wink as he fiddles with his cufflinks and turns for the hall. I feel the smile grow across my face at the thought of the argument that would ensue between the two of them and then wonder why Pascal would enjoy a beating. It's quite bizarre, but then so is he to be fair.

"When will we see you again?" I call as he passes through the door. It's more for preparation purposes than politeness.

"You may see me whenever you wish, Elizabeth. You have my card. Call me... For any reason. It would be my honour to entertain you, or fight for you should you request it," he says conspiratorially as he waves over his shoulder and ambles his way rather sexily up the hall.

"Goodbye, Pascal. Thank you," I whisper as I exhale a held in breath and shake my head at whatever it was that just happened.

"'Until the next time, my dear. I look forward to it and you are most welcome," he calls casually.

How the hell did he hear that? Definitely a vampire.

Another hour passes as I read a paper and listen to the radio, sipping at my third espresso and looking out into the wonderful garden. I keep recalling Pascal's words in my head and trying to make sense of the relationship I'm currently in with the enigmatic man upstairs. I'm just starting to wonder whether I should wake the beautiful Mr. White up when the news comes on so I listen to the random information that is thrown at me and crunch down on another piece of toast.

"And tonight, of course, is the much talked about charity ball in aid of Addisons at the Ritz. Since its humble beginnings, The Addisons Foundation has raised millions to help victims of childhood abuse and it continues to grow in stature year on year. Several celebrities and major business tycoons are likely to be in attendance and of course, patron and founder, Mr. Alexander White will be hosting as usual. The event

begins the season's festivities as it does every year and we're sure that the discerning and rather unfairly gorgeous Mr. White will be doing his damndest to relieve people of their money in aid of a very worthy cause. Well done, sir. And now to the weather..." the woman says as I try to process the information I have just heard.

The Addisons Foundation? Alex? Clearly I've heard of it but I never knew Alex had anything to do with it. How have I missed that piece of information? Mind you, until the last few weeks, someone could have said his name and I wouldn't have even known who he was. Wow! Millions for a charity that must be so close to his heart. No one could know why though, surely? A sudden thought hits me. Does he expect me to go with him tonight? If so, I certainly have nothing to wear with me. I doubt he'll want me with him at such a prestigious event anyway, will he?

Just as I move across the room to the coffee maker to start my fourth espresso, I hear footsteps padding down the hall. Smiling at the thought of him and feeling my body tighten, I flick the switch *all the way up* again. Damn that Pascal.

"Good morning, gorgeous," he says as he spins me around to face him, drags me towards his lips for a glorious kiss and then smiles his truly mouth-watering smile. It reminds me of how little Pascal actually has on this man. He's really not even close. So why I go all panty and ridiculous around him is a little annoying. I need to work on that and quickly.

"Good morning," I reply, looking into those hypnotizing blue eyes and draping my arms over his exposed shoulders.

"You must be wearing me out, young lady. I can't remember ever sleeping this late. I feel remarkably well rested now though. When did you get up?" he asks, reaching for a coffee glass.

"About two hours ago. Pascal said goodbye, by the way," I reply as I press the button, pouring two more coffees. He gazes at the glasses side by side for a moment and seems lost in thought then snaps out of it abruptly.

"You saw him, dressed like that?" he mutters, his body stiffening as he pushes away from me. Oh god, here we go with the pissed off thing.

"Yes, I did, and don't get all snippy about it. You could have told me he was staying and then I would have dressed more appropriately," I reply in my calmest voice, trying to quieten him before he launches. And given what actually happened, I really don't want to get into a conversation about it so I wander off casually.

"Right, well I hope he at least behaved himself. Although he more than often doesn't," he mumbles to himself as he sits at the table and pulls out a chair for me.

"He was a perfect gentleman, well, as gentlemanly he can be," I reply with a giggle. He rolls his eyes and picks up the paper I've been reading.

"What are you doing here anyway? I thought you'd be at work by now, although I'm very glad you're not," he asks, continuing with his slightly sulky face but winking at me.

"I could say the same, Mr. White. It seems making millions is easier than I thought," I reply with a raised eyebrow and a smirk. "I took the day off. I have the Stevely dinner to do on Sunday. Well, I do if the new cooker arrives on time, so we often swap days off when we can."

"Making millions is easier than you think, baby. It's keeping them that takes up the time," he says with a sardonic grin. "What do you mean new cooker?"

"Oh, I didn't tell you? I almost set the building alight yesterday. The old one blew up. Not a surprise really, everything's so old. We desperately need new premises really. It's just getting too small for us now. Just a few more clients and we'll talk to the bank about new investment. Hopefully they'll agree and we can get somewhere bigger and leave the shop as a bakery. Mum's struggling to help me with the larger parties now and I don't want to push her any further than I have to. She wasn't well a while ago and I'm not helping her go back that way," I reply, rambling with a resigned sigh as I sip my coffee and gaze longingly at the garden. The rain pelting against the window still doesn't lessen its appeal to me. If I had wellies with me, I'd be seriously considering going out in it.

"How much do you need?" Alex asks inquisitively, scrolling his thumb across his phone and frowning a little.

"Oh, I don't know exactly. It's a bit irrelevant at the moment anyway as we need more income for the sort of loan we're talking about. Mind you, White Industries have certainly helped our company profile. Belle is struggling to fit all the enquiries in lately," I say with a giggle. "Thank you, Mr. White."

"Mmm... Well I have very discerning colleagues, Miss Scott. Having said that, you are very good at what you do. In all areas, I might add," he replies with a smirk as he picks up my hand and sucks in a finger. "Now, since I have you all to myself, what would you like to do today?"

"Well, by the sound of it, you have a rather important charity ball to host this evening so I expect you'll want to relax a bit, won't you? Seriously, don't you ever damn well work?" He chuckles and raises an eyebrow.

"I don't do relaxing all that much and yes I do bloody work, very hard actually, you little minx. Let me take you out somewhere. I'm sure you probably need a dress for tonight. How did you know about the ball?" he says, reaching for my hand. Oh, he does want me to go.

"You want me to go with you?" I ask, genuinely bemused but secretly elated.

"Of course I do. I'm sorry I didn't mention it before but to be honest, I haven't really been sure if you'd still be willing to go with me. We have been a little at odds recently, haven't we?" he says as a quite adorably shy smile slides across his lips. I feel the blush rise over my cheeks as I think of coming home from Rome and then the fight. What the hell is actually going on between us now is still a slight quandary. If last night is anything to go by then maybe we're back on track.

"Yes, we have. Well, I'd love to go but I can get a dress from home, thank you. You will not spend any more money on me, Mr. White," I reply, looking to the table and fiddling with my bracelet. I can't accept it. I won't. Enough really is enough.

His eyes snap to mine and narrow. The crease of a frown crosses his brow as he speaks.

"The agreement was that you would do as you're told, Elizabeth, and not question me. I expect you to adhere to that. I'll buy you a new dress and shoes and the whole fucking shop if I choose to and you'll accept it graciously." He growls as he steels me with his ever-darkening eyes. Oh right, maybe I do have to accept it then - not quite as back *on track* as I thought, obviously. *It's only two weeks, Beth.*

"Okay," is all I can manage as I bite my nails and hope it's enough to cool his mood. His damn smirk does not go unnoticed.

"Well that was easier than I thought it was going to be," he says as he grins and looks back at his phone vibrating on the table. Bastard. I'm really not going to be able to play this game. I can feel my hackles rising at the thought, to be honest. "Now, how did you hear about the ball?"

Sudden images of that little boy with a blood soaked face hit me and all my anger disappears. Christ, it must be hell for him to deal with this charity, to have to feel it all over again and remind himself of his own trauma.

"The radio. Seems you're quite the hero, Mr. White. The Addison Foundation? Wow. Why didn't you tell me?" I say with soft eyes and the warmest smile I can find. I can't help but feel his pain at the very idea of the reason for the event.

"It never came up," he says with a shrug as if it's a small thing.

"I think it's wonderful. In fact, I think you're wonderful. It must make you feel fantastic to know that you're achieving something so important for others. You really are very special. You know that, don't you?"

He looks to the floor for a few moments, some odd emotion passing across his face, a little forlorn maybe, then quite abruptly stands and grasps onto my hand pulling me up to him with eyes suddenly full of desire and lust.

"Enough talking now. I think I want to take what's mine in my own home. Yes, I think that counter top looks very appealing. We have not christened enough of this house at all." Oh! Picking me up and depositing me on top of the counter, he pushes my legs apart and yanks me towards him. "I like you in my shirts - great access but these will have to go," he says as he rips the side of my panties and throws them over his shoulders. I immediately flood down below at the intensity of the situation. How the hell he manages to pull this out of me is anyone's guess. Unbuttoning the fly on his jeans, he lets himself spring free and pulls my hand down to his waiting erection. I grip on tightly and run my thumb over the top of him and watch as his mouth parts in ecstasy. I love that I can do this to him and it only increases the need to have him inside me, where he belongs. Groaning as my hand travels the length of him, he rips the shirt apart, sending buttons flying and takes my nipple into his mouth roughly, biting at it and massaging the other one between his finger and thumb.

"Oh god, yes..." I call as I tip my head back and let his mouth take me.

Quickly shoving me backwards and downwards so I'm stretched flat on my back on the peninsular, he climbs up and positions himself between my legs, then reaching in between us, he pushes his fingers inside me and draws them up to my mouth.

"Taste it, baby. Taste how ready you are for me. I fucking adore how you taste," he growls as he slides his fingers into my mouth and then kisses me, licking and sucking at my lips. "Tell me you want me inside you, Elizabeth. Ask me to fuck you."

"Yes, I want you. I want you inside me, Alex. Please..." I practically beg as my body starts to convulse while he rubs himself against my already very sensitive nub. Pushing my legs back and wrapping them around his waist, he forces his whole weight down on me and drives himself inside me with one fierce stroke.

"Oh Christ, that feels so fucking good. I could do this all day with you," he groans out as he continues his tortuous attack and pushes back in again, deeper.

"Yes... Oh, yes..." the feel of him inside me again, consuming me, it's like a drug I can't get enough of. Each movement of his hands or body seems to align with my mind, as if he senses exactly which part of me needs attention next so delivers it perfectly. That closeness comes flooding back into my mind, that ability to read where the other needs to be.

He raises himself up and pulls me back towards him with a violent tug, dragging my back up the counter as he kneels and wrenches me onto his cock again. My shoulders take my weight as he continues with his powerful thrusts and lowers his hand to my sex, rubbing slow circles and increasing the pressure gradually, easing the next round of pleasure from me.

"I can feel you're ready, baby. Just hold off. I want to come with you. Look at me. I want you to see me, see what you do to me. Fuck, yes." He groans as I feel him thickening inside me with every forceful drive forward. I open my eyes and am rewarded with the completely erotic vision of him slamming his hips against me, muscles straining and rippling with tension. Instantly I'm tipping over the edge and those bright lights start to glimmer as my body tightens around him and the ache in my core turns into an ecstasy of delight and pure pleasure. Clamping my legs, I raise my hips to meet his last stroke as he pours himself into me with another groan and hauls my limp body up by the neck to sit astride him. I wrap my arms around his neck and hang on as he grinds the last of his seed into me. Nuzzling into his neck and trying to get my breathing back to normal, I run my fingers up and down his back. Love swells in my heart, as he holds onto me tighter than usual, leaving me with feelings of belonging and hope. Maybe he is as close to this as I am? My lips can't stop licking their way around his throat as his hand rests on the back of my head and he pushes me in closer, tIlting his neck to give me greater access to it. God, I can't get enough of the taste of him, the sweat, the aftershave, him.

Eventually, when we've both started to regain our composure, I try to climb off, thinking he's probably quite uncomfortable kneeling on a countertop with my full weight on him.

"No. Stay," he says sharply as he grasps me tighter and kisses my shoulder tenderly. Oh. Okay.

"You're rather strong, Mr. White, and quite flexible to be honest. For an old man, you don't do badly at all," I say with a giggle into his neck. I instantly narrow my eyes at my own stupidity. That may have been not as funny as I intended. His chest shaking indicates that maybe I'm okay.

"You have no idea, Miss Scott," he replies, bringing my face towards him and kissing me again. "Grip on." I clamp my legs around him and tighten my arms around his neck. Spinning us around, he somehow manages to get us both down to the floor with me still attached and him still buried inside me, all the time growling into and nibbling my neck.

"Very impressive, Mr. White. Where to now?" I ask, grinning like a fool. God, I love playful Alex.

"Upstairs for a shower. If I make it that far without fucking you again, that is. The stairs are also looking very appealing at the moment. Although, I think Andrews might get a shock if he sees us and I think Mary will be here soon. She starts at eleven thirty," he replies as he shifts my weight and walks along the hall purposely.

"You can put me down, you know? And who's Mary," I ask, giggling and kissing his shoulder.

"I can't show any weakness now, can I? I'd look a right bloody idiot. Besides, I don't want to let you go just yet. I like having you wrapped around me. And she's my housekeeper. I think she's been at the apartment this morning, thankfully. I doubt she would have wanted to deal with our display of affection," he replies, taking the first step and chuckling.

"Affection...? Is that what you call having aggressive sex on the countertop?" I ask with another giggle. He quirks one of his eyebrows as a very devilish smile plays on his lips.

"That wasn't aggressive, Elizabeth. You haven't made me angry enough to see aggressive yet, or bored enough." He smirks while kissing my neck. "What do you think? Stairs or not?" Oh, Jesus, he means it? He twitches inside me for effect. I look down at the burgundy carpet and seriously consider the prospect, then Andrews flies into my head.

"Perhaps another time, but I think the shower could be invigorating, don't you?" I respond, pressing my lips against his and thinking of our last session in the shower.

"Yes, I think it could be, too. Brains as well as beauty," he says as he begins the climb easily, still smirking and now actually pulling me down onto him harder with another one of his mesmerising growls.

"Why thank you, Mr. White. Do you think you can make it all the way up? Not too hard?" My sarcasm apparently knows no bounds. He stops and instantly lowers my backside to the stairs with eyes sparkling with mischief.

"Leverage," he mutters as he pulls out of me, pushes me flatter to the floor and drops down across my chest, presenting me with his very impressive length. He rubs his fingers over my lips until I open them and smiles. "So now I'm going to deal with that smart mouth of yours, Miss Scott."

"Yummy," is all my brain can think of saying in response as I suck at his fingers and watch his eyes darkening again.

~

Slumping down onto his bed, I look at all the bags that are now adorning the bedroom floor. Bags of underwear, dresses, shoes, jewellery and if I'm not mistaken, there's also a bag over there with my make-up brand stamped all over it. Where has that come from?

While being with him has been utterly wonderful, the day in general has made me feel uncomfortable and awkward. What the hell is he trying to do? Shop me into submission now?

Well he can buy stuff as much as he likes. It will all be staying in his wardrobe in two weeks, or I will be taking the sodding lot back. One dress is all I need, *one*, and perhaps some shoes, but I don't even need that if I'm honest. I could easily have popped home and dug out one of my formal gowns. It's not like I haven't been to functions before. Okay, maybe not as high profile as this but still.

Pulling myself up and sighing, I start to unpack the clothes and hang them in the wardrobe. Bizarrely, a large space has been created to the side of his clothes, which I assume is for my benefit, but when the hell that happened I have no idea.

Sitting down on the seat in the walk in, I stare blankly at the exquisite burgundy lace over satin gown that hangs in front of me. It's strapless and very structured. The corset is built in to give it maximum oomph in the breast department and it then skims down to the floor and fishtails at the back, all beautifully peppered with thousands of hand stitched tiny crystals. Stunning, and so was the bloody price tag. I'd stopped looking by the time the personal shopper had reached for the fourth dress that was a mere snip at only twelve thousand pounds. The shoes... Well, by the time we'd reached the shoes I'd completely given up all hope of arguing and just begun accepting what was offered. Although, even I have to admit they are utterly beautiful. They have a timeless elegance about them and are a perfect match to the dress with crystals running down the back of the heel.

Looking around the rest of the clothes, I hold my head in my hands and sigh again. This whole thing is utterly absurd. This money could have gone to his charity or something else as deserving.

"What's the matter?" I hear softly from the entrance. I turn to see a worried looking Alex leaning against the frame, frowning with his arms crossed.

"Nothing," I reply, getting up and walking to him. I put my loveliest smile on, seriously not wanting an argument to ruin this evening.

His head tilts to the side as he smiles and reaches for me, pulling me into his arms and kissing my nose.

"It's because you didn't want it, you know?"

"Excuse me?" I say in confusion as I look at him.

"The reason I bought it all, it's because you didn't want it. You really did look adorable pouting like that all day. I couldn't help but keep dragging you into the next shop," he says, laughing at me, almost to the point of combusting, those blue eyes of his twinkling with devilment.

I stare in shock at his display of hilarity. Am I that damned amusing?

"You, Mr. White, are an arsehole," I practically shout as I storm out of his embrace and head for the bedroom. He catches up with me, quickly snagging my arm to turn me around. I try for affronted, failing as he smiles again. "I'm just not comfortable with it all, Alex."

"Of course you're not, and that is why I want to do it. You've never looked lovelier than you did when you threw my credit card out of the window," he says, kissing me quickly and launching - yes *launching* - like a sixteen-year-old towards the stairs.

I smirk at the thought of that credit card, slowly following him from the room. It had been my attempt to stop him spending money. Andrews, unfortunately, very quickly retrieved it and the shopping had continued. "Now, if you've finished with your temper tantrum, I'd like a drink and we have a ball to get ready for. We need to be there for eight thirty and we've got a great bottle of Krug to get through before we go. Come on, chop chop," he calls as he rounds the bottom of the stairs and takes off towards the kitchen. I continue to stare at him in amazement. Chop chop? Where the hell has this version of Alex come from?

~

Lights flash everywhere. I find myself holding my hand up to deflect the brightness that surrounds me as we exit the car and make our way toward the entrance. I've never seen so many paparazzi and apparently they all want a shot of the inimitable Mr. Alexander White and whoever it is that's with him. Yes, that would be me.

"Mr. White, Mr. White, over here. Who's the new girl and where is Rebecca Stanners. Can you give us a statement about your involvement with the charity, sir? What's happening with the shanghai deal, sir? Are you still involved with the Bruckstein takeover? Will you be apologising for delaying the property evaluation in the east end? When was the last time you took some time off? Any holidays planned?"

He rounds on them one by one, giving short and precise answers to each question as he pulls me close but slightly behind him. The ease of his voice is a complete revelation. He responds with true professionalism as if he's completely at ease with the whole situation. Of course, he probably is. I've never really seen that much of him in business mode so this is probably perfectly normal for him. His enigmatic smile is firmly in place as he almost flirts with each individual and gains both admiring and appreciative oohs and ahs from the interviewers. I, on the other hand, feel myself cowering behind him and hoping to hell they won't ask any questions of me.

"Miss? Can we ask your name? Who are you and how do you know Mr. White? How long have you been together? Are you an item? Is there an engagement we should be aware of?" Oh shit, no. What the hell do I say now? My mouth flounders over words I can't form as Alex moves in to deflect the questions with another gleaming smile just as a short and very beautiful dark-haired woman jumps in front of us and takes over. Alex smiles and starts to turn us away from the mob.

"Thank you, ladies and gentleman. Mr. White has said enough for now and after all, he does have a busy night sucking the money out of everyone. We wouldn't want to wear him out now, would we? How would that be of benefit to the charity? Please ask any furthering questions of the press office at White Industries," she says as she ushers us backwards and throws me a dazzling smile.

"Miranda, that was rather efficient timing." Alex chortles at her.

"No problem, Mr. White. Miss Scott, you look beautiful," she says to me. I have no idea who the hell she is but she's absolutely wonderful in my books.

"Thank you," I reply Miranda, who has saved my arse.

"Are you okay?" he whispers as he clasps onto my hand tightly and leads me into the Ritz.

"I don't know if I'm honest. That was quite bizarre. Is that normal for you?"

"Yes, that is very normal for me and with any luck, it will become very normal for you, too," he responds with a captivating smile as he pulls me towards his very inviting lips. A sudden flash breaks through our moment and Alex pulls back immediately and tucks me into his chest as he glares across my shoulder viciously.

"Get that fucker now, Miranda. I swear if that shot is in print tomorrow, you'll never work again," he seethes quietly as she launches herself at the man who has taken the picture, almost wrangling him to the floor in desperation. Andrews appears out of nowhere and quickly manhandles the photographer to the side of the room with rather impressive force, depositing him on a chair. The camera is wrenched from his neck and taken off somewhere by Miranda.

"Fucking parasites, the lot of them. I fucking hate this shit," Alex sneers as he put his hand on my back and gently pushes me into the lobby, looking over his shoulder. "Mind you, who wouldn't want to take pictures of you?" he says as his eyes soften and he takes us toward the bar.

Chapter 28

Elizabeth

I am completely out of my happy zone.

The venue is too stupendously extravagant, the food and company are astonishingly overwhelming and the table we are sitting at is so full of wealth I can't even begin to comprehend how to act around these people. No amount of Alex's encouraging words or gestures are making me feel comfortable here as they all discuss their various holiday homes, yachts and million pound deals. The diamonds that drip off the women around me are simply astounding and as they look down their noses at me with something close to disgust hiding behind their ridiculous smiles, I am shrivelling into a ball of mush.

After course three has been cleared and the table has resumed its cordial chatting, which, for the women anyway, is more like a constant quiet bitch fight, I know I have to get out of here. I have tried, really I have, but there are just too many of them. I thought I was getting good at this pretending, or even believing myself that I was actually getting the hang of discussing things with these people, but I can't keep it up. I just don't have enough interesting conversation to keep up with the amount of people who have pounced on us.

From the moment we entered the bar area, the highest of London's society and a good few of the European ones have hit us from all angles. Alex has, of course, been witty, charming and deceptively cunning in his sweep of the room, quickly moving between people, determining who has the most money and ensuring that they pledge as much as they can. He's also been ridiculously accomplished at his task and before we even sat down I was pretty sure he'd secured a fair few million. He has kept me close and given me nothing but beautiful smiles and adoring eyes all night, but I just can't shake the feeling of being absolutely out of place in this room with these people. Watching him manipulate the room with the precision of a panther has only reminded me of my incapability to do him justice. I just have to get some air and ten minutes of privacy. Maybe I can rally myself again after that. I can but hope anyway.

Excusing myself from the table, I make my way to the restroom, glancing back to see Alex in deep conversation with the stupidly stunning Mrs Bessie Stapleton, wife of Richard Stapleton, the right honourable owner of pretty much everything in London as far as I can tell. Taking a deep breath as I head out of the door, I hear my name being called from somewhere. Turning, I find a surprisingly friendly face attached to a body adorned in a deep blue dress that matches her eyes and I gratefully move toward her in the hope of some normalcy to the evening.

"Beth, what are you doing here? How wonderful to see you. I almost didn't recognise you. You look so... grown up, and bloody gorgeous by the way," Sarah says as she walks toward me and gives me a quick hug.

"Sarah, thank god for a friendly face. I am utterly at a loss as to what I'm doing here as well," I reply giggling. "If only I'd known, I probably would have told Alex to go to hell."

"Alex? A new boyfriend?" she enquires, smiling conspiratorially with her radiant smile and her blonde hair bouncing enthusiastically. "Show me which one is he."

"Sort of, and I doubt I'll need to show you. I'm pretty sure you know who Mr. White is. Everyone else seems to," I reply smiling. Her body stiffens a little, probably out of shock I suppose, and then she relaxes a little and links her arm in mine.

"Well, that's interesting. So when did that start up?" she asks as we walk into the restroom.

"Not that long ago, just beginning really. Anyway, I can't believe you're here. I don't think I've seen you for two years. It must have been Belle's twenty-fifth birthday," I reply, recalling the memory of the very drunken evening. "How's Henry?" She immediately frowns a little and waves her hand about.

"He's here somewhere, probably inspecting his newest conquest I should think." *Oh!*

"Anyway, let's not talk about him. How's Belle? I keep meaning to call her but you know how it is. I hear your business is doing very well lately. I dare say that's how you met Alexander. I heard you were doing his lunches now."

"Yes, we're doing well, thank you. I tell you what, why don't we finish up in here and then head to the bar for a while? I could really use a stiff drink and a happy chit chat for a bit."

"Fabulous idea. I think I've serviced the table well enough for a while," she replies as she applies her lipstick and I head into the toilet. "The bitches have been placated so to speak."

Almost an hour later, I watch Alex sweep into the bar with a slight frown marring his incredibly edible face. Having had a few more drinks and a very giggly catch up with Sarah, I've really begun to loosen up and enjoy the evening. I feel relaxed at last and after a severe ear bashing about how beautiful I look from Sarah, I have thankfully begun to believe I have a right to be here again. She left a while ago and now I'm talking to a very sweet young couple who are very interested in hiring us to cater for their wedding next year. Alex's eyes find mine in the crowd and I pretty much feel the growl as he stalks his way toward me. God, he looks divine, the crowd parting for him as he keeps his eyes fixed on mine.

The dinner suit is cut to perfection and only emphasizes his incredible physique. The white shirt with black buttons and black silk cummerbund accentuate his shoulders and pull me towards his delicious looking neck, which is of course, encased in a black bow tie that I tied for him before we left the house. He is sex personified. There isn't a man in the room that comes close to the masculinity that pours from his existence. Licking my lips and feeling my panties start their ridiculous combusting overture, I smirk and tighten my thighs.

"There you are. I've been looking everywhere for you," he says as he pulls me toward him and kisses me with more force than the situation suggests is appropriate. I couldn't care less.

"I met an old friend and then met Annie and Derek here who are in need of some catering," I reply as I look adoringly into rather darkened eyes and almost melt at the lust pouring out of them.

"All work and no play, Miss Scott? From you?" he says, raising that eyebrow. "I'm sorry, guys. I really am going to have to tear her away from you. The speech is in ten and I'd like a moment with my girlfriend alone if you don't mind," he says, looking at the very cute Annie and Derek and throwing them his award-winning smile. They smile and nod as we leave the bar and head up the stairs. Where the hell is he taking me now? Turning the corner, Alex starts sliding a card randomly into various doors and eventually one opens. Pushing me inside, he pulls the door closed and I find myself standing in a linen cupboard with him.

"A linen cupboard?" I ask, chuckling as he pushes me backwards into the racks of linen and grabs the bottom of my dress.

"Swiped the card off a receptionist," he says as he finds his way between my legs with his hand.

"That's very naughty, Mr. White. I think its called theft." I giggle.

"Been there, done that. Really quite good at it," he responds as he clasps his hands around my arse.

"Oh god. What are you doing? In here, really?" I ask in mock amazement. Nothing shocks me with him anymore.

"Fucking you, very quickly if I get my way. I've thought of nothing else since you stepped out of the car and I can't bear it anymore." He groans as he hooks his fingers into my g-string, rips it off and throws it over his shoulder. "I'll get you some more." *Okay, whatever.*

My breathing becomes shallow very quickly as it hits me that he's actually going to do this in a bloody linen cupboard. Unbelievably, my body reacts as quickly as it normally does when he's near me and I feel instantly ravenous for him. "I'd like to ravage those lips, Miss Scott, but I'm sure everyone will know what we've been up to so grab onto that rail and put those incredible legs around my waist." He growls as he indicates above my head with his chin and unzips his trousers, pulling himself free. As I lift my hands and find a solid hold, he grasps my thighs and lifts me straight onto his waiting and very impressive manhood.

"Oh, Christ." He grunts into my neck as he rams into me. Tugging at the back of my neck, he forces me to look at him and stills himself. "Look at me. Watch me show you how I feel about you."

Slowly pulling back, he keeps his eyes locked with mine. A small smile plays across his lips as he eases back in again. "Beautiful, and all mine. Mine," he growls as he pushes back in again, this time with more force and far more aggression. My mouth hangs open and my breathing shortens as the stretch overwhelms me with lust. He begins to increase his speed. The force with which he keeps pounding me is unbelievable. Where the hell does the man get his stamina? His mouth parts and his eyes bore into mine as he shows me what he has to give me, what he can do to me in only a few minutes. The vision of his feral glare has my core instantly tightening as I feel the familiar build of my orgasm start.

Tilting my head back, I try to keep a hold on the bar above me. My fingers are becoming wet from the tension of hanging on but I let the swirling sensations take over my body and just feel him, all of him, taking me. This isn't for me. This is him taking what he wants at the exact moment he decides he wants it, what he deserves and he can have me, anywhere he wants to and in any situation as far as I'm concerned. I'm all his.

"God, I love being inside you. Tell me you want me, Elizabeth. Tell me you're mine." He groans as I feel him thickening and my insides quivering for release.

"Yes, yours. Completely. Oh god. Yes... Alex..." I hiss as he changes his angle and plunges back in again. My insides start to explode as he pushes his body closer to me and wraps his arms around my back, whispering my name as he drives himself into me and finds his own moment of ecstasy. Regardless of the situation we're in, I couldn't feel closer to him. His fingers drop down to my backside to hold me up as he keeps gently moving in and out of me, groaning out his pleasure as if it's he's comforted.

Eventually, I release my grip on the rail and slide down his body, keeping one leg wrapped around him and nuzzling into his chest. One of his strong arms is still on my waist and the other is grasping onto my thigh as he tenderly kisses the top of my head and rubs his cheek against my hair. Minutes pass as we just stand there holding each other tight, in the bloody linen room.

"Well that's a first," he eventually says with a small chuckle, still panting. "I've never done that in a linen cupboard before." I giggle and look up at him.

"Neither have I, and I can assure you that I won't forget it a hurry either. You were quite unrelenting, Mr. White."

"What the hell do you expect? Look at you. I've had to watch every man ogle you and paw at you, which has incensed me to the point of breaking, I might add. I'm not sure how I made it this far through the evening before having you or fucking killing someone else," he grinds out as he scowls and draws his fingers across my chest. Lowering his head, he kisses my neck and looks back up with that disabling smile of his. "I may very well have to do it again before we leave." I smile softly.

"I'll take that as a compliment, I think." I chuckle in response as my head quirks. "Is that a hint of jealousy I hear, Mr. White?" I question cheekily, grinning at him.

"Where you're concerned, Elizabeth, I think my jealousy knows no bounds. Strange really, I've never been one to care that much before now." He smiles and gently places a kiss on my lips, lingering, pulling back and then doing it again. Grabbing a towel from the rack, he pulls out of me and softly cleans me up and then tucks himself away and gazes at me for a few moments. I have no idea what's going on in his head but I know mine is full of love for the man in front of me. He abruptly shakes his head and begins smoothing my dress down and messing with the hem until it looks perfect. I hear him muttering something to himself about devils again and as he rises back up in front of me, he takes my jaw in his hands and frowns. His piercing blue eyes look into mine as if he has so much to tell me with them.

"You, Elizabeth, are utterly astounding. You captivate me and I am completely unworthy of your affection, or attention for that matter. I don't know why you came into my life but I promise that I'll try to give you everything you need from me," he whispers as his face softens. "You're perfect. Do you know that? You make me want to give you everything, share everything, become more than I currently am." My heart almost melts under the heat of his gaze. It's beautiful, painfully truthful, as if he's trying desperately to show me something that he can't quite put into words. My hand goes to his jaw instinctively. God, I love him.

"And that is one of the main reasons why I love you so much," I reply without thinking at all, and then realise what has come out of my mouth.

My hand shoots back from his face to his arm as comprehension sets in and I become completely aware of what I've just admitted. I absolutely did not mean to say that out loud. His whole body stiffens as his face turns from soft and relaxed to confused, his smile suddenly replaced by something similar to bewilderment or maybe even panic.

Oh, shit. What the hell have I done? He said no emotion, you idiot. But he gave me emotion, didn't he? He said all those lovely things, and I had to say something. Maybe it was a bit too much but the words were out of my mouth before I even thought of stopping them. I couldn't have anyway. Actually, maybe I could if my brain to mouth filter was working more appropriately, but clearly it isn't. In fact, I'm not even sure if I wanted to stop it tumbling out. Regardless of whether he's ready or not, I love him, deeply, yes rather confusingly, but somehow I just know that he's everything I need and want. It's probably the stupidest part of me that believes this is possible between us but I have to trust that it might be okay, that we might stand a chance. Or rather, that I might.

He stares at me a while longer, as if he's trying to digest the information he's received. At least his face isn't impassive because that would be completely shit. His cheekbone seems to have a developed a twitch of some sort, and his eyes have narrowed slowly, showing his bafflement or maybe its displeasure. I'm really not sure but it's out there now so I just wait for some sort of response and hope it's going to be positive.

More time passes as he continues to look at me. Occasionally he opens his beautiful mouth and then closes it again before he's said anything. His hands are both firmly grasped at my hipbones as if clinging on for dear life while mine lie gently on his arms, not moving an inch. I have absolutely no clue as to what I'm supposed to say or do next and to be honest, it's probably his move now so I just keep staring back. I can feel my lips trembling. I also have no clue as to what I'm supposed to do with that either so I gaze into deep blue eyes hoping that he understands. Even if he doesn't feel the same, it doesn't matter. Oh god, I hope he does. Shit, what if he doesn't? Is this it? *Nice one, Beth.*

"...And now for the man of the night, Mr. Alexander White, ladies and gentlemen..."

Clap, clap, clap. Thunderous applause and cheering begins to emanate from downstairs, then stamping of feet ensues and more clapping.

I look into his unmoving eyes, which are still boring into mine. He clearly hasn't heard his name being called or even registered the announcement.

"Alex, they're calling for you. You have to go," I say quietly, trying to get his attention.

"No, they can fuck off," he responds abruptly, looking at my mouth and biting his bottom lip, still frowning.

"It's okay. This is important to you. You have to go. Go and make some more money for them," I say with a small smile as I push against his arms a bit to encourage him toward the door. There's no shifting him as he increases his grip on me.

"I can't. I haven't found the words yet and I don't know how to-"

"Alex, go. This can wait. It was stupid of me. I didn't mean to..." I cut across him and turn for the door myself. One of us has to get him down those stairs.

"Don't say that. Don't tell me that wasn't real, that you didn't mean it," he says from behind me.

I turn immediately to find him staring at the floor, unable to meet my eyes for the first time. The lost look of a little boy who feels alone and betrayed drifts through my mind, and for the first time I see the vision of torture and turmoil beneath the man in front of me. He's nervous, maybe even terrified. What have so many years of hiding the truth done to him? Has he no clue as to how he should react, what he should say. His face looks full of unknown emotions and his eyes hold what appears to be fear - the same eyes I saw at his father's house when he touched the banister rail, the same eyes he had while he stared at that damned door. That is absolutely not what my words are supposed to induce from him. I want him happy, elated, in love with me, not scared of the possibility.

Break the moment Beth, for God's sake. Get him back together. He has to be on stage now.

DO SOMETHING!

"Head up, unless I tell you not to." I smirk, gently trying to lift his chin. "I meant every word of it. I love you, Alex. I love you very much." His head comes up and as small grin starts to play around his mouth, I smile and relax a little, and then that bloody frown returns. "Stop whatever it is you're confusing yourself about and go, Alex. Show me what you're made of. I want to see you achieve this for yourself," I say as I gaze lovingly at the glorious man standing in front of me with all his emotions fighting underneath his skin. My insides still tremble as I desperately try to hold myself together for him, for this moment.

"...Well we appear to have lost our patron, ladies and gentleman. I dare say he's getting up to no good somewhere. The man really is intolerable sometimes." Applause and hysteric laughter erupt again. *"Please take your seats again and we'll find him for you. Be very prepared to get your wallets out. We all know how adamantly persuasive he can be..."*

I raise my eyebrow at him and as his grin grows wide again, he takes my hand in his and moves to the door.

"This isn't finished yet," he mutters, opening the door and glancing around the hall. "So bloody perfect, unbelievable," he continues as we leave the room and he drags me down the stairs behind him. I have no idea what to think about his reaction, but I know I haven't got time to think about it now as the door to the ballroom approaches fast.

He saunters into the main room with me in tow, his hand in his pocket and the most magnificent smile plastered across his face as he pulls me close to him and leads me to the table. I can't help but grin radiantly as every face watches us move across the floor. The crowd erupts with applause. Wolf whistles and cheers start up again as he pulls out my chair and sits me down. Filling my glass with champagne, he kisses the back of my hand and lets it go as he swaggers across to the stage, never removing his eyes from mine. God almighty, I've just told Alexander White that I love him. Why the hell did I do that? And in a fucking linen cupboard, for God's sake. What the hell is wrong with me? I'm completely insane or something.

I watch as a man shakes his hand and waves him onto the stage while whispering something in his ear. Alex beams at him and slaps him on the back. Finding my face again, he throws me a wink and goes to the centre of the stage. They were so talking about me. His whole demeanour changes in those seconds. Suddenly the arrogant and completely in control of himself man appears on the stage like the true professional he is and my heart leaps at the sight of his absolute superior presence again. How the hell he's just transformed himself is completely baffling but I thankfully relax a little, realising he's going to be okay. I lean back onto my chair, trying to calm the nerves that are now welling up inside me because of my catastrophic timing.

"Sorry I'm late, ladies and gentleman. I was a little preoccupied with a rather delightful distraction and I lost track of time," he says with that suggestive right eyebrow. Laughter and jeers ensue as the room looks toward me and I flush beet red. *Bastard!*

"Can't blame you for that, Alexander. I'd be distracted too," a large man at the next table shouts at him as his wife slaps him jovially and smiles at me.

"Watch it, Freddie or I'll tell Heidi about the Lamborghini you bought last week. Oh, fuck, I think I just did, sorry. Heidi, really it wasn't that much money at all," he says with a wicked chuckle and a smile. Large man looks momentarily irritated and then looks at his wife in shock as she kisses him. The crowd oohs and ahs, continuing with their laughter as Alex tries to find a way back to his speech. Eventually all heads turn and he begins speaking.

"So we all know why we're here and I am of course extremely grateful to all who have already donated, but I just wanted to give you a little something more to think about to see if I could persuade you to give me some more of that hard earned cash that sits uselessly in your bank accounts. It really could be doing so much more.

"A few years ago, I met a young girl called Sophie. She was found in an alleyway in Birkenhead with a broken arm, three broken ribs and a fractured skull. The cafe owner who took her to the hospital informed the nurse that she had been working the streets for a living for the last few years because she had a drug problem. Now, while some of you might be thinking that was her own fault, I can assure you it wasn't.

"Sophie grew up in a home with a mother who repeatedly beat her and a father and brother who continually raped her. She lost her virginity aged eleven as her mother held her down for her father, apparently telling her that this was perfectly normal and that if she just relaxed, she'd enjoy it."

My hand instantly shoots to my mouth as I gasp at the revolting thought, as do most of the women in the room.

"She was taken into the care system and in turn they passed her case to our people. So thankfully, because of your money and our time, Sophie has transformed herself into a new person. She's already working at one of our centres as one of our specialist counsellors and is taking her degree next year.

"She has a future to be happy with and people to talk to in the dark times that will more than likely haunt her for the rest of her life. She knows that, but she's prepared to try for normal, to accept that there might be a happily ever after and that maybe one day she'll find someone to spend the rest of her life with. Someone who'll protect her and hold onto her when the times get tough, because we all need that, don't we?" He looks across at me and smiles.

"Someone who cares enough to let you just be yourself and accept your complications." I beam back at him with every ounce of love I can find while trying desperately to contain my tears at what must be going through his mind as he recants this. He turns his head toward the back of the room and flashes a brilliant grin briefly before turning back to the rest of the crowd.

"She's here tonight, sitting amongst you. She wanted to be here to see the people who had changed her life. She wanted to say thank you and encourage you all to give more. If I could show you who she is, I would because she is undoubtedly a very beautiful and inspiring young lady, but she says she's not ready and I can understand that. So instead, I'll propose a toast. Maybe next year she'll be more ready. Well done, Sophie. You make me both humble and extremely proud. Oh, and by the way, could you call me? There's someone I want you to meet soon," he says as he raises his glass at no one in particular. The whole room responds and cheers as they clink glasses together. "Why the hell am I not seeing more cheque books, people? I won't be accepting no for an answer. You know I never do anyway and if you've already given, I want more from you anyway."

Wow! He really is extraordinarily good at this. I watch the room as several cheque books land on the tables and people begin to scribble amounts down, either in fear or compliance. I'm not sure which, but probably both if I'm honest.

"Good, that's a little better. Thank you. Now when you leave here tonight, after you have drunk the entire contents of my bar and had your fill of the wonderful food that has been traversing your tables, please - I am begging you here, and we all know how little I do that - please think of the thousands of children that are out there this evening with nothing and no one. They're not fed and I can assure you they are certainly not laughing. They may be on the streets like Sophie or maybe they're in their bedrooms, thinking of the man who is coming up the stairs to beat the crap out of them. Or maybe they're just trying to put enough drugs inside themselves to take the edge off the constant pain they're tortured with. They can't get out of it without you, so please give everything you can and help me make it better for as many of them as I can. I need you to help me because I can't do it on my own. No matter how much you think I'm worth, I still don't have enough for this. I know how they feel and saving just one more each day really isn't good enough. We need to be better than that. I damn well need to be better than that," he states as he wrenches off his bow tie and flicks the top button on his shirt. Rubbing at the back of his neck and looking at the floor, he wanders across the stage to the top hat full of cheques and frowns. He doesn't think it's enough. How can it ever be enough when you've lived through this shit yourself? My tears start falling as I look at the anguish in his eyes. The way he drops his head makes me want to soothe his soul and run to him, grab hold of him and tell him how wonderful he is. All I can see is that blood spattered little boy, cowering in a cupboard at the mercy of a bastard father, and I'm falling apart inside, trying to mentally send every loving emotion I've got up to him on that stage.

The entire room is silent apart from soft sobbing all around me. Tears are streaming down my face as I look up at the man I love. His face is strained with tension, his eyes glassy as if he might burst into tears at any moment, but as that wonderful smile starts to form again on his face, he looks at me with reverence and a beautiful solace takes over his eyes again. He lifts his eyes to the crowd again.

"Someone told me something tonight that was entirely unexpected and simply extraordinary to me. It has made me feel like a chance has been thrown my way to live a better life, that some kind of angel has been sent to help and to shine a light into the darkness. For the first time in a fair few years, I was speechless. I couldn't find the words I needed and I... I still can't. But I hope that with time, I will be able to show that person that I have become better, that I have become more than I currently am or have been. This is my way of showing that person how much more I want to be for them and how much more they deserve from me. I don't know if I'll ever be worthy of their praise or affection but I'll try, as hard as I can, I'll try."

He lowers his head a little and exhales softly at the floor, putting his hands in his pockets and kicking out at some imaginary piece of dirt on the floor while I stare at him in shock. I'm gobsmacked, utterly mind blown. Was that for me? That's... I don't know what that was. It was unbelievable; that's what that was... is. That's Alexander White up there, talking about me, Beth Scott, caterer.

My hand is on my heart, which is going ten to the dozen and I'm willing him to look down at me but he doesn't. He just keeps looking at the ground as if he's scared to death that he's just given too much of himself away or something. The room is silent again, apart from the occasional manly gasp and then another sob from some woman who's obviously as emotionally wrecked at his speech as I am. And still all I can think is oh my God. Did he really just say all that?

I try, really I do, but remaining casual just isn't possible. I can't help myself as the tears pour down my face. I desperately want to launch myself at him, to hold him and tell him I love him all over again, but just as I'm beginning to rise from my chair, the silence is broken.

"Here's twenty five thousand," a lady yells at the back of the room. His head shoots up and he finds her. Turning around and wiping at my tears, I see an older lady waving a cheque above her head.

"Thank you, Jean," Alex calls back at her shakily, his face still a little tense.

"Fifty," a man shouts from across the other side of the room.

"John, that's quite remarkable coming from you. Thank you," he replies with a small smile returning.

"Oh, you're all being pathetic. You buy cars worth more than that, you shits. One hundred and fifty," says large man from the next table. Alex begins grinning like a fool and jumps off the stage, walking over to Freddie and shaking his hand.

"Two hundred. To see Alexander White proving he's actually got a fucking heart in there somewhere is worth every penny," calls a man at the back. Alex turns and moves towards him.

I follow him around the room, watching as he thanks every single one of them and charms the pants off the entire room. My heart swells with pride and my stomach tightens with astonishment at the admission he's just made. He's pleaded with people, begged for their help with every fibre of his being and shown a softer side of the wolf that they normally see and they're reciprocating with generosity and kindness. Just beautiful, open emotion from people like these, astonishing really. Who would have thought it? Perhaps they're not all the venomous arses I thought they were after all.

Fifteen minutes later, he's leaping back onto the stage and dumping a rather large amount of cheques into the top hat at the front, which is now overflowing onto the table and floor.

"Right, now one more thing and I'll let you get back to enjoying yourselves. I have pleaded like a fool and you have rewarded me with extortionate amounts of money. Thank you. Obviously the pleading works. Tomorrow I will probably become the fucking irritable and conceited bastard you all know and love so much, so please, if you want to watch me beg again, come and find me. This is a one night only affair and it won't be happening again anytime soon so I suggest you make the most of it. For tonight and only tonight, you can pay me to beg for it. Well, for the right price anyway. There is only one person here who will ever hear me beg after this evening has finished, I can promise you that," he says with a chuckle as his eyes find mine again. I blow him a kiss while thinking of the things that I could make him beg for and hoping to hell that he actually did mean me.

"So anyway, that's enough from me. Enjoy your evening, and by the way, if I don't find signed cheques from every one of you by Monday morning, be warned that I will come after you relentlessly, and you all know how much I love to do that. It will be entirely your own fault if I get the money out of you in some other more sinister manner, and you'll have no one to blame but yourselves for not being quite as generous as you should have been." He smiles as his body language stiffens a little, showing the heartless and ruthless businessman again.

"Arsehole," someone shouts from across the room with a laugh attached. Alex grins wickedly.

"Ben, you're more than fucking welcome. Yours will be the first name I look for."

He does a mock salute with his hand at the band and they light up the room with the sound of Mack the Knife, which is slightly drowned out by the roars and screams that come from the rising crowd who stand and cheer him. They're idolising him, as am I, and as he ambles his way off the stage toward me with the most enchanting of smiles, I almost run to him. Trying to keep the elation from bursting from my seams any more than it already is doing, I throw my arms around his neck and pull him into me. He swings me in the air as I giggle like a triumphant child, and then lowering me down to the floor, he takes my hand in his and leads me to the middle of the dance floor. Kissing me tenderly, he reaches his arms around my waist and then slides them to a dance hold, dragging his finger seductively along my body as he does so and gazing into my eyes again.

"Are you ready, Elizabeth?" he whispers into my ear as he grazes his lips across my neck.

"Yes, I think so," I reply, trying not to notice the beautiful ache in my heart and groin, which is currently clenching wonderfully at the thought of love, connection and promises of more.

"Good, because I am, too. I've never been more ready for you," he says and I gaze back at him with unashamed love and adulation. "Say it again. Tell me again so I know it's real," he asks with a soft smile, his blue eyes darkening a touch and his lashes blinking.

"I love you, Alex White," I answer, knowing it's what he wants to hear, and before I have a chance to say anything else, he twirls us around the floor as if we're in some kind of Viennese waltz. My feet struggle to keep up but his relentless grasp of my waist holds me pinned to him. I could probably take my feet off the floor and just hold on while gazing at his beaming face. My heart swims with joy and from what I can tell from his smile, he's thankfully feeling the same. The music, the passion, the emotion of the evening is everything I could ever want from him. In his way, he's given me his all and I love him all the more for it, and it appears, as luck would have it, that he might just love me, too.

Slowly, other couples start to fill the floor and before I know it, we're inundated with requests for dances. Every woman wants a chance to hear Mr. White beg for it and every man wants to hear Mr. White begging to give me back to him. He makes an awful lot more money in the next hour or so.

Eventually though, my feet give out and I have to sit. Returning to the table and thankfully sitting, I rub at my feet and take a long drink of water. Alex is somewhere in the room, still begging for it. At one point I actually saw him on his knees in front of a very old lady who was blushing furiously and slapping him away from her.

"Well, well, Beth, how lovely to see you. I must say you've surprised us all." Henry chuckles as he sits down beside me.

"Henry DeVille. Or should I say sir?" I giggle. "You old scoundrel, how are you? I saw Sarah earlier and I was hoping I'd get to say hello to you," I reply, regarding the tall, blond man, who is now a Lord unbelievably.

"I'm fine, really very good actually, but I lost my chance at a dance. Do you think you've got one more in you?" he asks, his eyes twinkling in mirth as he grabs at my hand and hauls me back to my feet in the way that only Henry can.

"Of course I have. Come on, let's go," I reply with a smile. I don't really but I'm not about to let the side down. Just as we step onto the dance floor, a slower song starts and I look at him a little nervously. He simply wraps his arms around my waist and draws me towards him.

"I'm sure he won't mind, Beth. I know him quite well. Don't worry. Besides, I might make him beg for more money yet. I'm actually quite enjoying his begging. The suggestiveness of this dance might get him on his knees for me." I throw my head back and laugh as he pulls me in again and starts to move us about. "So tell me how you are."

We chat amicably as we dance. It's nice to catch up with him, and knowing that he and Sarah are a little at odds is disconcerting for me. Henry was like the big brother I never had. On many occasions while Belle and Sarah were giggling their way into the night, I would flag early and Henry would take me home, or take me to my room. He was a good and decent man and would never have thought of anything inappropriate, and besides, they'd always been so in love.

Belle and I watched the two of them fall in love and get married, although I didn't go to the wedding because I was sick. Belle was Sarah's best friend in school and even though the union was never really accepted by his parents because of Sarah not coming from a good enough family, they made it through the tough times, so why not now? Not wanting to alert anyone to the possible problems in their relationship, I move slightly closer so I can whisper in his ear.

"Are you and Sarah okay, Henry?" I ask softly.

"Fine," he clips abruptly and stiffens a little. Okay, so they're absolutely not.

"Oh, Henry, don't be an arse," I say as I raise my thumb to the crease in his forehead and smile. "You know you still love her. What's going on?" I continue with a small smile. He sighs.

"Things change, Beth. Life becomes more difficult. I'm sure you'll find out with the man you've decided to take on. He is challenging to say the least. Watch yourself. That's a predator I won't be able to protect you from," he replies with a rather tight squeeze as he brushes an escaping curl behind my ear sweetly.

"I'll worry about me, you worry about her," I say, grinning and pretending to tickle him.

"You always were a lovely girl. Such a shame..." he mutters as he dances us to the corner of the floor and kisses my hand, looking a little sad. I put both my hands on his arms and encourage him to open up if he wants to. He clearly doesn't.

"Look after yourself, Beth. It is lovely to see you. Please say hello to Belle for me." With that, he leans in and gives me a hug. Kissing me on both cheeks and then again on the hand, he sits me down onto my chair and frowns. "Your feet must be killing you," he says as he squats down to the floor, rubs his hands down my legs a tad too suggestively and slips off my shoes. Squeezing my feet and looking up at me, he chuckles. "Well I haven't done that for a fair few years, have I?" I giggle and beam down at him, realising how much I miss him in my life. He was always such a good influence, so caring, a very decent man.

"No, I think the last time was Belle's twenty fifth. If I remember rightly, I was just about to throw up on you. Thank you, kind sir," I reply with a snort of laughter.

"You're most welcome. I'll see you again soon, Beth. Take care," he says as he leaves me. I smile and wiggle my toes in the carpet, thanking heaven because my feet really are killing me.

Now, where is the man of my dreams? Oh no, my reality actually... I giggle again and take a drink of champagne as I scan the room in the hope of finding him somewhere, probably still on his knees.

Chapter 29

Alexander

*W*hore.
White, you're a fucking idiot. Of course she was playing you. You should have known better and trusted your instincts. Why would anyone love you? You're a worthless piece of shit and you know it. Using her ridiculous notions of sweet and charming to lull you into a false sense of security, fucking lies. Pretending to be in love with you, pretending to give herself to you simply to help that fucking bastard, DeVille distract you from his plan to demolish you.

Why they were doing it was still a source of consternation but that's what they were doing. Between them they were destroying him, and fucking laughing at him in the process.

He pretended to be asleep as he recounted the night's events and listened to her breathing beside him. He'd watched the whole charade from the back of the room. He'd been about to go to her and say the words she wanted to hear, but instead he'd quietly watched as Henry held her and whispered in her ear, as she'd pressed her body into him seductively and roared with laughter, probably at how well they were doing at playing their nasty little game. *Fucking bitch.*

He'd stupidly lost himself in her this evening as he so often did, but this time it had been with thoughts of a future, of love, of marriage and even children. The possibility of removing the constant shade that his life had always been under had been so enticing to him that he'd offered himself to her, body and soul, in front of people who knew nothing of the man beneath. What a fucking idiot.

He'd almost lost it and beaten the fuck out of DeVille, but then he'd realised that as much as he'd like to, he would be letting them know that he had found out what was going on. So instead, he'd continued watching as she'd laid her arms on the arsehole, the same way she had done when she'd lied to him about loving him. He'd stared at her lovely legs as the cock put his hands all over them, removed her shoes and rubbed her feet in the way that only a lover would. He'd felt his heart shatter in that moment - the heart that he'd idiotically allowed to become free again. His whole body had felt numb with something that felt like death, and it still did. Even the beatings from his bastard of a father hadn't made him feel quite that empty. She might as well have put a tie round his neck and dragged him across the floor, stamping on his face as she did it. Fuck.

Eventually he'd brought her home and fucked her again, just once more for good measure. Just one more time to rid himself of the ridiculous thoughts of more, and as she'd softly stroked his cheek and whispered those enchanting words again, all he could see was Henry and his conniving.

This was done, finished.

He needed to get his fucking house in order again and quickly. How much had he missed while he was busy thinking of peace and undeserved forever afters? Fucking ridiculous. What had the scheming shit being doing in his absence? What had he been planning? No wonder she constantly reminded him of time off and relaxing. She was doing it to make him forget about the fact that he had a major shit storm coming at him. Clever girl. Whore, yes, but very clever indeed.

He should have noticed it all really, her amazing witty retorts, her ability to manipulate others. Instead he'd thought it was her learning from him. God, he was just as egotistical as Pascal. He hadn't even seen her manoeuvring her way around him because he was so self-obsessed that he assumed her innocence was real. He'd been so busy being confounded by her that he hadn't even contemplated that she was a fake.

"All war is based on deception, Sun Tzu." The thought lingered in his mind like a snake winding its way around his brain cells, stimulating the senses and reviving the deadened man that he knew himself to be and letting the haunted child retreat to the furthest corners of his soul again, where it fucking belonged, where he could contain it and condemn it.

Suddenly she moved against him, kissed him on the shoulder and walked across the bedroom and out of the door. More than likely going to let her lover know what was going on, to tell him how much she loved him and what a pathetic waste of a human being Alexander White was.

He rolled onto his back and looked up at the ceiling. What the hell did he do now? Leave and be away from her, that's what he needed to do. He had to go and not let her know why. But he couldn't keep pretending with her and he knew it. She was just too good at it. He'd break if he had to keep lying to her. No amount of hatred for her was enough to convince himself that he didn't love her, because for the first time in his life, he was hopelessly in love and he felt it to his core.

No, he needed to be rid of her. It was the only way he could deal with Henry and the possible annihilation of his fortune. His pathetic heart would simply have to deal with it and move the fuck on.

He could tell her he didn't love her and let her go. That would force her out of the door. She'd presented the opportunity for him to decline her invitation of a blissful future. Yes, he'd made a complete fucking idiot of himself at the ball but he could blame that on the joy of making so much money from the callous bastards that surrounded him in the room. The callous bastards that had now seen his weaknesses, the ones she'd made him show. Christ, she was good.

After lying there for a few moments, he heard music coming from downstairs, soft and gentle classical music, the beginnings of Clair De Lune.

"Bitch," he muttered as he turned back onto his side and listened to his favourite piece of hopeful music, the only piece of music that soothed his core to some sort of peaceful rhythm. She probably knew and was using it to manipulate him, to make him feel relaxed and calm. She no doubt felt that he hadn't been entirely with her when he fucked her and probably knew that he wasn't really asleep. He almost laughed at the thought of his narcissistic self, thinking she was an amateur at playing these devious games of politics and business. Nobody was that good at playing chess if they didn't know how to manipulate everything around them. She'd pretty much told him herself when she'd explained her father's reason for teaching her. Another very clever man obviously.

"Chess is ruthless. You've got to be prepared to kill people." That he did laugh at. He couldn't imagine her even having the ability to kill a

spider let alone people. She'd completely dazzled him. Henry had taught her well.

Swinging his legs over the bed and reaching down for his trousers, he abruptly threw them down to the floor again. If she wanted to continue with her little game then she could, at least for the rest of the night anyway. It would do him good to have her again. Maybe if he screwed her from behind, he could imagine her sucking at Henry. That should get her out of his head. He felt himself shudder at the thought and shook his head. "You're a fucking fool, White. You know you want her again," he mumbled to himself.

As he walked to the door, he realised the music wasn't coming from the kitchen. She didn't know how to work the system in the lounge so where was she? He got to the bottom of the stairs and noticed along the corridor that the door to the music room was open. Not that it was his room really... When the last owners of the house went bankrupt, they just left everything in the house. He'd thrown most of it but the music room had filled him with a sense of pleasure he hadn't quite understood, so he'd just closed the door on it and left it all in there, waiting for him to find the meaning of it someday. As he realised that the piano was being played, he felt his heart constricting a notch tighter at the thought that this tragedy of love was apparently its meaning.

He moved closer and saw that the lamp in the corner was on and there, sitting at the grand under the window, was Elizabeth, her fingers travelling across the keys as if she were one with it while his shirt draped loosely around her body, moving with her as he should be. She wore the damn thing better than he did.

The sweet sound of Debussy filling the air with thoughts of hope and delicate whimsical visions made him suck in a breath at the sheer beauty that sat before him. She was, he had to admit, exceptionally good, and as he hovered in the doorway and traced the lines of her elegant legs with his eyes, the legs that had been in that bastard's hands a few hours before, rage welled up inside him again. He sneered quietly and leaned against the frame. Whatever his feelings for the woman in front of him, he loved this piece of music, the music she was ruining for him forever, but he wanted to watch her play it and play it she did.

Her body swayed to the melody effortlessly, her hands pausing with palpable effect over each note as if imagining every emotion contained within the notes. He itched to kiss her, to travel his mouth along her delicate collarbone and whisper words of love into her ear. Adoration leapt into his mind again before he could stop it and he felt himself moving forward, inexplicably drawn to her. He hated himself in that moment but he couldn't stop himself. He wanted to hold her again, to touch her again, just for one more night, to just pretend for one more fucking night. He wanted to feel her wrapped around him and to hear the words she said with ease even if they were lies. God, he'd loved hearing those words coming from her mouth, the feel of her against his skin as she moaned out his name and kissed him with more intensity than he'd ever felt before. He'd loved everything about her and yet here he was, preparing to throw her out in the morning, because tomorrow he would tell her it was over and then she would be gone and he would be alone, again.

Reaching his fingers towards her, he waited and let her finish the piece. As it started to peter out into its final notes, he could hear her soft sobs as she bought the piece to an end and closed her eyes. She gracefully fingered the last notes and chords as she tilted her head to the side and allowed the music to bring her back to reality as it so often did for him. The world of hopes and dreams was lost in those last few notes of the song for him. The reality of his world always hit him hard at that moment when the notes just seemed to die on the piano, as his life seemed to seep back towards him and the dull and deflated thoughts took hold again. Those tragic thoughts of his bastard father and of the violence that haunted him daily, that same violence that he'd rung down on so many others with the same ease and disregard. The blood, the pain, the disinterest in anybody else's life or care for their existence. It had been his job. He'd done it and enjoyed it, still would if it wasn't for this charade of a life he currently lived. No amount of love would ever erase his past and he was a fool for thinking that it could. She'd almost done it, made him believe he was worthy of something more and flashed visions of peace at him, but that was over now, destroyed.

Sighing and running a hand through his hair, he stepped forward to her.

"That was beautiful," he murmured. She jumped and swivelled around like a scared rabbit.

"Alex, I'm sorry. I didn't mean to wake you. I didn't know you were there. You made me jump," she said as she got up and walked across to him, smiling that sexy smile that disabled him so much. *Not this time, bitch.* He smiled back and held his arms out to her.

"I didn't know you could play," he said as he held her. Thoughts of warm, sunny days and fields of corn drifted through his mind, teasing him with happy no fucking mores. He quickly shook his head.

"You never asked and I suppose it never came up. I found the piano the other day. I hope you don't mind," she said quietly with her captivating face nuzzling into his chest.

"What were you thinking about?" he said, hoping to God she would say him but knowing it was a lie if she did. She was thinking of Henry and about how much she wished she was with him.

"You. You amazed me tonight. I was filled with such an overwhelming sense of pride and love for you that I think I just needed a little time to myself to process everything that happened this evening. I couldn't sleep. When I was little and I couldn't sleep, my grandmother would play the piano for me. I thought it might help me relax a little." Oh, and now come the stories of happy families and loving parents. God, she knew how to work him well. It was fucking pathetic really. How the hell had he allowed any of it to consume him so?

"Well, let's get you to bed now. You're tired and it's been a long day. Besides, I know something that might tire you out," he said as he scooped her up into his arms and carried her up the stairs. God, she felt good pressed against him as she giggled beautifully and nuzzled back into his chest.

"You're insatiable, Mr. White," she said suggestively, pressing a kiss to his heart. *Bitch.* He fucking hated her, hated those eyes, hated those lips, and hated that fucking glorious hair that was tickling his throat. The throat that belonged to her, only her.

"That I am, Elizabeth." *For you. Or I was, but no more. After tonight you will be gone and I will go back to mindless fucking with random women who will never fill your place in my heart.*

Laying her on the bed, he undid the shirt she had been wearing and gently pulled it off her. She rose immediately to kiss him and pulled him down to her.

"Make love to me, Alex. Show me how you feel." He gazed at her with longing for a reality he knew he could no longer have. She was so perfect, her lovely skin and her amazing contours, those big, beautiful brown eyes that now held nothing but lies and deceit in them.

I love you and you betrayed me. How could you? You've destroyed me.

"Turn over, Elizabeth." She complied, and as he slowly kissed his way down her body and savoured her taste, he barely held in the tears that were threatening to fall from his eyes, the damned tears that he had not cried since he was a young boy.

"I love you," she whispered in the darkness.

No you don't, but that won't stop me holding onto it for just one more night. Just one more time for a life I hoped I might have.

He slowly pushed himself inside her, closed his eyes and reached for her throat.

Damn you, Elizabeth. Damn you to hell.

By five am he was sitting in the back of the Bentley, travelling to the airport. He'd watched her sleep for another hour after he'd made love to her and then decided he couldn't do it. Try as he might, the connection had been too strong to deny and so he'd poured every emotion he had left into her and watched her take it and destroy him all over again in the process. So he knew with absolute certainty that he couldn't look at her and tell her he didn't love her. She'd see right through him and probably change his mind or something equally as frustrating. Guzzling another mouthful of whiskey out of the bottle, he stared out the window, gazed into the darkness and remembered the note he'd left her in the kitchen. A coward's way out, yes, but nonetheless, he knew himself well enough to know he couldn't look at her again. He just couldn't bear it. He was supposed to be furious and enjoy throwing her out of his house while he laughed at her, but that just wasn't possible with her. He honestly couldn't think of a time in his life when he'd been so unable to face someone head on and enjoy their torment. As long as she thought it was just his fucked up sense of appropriate, Henry would never work out that he knew what was going on.

Sighing, he swigged again and gazed at her bracelet in his hand. She hadn't worn it the night before. They'd been too busy laughing and giggling and trying to get out the door to the ball so he'd forgotten to give it to her. Her bracelet... He brought it to his nose and inhaled her perfume before tucking it into his pocket and drinking more Scotch.

Elizabeth, I'm sorry but I can't give you what you want. I don't love you and you deserve better than that. I am going to New York for a few weeks so you won't have to see me again.
I thought you were the one, but I was wrong. I'm sorry.
AW

The steps on the jet were down and Phillip waited at the top as he and Andrews boarded the plane.

"Good morning, sir," Phillip said.

"Is it? I don't fucking think so somehow," he replied as he frowned and made his way unsteadily to his seat. The alcohol was doing its job quite nicely.

He watched as Andrews muttered something to Phillip and then took the chair opposite him. Within minutes the jet started to move, thank fuck. He couldn't get away from London and the bitch quick enough.

"Good morning, sir," Tara said as she waltzed into the cabin and started doing her final checks. Did she fucking speak? Really? Who the fuck told her to speak?

"Don't open your fucking mouth again. You're a whore like the rest of them. Do your damned job and stay the hell out of my way," he roared. She visibly faltered and stared at him in shock. He simply averted his eyes and stared out of the window. Tara scuttled off to the front of the cabin and he sneered at the thought of fucking her, disgusted with himself at the very image of it. Actually, maybe he should do it again and break her fucking neck at the same time. That would shut the slut up, wouldn't it? Fucking women - better used as tools. It was easier, cleaner, less... whatever the hell the word for *"heart-wrenching"* or *"soul destroying"* was. And he could still smell her fucking perfume. Why could he still smell that? It had probably ingrained itself on his skin, just like her damn smile and perfect legs wrapping around him while she lied and thought of Henry. He needed a fucking shower to scrub the deceit off him. He rubbed at the bracelet in his pocket and heaved in a breath. *Bitch.*

"Do you want to tell me why we're going to New York?" Andrews asked calmly. He could fuck off, too with his, *"she won't hurt you"* damned pathetic lecture.

"I don't need to tell you anything. Just do as you're told," he replied abruptly as the jet took off.

Andrews fidgeted a bit and looked like he might say something, so he lifted an eyebrow, daring him to speak. Quite cleverly the idiot didn't so he simply took another gulp of whiskey and closed his eyes.

About an hour later, he woke up and rubbed his forehead, which fucking hurt. For a second he didn't remember and then it all came flooding back to him as the pain took hold again. Looking over at Andrews reading, he sighed and poured more whiskey down his throat.

Michael Andrews, six foot two of solid murdering machine and apparently he thought of himself as some sort of father figure. The irony was hilarious. If Michael knew half the things he'd done to people in his life, he wouldn't exactly be proud of his admission of fatherly intent. But he had always been there for him, dragged him out of all sorts of situations when he'd been too coked up to do it himself, fought for him and been hurt in the process. He supposed it was reasonably fatherly, not that he'd have a damn clue what a reasonable father was.

"You said she wouldn't hurt me," he said quietly while gazing out of the window.

"She wouldn't," Andrews replied, lifting his eyes up from his book with a quizzical expression.

"She's in it with Henry. I saw them together." Andrews flinched then frowned, putting his book on the table.

"Are you sure?" he asked, clearly very confused.

"Yes," he replied with an acid hiss as more Scotch was poured down his throat. Andrews sighed as he saw where Alex was deciding to take himself.

"Did you ask her about it?" he questioned.

"What, and completely degrade myself? I won't be her fucking toy anymore," he seethed as he poured some more whiskey. "I won't ever be anyone's plaything again. Twice is quite enough." He noticed his own slurring and smiled. Life was about to get much better.

"How do you know it's the truth then? What if you've got it wrong?"

"I know what I saw, Michael. It's all been a game to her. I guess she had us both wrapped around her fucking beautiful fingers. She really was very good at it though. I should employ her." He chuckled a little as the alcohol started to take hold of him again, the room spinning quite effectively. He reached for his glass and watched as it magically jumped out of his fingers and over the side of the table. "Really very special indeed. Il diavolo travestito da angelo," he continued as he lurched toward the bottle instead, missed and landed face first on the table with a thud and another chuckle. "Fairies. Damned pesky fuckers."

Andrews moved the whiskey away from him and stood up.

"Come on, let's get you to bed," he said as he reached for Alex and pulled him from the seat.

"Michael, if you're after sex I'm afraid I'm just not into men. Pascal couldn't get it from me so you definitely won't. Actually, I don't think I could get it up anyway. I'm properly fucked." He snickered as Andrews dragged him towards his bedroom, picking him up as he fell over and almost carrying him there.

"I don't want you for your body, you idiot," Andrews replied as he hauled him along the corridor.

"What do you want me for then? My money? Ha! You can't fucking have it. It's all mine, just for me," he slurred. "Nobody to fucking share it with anyway, and she doesn't want me. Why would she?" he said as he abruptly stopped and pushed Andrews up against the wall. "Why did she do this to me, Michael? Why?"

~

Andrews stared at him for a moment and contemplated an answer. What could he say? Suddenly Alex's legs gave way and he crashed to the floor in a heap. Andrews rubbed his forehead in

448

exasperation and looked down at the mess on the carpet. He hadn't seen him like this for quite some time. It didn't bode well in the slightest. Heaving him back up, he dragged him along towards the bed again and considered his options, which included calling Conner or following the dick until he got it out of his system. He'd go for the latter for the time being.

Laying him down, Andrews took off Alex's shoes and watched as he passed out. Watching him sleep for a few minutes, he resolved to go back in a while and check he hadn't choked on his own vomit, which was more than likely coming at some point. As he was about to leave, he saw something hanging out of Alex's pocket. Walking back in, he lifted the bracelet out and studied it for a few moments. He knew who it belonged to, and placing it on the table next to the bed, he hoped that the guy was wrong, that he'd misread the situation somehow. It was possible, but unfortunately Alexander White was exceptional at reading situations. He left the door open, took one last glance at him to check he was alright and left the room.

Well, at least he hadn't coked himself up. That was the last thing he needed. Michael had dealt with all this shit before when he'd first started working for him. Two years of drink and drugs had almost ruined the young and foolish Alexander White but somehow the man had managed to keep everything together, kept his fists from reacting too much as he survived on little sleep and cold comfort where he could find it in the arms of one of his whores.

The change in him over the next year had been inexplicable. Out of the blue, the guy had decided to get clean and so that's exactly what he'd done. Why was unknown. Who'd caused the shift in character was still a mystery, but at least he was clean, and even though the knock on effect had caused the mood swings to worsen, he'd at least become rational to some degree.

Michael sighed and returned to his seat. Picking up the glass on the floor, he poured himself a very large drink and studied it for a minute while he thought of the oncoming tornado that Mr. White would probably be unleashing on the world as of tomorrow. He downed his drink and decided that now was probably a good time to relax because he sure as hell wouldn't be getting any holiday any time soon. He would be far too busy looking out for his employer, who was bound to be getting himself in all sorts of trouble to amuse himself.

The guy's default setting to anything that sent him off kilter was to destroy as much as possible. Unfortunately, that might well include himself.

Definitely someone else.

"Oh, Elizabeth, what have you done?" he mumbled as he poured himself another drink and stared at the empty seat in front of him. "What have you done?"

Chapter 30

Elizabeth

Waking and stretching my arms above my head, I reach across for the man I love. Not here as usual. I chuckle to myself as I think of him probably working or checking out how much money he made for the foundation last night. Curling up into a ball again, I grab at his pillow and hug it tight to me, sniffing in his gorgeous Alex smell and glowing in a sense of post coital bliss, even though it's ages after the event actually happened.

Closing my eyes again, I let myself drift back to the night before, to the wonderful words he said in front of an audience and for the first time since we've been together, I realise that I actually feel secure - secure in the knowledge that he loves me. Okay, he hasn't actually said it, but he's said as much as he can. I know what he means. He's made it pretty obvious to me and that, for the time being, is all that matters. The rest will come later.

Sighing and deciding that I'm very ready for a hot shower, I haul my very hungover head upright and try to get up. The moment my feet hit the floor I'm reminded of my extremely high heels. I'm not wearing them again, ever. Well, maybe I will. His reaction to them is worth every second of the pain I'm currently feeling if I'm truly honest.

I need coffee, lots and lots of coffee, with aspirin or paracetamol. Damn him, he's even got me drinking his bloody espresso. I am so outrageously in love it's ridiculous. Giggling like a fool, I get up and gingerly cross the bedroom to go for a shower, noticing the time is eleven thirty. That's damned good sleeping, even for me.

Having had my very refreshing shower, I comb through my wet hair and cleanse my face with my very own make up cleanser that is sitting in the bathroom, next to his. Sweet. I smile at the notion of my make-up being permanently stored in his bathroom. I bet that's never happened before, Mr. White. The thought of being here and being happy with him has me giggling and bouncing about like a schoolgirl and I can't stop the huge grin that seems somehow permanently plastered across my face regardless of my bloody headache.

Deciding it's time to go in search of my beloved and the aspirin, I drag his shirt around my shoulders and pull on my underwear. Nearly skipping out of the door with delight, I laugh at my own absurdity and head for the stairs. *Where is he?*

Dragging my fingers down the banister, I take in the house around me in all its glory. It's so much like him, austere and manly in some respects and yet somehow there's a warmth flowing throughout when you scratch beyond the surface. Elegant paintings hang on the walls, portraying a passion that so few see and the flowers adorning the hall constantly remind me off his love of the fresh air outside of London. The clock chimes, reminding me of the time and I turn the corner to peek in his study. Nope, not in there, must be in the kitchen, where the coffee is, thank god.

Waltzing my way down the hall, I walk in and find that the kitchen is also empty. God, where is the man when you want a kiss? Thinking he must be in the lounge, I turn and head back up the hall and look around the door. Still nothing. Where the hell is he? Oh well, he must be somewhere. I'll go and sort my head out so I'll at least be semi lucid by the time he gets back.

Doing my stabbing on the remote again, I eventually find the radio and start the ritual of making a drink, of course remembering to turn the bloody thing all the way up. That reminds me that I didn't ask Alex about Pascal. I was surprised he wasn't at the ball last night. Maybe it wasn't his cup of tea. Or maybe he was back in Rome or at one of his other clubs. Who bloody knows? The man's a complete enigma.

Rattling about in the cupboards for a while, I eventually find some aspirin and hastily guzzle them back with a pint of water. The coffee machine starts to whine so I move across to it and hit the button. Tada! I giggle at myself again and move to the table. Sipping my drink and squinting rather painfully at the sunny garden, I close my eyes and drift back to thoughts of making love and rolling around in his arms. Strong, warm arms and a man who was made for loving a woman. He doesn't know it, but I'll show him. I'll show him exactly what he needs to rid himself of to finally accept how wonderful he is, because that woman is thankfully me and from now on that's my mission.

Remembering the words he used in his speech, I feel the tears brimming again. He gave me so much, so many of his thoughts and dreams and I can only hope that I can be the woman he needs me to be to help him through his tough times, to keep him safe and warm.

The radio cuts to the news and brings me back to the here and now. I keep my eyes closed, not quite ready to face the light again just yet.

"So the Addisons Foundation Charity Ball was, of course, a roaring success again this year and estimates for the total raised are averaging at about eight million pounds so far. Although we're told that this has only been counted from the beginning of the evening, so totals will be confirmed tomorrow. According to our insider, the rather dashing Mr. Alexander White was on very good form and did in fact show the privileged few who were inside the event that he isn't quite the heartless monster he is reputed to be. He also had a rather beautiful new young lady on his arm. There is no confirmation of her name at the moment but I doubt it will be long before she's announced. Perhaps she is the reason for his slightly warmer heart. I think perhaps Mr. White has been nabbed, ladies, so unfortunately we will have to keep searching for another Prince Charming. And now to the weather..."

Pulling my legs up onto the chair, I hug my knees and grin with triumph and joy. Mr. Alexander White, dream man, and all mine, every single inch of him. Opening my eyes and squinting again, I turn myself away from the garden in the hope that I might be able to see again. It's then that I notice a note propped up against the flower vase with my name on it. I sigh out a breath at his elegant writing, wonderful curling lines scrawling out my name as he imprints his name on my heart a little more. Picking up my coffee, I reach for the note and open it up.

Elizabeth, I'm sorry but I can't give you what you want. I don't love you and you deserve better than that. I am going to New York for a few weeks so you'll not have to see me again.
I thought you were the one, but I was wrong. I'm sorry.
AW

SEENING WHITE

My hand drops the coffee glass to the floor and as it smashes, I gasp and bend over, trying to process the note in my mind and feeling instantly sick. I heave repeatedly and eventually realise I can't hold it in anymore so run to the sink and throw the contents of my stomach up.

Eventually, after my stomach has stopped heaving, I stand shakily with my hands grasping onto the side of the unit and think of the note again. Swiping at my mouth with my hand, I quickly go back over to the table to read it again and sit down. What happened? Last night was so wonderful. I would have known if he'd changed his mind. Why would he say those things and then tell me he didn't want me? What's he doing? No, it's a lie. He can't mean it. It's all wrong. Why would he write this? Is he scared? What did I do wrong? Last night was... his words, his warmth, the caress of his hands on me as we danced, and his mouth, oh god his mouth. No, this isn't true. It can't be.

I place the note carefully on the table and stare at it, my mind frantically trying to find a new meaning to the message in front of me, but there isn't any other meaning to the words. He doesn't love me. He doesn't want me, and as those words slowly start to sink in, I feel my eyes fill with tears and then begin to cry. Uncontrollable sobbing takes hold of me to the point where I can't breathe through my tears. I stand awkwardly and try to get to the kitchen towel to wipe my face, but the effort is too much so I simply slide down the side of the peninsular unit and fall to a heap on the floor.

He doesn't want me and he doesn't love me. He thought I was the one, but he was wrong. He's sorry...

After what feels like an eternity, my sobbing stops a little and I pull my legs up to my chest, trying to somehow console myself. It doesn't work. I'm a fucking mess. I can't think clearly at all. But gazing out at the garden as I sniff and wipe at my cheeks and eyes, I start to feel my irritation niggle at me. Here I am in his bloody mansion, sitting on the floor and crying my heart out over a man who doesn't love me. What sort of sodding idiot sits here and mopes on the floor in the very house that he lives in? He could walk back in any minute. He doesn't fucking love me. It's that bloody simple and I need to get the hell out of here. But I love him, so much it feels like I'm dying inside. My heart is breaking in two at the thought of never seeing him again, of never touching him again or never hearing my name being breathed from his lips.

What did you expect, Beth? He's Alexander White and you, well you're just Beth Scott, cook.

Stupid Beth. Stupid, weak, pathetic Beth, useless and unwanted, tossed aside like a piece of rubbish that has amused him for only so long. You thought you could play in his world and he's shown you exactly how naïve you are. He knew it and he played with you. You must have been very entertaining for him. Sweet innocent Beth, what a treat you must have been.

What an utter wanker.

Pulling myself up, I look at the smashed coffee glass on the floor, smashed into a thousand pieces, something like my stupid heart. I always knew he was capable of it. He bloody told me as much himself when he decided it was his way or no way at all, and I took that risk believing that I was something special, that I could somehow change him. But I couldn't, could I?

You bastard, Alex. Damn you to hell.

Running up to the bedroom, I quickly gather my things and put them into my bag, making sure that I don't pack a single thing that he's bought for me. The arse can burn it for all I care regardless of how much it all cost. Perhaps he will give it to the next unfortunate girl who falls for his charms. I feel sorry for her instantly. I should leave a bloody note somewhere letting her know exactly what she's getting herself into.

How could he? I loved him. I still do and he's left me. I hurt so much. Tears start to pour down my face again and I scrub angrily at them with the back of my hand, refusing to shed one more tear in this farce of a home. Home. Fucking hilarious. The man has no heart to put in his house. That's what this place is, a house, no more, no less. A place to exist, maybe even breathe occasionally, but certainly not to be happy, or in love. Not that he knows what that means.

Pulling on my jeans and jumper, I drag my boots on and head for my bag.

SEENING WHITE

There on the dresser in front of me is his bow tie, staring at me, drawing me towards it. I can't damn well stop my feet from moving. Gently picking it up, I finger the smooth silk and raise it to my nose. Inhaling his scent and rubbing it against my cheek, I feel the tears bubbling again. His cheek, his mouth, and oh god the feel of his weight on me whirls around my brain, igniting the feelings of happiness and lust and desire. His body, the way he touched me and the way he held me, the way he made me feel every single emotion with a passion I've never known. The lone tear hits my chin and I gently wipe it away as I tuck the tie into my pocket and sigh. Just one thing to remind me of him, just one little thing to help me through the pain that is coming for me.

Grabbing my bag, I head to the front door and call for a taxi. The man says he'll be about ten minutes so I drop my bag and wait. I suddenly feel very awkward in this big house that stares at me silently, the house that I was beginning to feel very at home in, the house he *told* me to feel at home in. I glance around nervously, hoping for something to distract me from my thoughts. The heavy ticking of the clock echoes loudly around the hall and forces me to think of the first night when he carried me past it and up the stairs. My sodding tears start again at the vision so I turn my eyes away from the enticement and find the other hallway.

Looking at the music room door, I notice it's still open so I walk toward it. The lamp is still on but the lid on the grand piano has been closed. Lifting it, I tinkle with the notes and think back to playing in here last night, my favourite song, Debussy's Clair de Lune, the song I played while thinking of him and hoping for a wonderful life together. How stupidly wrong I was.

A sudden honking at the top of the drive alerts me to the taxi. As I turn to walk out, I kick something on the floor and glance down at whatever it is. A whiskey tumbler, in the middle of the floor? He's been in here. What was he doing in here? Reaching down, I pick it up and put it on top of the piano. Instant visions of his mouth wrapped around it invade my mind, so gazing at it for a moment more, I turn again for the door and walk out. I seriously can't cope with the image of his mouth a minute longer. I have to get the hell out of here so I can regain some sanity, or weep on my own and find a plan to make his fucking betrayal diminish somehow. I grab my bag from the floor and take a last look around. Sighing and desperately trying not to imprint every image into my mind, I open the front door hesitantly and swipe at another tear. It's over. The dream is finished. Alexander White has destroyed everything and probably enjoyed every fucking minute of it.

It will never happen to me again. Never. He's taught me a very valuable lesson.

Never, ever love a game player. Especially one who tells you how it is from the beginning.

God, I miss him.

As I hit the fresh air and slam the door behind me, I feel the wind whistle past my face and realise I've left my coat inside the house with my bloody keys in the pocket. Oh well, there's no getting back in now, so throwing my bag over my shoulder, I crunch my way along the gravel to the waiting taxi.

The journey home seems endless. I need to get keys really but that means seeing Teresa or Belle and I just can't face it, not yet. I phone through to the concierge at my apartment building and he informs me that he can let me in after we've gone through a few fucking irritating security questions.

"Arrggghhhhhh!" I scream out at the top of my lungs, having ended the call.

The taxi driver immediately slams on the brakes.

"What's wrong, love?" he asks with a look of shock.

"Nothing, sorry. I'm just a bit... upset. Sorry," I reply in a small voice.

"Is it a man, love?" he says. "'Cause if it is, he's not worth it. None of us are."

"Well I'm glad of your bloody insight but sod off, will you?" is my very loud response to the fount of all fucking knowledge sitting in front of me, who is a man, so is clearly a bastard.

"Alright, love. Just sayin', that's all," he mutters and then resumes his driving.

Within ten minutes I'm entering the building and apologising to Gavin for being rude to him on the phone. He leads me to our door and opens it for me.

"Are you alright, ma'am? You look a bit upset," he asks with a concerned face. Sweet. Belle's words ring in my ears. He's a man as well, therefore at the moment, he's a bastard too.

"Fine, Gavin... I'm fine, thank you," I say as I close the door behind me and drop my bag on the floor.

I am so not fine. I am a fucking wreck and it's all because of him.

~

I spend the afternoon curled up on the sofa, hoping to god that Belle won't come home, hoping desperately that she will miraculously understand my need for space and stay at Conner's house for the night. Where does Conner live anyway? Conner... Alex... Oh god, I'll never be rid of him if those two stay together.

I try to drink my way through a bottle of wine, thinking it will do some good, but the moment I bring it to my lips, I feel sick again so I decide against it and opt for sit on your arse and over think everything instead, which of course makes me cry all over again, repeatedly.

What have I done wrong? Why has he left so abruptly?

By eight thirty, it's becoming obvious that Belle isn't coming home any time soon, thankfully, so I get up and make myself a cup of tea. No sodding espresso machine here so I might as well have tea.

Just as I'm pouring it, the door opens and the two of them bound in like star crossed sodding lovers, gazing adorably at each other. My hand shoots to my mouth to stifle the instantaneous sob that rises up my throat and I run to my bedroom, slamming the door behind me and bursting into tears, again.

A few minutes later there's a soft knock.

"Beth, can I come in?" Belle asks as she opens the door anyway and walks over to my bed. I look up at her and she instantly wraps her arms around me and holds me while I cry my eyes out again, and again, and again. Eventually, she pushes me upright a bit and looks at me.

"What has he done to you?" she asks, her face full of emotion and worry.

"Gone. He's gone. He says he doesn't want me, that he doesn't love me and that... that he can't give me what I want," I splutter through my tears. The door flies open as a very pissed off looking Conner storms in.

"Get out, Conner. Can't you see we're a little preoccupied in here," Belle hisses at him as I lower my head.

"Where's he fucking gone?" Conner roars, scowling furiously. "Beth, tell me. Please?"

"Calm down, Conner," Belle says as she holds up her hand. "I won't tell you again. You'll fucking leave if you carry on," she continues as she frowns at him. I can't even look at him. I'm so pathetic but he reminds me too much. Alex, Conner, it's all the same damn thing.

"New York, the note said New York," I say quietly through my sniffs. He walks over to Belle and kisses her on the head, which makes me bawl again.

"A fucking note? The prick. I'll call you, babe. I need to go. Look after her and call me if I can do anything," he says as he picks up his phone and starts thumbing through the contacts.

"Where the hell are you going?" she says. "Don't do anything stupid, you idiot."

"It's not me I'm worried about," he mumbles as he calls someone on the phone and walks out. "Love you," he calls over his shoulder as the door slams. That also causes more fucking tears.

"Insensitive bastard," Belle mutters into my hair as she strokes it. I can't feel it. I can't feel anything but pain and hurt. "Can I do anything for you? Do you want to talk or do you want a bath?" she asks quietly.

"No, I just want to go to bed and forget it all," I reply through my sobs, preferably loaded with alcohol, or even drugs. I hate fucking drugs. The bastard has made me want to take drugs. I can't breathe. Oh, holy shit, what the hell am I going to do without him? I'm shaking again. Alex withdrawal, or maybe something equally as scary, is invading me, scratching at me and hurting me deep inside.

"Okay," she says as she lays me down and pulls back the covers. "We'll talk tomorrow. James is doing the Stevely dinner because our cooker didn't arrive so you don't have to get up. Just stay here as long as you like. I'll see you in the morning. Call if you need me," she says with a final stroke of my hair, then she gets up and leaves the room, closing the door softly.

I kick off my jeans and jumper and crawl into bed, trying not to think about the man who not only turned my world upside down but then destroyed it as if it were nothing. Half an hour later and with a snarl to myself, I reach for his bow tie and pull it up to my heart. He might not want me anymore but that doesn't stop this damned pining I've got hammering in my chest. Tomorrow I'll deal with it. Tomorrow I'll let the healing process begin, but for now, right at this moment, I'm just going to pretend that he's still wrapped around me and that it's all going to be okay. It's then that I begin to fall asleep, tired and exhausted, yes, but with him still beside me to keep me safe and warm, I finally close my eyes and sleep.

Chapter 31

Belle

"Hey, babe," Conner said sweetly.

It was pathetic really, this babe shit, but reasonably cute in its own way.

"Hi," she replied with as little emotion as she could manage, because he's a man, and therefore he's a dickhead. Mr. Bastard-Arsehole White just proved that, yet again.

"How is she?"

"Asleep for now, but she's not good," she said, picking at her nails and gulping back some more wine, wondering what the hell it was that he wanted, running away to find his little sodding friend, to what? Help him through his turmoil? Alexander White obviously has no heart at all, let alone any turmoil to deal with, but then why would he? Bastards with more money than sense are rarely able to do anything other than screw well.

"Okay. Is there anything I can do?"

Not fucking likely. You're a man, therefore you're a dick as well, who more than likely has no ability whatsoever to do anything right, regardless of how unfairly beautiful you are.

"Why has he done this to her, Conner? What the hell did she do to deserve this?"

As if Conner Avery could answer the question. Clearly Mr. White was just playing his normal bloody games like all the rest of them. She wouldn't be surprised if he smacked his women about as well with his "I'm in control" attitude.

"I don't know, babe, but I'm sure she didn't do anything." He sighed. "I'm going to find out though. I'm on my way now and as soon as I know something, I'll call you. I promise, okay?"

Too sodding right you will, because then I'll know where the arsehole is so I can kill him, or at least make him pay for his error in judgement.

"Okay. Don't let him get away with it, Conner. You find him, and you make him pay for this or I swear to god, I will," she hissed at him, trying to contain the venom spitting off her tongue and failing.

"Okay," he said quietly.

"Okay," she replied with a sneer as she refilled her wine. "I never liked him," she muttered.

"You never liked me and look where we are now?" he said softly in that voice that weakened her a little. She hated it.

We're nowhere, you idiot. You'll stay exactly where I put you while I control these stupid feeling things that are beginning to surface for some inexplicable reason, and damn you for making me sense this again. Love... stupid, pathetic, needy.

"I know, but she's not like me. She can't deal with this shit. He was too much for her. I knew he would be and I should have stopped it before it went this far," she replied, quietly chastising herself with every word uttered. "I love her. I can't watch her in pain."

"I know. But he's not the man you think he is, Belle. That's why I have to go. He needs me and I can't watch him in pain either. He's the only brother I've ever known. You wouldn't understand and now's not the time to go into it," he said with another sigh.

Pain, really? He didn't know the meaning of the word pain. If he did, he wouldn't have done this, would he?

Her eyes narrowed at the thought. Perhaps it was something she could use to get back at him.

"What do you mean?" she responded, now quite intrigued at the thought of an *in pain* Mr. White.

"He's... Oh shit, it's complicated, babe. I don't know how much to tell you. It's not really my place to say anything," he replied quietly with a slight crack to his voice.

It appeared that Conner was actually having some sort of real feeling regarding the dickhead. It was amusing in itself and she chuckled at the sensitivity he was having. He should learn to control that emotion before it consumed him to hell. But complicated? What was so complicated about him being a giant sized arsehole?

"Okay... You go find your little brother. But don't you dare bring him within a mile of her or me. I won't be responsible for my actions," she said, trying to find the anger and bring it to the surface again. Conner Avery's little emotional struggle was beginning to have a very negative effect on her. It was disconcerting. If she wasn't careful, she might actually have to respond kindly at some point or even admit that she gave a shit about his feelings.

"Okay, thank you. I do love you," he said in a small voice, clearly noticing her frosty behaviour.

He wasn't thick. She had to give him that. And he was hot as hell, but fundamentally she had to keep reminding herself that he was simply a man, and therefore a dickhead who would of course destroy her if she let him.

"I know," she said, fiddling with the wine bottle again and pouring herself another glass while shaking her head at the very thought of love. It was a revolting emotion. No good ever came of it at all.

"Will you ever tell me you love me?" he asked.

Would she? Unlikely. She didn't even understand what the sodding word meant anymore. The last time she'd said it, Marcus had literally beaten her half to death. The man she loved with all her heart had looked down on her and rained blow after blow because of what? Her skirt was too short. Bastard. That's what love apparently gets you.

"Possibly. If I'm ready," she replied, downing the wine and looking down the corridor towards the bedrooms. Conner's insecurity was the last thing on her mind. He was more than likely just as much of an arsehole as White was and she'd be damned if she'd get in that sort of trouble again, regardless of how much she liked him. Fucking men and their pathetic weaknesses.

"Then I'll wait."

Enjoy that.

"I know. I'm going to go and check on her again," she replied as she stood and made her way across the lounge, cringing with every step she made at the thought of her baby sister. Why hadn't she protected her from this? She'd even been so stupid as to push her toward it at one point, thinking it would help her confidence somehow.

"Okay, I'll call you tomorrow."

Whatever, just find the shit then kill him, or even better, get him back here so I can.

"Okay, bye," she said as she ended the call, threw the phone on the sofa along with her ridiculous feelings for Conner and walked to her sister's room.

She watched her for about ten minutes, and then, after deliberating the best thing to do, just got in bed next to her and pulled her into a hug, stroking her hair again like she did when they were children. It was just typical that she would meet someone like him. He had probably found her innocence and beauty appealing, but fundamentally, dickheads like Alexander White weren't capable of anything lasting or meaningful. They just wanted to break something that wasn't damaged to somehow prove their own superiority. She knew the feeling well. Marcus had done exactly the same to her and he was just like Mr. White. In fact, they probably went to the same school of how to screw women over and leave them. She blew out a breath and pulled her not so innocent anymore sister toward her again.

"Alex..." Beth murmured in her sleep. Belle closed her eyes and sighed at the torture that was coming, hoping her sister was stronger than she had been.

No, baby sister, it's just me. I'm so sorry. But I'm here and I always will be.

The End... For now.

Acknowledgements

There is only one person I have to thank for putting up with my constant keyboard tapping every evening and it's my wonderful partner. I love you more than words can say.
Without your support through the last year or so, I couldn't have achieved any of this and you'll never understand how much that means to me. But hopefully if you look inside the characters, you'll find a bit more of me that you've allowed to open up and free itself from its box.
Me x

Special thanks go out to all the Book Blogs who have supported me in this endeavour. Without the fabulous help of all these blogs my books would be nowhere at all. You are all stars in my eyes. But in particular:
Rachel Brightey at Orchard Book Club and Rachel Hill at Bound By Books Book Blog.
My editor - Heather Ross - thank you gorgeous x
My PA - Leanne Cook - Love you, honey. You know how wonderful you are x
And of course, you guys, anyone who's read my story and enjoyed it is warmly thanked and acknowledged as super wonderful. I hope you've liked my characters and if they've resonated with you in some way, be it small or large, then I've achieved my goal, which was to provoke thought and entertain you.
CEH x

****

THE WHITE TRILOGY CONTINUES

Feeling White
(White Trilogy 2)

And

Absorbing White
(White Trilogy 3)

Other Books By The Author

The VDB Trilogy
(Best read after The White Trilogy)

The VDB Trilogy begins a week after the end of The White Trilogy and is told from new POV's. It is, in some ways, a continuation.

****

The Parlour (Book 1)

Above all else Pascal Van Der Braak is a gentleman. Devastatingly debonair and seductively charming. Always styled and perfected.
He is also a cad, scoundrel, rouge and kink empire founder.
Tutored in the highest of society, having been born of royalty only to deny it, he found his solace in a world where rules need not apply.
Where he chooses to ensure rules and duty do not apply.
Some call him Sir, others call him master, and no one would dare risk his wrath unless they required the punishment he favourably delivers.
Except one, who has just strapped a collar around his throat, one he asked for. So, now he needs to appropriate his businesses correctly for peace to ensue. He needs to find the correct path forward for everyone concerned, so he can relax, enjoy, and finally hand over the responsibility to someone else.
Simple.
But where comfort and a safety of sorts once dwelled, there is now uncertainty, and a feeling of longing he no longer understands. A need unfulfilled. And as problems arise, and allies scheme, he finds himself searching for answers in the most unlikely of places.

Lilah

It's the same every day. I'd found it odd at first, but I'm used to it now. I was so tired and weak when I got here that it was helpful really. That small woman comes in to help me wash and get dressed. I don't know where the clothes come from, but they're nice enough, and at least they're clean and dry. Not like the rags I arrived in. They were taken from me the moment I took them off to get into the shower, the first shower I'd had in god knows how long. Nearly a year I'd been running the streets, a year without a real bed or a home of any sort. There isn't a long and awful story to tell about an abusive family member, or a broken home. I suppose I just slipped through the cracks and got lost at some point. I lost my job first, and then I couldn't afford the bills on my apartment, so the landlord threw me out. I don't blame him, he did the right thing by himself. And then it was just a long and never-ending road to nothingness.

So now I'm here, wherever here is.

And I don't know why.

****

This book is followed by:

Eden's Gate (VDB 2)

Serenity's Key (VDB 3)

Once Upon A (The Stained Duet #1)

Alana Williams is three published authors. She has been for years, but now she wants to add another voice to her whirlwind of deadlines and unachievable targets. Trouble is, she knows nothing of her latest literary undertaking.

*****
Alana

It began as research. Just research. The technical approach. One that delivers the content necessary for a hidden culture to seem plausible, even if it's not. Readers expect perfection from me. They want the experience. They need to be taken on a journey. That's my job as a writer.
Blaine Jacobs is his name. He's my research. A man who seems as logical and focused as me. A man who agrees to help. A man who, regardless of his stature in the community, seems to offer a sense of realism to this strange section of society. And even if he does occasionally interrupt my data with dark brooding eyes and a questionably filthy mouth, what does it matter? It's just research, isn't it? It's not real. None of this is. Nothing will come of it or change my mind.

So why am I confused?
I'm becoming lost.
Falling apart.

And Blaine Jacobs, no matter how calm he might have seemed at first, now appears to linger on the edges of sanity, pushing my boundaries with every whispered word.

The End (Stained Duet #2)

Blaine Jacobs knows nothing of love, but Alana Williams does and she's opening doors to truths he's never felt before. Walls will be broken and secrets revealed, regardless of consequence.

*****

Blaine

My throat growls out in distress, desperate for more alcohol to fuel this panic ridden hatred of myself. That's all this is. I know that. It's rage and indecision. A barrage of self-loathing and repugnance, one confused and trapped in its own irrational behaviour. The psychologist in me would tell me to quieten down. The magician would play for the fun of it, but the monster in me? He's ready to rut hell into anything that will take me, just so it can imagine her face and abandon the last drops of my resistance.

I'm confused.
Losing control.
Being torn into three.

And no matter how I try to avoid it, the layers keep peeling apart with no sense of clarification or psychological evaluation. They just split for her.

Innocent Eyes (A Cane Novel)

Co-authored with Rachel De Lune (Hart De Lune)

*****

"If he's gross, I'm bailing."
That's what I said to my supposed best friend when she asked me to take her place. A blind date, she said. What harm could it do?
He was charming. Beautiful. God's finest creation. He wined me and dined me. Made me do things I'd never before dreamt of in the bedroom. It was perfect. Dangerous. Arousing.
But Jenny didn't tell me the full story. She didn't tell me about the debt she owed. And now Quinn Cane wants his money's worth, and he's going to make me pay whatever way he can.

"A debt needs to be paid."
The woman who came to meet me didn't owe me money. I could tell by her innocent eyes. Still, the debt will be paid either way.
She was something to play with and use as I saw fit, but something about Emily Brooks made me want to keep her. So she became my dirty girl. Pure. Innocent. Mine.
Then she whispered my damned name and invaded my world, changing its reasoning.
She wasn't meant to break the rules. But she rolled my dice and won.

Shame. Forgiveness. Dark. Erotic. Romance.

All of Charlotte's books are intended for mature audiences. 18+ only.

Printed in Great Britain
by Amazon

17465993R00269